ROMAIN GARY

The Kites

Translated from the French by Miranda Richmond Mouillot

PENGUIN BOOKS

PENGUIN CLASSICS

UK | USA | Canada | Ireland | Australia
India | New Zealand | South Africa

Penguin Books is part of the Penguin Random House group of companies
whose addresses can be found at global.penguinrandomhouse.com.

First published in French as *Les cerfs-volants* by Éditions Gallimard 1980
First published in this translation in the United States of
America by New Directions Books 2017
First published in Great Britain in Penguin Classics 2018
001

Printed in Great Britain by Clays Ltd, St Ives plc

A CIP catalogue record for this book is available from the British Library

ISBN: 978–0–241–34561–0

The Kites

1

NOWADAYS, THE LITTLE MUSEUM IN CLÉRY DEVOTED to the works of Ambrose Fleury is only a minor tourist attraction. Most of its visitors drift over after lunch at the Clos Joli, a restaurant that guidebooks unanimously praise as one of France's most celebrated landmarks. These same guidebooks note the little museum's existence with the words, "worth a side trip." The museum's five rooms hold most of my uncle's work—the pieces that survived the war, the Occupation, the Liberation fighting, and all the vicissitudes and lassitudes our people has known.

Whatever their country of origin, all kites are born in the popular imagination, which is what gives them their slightly naive look; Ambrose Fleury's kites were no exception, even the final pieces he made in his old age bear that stamp of innocence and that freshness of soul. Despite lagging interest and the slim funding it receives from the municipal government, it's unlikely the museum will close its doors anytime soon—it's too much a part of our history. Mostly, though, its rooms are deserted. These days, the French are mostly looking to forget, not to remember.

The best existing photograph of Ambrose Fleury can be found at the museum's entrance. It shows him in his rural postman's outfit: his uniform and peaked cap, his big clodhoppers, his leather bag slung over his belly, standing between two of his kites, one in the shape of a ladybug, and one representing the fiery statesman Léon Gambetta, whose face and body form the balloon and the basket with which he made his famous flight during the siege of Paris. There are lots of pictures of the "certified postman," as he was long known in Cléry—most visitors to his workshop snapped a photo or two, just for a laugh. My uncle posed willingly for these portraits. He was unafraid of ridicule, and didn't mind being nicknamed the "certified postman" or labeled a "harmless eccentric." If he was aware that the locals had dubbed him "crazy old Fleury," then he seemed to see it more as a sign of their admiration than of their scorn. In the nineteen thirties, when my uncle's reputation began to grow, Marcellin Duprat, the chef and owner of the Clos Joli restaurant, came up with the idea of printing postcards that showed my guardian posed in uniform among his kites, with the words, *Cléry: Celebrated rural postman Ambrose Fleury and his kites.* Unfortunately, the cards were done in black and white, and so they betray no hint of the kites' joyful colors and forms, none of their smiling bonhomie—none of what I'd call the knowing winks the old Norman was always aiming skyward.

My father was killed in the First World War, and my mother died shortly thereafter. The Great War also took the life of Robert, the second of the three Fleury brothers; my uncle Ambrose came back from it after taking a bullet through the chest. For the sake of clarity in this story, I should also add that my great-grandfather Antoine perished on the barricades during the Paris Commune. I do believe that this little feature of our past played a decisive role in my guardian's life, though nothing left a deeper mark on him than the names of his two brothers carved onto Cléry's war monument. The man he was before the Great War—people say he was quick to go the knuckle back then—had come home someone very different. Many found it surprising that a decorated combatant like my uncle would take every opportunity to express his pacifist sentiments, defend conscientious objectors, and condemn violence in all its forms, with a glint in his eye that was probably just a reflection of the flame burning at the Tomb of the Unknown Soldier. Physically, there was nothing soft or gentle about him. His sculpted features and cropped gray hair gave him a hard and ready look, with one of those big bushy mustaches that are usually qualified as "Gallic"—thank God the French have managed to hang on to at least some of their historical memory, if only by the hairs. His gaze was somber, which is always a good foil for merriment. It was generally believed that he'd come back from the war a little bit "touched," which explained the pacifism, as well as his funny passion for his kites: he spent every spare minute with his *gnamas*, as he called them. He had discovered this word in a book about Equatorial Africa, where apparently it refers to everything that has a breath of life in it: men and mosquitoes, lions and ideas and elephants. Most likely he chose to become a rural postman because his Military Medal and his two War Cross citations gave him special priority for restricted civil service jobs. Then again, maybe he felt this was a good line of work for a pacifist. Often, he would say to me, "If you're lucky, my little Ludo, and you work hard, then someday maybe you can get a nice office job with the postal administration, too."

It took me many years to find my way through which things were matters of great consequence and faith to him, and which ones he drew from a wellspring of irony that seemed to flow from some pooled source where the French go to find themselves when they are lost.

My uncle always said: "Kites need to learn to fly, just like everybody else," and from the time I was seven, as soon as school let out, I would accompany him to what he called "practice." Sometimes we'd go to the field beside La Motte, and sometimes farther, to the banks of the Rigole, with a *gnama* that still smelled deliciously of fresh glue.

"You have to hang on tight to them," he would explain, "because they pull, and sometimes they break loose and fly too high—they take off in pursuit of the blue yonder and you never see them again, except when people bring them back here in pieces."

"But if I hang on too tight, won't I fly away with them, too?"

My uncle would smile, which made his big mustache look even kinder.

"It could happen," he'd say. "You can't let yourself get carried away."

My uncle gave all his kites pet names: Cracklemunch, Gambol, Hobbledehoy, Fatsy, Zigomar, Flutterpat, Lovey. I never understood why he picked the names he did. Why the name Bumble belonged to a kind of silly frog whose front legs waved "hello" to you in the wind, and not to Swash, who was a fish wreathed in smiles that wiggled its silvery scales and pink fins in the air. Or why he chose to fly his Patooty above the field by La Motte and not his Martian kite, Meemy, who I thought was a lovely creature, with round eyes and wings shaped like ears that quivered as the kite began to rise. I practiced until I could imitate him with great skill, and bested everyone in schoolyard competitions. When my uncle launched a *gnama* with a shape I didn't understand, he would explain, "You've got to try and make them be different from everything else in the world. Something really new—something that's never been seen or known before. Those are the leads you have to hold on to the hardest, though. They really go after the blue yonder if you let them go, and can do a lot of damage when they fall back down."

Sometimes it seemed to me that it was the kite holding Ambrose Fleury at the end of the line, and not the other way round.

For a long time, my favorite was the brave Fatsy, whose belly would puff up in the most wonderfully surprising way as soon as he got up in the air. With only a little breeze, he would execute comical flips by flapping his paunch with his paws, depending on how my uncle pulled or let out the line.

I allowed Fatsy to sleep with me, because on the ground, kites require a great deal of friendship. The shape goes out of them when they come down, and living flat on their faces like that makes them highly susceptible to the blues. For its beauty to really shine, a kite needs height, fresh air, and wide-open skies.

As a rural postman, my guardian spent his workdays crisscrossing the countryside, picking up the mail at the post office each morning and delivering it to the people in our community. But he was nearly always back home by the time I'd finished the walk from school, a good three miles away, standing in his postman's uniform in the field by La Motte—the wind at our place was always better in the late afternoon—gazing up at one of his "little friends" bobbing and fluttering high above us. And yet, when we lost our superb Fourseas—all its twelve sails filled up in one big burst and ripped kite and reel right out of my hands—I burst out sobbing and my uncle said to me, his eyes following his work of art as it disappeared into the blue yonder: "Don't cry. That's what they're meant to do. He's happy up there."

I was ten years old when the *Honfleur Gazette* published a slightly mocking article about "Ambrose Fleury, our fellow citizen, the country postman from Cléry: a charmingly original character whose kites will no doubt make a celebrated name of our region, like lace did for Valenciennes, porcelain for Limoges, and mints for Cambrai." My uncle cut out the page, framed it, and hung it on a nail in the workshop.

"You see I've got my share of vanity," he remarked to me, with a little wink.

A Paris newspaper picked up the *Honfleur Gazette* article and its accompanying photograph, and our barn, thenceforth known as "the workshop," soon began receiving not only visitors, but also orders. Marcellin Duprat, an old friend of my uncle's, began recommending this "local curiosity" to his customers at the Clos Joli.

One day, an automobile pulled up at our farm and a very elegant-looking gentleman emerged from inside it. What impressed me most about this man was his mustache, which went all the way up to his ears and disappeared into his sideburns, dividing his face in two. Later, I learned that he was the great English collector Lord Howe; he came accompanied by a valet and a trunk, which was opened to reveal a magnificent collection of kites from all over the world—Burma, Japan, China, Siam—carefully arranged against a custom-made velvet backing. My uncle was invited to admire them, which he did with the utmost sincerity: there wasn't a shred of prejudice in him. The one tiny point of national pride he clung to was his insistence that the kite had only acquired its true nobility with the French Revolution. After he had paid his respects to the English collector's showpieces, he brought out some of his own creations, including a Victor Hugo kite inspired by the famous Nadar photo: when flown, the poet seemed to be borne aloft by clouds, giving him a slight resemblance to God the Father. After an hour or two of inspection and mutual admiration, the two men went out into the field. Courteously, each one chose the other's kite, and then they entertained the Norman skies until every child in the area had run up to join the fun.

Ambrose Fleury's fame continued to grow, but it didn't swell his head at all, not even when his *Young Lady in a Phrygian Bonnet*—he was fiercely and viscerally devoted to the French Republic—won first prize at the Nogent competition, nor when Lord Howe invited him to London, where he demonstrated a few of his masterpieces at a gathering in Hyde Park. Europe's political climate was clouding over then; Hitler was consolidating power and occupying the Rhineland, and this was one of many demonstrations of Franco-British friendship taking place at the time. I saved a photo from the *Illustrated London News* that shows Ambrose Fleury holding his *Liberty Illuminating the World* as he stands between Lord Howe and the Prince of Wales. After this semiofficial vesting, Ambrose Fleury was elected to the Order of the Kites of France, first as a member and then as its honorary president. We saw more and more curiosity seekers. Lovely ladies and handsome gentlemen would motor in from Paris to lunch at the Clos Joli and then show up at our place to ask if the "master" might show them one or two of his pieces. The lovely ladies would sit in the grass, the handsome gentlemen would clench cigars between their teeth, hiding their smiles as they watched the "certified postman" hold his *Montaigne* or his *World Peace* at the end of a string, gazing up at the blue sky with the fixed stare of a great explorer. It occurred to me that there was something insulting in the titters of the lovely ladies and the superior expressions of the handsome gentlemen. Occasionally, I would overhear their comments, some of them unpleasant, some of them full of pity.

"Apparently he's not quite all there. Shell shock from the War, you know."

"He claims he's a pacifist and a conscientious objector but I daresay he's quite the clever self-promoter."

"Hilarious!"

"Marcellin Duprat was right, it's well worth the trip!"

"Don't you think he looks like Field Marshal Lyautey, with that crew cut and mustache?"

"Bit of a crazy gleam in his eyes, don't you think?"

"But of course darling, it's the creative spark, don't you know?"

Then they'd buy a kite, just like you'd pay for your seat at a show, and toss it carelessly into the trunk of their car. All the more upsetting was my uncle, who, when absorbed in his passion, became completely oblivious to what was going on around him. He didn't even notice that some of our visitors were poking fun at him behind his back. One day on the walk home, fuming about some comments I'd overheard while my guardian was flying his favorite kite of all time, a Jean-Jacques Rousseau with wings shaped like open books whose pages fluttered in the wind, I couldn't hold back my indignation any longer. I marched with giant steps along behind him, my eyebrows furrowed, my fists thrust into my pockets, stomping so hard that my socks fell down around my heels.

"Uncle, those Parisians were making fun of you. They said you were an old nutcase."

Ambrose Fleury stopped in his tracks. Far from being angry, he seemed rather satisfied.

"Really? They said that?"

I drew myself up to my full four and a half feet and repeated what

I'd heard Marcellin Duprat say about a couple of Clos Joli customers who'd complained about the bill: "They are lesser people."

"There are no lesser people," my uncle replied.

He leaned over, laid Jean-Jacques Rousseau carefully on the grass, and sat down. I sat down beside him.

"So they said I was crazy. Well, you know what? Those handsome gentlemen and those lovely ladies are right. Obviously, a man who's dedicated his entire life to kites is a bit touched. But really, that's a matter of interpretation. Some say it's touched in the head, some say it's touched by a sacred spark. It can be hard to tell the difference. But if you really love somebody or something, give them everything you have—everything you are, even. And don't worry about the rest." A flash of merriment appeared briefly in his big mustache. "That's what you need to know, Ludo, if you want to become a good employee of the postal administration."

2

OUR FARM HAD BEEN IN THE FAMILY SINCE ONE OF the Fleurys had built it, shortly after what my grandparents' generation still called "the events." When I became curious enough to ask which "events" they were referring to, my uncle explained that it was the French Revolution. In this way I learned that all the Fleurys have long memories.

"Oh yes, maybe it's the result of mandatory public education, but we Fleurys have always had surprising historical memories. I don't think a single one of us has ever forgotten anything we learned. Sometimes my grandfather would make us recite the Declaration of the Rights of Man, and it got to be such a habit with me that I still find myself doing it."

Though my own memory hadn't yet taken on its "historical" bent, I knew at the time—I'd just turned ten—that it was already a source of surprise, and ultimately of concern, for Monsieur Herbier, my teacher, who sang bass in the Cléry choir in his spare time. He ascribed the ease with which I recalled everything I learned—after reading them over once or twice I could recite pages at a time from my textbooks—as well as my unusual aptitude for mental math, to some kind of malformation of the brain, rather than to the skills, albeit the exceptional ones, of a good student. He was all the more inclined to distrust what he referred to not as my gifts, but my "predispositions"—the rather sinister accent with which he said the word made me feel almost guilty—because my uncle was touched in the head, which everyone took for granted in him, and which made it appear that I had been stricken by some hereditary defect, which might turn out to be fatal. The words I heard most frequently from Monsieur Herbier's mouth were, "Moderation in all things." He would stare at me grimly as he pronounced this dire warning. When my predispositions became so glaring that a schoolmate ratted on me for pocketing an ample sum after successfully betting that I could recite ten full pages of the Chaix railway timetable, I learned that Monsieur Herbier had referred to me as a "little freak." I made matters worse for myself by trotting out square roots from memory and executing rapid-fire multiplications of very long numbers. So Monsieur Herbier came to La Motte and spoke for a long time with my guardian. His advice was that I be sent to Paris and examined by a specialist. My ear pressed up against the door, I took in every word of their exchange.

"Ambrose, this is not a normal proficiency we're talking about here. It's happened before, children with amazing gifts for mental calculation turning out abnormal. They end up as circus freaks and that's the end of it. One part of their brain develops at lightning speed, but they're gibbering idiots when it comes to everything else. In his current state, Ludovic could practically sit for the entrance examinations at the Polytechnic Institute."

"That *is* very curious," observed my uncle. "With us Fleurys it's always been historical memory. One of us even ended up in front of a firing squad, under the Commune."

"I don't see the connection."

"Just another one who remembered."

"Remembered what?"

My uncle observed a moment of silence.

"Everything, probably," he replied, finally.

"You're not saying that your ancestor was executed for an excess of memory?"

"That's exactly what I'm saying. He must have known it all by heart, every single thing the French had been subjected to over the ages."

"Ambrose, you have a reputation in these parts … I'm sorry to say this, but as a … well, as a bit of a fanatic, but I didn't come here to talk about your kites."

"Well, yeah, what about it? So I'm a nutter, too."

"My visit today is simply to warn you that little Ludovic has an abnormal memory for his age—abnormal for any age, really. He recited the Chaix timetable from memory. Ten pages. He multiplied a fourteen-digit number by another one just as long."

"Well, so with him it's numbers. I guess he's not troubled with the historical memory. Maybe that'll keep him away from the firing squad, next time."

"Next time? What next time?"

"How am I supposed to know that? But there always is a next one."

"You should have him examined by a doctor."

"Listen, Herbier. You're pushing it, now. If my nephew were truly abnormal, he'd be an imbecile. Good day, and thank you for your visit. I understand you're saying this with the best of intentions. Tell me, is he as gifted at history as he is at mathematics?"

"I'm telling you, Ambrose, you can't call it a gift—or even intelligence. Intelligence implies *reason*. I'll repeat that: *reasoning*. And in that department he's no better or worse than any other kid his age. As for French history, he can recite every bit of it, from A to Z."

There was an even longer silence, and then suddenly I heard my uncle bawl, "To Z? What Z? Because there's already a Z in sight?"

Monsieur Herbier had nothing to say to that. After the defeat in 1940, with the Z hovering distinctly on the horizon, I often found myself thinking back to that conversation.

The only teacher who did not seem the least bit worried about my "predispositions" was my French teacher, Monsieur Pinder. The one time he got upset with me was when, in an attempt to outdo myself, I took it upon myself to start with the last verse of the José-Maria de Heredia poem "Los Conquistadores" and recite it backward. Monsieur Pinder interrupted me with a menacing shake of his finger. "Young Ludovic," he warned, "I don't know if this is your way of preparing for what appears to be threatening us all, by which I mean a backward life in a backward world, but I shall ask you to leave poetry out of it, at the very least."

Later on, it was this same Monsieur Pinder who assigned us a composition topic that would play a certain role in my life later on: "Examine and compare these two expressions: *to live reasonably* and *to keep your reason to live.* Do you see a contradiction between the two ideas? Explain."

It should be acknowledged that Monsieur Herbier was not entirely incorrect when he came to my uncle with his concerns, with his fears that my knack for remembering anything and everything wasn't accompanied by any growth in maturity, moderation, or plain good sense. Maybe that's how it is, more or less, for everyone who suffers from an excess of memory—how it turned out for so many Frenchmen a few years later when they were deported, or taken down by the firing squad.

3

OUR FARM WAS LOCATED BEHIND THE HAMLET OF Clos, at the edge of the Voigny woods. Fern and broom crowded together with beech and oak trees there, and deer and boar roamed wild. Farther on there were marshes, where the peace of teal, otters, dragonflies, and swans reigned.

La Motte was fairly isolated. Our closest neighbors, the Cailleux family, were a good half-hour's walk away. Little Johnny Cailleux was two years younger than I, so to him, I was "the big boy." His parents had a dairy in town; the grandfather, Gaston, who had lost a leg in a sawmill accident, kept bees. Further on, there was the Magnard family, a taciturn lot who didn't care for anything besides cows, butter, and fields. The father, the son, and the daughters, two old maids, never spoke to anyone.

"Except to tell or ask a price," Gaston Cailleux would grumble.

Other than that, the only farms between La Motte and Cléry belonged to the Monniers and the Simons, whose children were in my class at school.

I knew the surrounding woods all the way down to their smallest, most secret corners. My uncle had helped me build an Indian wigwam, a little hut made of branches and covered in oilcloth, at the bottom of a ravine in a place known as Vieille-Source. I'd slip over there to read the books of James Oliver Curwood and James Fenimore Cooper, and dream of the Apaches and the Sioux, or else, besieged by enemy forces—which, as tradition requires, were always "superior in number"—I would defend myself down to the last bullet cartridge. I was dozing there one day in mid-June, having gorged on wild strawberries, when I opened my eyes to see a very blonde little girl gazing severely at me from beneath a big straw hat. Sun and shadow were dappled beneath the branches, and even today, after so many years, it seems that dark and light have never ceased to play around Lila—that somehow, in this instant of emotion, whose reason and nature I didn't comprehend, I was forewarned. Instinctively, driven by some unknown inner force or weakness, I made a gesture whose definitive, irrevocable nature I was far from understanding at the time: I held out a handful of strawberries to the severe blonde apparition. I had no idea how much more than that I was offering. The little girl came and sat down beside me, and without paying the least attention to the berries I proffered, took the entire basket. And that was how the roles were dealt, for all time. When there were only a few strawberries left at the bottom of the basket, she handed it back to me and said, with a certain degree of reproach, "They're better with sugar."

There was only one thing to do, and I didn't hesitate. I leapt up and took off running, fists at my side, through the woods and fields to La Motte, where I shot into the kitchen like a cannonball, grabbed a box of powdered sugar from the shelf, and retraced my steps at the same speed. There she was, sitting in the grass, her hat lying beside her, contemplating a ladybug on the back of her hand. I held the sugar out to her.

"I don't want any more. But that's nice."

"We'll leave the sugar here and come back tomorrow," I said, with inspiration bred from despair.

"Maybe. What's your name?"

"Ludo. What's yours?"

The ladybug flew off.

"We don't know each other well enough yet. Maybe someday I'll tell you my name. I'm pretty mysterious, you know. You'll probably never see me again. What do your parents do?"

"I don't have any parents. I live with my uncle."

"What does he do?"

I sensed vaguely that "rural postman" wasn't quite the right thing.

"He's a kite master."

She seemed favorably impressed.

"What does that mean?"

"It's like a great captain, but in the sky."

She thought for a little while longer, then got up. "Maybe I'll come back tomorrow," she said. "I don't know. I'm very unpredictable. How old are you?"

"I'm almost ten."

"Oh, you're far too young for me. I'm eleven and a half. But I like wild strawberries. Wait for me here tomorrow at the same time. I'll be back if there's nothing better to do."

She left me, after shooting me one last severe look.

I must have picked six pounds of strawberries the next day. Every few minutes, I ran to see if she was there. She didn't return that day. Nor the next day, nor the day after that.

I waited for her every day in June, July, August, and September. At first I had the strawberries to count on, then blueberries, then blackberries, then mushrooms. The only other time waiting would cause me such torment was from 1940 to 1944, keeping watch for France's return. Even when it came time for the mushrooms to abandon me, too, I kept returning to the forest, to the place we had met. The year passed, and then another and another again, and I discovered that Monsieur Herbier had not been entirely wrong when he warned my uncle that there was something unsettling about my memory. There must have been some kind of hereditary weakness in the Fleury family: we did not possess the soothing ability to forget. I studied, I helped my guardian in the workshop, but rare were the times when a little girl in a white dress did not dog me, clutching a big straw hat in her hand. It was indeed an "excess of memory," as Monsieur Herbier had so rightly pointed out—something that must not have plagued him too much, given how carefully he avoided memory's dangerous, ardent clamor under the Nazis. Three or four years after our encounter, when the first strawberries appeared, I still found myself filling my basket and stretching out under the beeches with my eyes closed, to encourage her to surprise me. I even remembered the sugar. Of course, as time went by, there was a certain amount of fun in it. I had begun to understand what my uncle called "the pursuit of the blue yonder," and I was learning not to take myself, or my excess of memory, too seriously.

4

I SAT FOR MY BACCALAURÉAT EXAMS AT FOURTEEN,
thanks to a "special dispensation" obtained with the help of Monsieur Julliac, the secretary at our town hall, who "adjusted" my birth
certificate to make me fifteen. I didn't yet know what I was going
to do with my life. In the meantime, my gift for numbers had led
Marcellin Duprat to entrust me with the accounts of the Clos Joli.
I worked there twice a week. I read everything I could get my hands
on, from medieval fabliaux to works like Henri Barbusse's *Under Fire*
and Erich Maria Remarque's *All Quiet on the Western Front*, both
gifts from my uncle—although, with his confidence in "mandatory
public education," he rarely recommended books to me. Beyond
that confidence, I believe Ambrose Fleury had a trust even greater
in something he seemed to consider a certainty, despite the debate
it has provoked before, during, and after: the heredity of acquired
traits—above all, he'd add, among "our kind."

Several years had passed since my uncle had left his job as a rural
postman, but Marcellin Duprat, with no little zeal, advised him to
receive visitors in his old uniform. The owner of the Clos Joli had a
keen sense of what nowadays we'd call "public relations."

"You understand, Ambrose? You're a legend now. You've got to
uphold that legend. I know you could care less about it for yourself, but you owe it to your country. My customers are always asking

about you: 'That Fleury, the famous postman with his kites—is he still around? Can we go see him?' Your whatsits, whatever you call them—I mean, you do sell them, after all. They're your livelihood. Well, so you have to keep up your name. Someday people will be saying 'the Postman Fleury' like they say 'le Douanier Rousseau.' Look at me, when I come out to greet customers, I keep my chef's hat and jacket on. Because that's how they want to see me."

Although Marcellin was an old friend, his little recipe didn't please my uncle one bit. They had a few first-rate shouting matches over it. The owner of the Clos Joli saw himself as something of a national treasure, and the only people in his field he would acknowledge as equals were Point in Vienne, Pic in Valence, and Dumaine in Saulieu. He had a stately presence: a faintly receding hairline, clear, steel-blue eyes, and a little mustache that gave him a haughty, authoritarian air. There was something military in his bearing, perhaps acquired during his years in the trenches of the Great War. In the thirties, it had not yet occurred to France to retreat into its culinary grandeur, and Marcellin Duprat deemed himself its unsung hero.

"The only man who understands me is Édouard Herriot. The other day, as he was leaving, he said to me, 'Every time I come here is a comfort. I can't say what the future holds for us, but I'm sure the Clos Joli will survive it all. The only thing is, Marcellin, you're going to have to wait awhile for your Legion of Honor Medal. The abundance of cultural riches we still enjoy in France makes us neglect some of our more modest values.' That's what Herriot said to me. So do me a favor, Ambrose. You and I are the only famous people around here. Please, every so often, for the sake of the customers, if you'd just put on your postman's uniform—I promise, you'll look a hell of a lot better than in those hick corduroys."

In the end, my uncle couldn't help but laugh. I was always happy when I saw those nice little wrinkles—the kind that live off merriment—appear on his face.

"Good old Marcellin! All that grandeur can weigh heavy on a man's shoulders. But you know what? He's not all wrong. Popularizing the peaceful art of kite-making is worth sacrificing a little pride for."

I don't think it actually bothered my uncle all that much to button up his old postman's uniform when he went out into the fields surrounded by children, two or three of whom came regularly to La Motte for "practice" after school.

As I mentioned, Ambrose Fleury had been elected honorary president of the Order of the Kites of France, and God knows why he resigned from it after Munich. I never did understand how it was that an ardent pacifist could feel so indignant, so beaten, the day that peace—shameful as some people said it was—was kept at Munich. No doubt it was the old Fleury historical memory flaring up again.

My own memory wasn't letting up any, either. Every summer, I returned to the forest and remembered. I asked around and learned that I had not been the victim of some kind of "apparition," as I had occasionally begun to fear was the case. Elisabeth de Bronicka really did exist; her parents owned Le Manoir des Jars, an estate bordered by the road from Clos to Cléry, whose walls I passed every day on the way to school. They hadn't been back to Normandy for several summers. From my uncle, I learned that they had their mail forwarded to Poland, to their estate on the shores of the Baltic, not far from the Free City of Gdańsk, better known back then as Danzig. No one knew if they were ever coming back.

"This isn't the first kite you've lost in your life, Ludo," my uncle would remind me when he saw me returning from the woods with my basket of strawberries still disconsolately full. "And it won't be the last, either."

By that point, I hoped for nothing more. Even though my game had become a bit childish for a boy of fourteen, I had before me the example of a grown man who'd succeeded in preserving in himself the scrap of naïveté that turns into wisdom only when it ages badly.

It had been nearly four years since I'd seen "my Polish girl," as I called her, but my memory had held up perfectly. The finely sculpted features of her face made you want to cup it in the palm of your hand, and the harmonious vivacity of her every movement got me excellent marks on my philosophy finals. I had chosen aesthetics as the subject of my exams, and the examiner, who I imagine was worn out after a long day's work, said: "I shall ask you only one question: What characterizes grace?"

I thought of the Polish girl—her neck, her arms, her floating hair—and did not hesitate: "Motion."

He gave me nineteen points out of twenty. I owe my *baccalauréat* to love.

Aside from Johnny Cailleux, who would occasionally come sit in a corner and watch me, a little sadly—"at least you have somebody," he said to me one day with envy—I had no real ties to anyone. I had become almost as indifferent to my surroundings as the Magnard family. I would run into them from time to time, the father, the son, and the two daughters, clutching their crates as they lurched down the path in their cart on the way to market. I said hello every time, and they never answered.

Early July 1936 found me sitting in the grass with my basket of strawberries, reading José-Maria de Heredia, whose poems still seem to me to have been quite unjustly forgotten. In front of me, in a tunnel of light between two beeches, sunshine rolled over the ground like a voluptuous cat. From time to time, a titmouse fled from the nearby marsh.

I lifted my eyes. There she was before me, a girl whom the past four years had treated with a piety that was like a tribute to my memory. My heart leapt from my chest and clutched at my throat. I froze.

And then the emotion passed.

Calmly, I laid down my book.

She had been a little late in returning, that was all.

"I hear you've been waiting for four years to see me …" She laughed. "You didn't even forget the sugar!"

"I never forget anything."

"I forget everything so easily. I don't even recall your name."

I let her play with me. If she knew I had been looking for her everywhere, then she had to know who I was.

"Wait … Let me think … Oh yes. It's Ludovic. Ludo. The son of Ambrose Fleury, the famous postman."

"His nephew." I held out the basket of strawberries. She tasted one, sat down beside me, and picked up my book.

"My God. José-Maria de Heredia! That's so unfashionable. You should read Rimbaud and Apollinaire."

There was only one thing to do. I recited:

> She he once called his Angevin sweet
> O'er trembling chords erred spirit fleet
> As love's anguish struck her heart; in pain
>
> Her voice cried to the winds that lured him away
> To caress him; perchance his fickle heart swayed
> With his song, made for a thresher of grain.

She appeared flattered, and pleased with herself.

"Our gardeners told me that you came and asked questions about whether I was ever coming back. Crazy in love, or something."

I saw that I'd be lost if I didn't stand up for myself. "You know, sometimes the best way to forget about someone is to see them again."

"Hang on a second, don't get all worked up, I was only teasing. Is it true, what they say—that you're all like that?"

"Like what?"

"That you don't forget?"

"My uncle Ambrose claims the Fleurys have such good memories that some of them even died from it."

"How can you die from memory? That's ridiculous."

"That's what he thinks, too—it's why he hates war and became a rural postman. He's only interested in kites, now. They're beautiful when they're in the sky, but at least you can stick a string to them, and even when they get away from you and crash, it's just paper and bits of wood."

"I'd like you to explain to me how you can die of memory."

"It's pretty complicated."

"I'm not an idiot. I might be able to understand."

"All I mean is that it's kind of difficult to explain. Apparently all the Fleurys are victims of mandatory public education."

"Of what?!"

"Of mandatory public education. They were taught too many beautiful things and they remembered them too well, and believed in them completely, and passed them down from father to son, because of the heredity of acquired traits, and ..." I sensed that I was not explaining myself as well as I should have; I wanted to add that there was in all of this a battiness that some would call a sacred spark, but, riveted, by the severe blue gaze that she had turned on me full force, I only dug myself further in. I kept repeating obstinately, "They were taught too many beautiful things that they believed in—they even got killed for them. That's why my uncle became a pacifist and a conscientious objector."

She shook her head with a *humph*. "I can't understand a word you say. It doesn't hold together, what your uncle says."

Suddenly, what seemed like a clever idea struck me: "Well, come see us at La Motte, and he'll explain it to you himself."

"I have no intention of wasting my time listening to old wives' tales. I read Rilke and Thomas Mann—not José-Maria de Heredia. Besides, you live with him, and he doesn't seem to have been able to explain it to you."

"You have to be French to understand."

She grew angry. "Oh, nonsense. Because the French have better memories than the Polish?"

I had begun to feel crazed. This was not the conversation I was expecting after a tragic, four-year separation. At the same time, making a fool of myself was out of the question, even if I hadn't read Rilke and Thomas Mann.

"It's a question of historical memory," I insisted. "There are lots of things that French people remember and can't make themselves forget, and it lasts your whole life, except with people whose memories go blank. I already explained, it's an effect of mandatory public education. I don't see what's so hard to understand about that."

She stood up and looked at me pityingly. "You think that you French are the only ones with this 'historical memory'? That we Poles don't have one, too? I never saw such a silly ass as you. One hundred and sixty Bronickis have been killed in the past five centuries alone, most of them in heroic circumstances, and we have the documents to prove it. Goodbye. You will never see me again. Well, no. You'll see me again. I feel sorry for you. You've been coming here to wait for me for the past four years, and instead of just admitting that you're madly in love with me—like all the rest of them—you insult my country. What do you know about Poland anyway? Go ahead. I'm listening."

She crossed her arms over her chest and waited.

Tears pricked my eyes: everything was so different from what I had hoped for and imagined when I dreamed of her. This was all my crazy old uncle's fault. He had filled my head with stacks of ridiculous notions, instead of keeping them for his paper darlings. I was making such an effort to hold back tears that suddenly she became worried.

"What's wrong with you? You've turned green."

"I love you," I whispered.

"That's no reason to turn green. At least, not yet. You'll have to get to know me better. Goodbye. I'll see you soon. But don't ever try to give us Polish people lessons about historical memory. Promise?"

"I swear to you, I wasn't trying to … I think very highly of Poland. It's a country known for …"

"For what?"

I was silent. I realized with horror that the only thing I could come up with that had anything to do with Poland was the expression "drunk as a Pole."

She laughed. "Well, all right. Four years isn't bad. You could do better, obviously, but you'd need more time."

And having stated the obvious, she left me—a white, lively silhouette drifting off through the beech trees, into the light and shadow.

I dragged myself back to La Motte and lay down with my face to the wall. I felt like I had ruined my life. I couldn't understand why or how, instead of proclaiming my love to her, I had let myself get into some senseless conversation about France, Poland, and their respective historical memories, which I didn't give one good goddamn about. Clearly, this was all my uncle's fault, with his rainbow-winged pacifist Jean Jaurès and his Arcole—of whose name, rightly or wrongly, as he'd once explained to me, nothing remained but the bridge.

That evening, he came to see me. "What's gotten into you?"

"She came back."

He smiled affectionately. "And I'll wager she's not at all the same. It's always a safer bet to make them yourself," he added, "with pretty-colored paper and string."

5

THE NEXT DAY, AT AROUND FOUR IN THE AFTER-
noon, just when I had begun to tell myself that all was lost, and that
I would have to accomplish what is sometimes the most superhuman
effort of all—forgetting—a gigantic blue convertible with the top
down stopped in front of our house. A distinguished-looking driver
in a gray uniform announced my invitation to tea at "the manor."
As quickly as I could, I polished my old shoes, put on my only suit,
which was now too small, and seated myself beside the chauffeur,
who turned out to be English. He informed me that Stanislas de
Bronicki, "Mademoiselle's" father, was a wizard financier, and that
his wife had been one of Warsaw's greatest comediennes. She had
given up her career, but compensated for the sacrifice by constantly
making scenes.

"They have extensive properties in Poland, including a castle
where Monsieur the count receives statesmen and celebrities from
all over the world. Believe it, my boy, he's really somebody. If he takes
a shine to you, your life's not going to end with a career in the postal
service."

Le Manoir des Jars was a great wooden structure, three stories
high, with verandas and sculpted balustrades, turrets, and lattice-
work balconies. Resembling nothing else in our region, it was an exact copy of a house that cousins of the Bronickis, the Ostrorog family, owned on the Bosporus, in Istanbul. It was built tucked away into

grounds whose drives and pathways you could just glimpse through the gate, and figured prominently among the picture postcards sold at the *Petit Gris*, the Cléry café and tobacconist's shop, in the rue du Mail. Its Turkish style was all the rage in 1902, when it was built by Stanislas de Bronicki's father as a tribute to his friend Pierre Loti, who was a frequent guest there. Age and dampness had darkened the wooden boards of the house with a blackish patina, which Bronicki refused to touch, for authenticity's sake. My uncle knew the manor well, and had often spoken of it to me. His work as a postman had once brought him there almost daily, for the Bronickis received more mail than all the rest of Clos and Cléry combined.

"Rich people don't have their heads on straight," he grumbled. "Building a Turkish house in Normandy—I bet they had a Norman manor built in Turkey, too."

It was the end of June, and the park was fully resplendent. Never before had I seen nature so carefully tended—the nature I knew was raw and simple. The flowers looked well nourished enough to have been fed by the hand of Marcellin Duprat himself.

"They've got five full-time gardeners working here," said the chauffeur.

He left me alone in front of the veranda.

I tugged off my beret, licked my hand and slicked down my hair, then climbed the steps. As soon as I rang, a frantic chambermaid pulled open the door, and I saw that I couldn't have come at a worse time. A blonde woman, dressed in what appeared to be a tangled heap of blue-and-rose-colored chiffon, was half prostrate in a chair, sobbing; a worried-looking Dr. Gardieu held his old pocket watch in one hand while feeling her pulse with the other; a smallish but powerfully built man, wearing a silver dressing gown that shone like a suit of armor, paced the length of the sitting room; a butler followed behind him, bearing a tray full of drinks. Stas de Bronicki had a head of curls as blond as a baby's, sideburns that went halfway down his cheeks, and a face you might have said was lacking in nobility, if such a thing could be detected with the naked eye, without any recourse to supporting documentation. It was round, with heavy, ham-colored jowls; a face you could easily imagine leaning over the block at a butcher's stall; a thin mustache, little more than a downy fuzz, ornamented lips that pursed and protruded like the back end of a chicken, giving him a constantly aggrieved look that was particularly evident at the moment of my arrival. His big, slightly bugged eyes were a faded blue—their gleam bore more than a passing resemblance to the bottles on the butler's tray, and the fixedness of his gaze must have had something to do with the contents of these same bottles. Lila was seated tranquilly off to one side, waiting for a miniature poodle to stand up on its hind legs and be given a treat. A predatory-looking individual dressed all in black sat at a desk, so hunched and absorbed in the pile of papers through which he was rifling that he seemed to be examining them with his long, ferrety nose.

I waited timidly, beret in hand, for someone to notice me. Lila, first throwing me a distracted look, finally bestowed the treat upon the poodle. Then she came over to me and took my hand. At this same moment, sobs overcame the beautiful lady again, even more wracking than before, which the assembled company greeted with total indifference.

Lila said: "It's nothing, just the cotton again."

And, as I must have looked at her with a face flooded with incomprehension, she added, as an explanation, "Papa went and got himself into cotton again. He can't help it." With a little shrug, she added, "We did a lot better in coffee."

I did not yet know that Stanislas de Bronicki made and lost fortunes on the stock exchange with such speed that no one could ever say for certain whether he was ruined or rich.

Stanislas de Bronicki—Stas to his gaming circle and racetrack friends as well as to his lady escorts at Le Chabanais and Le Sphinx—was forty-five at the time. I was always surprised and a little uneasy at the contrast between his massive, heavy face and its features, which were so tiny that, to use the words of the Comtesse de Noailles, "you had to look for them." There was also something incongruous in his curly, baby-blond hair, his rosy complexion, and the blue Saxon gaze—the whole Bronicki family, except for the son, Thaddeus, seemed entirely blue, blond, and pink. A speculator and a gambler, Stas de Bronicki sent money tumbling across the gambling table as offhandedly as his ancestors had once sent their soldiers charging into the field of battle. The only thing he hadn't ever gambled away was his title: he belonged to one of Poland's four or five great aristocratic lineages, like the Houses of Sapieha, Radziwiłł, and Czartoryski, which had for so many years divided Poland up among themselves, until the country passed into other hands and was subjected to other divisions. I noticed that his eyes tended to roll around a little in their sockets, as if following the motions of all the balls he'd seen rolling around the roulette wheel.

Lila led me to her father, but he, with his hand to his forehead and his eyes directed toward the ceiling, from whence the ruin had apparently fallen, paid not the slightest attention to me. So I was led before Madame de Bronicka. There was a pause in her crying, and a human eye with more eyelashes around it than I had ever before encountered in my life was trained upon me. The handkerchief was removed from her sobbing lips, and a small, still-stricken voice demanded: "Where does this one come from?"

"I met him in the forest," Lila said.

"In the forest? Good heavens, how horrible! I hope he isn't rabid. All the animals are getting rabies right now. I read it in the paper. If you get bitten, there's a treatment you have to take, it's very painful … you can't be too careful …" She leaned over and picked up the poodle. Clasping it to her, she regarded me with suspicion.

"Mother, please. Calm yourself," Lila told her.

And so it was that I met the Bronickis for the first time, in their natural state, which is to say, in crisis. Genia de Bronicka—later I learned that the "de" disappeared whenever the family returned to

Poland, where the name did not take a preposition, and then resurfaced in France, where they weren't as well known—was a beauty of a kind once known as devastating, an expression that is no longer in fashion, most likely due to inflation among the devastations the world has known since it was. She was quite slender, but it was the variety of slender that makes a respectful detour at the hips and the chest—one of those women who are so beautiful they don't know what to do with themselves.

A motion of the handkerchief, and I was waved aside definitively. Lila, still holding me by the hand, drew me down a corridor and up some stairs. There were three floors between the grand entry hall, where the cotton crisis was occurring, and the attic, but I believe that during this brief ascension I learned more details about certain odd things that happen between men and women than I had heard in my entire existence up to that point. We had just made it up the first few steps when Lila informed me that Genia's first husband had killed himself on their wedding night, before entering the bridal chamber.

"Performance anxiety," Lila explained to me, still holding me firmly by the hand, perhaps fearing that I'd turn tail and run.

Her second husband, on the other hand, had died from an excess of self-confidence. "Exhaustion," Lila informed me, looking me straight in the eye, as if to warn me, and I wondered what on earth she could mean.

"My mother was the greatest actress in Poland; she had to have a special servant just for the flowers she received all the time. She was kept by King Alphonso XIII, by King Carol of Romania ... but she only ever loved one man in her life, I can't tell you his name, it's a secret—"

"Rudolph Valentino," said a voice.

We had just arrived in the attic, and, turning in the direction of the sarcasm-laden remark, I saw a boy sitting cross-legged on the floor beneath a gabled window, an atlas open over his knees. Beside him was a globe. He had the profile of a young eagle, with a nose that presided over the rest of his visage as if it were master of his face and features. His hair was black, his eyes brown, and although he was only a year or two older than I, the thinness of his lips seemed already to have been shaped by irony; it was impossible to tell whether he was smiling or if he'd been born that way.

"Listen carefully to what my little sister tells you, because there's never a word of truth in it, and that shapes the imagination. Lila's need to lie is so great that you can't hold it against her. It's a calling. I, on the other hand, have a scientific and rationalist mind, which is totally unique in this family. My name's Tad."

He got up and we shook hands. At the other end of the attic was a red curtain, and behind it, someone was playing the piano.

Lila didn't seem at all bothered by her brother's words, and observed me with a slightly amused expression.

"Do you believe me, or not?" she asked me.

I didn't hesitate: "I believe you."

She shot her brother a triumphant look and went and sat down in a big, shabby armchair.

"Oh well, already in love, I see," Tad observed. "In that case, reason is out of the question. I live with a mother who's completely mad, a father who would gamble away all of Poland if given the opportunity, and a sister who considers truth as her personal enemy. Have you two known each other long?"

I started to answer, but he held up his hand.

"Wait, wait—since yesterday?"

I nodded, yes.

Admitting to him that I had seen Lila one single time four years ago, and that I hadn't stopped thinking of her since, could only expose me to some other form of blistering sarcasm.

"Just as I thought," said Tad. "She lost Shako the poodle yesterday and she needed a quick replacement."

"Shako came back this morning," Lila announced.

The siblings were clearly used to these verbal jousts.

"Well, I hope she won't send you away, then. And if ever she starts leading you round in circles come and see me. If you need a little reminder that two and two still make four, I'm your man. And if you do want my advice, get out while you can."

He returned to his corner, sat back down, and took up his atlas again. Lila, her head leaning against the back of the armchair, stared off into space, oblivious. I hesitated a moment, then went over to her and seated myself on a cushion at her feet. She drew her knees up beneath her chin and regarded me pensively, as if she were wondering how best to make use of her new acquisition. I bowed my head to this examining gaze while Tad, furrowing his brow, traced his finger over the globe, following a route down the Niger, the Volga, the Orinoco—I couldn't say. From time to time, I lifted my eyes, met Lila's meditative gaze, and lowered them again, fearing I might hear her say, "No, you won't do after all; I was wrong." I felt I was at a turning point in my life—the world had a center of gravity different from the one I'd learned about in school. Half of me wished to stay there, at her feet, till the end of my days, and the other half of me wanted to flee; even now, I don't know whether I succeeded in life because I didn't take off running, or whether I came to ruin because I stayed.

Lila laughed and touched my nose with the tips of her fingers.

"You seem completely beside yourself, you poor boy," she said. "Tad, he's only seen me twice in four years and he's already lost his mind. What is it about me, anyway? Why do they all fall in love with me so madly? They take one look at me, and just like that, intelligent conversation is impossible. All they do is sit there staring at me, going 'um' and 'ah' from time to time."

Tad, keeping a finger on the globe so he wouldn't lose his place in the Gobi or the Sahara Desert and die of thirst, glanced coldly at his sister. At sixteen, Tad Bronicki seemed to have such knowledge of the world that the only thing left for him to do was add a few small corrections to the planet's history and geography.

"The child suffers from an excess of herself," he said.

This whole time, the piano behind the curtain at the far end of the attic had continued to play; the invisible musician must have been a thousand miles away, carried by the melody to some faraway realm that neither our voices, nor likely any echo of anything else of this world, could reach. And then the music stopped, the curtain was drawn back, and I saw a very gentle face beneath a tousled thatch of hair, with eyes that still seemed to be following the notes, flown off to the unknown. The rest of him was the big body of a teenage boy of about fifteen or sixteen, hunched down as if encumbered by his size. At first I thought he was watching me, but the more attentively Bruno seemed to be looking at you the less he actually saw you. The concrete reality of this world—"an object of utmost importance," as Tad said—inspired in Bruno an indifference mixed with surprise.

"That's Bruno," announced Lila, inflecting the word "that" with a mixture of tenderness and pride of ownership. "He'll be awarded first prize at the Conservatory for his piano playing someday. He's promised me. He'll be famous. Actually, in a few years we'll all be famous. Tad will be a great explorer, Bruno will be applauded in concert halls everywhere, I'll be the next Garbo, and you …"

She studied me for a moment. I blushed.

"Well—it doesn't matter," she said.

I lowered my head. The efforts I was making to hide my humiliation must have been utterly useless, for Tad leapt to his feet and bounded over to his sister. In Polish, the two teenagers exchanged what appeared to be a flood of insults, during which my existence was completely forgotten, allowing me to regain my composure a little. Upon which a manservant dressed in a white coat entered the attic, followed by a chambermaid. I recognized him as Monsieur Julien, the waiter at the Clos Joli. They were carrying two trays laden with pastries, plates, cups, and teapots; a cloth was spread over the floorboards and tea was served upon it. At first I thought this might be a Polish custom, but Tad explained that it was to "bring a little bit of simplicity into this household, with its intolerable habit for luxury … Actually, I'm a Marxist," he added. This was the first time I'd heard the word, and I took it to mean the habit of sitting on the floor to eat.

Over tea, I learned that Tad had no intention of becoming an explorer, as his sister demanded. Instead he had set himself the goal of "helping men to change the world"—he gestured toward the globe near the window as he declared that Bruno was the son of an Italian butler, now deceased, who had worked for the Bronickis in Poland; the count, having discovered that the boy possessed an extraordinary gift for music, had adopted him, given him the Bronicki name, and was helping him to become "the next Rubinstein."

"Another investment," Tad informed me. "My father's planning on becoming his impresario and making lots of money."

I also learned that the whole family would be leaving Normandy at the end of the summer.

"That is, if Papa's creditors let him, and if he hasn't sold off our estate in Poland," Lila commented. "But none of that matters a bit, really. Mama will get us out of it again. She always finds some very rich lover to come to the rescue at the last minute. Three years ago, it was Basil Zaharoff, the world's biggest arms dealer, and last year it was Monsieur Gulbenkian—they call him 'Mister Five Percent' because he gets 5 percent of the revenues of every English petrol company in Arabia. Mama loves Papa, and every time he ruins himself and starts threatening suicide, she … well … how shall I say it?"

"She heads for the coal mines," Tad summed up briefly.

I'd never before heard children talking about their parents that way, and my astonishment must have shown, because Tad gave me a friendly slap on the back. "Come now," he said. "You're as red as a beet. What can I say, we Bronickis are all a bit decadent. Do you know what decadence is?"

Silently, I nodded yes.

But search as I might through the famous Fleury "historical memory," I couldn't for the life of me find that word.

6

I RETURNED HOME RESOLVED TO BECOME "SOME-
body" as rapidly as possible, preferably before the departure of my
new friends, but my resolve expressed itself in the form of a high
fever, and I was obliged to stay in bed for several days. Within me,
my delirium revealed the power to conquer galaxies: I received a
kiss from Lila's lips in thanks. I remember that, returning from a
particularly hostile planet, following an expedition where I'd taken
a hundred thousand Nubian prisoners—I didn't know what the
word Nubian meant but it seemed to fit these interstellar predators
admirably—I dressed to offer up my new kingdom to Lila in a suit
adorned with such a profusion of gemstones that at once, at the sight
of such intense brilliance beaming up from an earth that had until
then held only a very modest position among the light years, a veritable panic broke out among the brightest stars.

My illness ended in the sweetest of ways. The room was very dim:
the shutters were closed, the curtains drawn, for it was feared that
measles might, following these few days of hesitation, break out
abruptly. Back then, one aspect of treatment was to keep patients
in the dark, in order to protect their eyes, and Dr. Gardieu was all
the more concerned because I was already fourteen—the measles
were running late. It must have been noon, judging by the light that
poured into the room as the door opened and Lila appeared. She
was followed by the chauffeur, Mr. Jones, his arms loaded with an

enormous fruit basket; behind them came my uncle, who kept warning Mademoiselle of the risk of fatal contagion. Lila stood in the
doorway for a moment, and despite my extreme agitation, I could
not help feeling the premeditation in the pose she struck against the
bright background, one hand toying with her hair. While the visit
was about me, it was above all a dramatic moment: a young girl in
love arriving at a deathbed, and although one could not leave out the
love and the death, they nevertheless ranked as accessories. Lila held
her pose a few moments more as the chauffeur deposited the exotic
fruit basket on the table. Then, rapidly, she crossed the room, leaned
over me, and brushed my cheek with a kiss, despite my uncle's repeated reminders to Mademoiselle of the powerfully dangerous and
contagious nature of the microbes that quite possibly filled my body.

"You're not going to die of sickness are you?" she demanded, as if
she expected me to depart from this earth in some entirely different
and admirable way.

"Don't touch me, you might catch it."

She sat down on my bed. "What's the use of loving someone, if
you're afraid of catching it?"

A wave of pleasant heat rose to my head. My uncle smoothed his
mustache. Mr. Jones stood guard over the exotic fruit basket, whose
lychees, papayas, and guavas evoked Parisian luxury more than they
did tropical climes. In carefully chosen terms, Ambrose Fleury stated
the gratitude that, according to him, only my state of weakness prevented me from expressing. Lila went and drew the curtains, opened
the shutters, and became all light; she leaned over me in the flood
of her hair, where the sun, knowing a good thing when it sees one,
supplied itself liberally.

"I don't want you to be ill, I don't like illness, I hope you won't
make a habit of this. You can have a little cold from time to time but
not more. There are enough sick people without you. There are even
people who die, and not at all from love, but from God knows what
horrible filth. I understand dying of love, because sometimes it's so

strong that life can't withstand it, it snaps. You'll see, I'll give you books where that happens."

My uncle, aware of Slavic custom, proposed a cup of tea; Mr. Jones glanced discreetly at his watch and "permitted himself to remind Mademoiselle that she was expected for her music lesson," but Lila was in no hurry to leave; it was pleasurable for her to see herself in my silently adoring gaze, where she reigned—I was her kingdom; seated on the edge of my bed, leaning tenderly over me, she let herself be loved. As for me, I only truly regained my wits after she departed: I was more conscious of her visit after it ended than while it lasted, this perfumed half hour during which, for the first time in my life, I felt the first wafts of femininity drifting over my face, my first sensual proximity. After Lila had left me, I waited a quarter of an hour, then got up and crept from my bed, so that my uncle would not notice my troubled state. It lasted all day. I dressed and spent the afternoon walking through the countryside, but there was no palliating it until nighttime, when nature, in her benevolence, took it upon herself to relieve me as I slept.

The sky-blue Packard convertible came to collect me every day, and my uncle began to grumble. "These people are inviting you into their home to show they aren't prejudiced, that they're open-minded and allow their daughter to be friends with a little peasant boy. I ran into Madame de Bronicka in Cléry the other day. You know what she was doing? She was visiting the poor, like in the Middle Ages. You're an intelligent boy, but don't aim too high. It's a good thing they're going away. You'd end up picking up bad habits."

I pushed my plate away from me. "Well, I don't want to be a postal employee, at any rate," I announced. "I want to be someone entirely different. I have no idea of what I want to do because it's too big, the thing I want; it doesn't exist yet, I'll have to invent it."

I spoke in a loud, confident voice with my head held high. I wasn't thinking of Lila. I didn't even know that inside what I was saying, inside this desire to surpass myself, to fly so high, to achieve great things, was a young girl, was her breath on my lips and her hand resting on my cheek.

I returned to my soup.

My uncle seemed pleased. He squinted one eye ever so slightly and smoothed his mustache to hide his smile.

7

A FEW MILES FROM LA MOTTE, BEYOND THE MAZE pond, surrounded by ash and birch trees, was a ravine. Long ago, this forest had been maintained for Colbert's navy; now it was a wilderness; many red oaks grew there—where the axes had once done their work, snarls of bushes and ferns. It was down in this ravine that my uncle had helped me to build my wigwam, by a spring whose extreme old age had left it mute and infirm. Due to some strange play of currents, kites launched at the edge of this ravine took to the air with an ease that was explicable to my knowledgeable guardian, but which I ascribed to the sky's friendly benevolence toward me. It was there I ended up some two weeks before the Bronickis' departure, looking up at Ambrose Fleury's latest creation whose nickname was Bastle, a kite shaped like a split-open fortress, with a crowd of little men that fluttered as if they were storming its walls. I was giving it a little more freedom up there, up where it was at home, letting out the line, when suddenly I was pushed and punched. Still holding the reel, I found myself on the ground, my assailant bearing down on me with all his weight. Rapidly, I saw that he did not have the force or the skills to match his bellicose intentions, and, although I had only one fist free, I had no trouble extricating myself from the situation. He fought courageously, throwing big, disorganized punches, and as I settled down on his chest, pinning one of his arms with my knee and the other with my hand, he strove to butt at me with his head. The only effect this had was surprising me, for certainly it was the first time I had inspired such strong emotions in anyone. He had fragile features, an almost feminine face, with long blond hair. The energy he gave to the fight could not compensate for his narrow shoulders and weak hands. Finally, exhausted, he grew still, rallying his forces, then commenced to wriggling again. I stuck to the task of keeping him on the ground, without letting go of my kite.

"What do you want from me? What's your problem?"

He struggled to butt my stomach with his head, but succeeded only in smacking his neck against a rock.

"Where did you come from?"

He didn't answer. I began to feel a little awed by his blue gaze, which he clamped on me with a kind of limpid fury.

"What did I do to you?"

He remained silent. His nose was bleeding. I didn't know what to do with my victory, and, as I always did when I felt I had the upper hand, I rather wanted to spare him, even to help him. I leapt to my feet and backed away.

He remained on the ground for a moment, then stood.

"Tomorrow. Same time," he said. With that, he turned his back on me and departed.

"Hey, listen!" I yelled. "What did I do to you?"

He stopped. His white shirt and handsome golf trousers were soiled with dirt.

"Tomorrow. Same time," he repeated, and, for the first time, I noticed his strange, guttural accent. "If you don't show up, you're a coward."

"I'm asking you: what did I do to you?"

He said nothing and stalked away, one hand in his pocket and the other arm bent, his elbow against his side, a posture I found extremely elegant. I watched him until he disappeared among the ferns, then I reeled Bastle back to earth, and spent the rest of the day racking my brains to try and understand why I had been attacked by this boy I had never seen before in my life. My uncle, when I confided my encounter to him, expressed the opinion that my assailant had intended to steal our kite, having been unable to resist the sight of such a masterpiece.

"No, I think it was me he was after."

"But since you didn't do a thing to him?"

"Maybe I did something without realizing it."

Actually, I was beginning to feel guilty of the very cruelest kind of transgression—that is, the one we have no idea of. No matter how hard I thought, the only wrongdoing I could come up with was having followed Lila's suggestion that I release a snake in the middle of mass a few days earlier, which had had an extremely satisfying effect on the assembled company. Impatiently, I waited for the moment I'd meet my adversary again, and would oblige him to tell me the origins of his vengeful rancor, and what wrong I had done him.

The next day, he appeared just as I was arriving at the wigwam. I think he had been waiting for me behind the blackberry hedges that lined the ravine. He was wearing a blue-and-white-striped jacket—a *blazer*, as I learned to call it once I had gotten the knack of high society—white flannel trousers, and, this time, instead of pouncing on me, he took up a boxer's stance, with one foot in front of the other and his fists in front of him. I was unnerved. I didn't know a thing about boxing, but I'd seen Marcel Thil, the world middle-weight champion, strike exactly the same pose in a newspaper photo. He took a step toward me, and then another, pumping his fists as if savoring ahead of time the knockout blow he was about to land on me. Once he got near, he began to hop and dance around me, occasionally touching his cheek with his fist, sometimes hovering up closer, then springing back or hopping to the side. He danced around like that for a while, then he hurled himself at me. I met him with my fist, which he took square in the face. He fell to a sitting position, but got up immediately and went back to dancing, occasionally reaching out his arm to strike at my body with blows I barely felt. Finally, when I'd had my fill, I gave him a good old Norman slap across the face with the back of my hand. Though I didn't intend to, I must have hit him hard, for he fell yet again, his lips bleeding this time. I'd never seen such a fragile kid. He wanted to get up, but I held him pinned to the ground.

"How about you explain yourself now."

He kept silent and looked me straight in the eye, with a defiant air. I was at a loss. I couldn't give him a good thumping: he really was too feeble. The only way to get him was to wear him down. I held him on the ground for half an hour. Nothing doing: he wouldn't speak. I couldn't very well spend the entire day sitting on him. I was worried I'd hurt him. He had courage and resolve, the poor fool. When I finally let him go, he stood up, smoothed out his clothes and his long blond hair, and turned to face me.

"Tomorrow. Same time."

"Oh, go shit in your hat."

I went over my conscience again, and, finding nothing anyone could possibly reproach me for, concluded that my stubborn adversary had mistaken me for someone else.

That afternoon, as I was reading the volume of Rimbaud that Lila had given me, I was interrupted by the familiar sound of the Packard's horn in front of my house. Quickly, I ran outside. Mr. Jones winked and greeted me in his habitual and affably mocking way: "*Monsieur* is invited to take tea."

I ran upstairs to freshen up, put on a clean shirt, slicked down my hair with a splash of water, and, finding the results of my efforts unsatisfactory, ducked into the workshop for some glue, which I used as hair pomade. Solemnly, I climbed into the back seat, spread the Scottish rug over my lap; and then, to the great displeasure of Mr. Jones, who had just started the car, I leapt out of it again and dashed up to my room—I had forgotten to shine my damn shoes.

8

THE BRONICKIS' SITTING ROOM WAS FULL OF PEO-
ple, and the first to catch my eye was my mysterious attacker: he was
standing with Lila, showing not the slightest hostility toward me
when my friend took his arm and led him over to me. "This is my
cousin Hans," she told me.

Hans bowed slightly. "A pleasure," he said. "I believe we've met
before. And that we'll have the occasion to meet again." Nonchalantly, he walked away.

"What's going on?" Lila demanded with surprise. "You look
strange. I hope you'll be friends. You have at least one thing in common: he's in love with me, too."

Madame de Bronicka was in bed with a migraine and Lila wore
the role of hostess with ease, making the rounds of her guests with
me. "I'd like to introduce our friend Ludo, the nephew of the celebrated Ambrose Fleury."

Most of these Parisian personages knew nothing of my uncle,
but nodded knowingly so as not to be caught red-handed in some
monstrous ignorance. The elegance of their dress astounded me; an
intimidating pageant of jewels, hats, jackets, spats, and suits equaled
only in what I had seen on the backs of the customers at the Clos
Joli; I felt uneasy there with my worn-down shoes, my shiny jacket
sleeves, the beret sticking out of my pocket. I battled my feelings of
inferiority bravely, picking out a guest and imagining him floating

in the air at the end of a line I held in my hand, with his stiff-legged trousers, his checked vest, and his yellow tie, propelled this way or that with a flick of my hand. It was the first time I had wielded my imagination as a weapon of defense, and nothing ever turned out to be more beneficial to me in this life. To be sure, the beginnings of social awareness were still far off for me at this point, but all the same, I was engaging in a kind of protest that, without blowing anything out of proportion, smacked ever so slightly of subversion, if not revolution. When it came time for a corpulent gentleman by the name of Oustric, whose smoothly hairless face, powerfully endowed with fat, sheltered a round baby nose perched above plump little lips, to learn from Lila that I was the nephew of "the celebrated Ambrose Fleury," he shook my hand as he told me, "I congratulate you. France could use a lot more men like your uncle."

I caught the flash of mischief on Lila's face that I had begun to know well.

"You know," she said, "they're talking about appointing him minister of the postal service in the next government."

"A great man! A great man!" Monsieur Oustric hastened to affirm, inclining his torso slightly toward the petit four already in reach of his lips.

I felt a sudden desire to deliver the little cake from its impending fate. Among all these bigwigs, who made me feel as if I'd been reduced to dust, it seemed to me that if I wished to affirm my existence in the eyes of my beloved, my only possible course of action was some sort of crazy feat.

Delicately, I withdrew the petit four from Monsieur Oustric's chubby hand and brought it to my own lips. It took almost everything I had, my heart was pounding—not yet did I equal my Fleury forefather finding death on the barricades in 1870, not yet was I charging into Berlin with my troops to dazzle Lila as I locked Hitler away, but at least for now I was showing her what I was made of.

When Monsieur Oustric saw the petit four disappear into my

mouth, the look of stupor that appeared on his face was such that I suddenly measured the true boldness of my exploit. More dead than alive, for I hadn't yet forged the strength of character of a true revolutionary, I turned to Lila. In return I received a little look of amused tenderness. She took my hand, pulled me behind a screen, and kissed me.

"What you did is very Polish, you know. We are a nation of dare-devils. You would have made a splendid Imperial Guardsman under Napoleon and you would have ended up a field marshal. I'm sure you'll do great things in life. I'll help you."

I decided to test her. I wanted to know if she loved me for who I was or only for all the feats I would accomplish for her. "You know, as soon as I'm old enough, I hope I'll be able to get a nice position as a clerk in the postal administration."

She nodded her head and stroked my cheek in an almost maternal fashion.

"You don't know me," she said, as if I had been talking about her life and not my own. "Come."

A few of the most gleaming personalities in the who's who of the upper crust of the time were present that day at the Bronickis', but their names were as unknown to me as my uncle's was to them. Only one man among them showed a friendly interest in me. It was a fa-mous aviator, Corniglion-Molinier, who had just failed in a highly courageous manner in his attempt to fly from Paris to Australia, in the company of the English Mollison. The *Gazette* had gratified the failure with the following attempt at commentary: "Mollison and Molinier will never make a hit!" He was a short southerner with languorous eyes rimmed with long, almost feminine eyelashes, and when Lila introduced me with her obligatory, "He is the nephew of the celebrated Ambrose Fleury," Corniglion-Molinier replied amusedly, "Your uncle gave me one of his kites after my failure, I'm not sure if it was to encourage me to change careers ..."

Having made my tour of the sitting room in this manner I was finally able to join the other young people in the next room, around a table attended by a white-gloved waiter. I hardly touched the pastries, ices, creams, and exotic fruit, all presented on silver platters marked with the vermeil she-wolf of the Bronicki coat of arms. This atmosphere of luxury and elegance made me all the more uneasy because I had been seated across from Lila's cousin, Hans von Schwede. My fragile yet intrepid woodland attacker held himself very straight, keeping his elbow pinned at his side as he lifted his cup of tea, his legs crossed. His hair was almost as blond and long as Lila's, and his face had a fineness to it that I would not yet have known to qualify as aristocratic at that phase of my life, still being unschooled in the rapport between the word and its aesthetic. He showed no hostility toward me and at no moment did he try through any sort of mockery to gain advantage over me through the difference in our appearances—between his silver-buttoned blazer and white flannel trousers and my old ill-fitting suit, which could not have gone worse with my current company. He simply acted as if I weren't there, and I consoled myself by noting the incontestable marks of my existence on his face: a slightly swollen lip and a black eye. Distractedly, he was sculpting his black-currant sorbet into the shape of a rose with his dessert spoon. Tad cast cold looks at the guests of this *raout*, a word that was living out its last years of use in the French language. The thinness of his lips had an easy affinity with what I would, a good many years later, come to describe as "terrorist irony," whose traces I recognized in Houdon's famous sculpture of Voltaire. With one arm dangled over the back of his chair, he observed the tables around which the Bronickis' guests embodied to perfection the high tone of the nineteen thirties, when the Azure Coast was not a thing in summer because its hotels still only opened for the winter season, and Cabourg had not yet acquired the "old fashioned charm" that ennobles the poor taste of the past. As for Bruno, he sat peacefully among us, always a little hunched, always a little absent, crouched in the underbrush of his tangled curls, which, though he was only sixteen, were already shot with a few strands of gray. He had one of those very gentle faces that seem made for maturity, which stands ready for its snowfall even in the springtime of youth. The three boys had risen as Lila approached; she had seated me beside her. I remember feeling horribly conscious of my too-short trousers, which left my ankles bare above my socks. And that was how, on that memorable afternoon in the last days of July 1935, we all ended up together for the first time, and in my memory not a single one of the tutti-frutti ices, pastries, or other sweet things will ever melt or turn.

"Observe," Tad said, "the hopeless battle of the *couturiers*, the tailors, the beauticians, and the hairdressers against the blandness, the vulgarity of soul, and the intellectual poverty of society's best here. And their song matches their fancy feathers: I'll bet they're all warbling on about the stock market, horse racing, and gala evenings, while at this very moment civil war is spreading across Spain, Mussolini is gassing the Ethiopians, and Hitler's demanding Austria and the Sudetenland. That very thin man, the one with a title to a case of baldness—his head would remind you of an ostrich egg if El Greco hadn't ennobled it by painting it into *The Burial of the Count of Orgaz*—he's no Spanish grandee; he's a usurer who lends to my father at 20 percent interest … The man in the gray jacket and waistcoat is a lawyer with access to every minister of the cabinet—with his wife as his calling card. As for our dear parents, I shudder to think what would become of them if our family tree didn't offer them such good cover. The aristocratic air would go right out of my father, he'd be taken for a butcher; and if my mother stopped being able to afford Miss Chanel, Antoine the hairdresser, Julien the masseur, Fernande the beautician, and Nino the gigolo, she'd start to resemble a myopic chambermaid who's lost her iron …"

Lila nibbled at an éclair. "Tad is an anarchist," she explained.

"Which means he's a born elitist," Hans remarked.

I was pleased to note that he had a German accent. Since France and Germany were hereditary enemies, I felt that, whatever the motive behind his aggression, I had done right in giving him a thrashing.

Bruno looked pained. "Tad, it seems to me that you have at least as many prejudices as you're attributing to these people. You can do the exact same thing with nature: you can say that birds look stupid, that dogs are foul because they lick their own rear ends, that there's nothing stupider than a honeybee when you count up how many hours they've spent making honey for everyone else. Watch out. First it's a way of looking at the world, then it becomes a way of life. Seeing everything as twisted gives you crooked vision."

Tad turned to me. "That, young sir, is the voice of a juicy pear whose purpose in life is to be eaten. It's what they call an idealist."

"I'd like to know why you've suddenly turned all formal with our friend," Lila demanded.

"Because he isn't yet my friend, if indeed he ever becomes one. At seventeen, I no longer throw myself body and soul into friendships—or anything else, for that matter. I may be Polish, but 'body and soul' is not my forte. It was all well and good for our ancestors in the Imperial Guard—those righteous asses had it in them."

"I'll ask you not to use that kind of language in the presence of a young lady," Hans shot out at him.

"There you go, the Prussian Junker's awake now," Tad sighed. "Which reminds me, where did you get your face all done up like that? In a duel?"

"Fighting over my pretty face," Lila declared. "They're both madly in love with me, but instead of realizing that it should bind them together as brothers, they beat each other up. They'll get over it when they figure out I love them both, so I won't be playing favorites."

I still hadn't said anything. I felt, however, that the moment had arrived to make myself known in one way or another; I couldn't forget that I was the nephew of Ambrose Fleury and therefore came by it honestly. I was not versed in the art of scintillating socially, despite my ardent wish to make a demonstration then and there of something exceptionally superior in Lila's eyes, something that would leave them all gaping. Had there been any justice in the world, I would've been granted the power to fly on the spot, or had a lion bestowed upon me so that I could face it down and vanquish it, or been deposited in a ring with Lila seated at its edge while I won the title of all-weight champion. But the only thing I could do was ask, "What is the square root of 273,678?"

I must say that at least I succeeded in surprising them. The three boys stared at me fixedly, then exchanged a few glances with one another. Lila seemed enchanted. She had a horror of mathematics, as she found that numbers had the annoying habit of proclaiming that two and two are four, which to her seemed somehow contrary to the very spirit of Poland.

"Well, since you don't know, I'll tell you," I declared. "It's 523.14242!"

"I presume that you memorized that before coming here," Hans said disdainfully. "I call that taking precautions. Incidentally, I have nothing against showmen sawing women in half or pulling rabbits out of hats, it's a living … if that's what you need to do."

"Well, pick a number yourself, then," I answered, "and I'll tell you its square root straightaway. Or any multiplication problem. Or, well, give me a list of a hundred numbers and I'll repeat it in the order you gave it to me."

"What's the square root of 7,198,489?" Tad asked.

It took me a few seconds more than usual, because I was feeling emotional: it was a matter of life and death.

"Two thousand, six hundred and eighty-three," I proclaimed.

Hans shrugged. "What the good in that? We can't check him."

But Tad had pulled a notebook and pencil from his pocket and did the calculation. "Correct," he said.

Lila applauded. "I told you he was a genius," she declared. "It's actually obvious even without that utterly unnecessary mental math exercise. I don't choose just anyone."

"It'll have to be looked into a bit more closely," Tad murmured.

"But I admit I'm interested. Perhaps he'll agree to submit to a few more challenges."

It was hard, but I made it through without a single mistake. For half an hour, they recited lists of figures to me and I repeated them back from memory, produced the square roots of interminably long numbers, and answered multiplication problems so astronomical they could have turned the solar system green with envy. Not only did I succeed in convincing my audience of what my friend called my "powers," but in the end, Lila got up from the table, went and found her father, and informed him that I was a mathematical wunderkind who merited his attention. Count Bronicki came to see me immediately; he must have thought that somewhere in the depths of my brain slumbered a winning combination that only needed awakening to achieve triumph at roulette, baccarat, and the stock market. He was a deep believer in miracles—in the form of money. I was forthwith invited to stand at the center of the sitting room, before an audience that included some of the era's biggest wheelers and dealers, people with an irresistible attraction to numbers. Never before had I engaged in mental calculations with such a desperate desire for victory. To be sure, no one in the family had ever called me a peasant, nor had I ever been made to feel my social inferiority: the aristocratic bloodline of the Bronicki family was so old that they had come to feel toward the popular classes the attraction and melancholy-tinged nostalgia that inaccessibility inspires. But just imagine a boy of fifteen, raised in the Normandy countryside, wearing too-short trousers and a faded shirt, his beret in his pocket, surrounded by half a hundred ladies and gentlemen dressed with a kind of splendor that seemed to me to indicate their place in a world that, to quote Ravachol—though I wouldn't have known to do so at the time—"can be made accessible only by ending it." Imagine all this and you'll understand the feverish excitement, the anxiety with which I threw myself into this battle for honor. I have lived long enough to find myself in a world where the term "fighting for honor" has ceased to evoke anything but the absurd panache of a bygone era, barely worthy of jest. But all this means is that the world went one way and I another, and it's not my place to decide which one of us took the wrong turn.

Standing on the gleaming parquet, one foot forward, my arms crossed over my chest, my face ablaze, I multiplied, divided, found the square roots of enormous numbers, and recited from memory some hundred telephone numbers that were read aloud to me from the telephone book, my head high beneath the strafe of figures, until Lila, worried, came to my rescue. She seized my hand and cried out to the audience in a voice trembling with anger, "That's enough! You're exhausting him."

She dragged me to the office behind the sideboard, where the Bronickis' maid busied herself with reinforcements of layer cakes, ices, and sorbets that had just been sent over from the Clos Joli. I did not know why, but although I had emerged victorious from this showdown, I felt defeated and humiliated. It was Tad, as he appeared with Bruno from behind the velvet curtain that separated us from the fancy folk, who provided the explanation for my unease.

"Please forgive us, my friend," he said. "My little sister should have known that our father would never miss an opportunity to entertain his guests. You've got quite an unusual gift there. Do try not to become a circus dog."

"Pay no attention to Tad," instructed Lila, who, to my horror, was smoking a cigarette. "Like all very intelligent boys, he can't stand genius. It's just envy. Really, dear brother, with a sense of humor like that you should take up meteorology—you just love to rain on people's parades!"

Tad kissed her on the forehead. "I love you. Too bad you're my sister!"

"I'm only her cousin, so perhaps I've got a chance!" called out a voice whose German accent I recognized instantly.

There was Hans, holding a bottle of port. I'd been having some difficulty shaking off my nervous tension, but the sight of that face, all blondness and fine features, fully returned me to my senses. I already knew that it was him or me, and, since he had been drinking, and was looking me up and down defiantly, I set about wishing for war to break out immediately between France and Germany, so that fate could decide it for us. I detested his affected elegance, his stiffness, that hand in his pocket, that elbow against his side—he might well have been the descendant of Teutonic conquerors and Baltic barons, but for all his pretensions I'd managed to thrash him single-handedly.

"Nice little number you've got there, Monsieur Fleury," he said. "You've got a great future ahead of you."

"Don't be so formal," Lila protested. "We'll all be friends …"

"You have a lovely career ahead of you, Monsieur Fleury," Hans repeated. "No doubt about it: numbers are the future. The world's been learning to count since the days of chivalry ended and it's only going to get worse. We're about to witness the end of everything that isn't quantifiable—honor, for example."

Tad observed him with a look of amusement. Lila's brother had an almost physical gift for nonchalance: it was as if he were constantly trying to attenuate the excessive, passionate side of his personality with an attitude of detachment, a slightly weary boredom. I sensed that he had a stinging retort at the tip of his tongue, but as I had observed for myself during our two "battles," Hans was a boy you wanted to spare. At fourteen, he was the youngest of all of us, and the frailest. He was nevertheless being prepared for a military career, as every man in the von Schwede family was. I learned from Lila that there were certain parallels between his destiny and mine, although it wouldn't have occurred to me to speak of "destiny" in relation to the Fleurys—the word "fate" was the only one I had heard when it came to my own relations. His father had been killed during the Great War, and his mother, like mine, had died shortly after his birth; he had been raised by an aunt in the castle of Kremnitz in Eastern Prussia, just a few miles from the Bronicki estate in Poland.

As we exchanged more or less friendly repartee, Bruno stood off to one side, tapping out an imaginary melody on the edge of a table.

"Let's go for a boat ride," Lila proposed. "It's going to rain. Maybe there'll be a storm, lightning ... an *event*!" She lifted her eyes heavenward, which, as is all too often the case, was only the ceiling. "Oh God," she exclaimed, "give us a nice thunderstorm, and if it's in your power, how about a volcano to bring all this Norman placidity to a crashing end!"

Tad put a kindly arm around her. "Little sister, there's certainly no lack of volcanoes with exotic names in this world, but the fires smoldering in Europe right now are far more dangerous—and they have nothing to do with the insides of the earth, but everything to do with those of men!"

A few raindrops fell as we reached the pond. It had been designed by Sanders, the great English landscape architect, whose floral triumphs bloomed all over Europe. Lila's father had spent millions improving the estate, in the hopes of selling it to some dazzled parvenu for five or six times what he'd paid. The Bronickis were never far from the "ultimate" financial catastrophe, as Tad not unhopefully prognosticated; their opulent lifestyle concealed disasters and near desperate situations of the kind only conspicuous consumption is able to dissimulate. As we took the oars, Lila lounged languorously on some cushions. There was just enough rain to testify to the sky's beneficence in sparing us from a downpour. The clouds had that heaviness that could have won the day with a few gallops, but the wind was in no hurry. The pre-rain birds took it lazily. Far away, you could hear a train whistle, but not too nostalgically—it was only the Paris–Deauville, not enough to evoke long journeys. You had to row carefully to avoid disturbing the water lilies. The water smelled good, of cool and silt, and the insects dropped down in just the right places to set the ripples running. It wasn't the season for my friends the dragonflies. A fat and foolish bumblebee occasionally clowned up to us. Lila, in her white dress, draped among her oarsmen, hummed a Polish lament, bestowing her gaze on the lucky sky. I was the strongest of the rowers, but she did not seem to pay that any mind, and at any rate I had to match my strokes to the others. We had to watch out for the ever-so-carefully tended branches, to keep all their flowers in place. There was, of course, a cunning little bridge, covered in white lanterns brought specially from Asia. That was the only obvious trace of premeditation—all the other flower beds had been carefully designed to look wild.

Lila had ceased her song; she was playing with her hair, and her eyes, so blue that it must have been hard on the sky, had taken on a grave expression that always seemed like her tribute to dreaming.

"I'm not sure I want to be the next Garbo—I don't want to be the next anything. I don't know what I'll do yet, but I'll be *unique*. Obviously, the time has passed when a woman could change the face of the world—really you'd have to be a man, and a pitiful one at that, to want to change the face of the world. I won't be an actress, because an actress only gets to become someone different for the span of an evening, and I need to change all the time, morning to night, there's nothing more depressing than only being who you are, some small work that's the result of circumstance . . . I have a horror of anything once and for all."

I rowed, listening religiously to Lila "dreaming of herself," as Tad put it; Lila crossing the Atlantic solo, like Alain Gerbault; Lila writing novels translated into *every* language; Lila becoming a lawyer and saving people's lives with feats of eloquence. That blonde head, reclining on the Oriental cushions among her four oarsmen, had no idea that to me, she already was a creation far more extraordinary and overwhelming than any of those she evoked in her unknowing of herself.

The heavy odor of stagnant water rose around us each time the oars moved; hirsute grasses caressed my face; from time to time among the bushes appeared false jungle scenes so skillfully imagined that you had to be very levelheaded and indeed bear in mind that it was only an English garden.

"I can still fail at everything," Lila was saying, "I'm young enough. When you get old you have less and less opportunity to mess everything up because you run out of time, so you can live an untroubled life and be happy with what you've already made a mess of. That's what they mean by 'peace of mind.' But when you're only sixteen you can still try everything and fail at it all, that's what they usually call 'having your future ahead of you.'" Her voice trembled. "Listen, I don't mean to scare you, but there are times I think I have no talent for anything…"

We protested volubly. I say "we," but it was mostly Tad and Bruno predicting her amazing future. She was going to be the next Marie Curie, but even better, in another field entirely, perhaps one that hadn't even been invented yet. As for me, I hoped—to be sure, a little shamefacedly—that Lila was right: if she had no talent for anything, then I still had a ghost of a chance. But Lila remained inconsolable, and a tear glided slowly down her cheek, stopping in just the right place to gleam. She carefully abstained from wiping it away.

"I do so want to be someone, too," she murmured. "I'm surrounded by geniuses. Bruno will have crowds at his feet, everyone knows Tad will be more famous than Sven Hedin as an explorer, and even Ludo has an astonishing gift for memory…"

I swallowed the "even Ludo" without too much difficulty. I had good reason to feel satisfied: Hans was silent. He had turned his head away, and I couldn't see his face, but secretly, I rejoiced. I had trouble seeing how he could explain to Lila that he, too, had a brilliant future ahead of him, that he was entering a German military academy, because he was in love with a Polish girl. In that regard, I felt I had my hands on something good and solid, as we say around here, and I was not about to let go of it. I even allowed myself the luxury of feeling a little bit of pity for my rival. Times were hard for Teutonic knights. Indeed, it was undeniable that pleasing a woman was becoming a taller and taller order: America had already been discovered, as had the sources of the Nile; Lindbergh had already crossed the Atlantic; Mallory had scaled Mount Everest.

The five of us were still near to the naïvetés of childhood—which may be the most fertile portion life gives us, and then takes away.

9

THE VERY NEXT DAY, STAS BRONICKI CAME TO SEE my uncle. He arrived with due pomp; such a man would not have had the vulgarity to change into ordinary clothes to visit ordinary people. The blue Packard gleamed; Mr. Jones, the chauffeur, lifted his cap as he opened the door with a solemnity that was as much an announcement of the servant's importance as the master's; and the Polish Imperial Guardsman of finance, as he was known in the Paris stock exchange, appeared in all his sartorial splendor: a rosewood-colored suit, a necktie in the colors of the best London club, butter-yellow gloves, a cane, a carnation at his buttonhole, and, as always, the slightly anxious expression of a man whose martingales have been treacherously foiled on the trading floor, the baccarat table, and the roulette wheel.

We had just tucked into a snack, and our visitor, having glanced with great interest at the fat sausage, the peasant loaf, and the butter slab, was invited to join us, which he did immediately, wielding the big kitchen knife with panache and coughing only a little as he drained a few glasses of our rough *pujol*. Then he made my uncle an unexpected proposal. I was—he affirmed, in a Polish accent whose singing vowels and slightly abrupt consonants recalled Lila's voice to me—I was, he repeated, a prodigy of mathematics and memory; my future merited great care. He proposed to be the one to guide my steps, and to initiate me little by little into the secrets of the stock market, for it would have been criminal to neglect my capabilities and even to see them waste away for lack of a proper nurturing environment. And since my young age prevented me from sitting for entrance exams for the Ministry of Finance, not to mention striking out on my own in a field where mathematical genius must be accompanied by a maturity of mind and certain kinds of indispensable knowledge, he proposed that in the meantime I stick with him each summer, as his personal secretary.

"My dear sir, you must understand that your nephew and I possess complementary gifts, as it were. I am highly versed in the science of predicting stock market fluctuations, and Ludovic is capable of instantly translating my predictions and theories into the language of numbers. I have specialized offices in Warsaw, Paris, and London, but we summer here, and I cannot spend the entire day tied to the telephone. Yesterday your nephew demonstrated a speed in calculation and a memory that could gain me precious time in a world where time is money, as the expression so rightly goes. If you agree to it, my chauffeur will come to fetch him every morning and will bring him home at the end of the day. He shall be paid a monthly salary of one hundred francs, a portion of which he can place in the promising investment opportunities I shall indicate to him."

I was so overcome at the idea of spending my days close to Lila that I was tempted to see this proposition as influenced by Albatross the kite, who had flown off into the heavens the day before and perhaps had intervened up there on my behalf. As for my uncle, he lit his pipe and observed the Polish gentleman with a meditative eye. Finally, he pushed the sausage and the bottle toward him; Stas Bronicki helped himself, and this time, without any thought for elegance, he bit straight into it. Then, his mouth full, he exhaled a big garlicky breath and cried out to us from deep in his soul.

"You probably find me excessively preoccupied with money—in your own way your passion is for winged and elevated things, so it probably seems a bit too down-to-earth for you. But, Monsieur

Fleury, please know that truly, my battle is for honor. My ancestors conquered every enemy who ever tried to bring us to heel—money is the latest invader, the natural enemy of nobility, and I intend to vanquish it in its own territory. Do not think that I seek to defend the privileges of the past—I am sufficiently democratic to allow myself to be dispossessed in this respect with pleasure, but not by money. And …" He stopped there and, raising his eyebrows very high in a look of surprise, suddenly stared fixedly straight ahead of him. We were at that time in the last days of the Popular Front. My uncle, although he had no affiliations, as he put it, had nevertheless been sufficiently inspired by this historic moment to put together a Léon Blum out of paper, string, and cardboard, with a stunt tail. In the sky, the prime minister looked very fine, with his black hat and eloquently raised arms, but at the moment, he was, with little concern for chronology, hanging his head from a beam beside a kite that depicted the poet Musset holding a lyre.

"What's that there?" Stas Bronicki asked, putting down the sausage.

"That's my historical series," Ambrose Fleury replied.

"It looks like Léon Blum."

"I stay informed, that's all," explained my uncle.

Bronicki gestured vaguely with his hand and turned away. "Anyway. Enough of that. As I was saying, your nephew's talents could be extremely useful to me—no machine is capable of such rapid calculations. High finance is like fencing: speed is everything. You have to stay ahead of everyone else."

He glanced worriedly at Léon Blum again, pulled out his pocket square, and mopped his brow. In the periwinkle blue of his eyes he had the desperate gleam of some knight setting off on a quest for the Holy Grail, whom circumstances had obliged to pawn his horse, armor, and lance.

It took me quite some time to discover that Bronicki's financial genius was actually real. In fact, he had been among the first to perfect what is a now widely used financial technique, one that ensured that the banks were unstinting in their support of him: he was so deeply in their debt that their shareholders could not afford to corner him into bankruptcy.

My uncle reacted cautiously. With the total absence of irony that he showed in his most ironic moments, he informed my future mentor that my path in life was, so to speak, already laid out for me, and that it did not soar to any great heights: "A nice little job as a postal worker, with pension guaranteed. That's what I have in mind for him."

"But good God! Monsieur Fleury, your nephew is a genius of memory!" Stas Bronicki thundered, pounding his fist on the table. "And your only ambition for him is a job as a lowly clerk?"

"Sir," my uncle retorted. "Given the times that are ahead of us, lowly clerks may well have the very best position of all. They'll be able to say, 'At least I didn't do anything!'"

Nevertheless, it was agreed that during the summer months, I would make myself available to the Bronickis as a "mathematical clerk." Whereupon my uncle and Mr. Jones each took the count, under the influence of the sausage—discretion prevents any mention herein of the two bottles of wine—by an elbow and helped him to the car. As he got in behind the wheel, the impassive Mr. Jones, who until that moment I had taken to be the embodiment of the very British virtues of phlegm and discretion, turned to my guardian, and, in a French strongly accented by English but which suggested incontestably that he had spent time in pursuits very different from those of a gentleman chauffeur, declared, "Poor bugger. Never saw such a patsy. Made to be stiffed." Whereupon, having pulled on his gloves, he regained his imperturbable air and started up the Packard, leaving us dazzled by this sudden revelation of his linguistic abilities.

"Well, well," said my uncle. "Now you're on your way. You've got yourself a powerful mentor, there. I'll just ask one thing of you." He looked at me gravely, and knowing him as I did, I began to laugh before he finished: "Just don't ever lend him any money."

10

OVER THE NEXT THREE YEARS, FROM 1935 TO 1938, my life knew just two seasons: summer, which began in June when the Bronickis arrived from Poland, and winter, which came with their departure at the end of August, and lasted until their return. The interminable months I spent without seeing Lila were entirely devoted to memory, and I think that those absences rendered me eternally incapable of forgetting. She did not write often, but her letters to me were long and resembled the pages of a personal journal; Tad, when I heard from him, informed me that his sister was continuing to "dream of herself—right now she's thinking of going to care for lepers." Certainly, there were words of tenderness and even love in her letters, but they struck me as strangely impersonal; their effect seemed purely literary—so much so that I was not too surprised when, in one of her letters, Lila told me that she had been sending me passages from a much vaster work she was writing. Nevertheless, when the Bronickis returned to Normandy, she would run to me with open arms, covering me with kisses, laughing and sometimes even crying a little—these few instants were enough to make me feel that life kept all its promises and that doubt was not permissible. As for my functions as the "secretary calculator"—as I had been nicknamed by Podlowski, my employer's factotum, a glabrous individual always ready to bow and scrape, all chin and jaw, with a part down the middle of his hair, and clammy hands—the work demanded of me was hardly gripping. When Bronicki received some banker, stockbroker, or fellow speculator, and together they plunged into complicated estimates of interest rates, increases, and profit margins, I would sit in on the meeting, juggling with millions and millions, making vast fortunes, deducting bank charges and loans, and then multiplying the prices of the shares to be bought that day by the morning's projected profits, indicating that so many tons of sugar or coffee — presuming growth continued according to the intuitions of the great Imperial Guardsman of finance — multiplied by the day's stock prices, in pounds sterling, francs, or dollars, would give this or that amount. I fell into the habit of millions so quickly that I have never again felt poor. As I engaged in these high-flying acrobatics, I would watch through the slightly open door for Lila to appear. She never failed to materialize, which would lead me to lose my head and commit some glaring error: ruining her father in the blink of an eye, causing cotton prices to plummet, dividing instead of multiplying, provoking flat panic in the Imperial Guardsman and peals of laughter in his daughter. When, having slowly habituated myself to the maneuvers she deployed to measure — oh, how needlessly! — the force of her hold on me, I did manage to keep my head and avoid mistakes, her mouth would pucker into a *moue* of resentment and she would depart, more than a bit piqued. And then I'd feel as though I'd sustained an enormous loss, far graver than any stock-market crash.

Every day at around five we would find each other at the far end of the gardens, in the shed behind the pond where the gardener disposed of the flowers that had "hit the age limit," as Lila put it; they had lost their shine and freshness and had come there to breathe out the last of their perfume. We waded in petals, in red, blue, yellow, green, and violet, and in the plants we call weeds when they're alive because they obey only themselves. It was here in these moments that Lila, who had learned to play the guitar, would "dream of herself" with a song on her lips. Seated among the plants, her skirt hitched up over her knees, she would tell me of her triumphant future: the

American tours, the adoring crowds. So convincing was she in her fantasies, or rather, I adored her so much, that all those flowers at her feet already seemed to have been thrown there by her fervent admirers. I could see the tops of her thighs; I was dying of desire, dared nothing, didn't move, wasted slowly away, that was all. In an uncertain voice she would launch into some song whose lyrics she had written herself and whose music had been composed by Bruno, and then, horrified by her old enemy—reality—which refused to bestow upon her vocal cords the divine accents she demanded of them, would throw down the guitar and weep.

"There you go. I have no talent for anything."

I would console her. Nothing gave me more pleasure than these moments of despair, which allowed me to take her in my arms, to brush over her breasts with my hand and her lips with mine. And then a day came when, losing my head, I abandoned my lips to their mad inspiration and, not encountering any resistance, heard a voice of Lila's that I did not know, a voice that no virtuoso singer can surpass. Even as the voice went to my head and bore me away beyond everything I had ever known in life of happiness and of myself up until then, I remained on my knees. The cry rose so high that I, who had until that moment never been a man of faith, felt as if I had finally rendered unto God what was His due. Afterward, she remained motionless on her bed of flowers, both of her hands forgotten on my head.

"Ludo, oh Ludo, what have we done?"

All that I could say, from the very deepest reaches of the truth, was: "I don't know."

"How could you have?"

And, when you think of all the ways there are to encounter faith, the sentence I came up with was utterly comical: "It wasn't me, it was God."

She straightened herself a little, sat up, and wiped away her tears.

"Lila, don't cry, I didn't want to make you unhappy."

She sighed and brushed me aside with a wave of her hand. "You idiot. I'm crying because it was too good." She looked at me severely. "Where did you learn that?"

"What?"

"Goddammit," she said. "I never saw such a fool."

"Lila …"

"Shut up."

She fell back. I lay down beside her. I took her hand. She withdrew it.

"Well, that's that. I've become a whore."

"Good God, what are you talking about?"

"A fallen woman. I'm a fallen woman."

I realized that she was saying it with a great deal of satisfaction in her voice.

"Finally, I actually managed to become something!"

"Lila, listen …"

"I have no talent for singing!"

"But if only …"

"Yes, only. Shut up. I'm a whore. Well, I might as well become the greatest and most celebrated whore in the world. *The Lady of the Camellias*, minus the tuberculosis. I have nothing more to lose. My life is all traced out for me now. I have no choice anymore."

As well as I knew the ups and downs of her imagination, I was appalled. It was a kind of superstition: it seemed to me as if life were listening and taking notes. I sat up.

"I forbid you to say that kind of horseshit!" I yelled. "Life has ears. And besides, what, all I did was li …"

"Ah," she said, and placed her hand on my lips. "Ludo, I forbid you to say such things. It's monstrous! Mon-strous! Go away! I never want to see you again. Never. No, stay here. It's too late, in any case."

One day I was returning from our daily rendezvous in the shed when I ran into Tad, who was waiting for me in the hall.

"Say, Ludo."

"Yes?"

"How long have you been sleeping with my sister?"

I was silent. On the wall above my head, the colonel of the Imperial Guard, Jan Bronicki, hero of Saint Domingue and Somosierra, raised his sword.

"Don't make that face, old boy. If you think I'm here to have a talk with you about the honor of the Bronickis, you're very silly. I just want to prevent any misfortunes. I bet you don't even know that the cycle exists—neither of you."

"What cycle?"

"There you go, that's just what I thought. There's a time—about seven days before the period and seven days after—when women cannot be impregnated. You therefore risk nothing. So since you're so good at calculations, don't forget it. And don't be stupid, either of you. I don't want to have to go see some farmer's wife with her knitting needles. Too many girls die from that. That's all I have to say and I'll never mention it to you again."

He slapped me on the shoulder and began to walk away. I couldn't let him go like that. I wanted to justify myself. "We love each other," I told him.

He looked me over attentively, with a sort of scientific curiosity. "You feel guilty because you're sleeping with my sister. You must have about two thousand years of guilt, there. Are you happy? Yes or no?"

Saying "yes" seemed so inadequate that I kept silent.

"Well, there's no other justification to life or death. You can spend your whole life in libraries, you'd never find another answer."

He departed, his gait nonchalant, whistling softly. I can still hear those few notes of the *Appassionata*.

Bruno avoided me. I tried to tell myself that there was nothing to feel bad about, that if Lila had chosen me, it was as independent of my own will as when a ladybug lands on your hand. But I was haunted by the pain I saw in his face when we happened to catch each other's eye. He spent all his days at the piano, and whenever the music stopped, the silence that followed, of all the Chopin pieces I knew, seemed to me the most devastating.

11

MY WORK WITH BRONICKI WAS NOT LIMITED TO HIS financial enterprises. I was also assisting him in the creation of a scheme intended to help him win a crushing and final conquest of the casino, which up until then had remained an impenetrable stronghold that he dreamed of storming and overtaking once and for all. Stas would place a roulette wheel on the bridge table and throw the ball, even calling out, "No more bets, please!" for heightened realism—a cry, I must say, that seemed to well up from those hidden depths of the soul we like to call the subconscious. My only contribution to this desperate quest for a "system" was to memorize the order of the numbers as the ball fell and then recite them back to Stas ten or twenty times over so that he could try and detect a little wink from destiny somewhere in them, while at the same time I searched his sideburn-flanked face for the death of that same dream. At the end of a few hours' pursuit of the blue yonder, he would mop his brow and murmur, "My little Ludovic, I believe that I have overtaxed your forces. Go and get some rest so you'll be at the top of your game."

My compassion for him and my desire to help grew so strong that I began to cheat. I knew that the count was searching my recitations for numbers and combinations of numbers that repeated in a certain order. Only vaguely aware of the potential consequences of my very poorly placed goodwill, I set about rearranging the numbers as they fell, much in the way that séance participants cannot help pushing at the table to maintain the illusion. It was a disaster. Having asked me to recite several times over the numbers I had arranged into series, Stas Bronicki was suddenly overcome by an expression I can only qualify as wild-eyed. He remained frozen for an instant, his pencil in hand, ears cocked as if he were hearing some divine music, and then invited me, in a voice hoarse with emotion, to make my recitation over again. I did so immediately, with the same well-meaning deceit as before, and he brought his fist down on the table with formidable force and thundered in the same voice his ancestors must have used when they drew their swords and led the charge into battle: "*Kurwa mać!* I've got the bastards! They'll cough up for me now!" He leapt to his feet and departed from his office, and I, in my innocence, felt very pleased with my good deed.

That evening, Bronicki lost a million at the Deauville Casino.

I was with Lila the next morning when the count returned home. An hour before, Podlowski had warned us of the disaster, adding, "He's going to blow his brains out again." Lila, who was having tea and honey on toast, did not seem particularly moved.

"My father can't have lost that much. If he did, it can't have been his money. So he's only lost debts. He must be feeling relieved."

These Polish men and women before me really did possess the admirable sturdiness that had made it possible for their country to withstand every catastrophe. I expected to see Genia Bronicka in full hysterics, with telephone calls to doctors and fainting spells, upholding the fine tradition of her theatrical techniques; instead, I witnessed her descend to the dining room in a pink negligee with the poodle under her arm. She dropped a kiss on her daughter's forehead, tossed a friendly hello my way, called for her tea to be served, and observed, "I put the revolver in the safe. He mustn't find it: he'd sulk at us for a week. I don't know if he borrowed the money from the Potockis, the Sapiehas, or the Radziwiłłs, but for heaven's sake it's all the same—a gambling debt is a debt of honor, they understand that well enough. So one or the other of them will pay, what matters is that the Polish nobility uphold its traditions."

Tad walked down the steps in his robe, newspaper in hand, yawning. "What's going on? Mama looks so calm—I fear the worst."

"Father has ruined himself again," Lila said.

"That means he's gone and ruined someone else again."

"He lost a million at Deauville last night."

"He must have really had to scrape around for that," Tad grumbled. The chambermaid had just arrived with warm croissants when Stas Bronicki made his entrance. He looked haggard. Behind him followed the impeccable Mr. Jones, carrying his coat, and then Podlowski, the factotum, the blue-black of his five-o'clock shadow giving him twice the jaws and chin as usual.

Bronicki contemplated all of us in silence.

"Can someone here lend me a hundred thousand francs?" His gaze came to rest on me. Tad and Lila burst out laughing. Even kindly Bruno had a hard time hiding his mirth.

"Sit down, my friend. Have a cup of tea," said Genia.

"Fine. What about ten thousand?"

"Stas, please," said the countess.

"Five thousand!" roared Bronicki.

"Marie, heat some more croissants and some tea," called Genia.

"A thousand francs, for God's sake!" bawled Bronicki in despair.

Archie Jones put his hand inside his jacket and stepped forward, still carefully holding the count's checked overcoat. "If Monsieur will permit ... A hundred? *Fifty-fifty*, naturally."

Bronicki hesitated a moment, then grabbed the note from the chauffeur's hand and dashed outside. Podlowski raised his own hands and shoulders in a helpless motion and followed. Archie Jones bade us a polite goodbye and departed as well.

"Well, there you go," said Genitchka with a sigh. "The English really are the only people you can count on."

That was a phrase I would come to hear often, albeit in very different circumstances.

12

I DON'T KNOW WHETHER IT WAS THE SAPIEHA
princes, the Radziwiłł princes, or the Potocki counts who provided
my employer with the funds lost through the scheme for which I was
so innocently responsible, but in the days that followed, Le Manoir
des Jars was overrun with Polish gentlemen looking extremely elegant and swearing like sailors. Terms such as "that asshole Bronicki,"
"that walking shit," and "that son of a bitch" rained down from all
quarters, so much so that it seemed as if those same phrases were falling from the lips of the colonel of the Imperial Guard, Jan Bronicki,
in the aforementioned portrait. Poland's greatest names seemed to
be swooping down upon the roulette wheel's unhappy victim, who
faced the tempest with the utmost composure, as befits the citizen
of a country accustomed to being reborn from its own ashes. He was
unwavering in his line of reasoning: he hadn't had the second million his "system" required to break the bank. Therefore, if someone
would only be willing to advance him those two million, he would
return to the front, and no later than tomorrow the men cursing
him now would be the first to send up victory cheers in his honor.
But for once, it appeared that even the staunchest of Polish patri-
ots were furling the flag and losing confidence in victory. Bronicki
held long and secretive meetings with his factotum, to which I was
invited, although there was no need for calculations, since the only
figure emerging from the whole situation was a big fat zero. It was

decided that the family jewels should be sold, and Bronicki went to request them from his wife. He was met with refusal. Lila, who had witnessed the scene, settled comfortably in an armchair, eating candied chestnuts—"Since we're going to be poor, I might as well enjoy things while I can," she said, laughing, as she told me how her mother maintained that the diamonds and pearls in question had been given to her by the Duke of Ávila when he was the Spanish ambassador in Warsaw, so it would have been immoral for her to part with them for her husband's profit.

"As usual in our family, honor comes first," was Tad's comment.

Only one fallback position remained to the last of the Imperial Guards: to return to his properties in Poland. They were impregnable to the enemy, as they were part of a set of historic landholdings jealously guarded by the regime of colonels that had succeeded Marshal Piłsudski and his officers. The castle and estate were located at the mouth of the Vistula River, in the "Polish Corridor" that separated East Prussia from the rest of Germany. Having already installed a Nazi government in the Free City of Danzig, Hitler was now demanding its "restitution." The property had been declared inalienable in 1935 and the Bronickis received substantial aid for its upkeep.

I was horrified. The cruelty of losing Lila seemed to me to be incompatible with everything I knew of being human. The months or even years that I would be obliged to live apart from her revealed the existence of a duration that reflected nothing I was capable of calculating. My uncle, watching me wilt away as the fatal hour approached, attempted to explain to me that literature contained examples—in cases of extreme affliction—of loves that had survived years of separation.

"Definitive departure is better. You just turned seventeen, you need to make a life for yourself, and you can't become solely dependent on one woman. For years now, you've lived for her and by her alone. They may call us the 'crazy Fleurys' but even we need to be a little reasonable, which in French is also known as 'seeing reason,' though I'll be the first to acknowledge that this expression stinks of renunciation, giving up, and submission. If the French had all 'seen reason,' France would have disappeared a long time ago. The truth is, you can't have too much reason or too little madness—but I'll admit that while not too much and not too little might be a fine recipe for the Clos Joli and our friend Marcellin when he's in the kitchen, sometimes you've got to know to lose your head. Good gracious, here I am saying the exact opposite of what I'd wanted to say. Might as well suffer a whole lot and get it over with. And even if you must love this girl your whole life long, she's better off going away forever, it will only make her more beautiful."

I was patching up his *Blue Bird*, which had taken a tumble the day before. "What exactly are you trying to tell me, uncle? Are you advising me to live reasonably or to keep my reason to live?"

He lowered his head. "All right. I'll say no more. I'm the last person to be giving out advice. I've only ever loved one woman in my life and since it didn't work out ..."

"Why didn't it work out? She didn't love you?"

"It didn't work out because I never met her. I could see her in my head, I saw her every day in my head for thirty years, but I never found her. We didn't meet. Sometimes imagination can play really dirty tricks with you. It's true with women, with ideas, with countries—you love an idea, it seems like the most beautiful idea of all, and when it materializes, it doesn't look a thing like itself anymore, or it even becomes complete horseshit. Or you love your country so much you end up not being able to put up with it at all anymore, because it's never the right one." He chuckled. "And so you make your life, your ideas, your dreams into ... kites."

Only a few days remained to us, and our goodbyes were made of looking at the woods, ponds, and old paths we would never again see together. The end of the summer came in soft tints, as if it felt a certain tenderness toward us. The sun itself seemed reluctant to leave us.

"I want so very much to do something with my life," Lila said to me, as if I weren't there.

"That's only because you don't love me enough."

"Of course I love you, Ludo. But that's what's so awful. It's awful because it's not enough for me, because I still keep thinking about myself. I'm only eighteen, and already I don't know how to love. If I did I wouldn't be constantly thinking about what I am going to do with my life—I'd forget myself entirely. I wouldn't even think of being happy. If I truly knew how to love, I wouldn't be here anymore, there wouldn't be anyone but you anymore. True love is when there's nothing but the other person anymore. So there you go …"

Her face took on a tragic expression. "I'm only eighteen, and already, I cannot love," she exclaimed, and she burst out sobbing.

I was not particularly moved. I knew that she'd begun renouncing things several days ago—first medicine, then architecture—in order to enter the Warsaw Conservatory for the Dramatic Arts, and thus to rapidly become the darling of the Polish stage. I was beginning to understand her now, and I knew that my duty was to be a connoisseur of the sincerity of her voice, of her chagrin, of her distress. As she brushed a strand of hair from her face—a movement that still to this day is a woman's most beautiful gesture to me—watching for me from the sky-blue corner of her eye, she did everything but ask it aloud: "Don't you think I have talent?"

And I would have sacrificed anything to preserve the sublime grandeur of those heights in her eyes. I was, after all, dealing with a girl whose idol, Chopin, had gone and aggravated his tuberculosis in the damp of the Majorca winter just to please George Sand; a girl who had often reminded me, her eyes shining with hope, that Russia's two greatest poets, Pushkin and Lermontov, had both been killed in duels, the former at thirty-seven and the latter at twenty-six; that Hölderlin had gone mad with love; and that Heinrich von Kleist had died in a suicide pact with his beloved. All of that, I told myself, for once in my life throwing the Slavs in with the Germans, was Polish stuff.

I took her arm and tried to reassure her, even as I felt the beginning of something on my lips that bore a marked resemblance to my uncle Ambrose's ironic smile.

"It may just be that you don't love me," I repeated to her. "Now obviously, that's not what you've been expecting. But it will come. It might be Bruno. Or Hans, you'll be seeing him again soon—they're saying that the German army is all ready for business at the Polish border. Or maybe you'll meet somebody else you truly love."

She shook her head, in tears.

"But no, that's exactly it, I love you, Ludo! I really love you. But this, this can't be all there is to it—all there is to loving someone. Or maybe I'm just mediocre. I have a tiny heart, I'm superficial, incapable of depth, of grandeur, of intensity!"

I remembered my uncle's advice, and, once again taking a firm hold, so to speak, of the line of my beautiful kite to keep it from flying off and losing itself in all that Slavic torment, I pulled her to me; my lips pressed to hers, my last conscious thought being that if what Lila was giving me was not, as she had cried out to me, "true, great love," well, then life was even more abounding in beauty, joy, and happiness than I had imagined, even as she departed for Paris that very evening—here, without premeditation but not without a smile, I have created a syntactic confusion between "she" and "life"—where her parents were waiting for her.

Having been backed into a corner, the Radziwiłłs, Sapiehas, Potockis, and Zamoyskis had patriotically renounced their pursuit, so as not to tarnish one of Poland's most illustrious names, at a moment when statesmen less committed to honor were abandoning themselves to shame and bowing at Munich before the Nazi rabble. I returned once more to Le Manoir des Jars; Tad and Bruno were overseeing the packing of the artworks and managing "details" such

as the payment of the gardeners' and servants' salaries. This was causing some difficulties. The portrait of Colonel Count Jan Bronicki in
Somosierra had already come down from the wall and was waiting to
be crated and returned to its native soil. Podlowski wandered from
room to room, choosing which of the interior furnishings were to
be sold off to pay salaries and settle the bill at the Clos Joli, which
Marcellin Duprat refused to forget. The Bronickis' suppliers in Clos
and Cléry were no more inclined to relent, and attempted to seize
hold of anything that might serve as compensation. A few weeks
later, Genitchka finally agreed to part with a diamond "souvenir,"
and everything worked out. A significant proportion of the house's
contents, including the piano and the globe, were even left there in
the hopes of a return. In the meantime, however, Bruno despaired
at the thought that he might lose his Steinway. As for Tad, he was
more preoccupied with current political events than such material
concerns, and greeted me from where he was sitting, a stack of newspapers in his lap.

"We probably won't be back," he told me, "but that's nothing,
because I'm pretty sure that pretty soon millions of men won't be
back anywhere."

"There won't be a war," I said firmly, as I was ready to sacrifice
whatever it took to see Lila again. "I'll come and visit you in Poland
next summer."

"If there still is a Poland," Tad answered. "Now that Hitler's taken
full measure of your cowardice, he'll stop at nothing."

Bruno was packing his sheet music into a crate. "The piano is
done for," he said to me.

"What egotism," Tad grumbled. "That one, I tell you. The world
can go to hell in a handbasket, the only thing he cares about is a little
more music."

"France and England won't allow it," I said, and Tad must have
been very right to speak of egotism because immediately and with
utter clarity I realized that when I said "France and England won't

allow it," what I meant was that my definitive separation from Lila wouldn't be allowed.

Disgusted, Tad tossed the stack of newspapers to the floor. He observed me with only marginally less displeasure. "Oh yes, 'the most desperate songs are the most beautiful.' And we could also add, 'blessed are those who have died in a just war; blessed are the ripe sheaves and the wheat gathered in.' Poetry will march hand in hand with music, and the irresistible force of culture will sweep Hitler away. It's all over, kids." He looked at me again and pursed his lips. "You're welcome in Gródek next summer," he added. "It's possible that I'm wrong. Perhaps I underestimate the all-powerful force of love. Maybe there are gods I don't know about who make sure that nothing prevents lovers from reuniting. Oh, goddammit all! Goddammit! How could you have capitulated like that?"

I informed him that my uncle, the complete pacifist and conscientious objector that he was, had just stepped down from his post as honorary president of the Order of the Kites of France, because of Munich.

"What's surprising about that?" he snapped at me. "That's exactly what you call a conscientious objector. But who knows, things might drag on like this for two or three more years. So, see you next year, Ludo."

"See you next year."

We hugged goodbye and they saw me out to the terrace. I see the two of them again now, waving at me. I was certain that Tad was wrong, and I felt a bit sorry for him. He passionately loved all of humanity, but really, he had nobody. He believed in misfortune because he was lonely. You need two to hope. All laws of large numbers begin with that certainty.

13

DURING THE WINTER OF 1938–1939 MY MEMORY AS-
serted itself in a manner that justified the worst fears once expressed
by Monsieur Herbier when he came to warn my uncle that "the boy
seems entirely lacking in the ability to forget." I don't know if it actually was that way for all the Fleurys, as I had so often heard it said,
because this time it had nothing to do with liberty, human rights,
or France, which was still around and appeared not to demand any
particular effort of memory. Lila now accompanied me everywhere.
I had returned to my job as an accountant at the Clos Joli, and had
begun working for other businesses in the area as well, in order to
save up the money I needed for my trip to Poland; I kept up with
the farm, but during that whole time Lila's presence at my side took
on such physical reality that my uncle, with or without irony, had
begun setting a third place at the table for the one who was absent so
presently. He consulted Dr. Gardieu, who diagnosed a state of obsession and recommended jogging and team sports. I was not surprised
by the physician's lack of understanding, but my guardian's attitude
pained me, although I understood his long-standing mistrust of any
absolute loyalties, as they had already caused so much trouble in the
family. We argued a few times. He claimed that the trip to Poland
I was planning for that summer would be full of the worst kind of
disappointment, and, what's more, that the expression "first love" by
definition signified something that was meant to end. Nevertheless,

it seemed to me from time to time that my uncle's gaze, when he looked at me, wasn't lacking in pride.

"Anyhow, if you don't have enough money for the trip," he ended up saying, "I'll give you some. You'll need to buy some clothes, because there's no way you're going to visit those people dressed like a hobo."

Over the winter, Lila wrote me a few letters; they became shorter and shorter until they were only postcards. That was normal, we would be reunited soon, and the very brevity of her words, "We're all expecting you," "I'm so happy to think you'll finally see Poland," "We're thinking of you," "June's coming!" seemed to shorten the time, leapfrogging over the months and weeks. And then, in the time leading up to my departure, a long silence, as if to further abridge the last weeks of the wait.

I took the train from Cléry on June 20. My uncle accompanied me to the station. He said just one thing to me, as we pedaled side by side on our bicycles: "It'll be a change in landscape."

Landscape, lands—the earth was the farthest thing from my mind. The world was not invited on this trip. All I could think of was being whole again, of getting back my two missing arms. When the train began moving and I leaned out the window, Ambrose Fleury called out to me, "I hope you won't take too big a tumble. I hope I won't have to pick you up all dented and banged up like our old *Fourseas*! You remember?"

"You know I never remember anything!" I called back to him, and we left each other like that, in a burst of laughter.

14

NEVER BEFORE HAD I LEFT MY NATIVE NORMANDY. Of the world I knew only geography, and of history I knew only what I had learned in my textbooks, or from looking at my father and his brother Robert's names on the Cléry war monument, or from listening to my guardian comment about one or the other of his kites. It did not occur to me to think of history in the present tense. Of politics and those who engaged in it I knew only the faces of Édouard Herriot, André Tardieu, Édouard Daladier, Pierre La-val, Pierre-Étienne Flandin, or Albert Sarraut, who I glimpsed from time to time as I left Marcellin Duprat's little office in the Clos Joli. Of course I knew that Italy was fascist, but whenever I saw *A bas le fascisme!* written across a wall I wondered what the inscription was doing there, since we were in France. The Civil War in Spain, of which Tad had so often spoken, seemed to me a far-off affair of other people with other customs; after all, everyone knew—and said all the time—that the Spanish had blood in their blood, so to speak. I had been indignant over Munich, the year before, mostly because Hans was German, and it had seemed to me that I'd lost a point in our rivalry. The only thing I was sure of was that France would never let Poland down—or, to be more specific, Lila. Today, such igno-rance and indifference in a young man of eighteen seems difficult to understand, but back then, France was still the land of grandeur, peaceful strength, prestige—a country so certain of its "spiritual mission" that nothing was more natural in my eyes than to let it take care of itself; this, it seemed to me, saved the French a lot of worry. I can't even say I was one of the uneducated; quite the opposite, in fact: mandatory public education had simply taught me too well that liberty, dignity, and human rights were unassailable so long as our nation remained faithful to itself. And I had no doubt it would, since I remembered everything I had been taught. Whatever was happening with our neighbors, however nearby, took place beyond our borders, and to me, news of it evoked only surprise, tinged with disdain, while confirming our superiority in my eyes. Besides that, my uncle and Marcellin Duprat and all of my teachers at school were unanimous in affirming that a dictatorship had no chance of enduring, since it did not benefit from the consent of the people. To Ambrose Fleury, the *people* was a sacred notion, one that came with the fall of Mussolini, Hitler, and Franco all wrapped up inside it. No one saw Fascism and Nazism as popular regimes. Such an idea would have been an actual negation of the very building blocks of my mandatory public education. My guardian's resolute pacifism had done the rest. Certainly, at times I sensed a kind of confusion in him, and contradictory feelings; in this way he admired Léon Blum for refusing to intervene in the war in Spain, while Munich had left him overcome by fury. On that occasion, I ended up concluding that despite all his efforts, he had succumbed to the Fleury "historical memory," and that even the many years he had spent in his peaceful job as a rural postman were not enough to prevent the occasional relapse.

And so I couldn't have been more poorly prepared for the sight of the Europe I crossed in 1939. At the Italian border, which was overrun with black shirts, daggers, and Fascist emblems, I had my pocketknife confiscated, though it was barely three inches long. The steps outside of railway stations echoed with the footsteps of military detachments; a compatriot translated a Malaparte editorial for me that compared "degenerate France" to a submissive girl. Just after we crossed over the Austrian border, a small, sad, bald man who had taken a seat in my compartment was asked to leave the train, which he did in tears. Swastikas were everywhere, on flags, armbands, and walls, and from every poster, Hitler's gaze met mine. When my passport and visas were checked and it emerged that I was traveling to Poland, eyes hardened and papers were returned to me with a brusque gesture and a look of contempt. Twice, the windows of the train car were covered over with a special adhesive and cameras were collected and held for the duration of that leg of the journey; doubtless the train was passing through some "military zone." Some SS officers who had taken seats across from me on the way from Vienna to Bratislava glanced with amusement at my French beret and saluted me with a triumphant "*Sieg heil*" on their way out.

At the train's first stop in Poland, the atmosphere transformed abruptly and completely. Even my beret seemed to have changed expression, if not personality: the Polish passengers kept giving it friendly looks. Those who knew no French and had no other way to demonstrate their fellowship clapped me on the shoulder, shook my hand, and shared their beer and food with me. On the way to Warsaw, and then, once I changed trains, all along the "Corridor" that followed the Vistula River to the Baltic, I heard "Vive la France!" more times than ever before in all my life.

The Bronickis had cabled to say they would meet me at the station, and, as soon as the conductor came to tell me we were approaching Gródek, I left my third-class coach and moved to the first-class one, where I prepared to descend in a fittingly dignified manner. Marcellin Duprat had lent me a real leather suitcase. Reminding me that, after all, "You'll be representing France over there," he'd also suggested that I affix the three-star tricolor insignia of the Clos Joli to my jacket lapel, or even my beret. I had pretended to accept it, but then left it in my pocket—at the time I hadn't even the slightest premonition that it would one day constitute the last universally recognized distinction of my country. Famous as he was, it would not have occurred to anyone to consider Marcellin Duprat a visionary—"France's three stars," as the master chef called them, did not yet shine with anywhere near the same brilliance as they do today.

With the exception of a few farmers and their crates, almost no one remained in the train as it pulled up to Gródek's little redbrick station. However, they appeared to be expecting some sort of official visit, for as I set foot on the steps, I found myself surrounded by a military marching band composed of some dozen men. I also saw that the station roof had been decorated with crossed French and Polish flags, and as soon as I'd stepped forward with my suitcase, the band struck up "La Marseillaise," followed by the Polish national anthem. Rapidly removing my beret, I stood and listened at attention, all the while glancing around in the hopes of catching a glimpse of whatever French celebrity was being welcomed in this manner. I could see Stas Bronicki, bareheaded, his hat over his heart, listening to the national anthem; Lila waved at me; Tad, with eyes lowered, struggled visibly to keep from laughing; behind them, Bruno regarded me with a smile of both friendship and embarrassment, looking, as usual, a little bit lost. I figured it out only when a little girl bedecked with tricolor ribbons presented me with a bouquet of blue, white, and red flowers and articulated very carefully, in French: "*Vive la France éternelle et l'amitié immortelle du peuple français et du peuple polonais!*" which seemed to me to be a lot of eternity and immortality all at once. Following a moment of panic when I finally grasped that I was the object of this quasiofficial welcome—it was the first time I had ever represented France in another country—I responded bravely and in Polish, "*Niech zyje Polska! Vive la Pologne!*"

The little girl burst into tears, the musicians from the brass band broke ranks and came over to shake my hand, Stas Bronicki grabbed me in a hug, Lila threw her arms around my neck, Bruno pecked me on the cheek and slipped away, and, as soon as everyone's patriotic enthusiasm had settled down, Tad took my arm and whispered in my ear, "You see, it's like we've already won!"

Such a note of distress sounded from his mocking tone that I felt indignant in my new role representing France; I pulled my arm away and retorted, "My dear Tad, there is what we call cynicism, and there is what we call history in France and Poland. The two do not go together."

"Besides, there won't be any war," Bronicki put in. "Hitler's regime is on the verge of collapse."

"I believe I remember Churchill saying something about that to the British Parliament right around the time of the Munich pact," growled Tad. "He said, 'You were given the choice between war and dishonor. You chose dishonor and you will have war.'"

I was holding Lila's hand in mine. "Well then, we'll win it," I said, and was rewarded with a kiss on the cheek.

I could practically feel the weight of the crown of Frenchness on my head. When I recalled that Marcellin Duprat had dared to suggest that I travel to Poland with the insignia of the Clos Joli sewn to my chest, I regretted not having given him a good pair of slaps. Feeding all the big wheels of the Third Republic at his little restaurant had caused the good cook to lose sight of the true meaning of his country's grandeur, and all it represented in the eyes of the world. On the way from the station to the château, in an old Ford Bronicki drove himself—the blue Packard had been seized by creditors in Cléry—with Lila at my arm, I gave my friends the latest news from France. Never had the nation felt so sure of itself. Hitler's ranting was risible. There was not a single trace of nervousness anywhere, nor even apprehension. The entire country, peacefully confident in its strength, seemed to have acquired a new character trait, a phlegmatic cool once attributed to the British.

"President Lebrun made an amusing gesture that's apparently sent Hitler into a mad rage. He visited the rose garden our soldiers have planted along the Maginot Line."

Lila was sitting by my side, and her profile, so pure against the background of her pale hair, her gaze like the end of every question and all doubt, awoke within me a certainty of victory that was no illusion, for it could not and would not ever know defeat. So that makes one thing I have never been wrong about in my life, at least up until now.

"Hans tells me that the top brass in the German army are just waiting for the right moment to oust Hitler," she said.

So that was how I learned Hans was at the château. Goddammit, I thought suddenly, and wasn't even ashamed of this steep drop in my elevated thoughts—or rather of this irrepressible outbreak of popular indignation. "I don't know if the German army will oust Hitler, but I do know who will oust the German army," I declared. I really think I believed that the answer was: *it's me.* I'm not sure which of these had gone to my head: the euphoria of the patriotic welcome I had just received, or Lila's hand in mine. "We're prepared," I added, taking refuge in the plural, for modesty's sake.

Tad kept silent, with one of those thin smiles of his that further accentuated his eaglet profile. His sarcastic expression was difficult for me to stomach. Bruno attempted to set things a bit at ease. "And how are Ambrose Fleury and his kites?" he asked. "I think of him so often. He truly is a man of peace."

"My uncle never got over the Great War," I explained. "He's of another generation—they witnessed too many horrors. He mistrusts anything that gets people carried away; he thinks men should keep even their noblest ideas firmly tied to a solid line and hold on tight to the other end. Without that, he's convinced that millions of lives will be lost 'in pursuit of the blue yonder,' as he calls it. He's only happy when he's with his kites. But we, the youth of France, we cannot be satisfied with paper dreams—with any dreaming at all, for that matter. We're armed and ready to stand and defend, but not our dreams—our realities. The names of those realities are freedom, dignity, and human rights…"

Gently, Lila withdrew her hand from mine. I don't know if she felt uncomfortable with my patriotic fervor and my prolonged verbiage, or whether she was a bit vexed because I seemed to have forgotten her. But I hadn't forgotten her at all: it was Lila I was talking about.

15

THE BRONICKI CHÂTEAU RESEMBLED A FORTRESS, which indeed was what it had once been. It was a few hundred yards from the Baltic Sea, and half a dozen miles from the German border, surrounded by gardens, a forest of pine trees, and sand; there was still a moat, but a wide staircase and a vast terrace had been built where the drawbridge once stood. History and salt air had eaten away at the walls and the old towers; the entry hall bristled with so many suits of armor, banners, shields, arquebuses, halberds, and heraldic devices that arriving there made me feel naked as a jaybird.

I had walked only a few steps through this auction house atmosphere when I noticed Hans sitting in a tapestried armchair beside a marble table. He wore a pullover, riding breeches, and boots, and was reading an English magazine. We waved to each other from afar. I didn't understand his presence there, knowing as I did that he was studying at a military academy in Preuchen, and that the tension between Poland and Germany grew from one week to the next. Lila explained to me that the "poor darling" was convalescing from pneumonia at the estate of his uncle, Georg von Tiele, across the border, which he traversed on horseback from time to time to visit his Polish cousins, over paths he had known since childhood—which to me simply meant that he was as in love with his cousin as ever.

I found Lila changed. She had just turned twenty, but, as Tad had confided in me, she was still dreaming of herself.

"I want to do something with my life," she kept repeating to me.

Once, I couldn't resist snapping back at her, "Well, at least wait till I've gone home!"

I really don't know where I had come up with the idea that love could constitute the whole of life's work and meaning. Probably I had inherited this total lack of ambition from my uncle. Perhaps, too, I had loved too early, too young, with all my being, and there was no room left over in me for anything else. Of course I had moments of lucidity, when meager reality and the banality of my actual self seemed infinitely distant from the expectations of the blonde, dreamy head resting on my chest, her eyes closed, a smile on her lips as she wandered off down some glorious future path. I had a premonitory sense that she actually found a kind of comforting strength in my simplicity, but it's not easy to come to terms with the idea that a woman is attached to you because you help keep her feet on the ground, so as not to fly too far off. At the end of whole days spent "looking for herself in the forest," as she'd say to me, she would come find me in my room and snuggle against me sadly, as if I were her resigned answer to all that she asked herself.

"Love me, Ludo. That's all I deserve. I'll probably end up being one of those women who's only good at being loved. Whenever I hear a man's voice behind me murmuring, 'She's so pretty!' I feel like they're saying that my entire life could be contained in a mirror. And since I have no talent for anything—" she touched the tip of my nose, "—except you ... I'll never be a Marie Curie. I'm going to apply to medical school this year. With a little luck I might eventually heal someone."

I gleaned just one thing from her sadness: I was not *enough*. Seated beneath the tall pines at the edge of the Baltic, Lila would dream of herself with a stalk of grass between her teeth, and it seemed that the stalk of grass was me, and that I would be tossed to the wind at any moment. She became upset when I murmured to her, "You are my whole life," and I didn't know if it was the banality of the expression that made her indignant or the puny size of the unit of measurement.

"Come on, Ludo. Other men have loved before you."

"I know, I've had precursors."

Today, I believe she harbored a bewildered desire that she was incapable of articulating: not to be reduced to her femininity alone. How, at my age, knowing so little of the world in which I lived, could I understand that the word "femininity" could be a prison for women?

Tad said to me, "My sister is politically illiterate, but she dreams of herself like the revolutionary she hasn't figured out that she is."

In mid-July, the police came and placed Tad under arrest, taking him to Warsaw and interrogating him for several days. He was suspected of having written "subversive" articles in one of the banned journals then circulating in Poland. He was released with apologies by orders from above: whether or not he was guilty, it was unthinkable that the historic house of Bronicki could be mixed up in such an affair.

Rumors of war clamored louder every day, like the continuous pealing of thunder on the horizon; I walked through the streets of Gródek and strangers would come up and shake my hand when they saw on my jacket lapel the little tricolor insignia from which I had removed, thread by thread, the words "Clos Joli." But no one in Poland believed that after barely twenty years, Germany would rush into a new defeat. Only Tad was convinced that a global conflagration was imminent and I sensed that he was torn between his horror of war and his hope that a new world would be born from the ruins of the old one; I was embarrassed when he, too, though well aware of my naïveté and my ignorance, asked anxiously: "Do you really think the French army is as strong as they say it is here?" Immediately, with a smile, he caught himself. "You have no idea, obviously. No one knows. That's what history calls 'unforeseen circumstances.'"

When the sun agreed to it, we would steal off to a secluded spot on the Baltic shore, from which nothing seemed further than the end of this world, although it was just a few weeks away. And yet, I sensed a nervousness, even a terror in my companion, which I would ask vainly for her to explain to me; she would shake her head and press herself to me, her eyes widened, her chest heaving. "I'm frightened, Ludo. I'm frightened."

"Of what?" And then I'd add, as was the right and proper thing to do, "I'm here."

Every great sensibility is a bit clairvoyant and once Lila murmured to me, with strange calm, "The earth will shake."

"Why do you say that?"

"The earth will shake, Ludo. I'm sure of it."

"There's never been an earthquake in this region. That's a scientific fact."

Nothing gave me more tranquil strength and self-assurance than those moments, when Lila lifted her almost imploring gaze to me. "I don't know what's gotten into me." She touched her hand to her chest. "I feel like I don't have a heart anymore. It's become a frightened little rabbit."

I blamed the Baltic, the frigid waters, the sea mist. And for goodness' sake, I was there, wasn't I?

Everything seemed so calm. The old Norse pines joined hands above our heads. The cawing of the crows announced nothing more than nightfall, and a nearby nest. Before my eyes, Lila's profile against its backdrop of blondeness traced out the horizon of our destiny with more sureness than any cry of hatred or threat of war. She lifted grave eyes to mine. "I think I'm finally going to tell you, Ludo."

"What's that?"

"I love you."

It took me some time to regain my composure.

"What is it?"

"Nothing. But you were right. The earth just shook."

Tad, who now almost never left his wireless, observed us sadly. "Hurry up. You may be having the world's last love affair."

But our youth rapidly reasserted itself. The castle possessed a veritable museum of historical costumes, occupying three rooms of the so-called memorial wing; its wardrobes and glass cases were filled with castoffs from the venerable past; I slipped on a uniform from the Imperial Guard, Tad allowed us to talk him into trying on the garb of the *kosynierzy*, those peasants armed with nothing but their scythes who had marched with Kościuszko against the Czar's army; Lila appeared in a gown sparkling with gilded embroidery, which had belonged to some royal great-grandmother; Bruno, dressed as Chopin, took his seat at the piano. Lila, laughing helplessly at our masquerade, danced the polonaise with each of us in turn, while the mirrors, although they had been party to those bygone eras, observed benevolently. Nothing seemed surer to us than world peace when it became the countenance of my companion; as I bounded heavily across the parquet, Lila in my arms, everything was there, present and future; so it came to pass that a bold Norman Imperial Guardsman floated high above the earth after a queen whose name the history of Poland did not yet know—in those last days of July 1939, Polish history had little time for matters of the heart.

Then we would exit the "memory wing" to skip off through the pathways of the estate; discreetly, Tad and Bruno would slip away and leave us to ourselves; the forest began at the end of the path and alternated in its murmurs between the voices of its pines and the voice of the Baltic; among the tall heather there were patches of earth and rock where time seemed never to have set foot. I loved these lost places, suspended in the secret reveries of the geological eras that held them captive. The marks of our bodies in the sand still remained from the preceding days. Lila caught her breath; I shut my eyes on her shoulder. But soon the red and white Imperial Guardsman's uniform would join the royal robe in the heather, and then sea, sky, and earth were no longer; each embrace rescued life from all peril and error, and each made me feel as if I had known only spurious imitations until then. When consciousness returned, I felt my heart arriving slowly at its anchorage with all the peace of great sailing ships after years of absence. At the end of each caress, to take my hand from Lila's breast and touch a rock or a tree was enough to banish all harshness there. Sometimes I tried to love with my eyes open, but closed them always, for seeing took up too much space and cluttered my senses. Lila pulled away from me a little and examined my face with a trace of disapproval in her gaze.

"Hans is handsomer than you and Bruno has much more talent. I wonder why I prefer you to everyone else."

"Me, too," I said.

She laughed. "I certainly never will understand anything about women," she replied.

16

IT SEEMED TO ME THAT BRUNO WAS AVOIDING ME. The pain I saw in his face was haunting. Normally, he would spend five or six hours a day at the piano, and I'd sometimes linger below his window, listening to him. But for some time, everything had been silent. I went up to the music room: the piano had disappeared. What occurred to me then seemed mad, but was in fact how I thought of heartbreak: *Bruno had thrown his piano into the sea.*

That very afternoon, having followed a footpath in search of Lila, I heard notes of Chopin mixed in with the murmuring of the waves. I took a few steps down a sandy walkway covered in green fir needles and arrived at the beach. To my left, I caught a glimpse of the piano, beneath a great pine, which was leaned in the way very old trees do, whose tops seem to dream of the past. Bruno was seated at the piano about twenty paces away from me; I saw him in profile, and in the sea air his face seemed to have an almost ghostly paleness, for it was that end-of-day light, which dims more than it illuminates and which gulls' cries rip through suddenly, like foghorns.

I stopped behind a tree, not to hide, but because everything was so very perfect in this northern symphony of paleness and sea that I feared I would interrupt one of those moments that could last a lifetime, if there were memory enough for it. A seagull escaped from the fog, traced its brief signal above the water, and flew off like a note. The swishing of the surf, although it was only that, the Baltic, nothing more than a stretch of sea, a plain mixture of water and salt, ended in the sand before the piano like a dog lying down at its master's feet.

Then Bruno's hands went silent. I waited a little longer and approached him. Beneath his thick and tangled hair, his face still had the look of a bird just fallen from the nest. I searched for something to say, since you always have to fall back on words to prevent silence from speaking too loudly, then I sensed a presence behind me. Lila was there, barefoot in the sand, wearing a dress she must have borrowed from her mother, a striking ripple of sheerness and lace. She was weeping.

"Bruno, my little Bruno, I love you *too*. As for Ludo, it could be over tomorrow or it could last a lifetime—it's not my decision—it's life!"

She went over to Bruno and gave him a kiss on the lips. I was not jealous. It wasn't that kind of kiss.

I dreaded another rival altogether: I would see him on the paths, beneath the pines, holding two horses by their bridles—Hans, who had once again managed to cross the border to be with Lila. Despite her explanations that it was an accident of centuries and family trees that the Bronickis had grown a branch all the way into Prussia, the presence of this "cousin," a cadet in a Wehrmacht military academy, was intolerable in my eyes. I could see it in the very way he stood there, indifferently, in the outfit of a English gentleman rider, an intrusion and an arrogance that left me beside myself. I clenched my fists and Lila looked worried.

"What's gotten into you? Why are you making that face?"

I left them and ran off into the forest. Yet again, I could not understand, whatever their family ties, how the Bronickis could tolerate the presence of someone who might very well, from his position in the ranks of the German army, be preparing to invade the sacred "Corridor." I had only once heard Hans himself begin to discuss the subject, after a particularly virulent speech by Hitler. We had all come together in the sitting room, gathering around the fireplace, in which the fire leapt and roared with the voice of an old lion dreaming of its tamer's death. Tad had just shut off the wireless; Hans contemplated us.

"I know what you're thinking but you're wrong. Hitler isn't our master; he's our servant. The army will have no trouble getting rid of him, once he's outlasted his usefulness. We'll put an end to all this ignominiousness. Germany will be back in the hands of those who have always tended to its honor."

Tad was sitting in an armchair that had been worn threadbare by many historical Bronicki bottoms.

"My dear Hans, the elite has taken its shit. Time to get off the pot. It's over. The only thing left for them to bring into this world now is their own end."

Lila was half-reclined on one of those high-backed quadrupeds, stiff and monastic, which must have been the local equivalent of Louis XI style.

"Our Father who art in heaven," she murmured.

We looked at her in surprise. Her attitude toward churches, religion, and priests was very Christian in its pity; as she said, "they must be forgiven, for they know not what they do."

"Our Father who art in heaven, make the world feminine! Make ideas feminine, make countries feminine, make heads of state feminine! Do you know, children, who the first man to speak in a feminine voice was?"

Tad shrugged. "The idea that Jesus was a homosexual is just another Nazi rant—it has no grounding in historical fact."

"There's a masculine thought for you, my little Tad! I'm not stupid enough to claim anything like that. I'm simply saying that the first man in the history of civilization to have spoken in a feminine voice was Jesus. I say it and I can prove it. After all, who was the first man to preach pity, love, tenderness, gentleness, forgiveness, and respect for weakness? Who was the first man to have said that strength, hardness, cruelty, fisticuffs, and bloodshed could all go to hell? Well, so to speak. Jesus was the first man to demand that the world be made feminine, and I demand it, too. I'm the second person after Christ to insist upon it, there you go!"

"The second coming," Tad muttered. "That's all we needed."

Some days, I barely saw Lila at all. She would disappear into the forest with her pencils and a fat notebook. I knew that she was writing a diary that was to eclipse the then-celebrated journal of the painter and sculptor Marie Bashkirtseff. Tad had given her Mary Stanfield's *History of Feminist Struggles*, but the word "feminist" displeased her.

"We need to come up with something without an *–ist*," she'd say.

I was jealous of her solitudes, of the paths she walked down without me, of the books she took with her and read as if I did not exist. I now knew how to poke fun at myself in these excessively demanding moments, to make light of my tyrannical terrors. I was beginning to understand that you must learn to let all things leave you every so often—even your reason to live. That you must grant them their right to be a little inconstant, even: to take up with solitude, with the horizon, or with those tall plants whose name I didn't know, the ones that lose their white heads at the tiniest gust of wind. When she abandoned me in this way to go off and "look for herself"—in a single day she might start out at the École du Louvre in Paris and end up studying biology in England—I felt I'd been chased out of her life for being insignificant. And yet I was awakening to the idea that it was not enough to love, that you also had to learn how to love, and I recalled my Uncle Ambrose's advice to "hold tightly to the end of the line, so your kite doesn't fly away and get lost in pursuit of the blue yonder." I dreamt too high and too far. I had to accept the idea that I could only be my own life, and not Lila's. Never before had the notion of liberty seemed so stern, so demanding, and so difficult. Liberty had, for all time, demanded sacrifices: I was too accustomed to the Fleury family history—"victims of mandatory public education" every last one of them, as my uncle put it—to contest that. But it had never occurred to me that loving a woman could also be a lesson in liberty. I set about it with courage and application: I no longer wandered the forest in search of Lila; I fought against the feelings of insignificance and inexistence that overcame me when her absences wore on; my feeling "less and less" very nearly became a kind of game, which I played until the moment when, the better to laugh about it, I would go and check in a mirror to be sure I had not shrunk to dwarf size.

It must be said that my damn memory didn't make things any easier. When Lila left me, I could see her so clearly that from time to time I would reproach myself for spying on her. Is it necessary to have loved several women to learn to love a single one? Perhaps. Nothing can prepare us for a first love. And when Tad would say to me, as he did occasionally, "Come now, you'll love other women in this life," it seemed like an awfully harsh thing to say about this life.

In the castle were three libraries, each with crimson- and gilt-edged volumes lining the walls, and I visited them often, to search their books for a reason to live other than Lila. There wasn't one. I was getting scared. I wasn't even sure Lila truly loved me—was I just her "little French whim," as Mama Bronicka had said to me one day? Lila had dubbed us—Tad, Bruno, Hans, and I—her "four horsemen of the anti-Apocalypse," and all of us were to become champions of humanity, yet here I was with no idea of how to ride a horse. So when she abandoned me to myself, I took refuge in reading. We rarely saw Stas Bronicki in Gródek—he was tied up with an affair of honor in Warsaw; Genia, it was being said, had become the mistress of a leading statesman, and if her husband left her alone in the capital, the excess of obviousness might tarnish the Bronicki name—but one day, he happened upon me absorbed in a first edition of Montaigne, and declaimed, with an expansive gesture at his bibliophilic treasures: "I spent the most exalting and inspired hours of my youth here, and it is here I shall return, in my old age, to my true raison d'être: culture …"

"My father never read a book in his life," Tad whispered in my ear. "But the sentiment is there."

When Lila's absences were long or when—in the very height of misfortune—Hans appeared and the two of them went riding together through the forest, the trancelike state I entered did not go unnoticed by my friends. Bruno would reassure me that I mustn't feel jealous—you had to admit it: Hans was an excellent horseman. Tad would make an effort not to seem sarcastic, which for him was a truly unnatural act. Once, though, he lost his temper, when the Polish radio announced new concentrations of German troops along the "Corridor": "Oh, please, what's one pip-squeak heartache compared to Europe and freedom heading down the road to ruin?"

In one of the narrow little streets of Gródek, an old man with a handsome white mustache waved hello to me and invited me "into his humble abode." On the sitting-room wall was a full-length portrait of Marshal Foch.

"Long live immortal France!" said my host.

"Long live eternal Poland!" I replied.

There was something all too mortal in these declarations of immortality. Of my entire stay, it was probably the only moment I felt doubt brush against me with a wing of misgiving. In the trust showed by every Polish person I encountered for "invincible France" was something that suddenly seemed to me to be closer to death than to the invincible. But that only lasted an instant. Immediately, I searched the Fleury "historical memory" and located the certainty that allowed me to return to Lila's side and take her in my arms with the tranquil assurance of someone who, in so doing, is preserving world peace. I won't try today, after forty million deaths, to find any excuses for myself, except perhaps for the naïveté from which both supreme sacrifice and shameful blindness can be born; but to me, nothing quelled the threat of war with such serenity as the heat of her lips on my neck, on my face—a heat I would never cease to feel there, even after they were long gone. When we are too happy, we run the risk of becoming monsters of contentment. When Polish people, seeing my tricolor insignia, would approach me in the street, I would reply curtly, "France is here," brushing off anything that took the liberty of casting shadows over *our* future. Reluctantly, I accompanied Tad to a clandestine student meeting in Hel, where two rival schools of thought clashed: the one demanding immediate mobilization and the one affirming, if I understood correctly, that you had to know how to lose a purely military war in order to triumph in a different one, the one that would bring an end to a society of exploitation. My very rudimentary knowledge of Polish did not allow me to keep my bearings between these dialectics, so I sat there, politely but a bit ironically, my arms crossed over my chest, certain that my tranquil French presence was the answer to everything.

17

IT WAS UPON MY RETURN FROM THIS MEETING THAT Count Bronicki held a solemn interview with me in the great oval hall known as the "Hall of Princes," where some victorious treaty or another had been signed. I had been summoned to appear there at four o'clock in the afternoon and was waiting for him beneath the paintings, where Napoleon's field marshals hung just a few yards away from Hetman Mazepa, fleeing in shame after his defeat; and from Jaroslav Bronicki, the hero whose celebrated charge had sealed the Turks' defeat at Sobieski, before they reached Vienna. In various parts of the country, half a dozen painters labored for Stas Bronicki to preserve the oldest and noblest traditions of Polish history in paintbrushes and oils. The count was at that time engaged in a vast trade operation: eight million skins ordered from the Russians, including two-thirds of the total production of astrakhan and Persian lamb, sapphire mink, and longhairs: lynx, fox, bear, and wolf, which he was proposing to sell at a 400 percent profit on the other side of the Atlantic. I don't know how the idea for this business had sprouted in his genius brain; today I believe he must have had some sort of intuition or premonition—just about the wrong kind of skin.

I spent several hours a day calculating potential profit margins based on prices in different world markets. The business was supposed to include nearly the entire pelt production of the Soviet Union in the years 1940, 1941, and 1942, and enjoyed the support of the Polish government; it appeared to be a matter of high-level diplomacy: Colonel Beck, the foreign minister, having failed in his efforts to reach an agreement with Nazi Germany, was seeking to establish good relations with the USSR through trade relations. Probably never, in the entire history of humanity, had a bigger mistake been made as to the nature and the price of skins. You can still find the details of the affair in the Polish National Archives. One of the most awful sentences I've ever had occasion to hear uttered was from the mouth an eminent member of the Wildlife Society after the war: "We can at least be grateful that tens of millions of animals escaped massacre."

I waited for Bronicki a good half hour. I didn't know what he wanted from me. That same morning, we'd had a long work session about finding a place to store the furs, somewhere they could be preserved carefully so as not to flood the market and cause prices to collapse. There were also other complications: apparently Germany wanted in, too; rumor had it that they were prepared, over the next five years, to acquire every single Soviet skin. Bronicki had given no hint of this slightly ceremonious convocation during the course of the business meeting. "Wait for me at four o'clock in the Hall of Princes," was all he had said, somewhat curtly, at the end.

When the door opened and Bronicki appeared, I noticed immediately that he was slightly "under the influence," as the Polish tactfully say—*pod wpływem*. It was not out of character for him to empty half a bottle of cognac after a meal.

"I think the time has come for you to have a frank and open conversation with me, Monsieur Fleury."

It was the first time he had bestowed a "Monsieur" on me and called me by my surname, placing what seemed to me to be a particular emphasis on the "Fleury." He stood before me, in golfing trousers and jacket, his hands behind his back, from time to time lifting himself slightly onto his toes.

"I am fully aware of your relationship with my daughter. You are her lover." He held up his hand. "No, no, there's no use denying it. You are, I'm sure, a young man with a sense of honor and of the obligations this imposes. I believe, therefore, that your intentions are honorable. I just want to be sure of it."

It took me a few seconds to return to my senses. All I managed to stammer was, "I do indeed wish to marry her, sir." The rest, through which shuffled phrases like "the happiest of men" and "the very meaning of my life," was lost in a mumble.

Bronicki looked me up and down, his chin thrust forward. "But I thought you to be an honorable man, Monsieur Fleury," he said.

I no longer understood.

"I believed, as I have said to you, that your intentions were honorable. I regret to observe that they are not."

"But …"

"That you are sleeping with my daughter is … how shall I say it? A pleasure that bears no consequences. We do not require sainthood of the women in our family: pride is sufficient for us. But my daughter marrying you, Monsieur Fleury, would be out of the question. I am sure that you have a brilliant future ahead of you, but given the name she bears, my daughter has all the chances in the world of marrying someone of royal blood. As you are well aware, she is regularly invited to the courts of England, Denmark, Luxembourg, and Norway …"

It was true. I had seen for myself the engraved cards lined up on the marble table in the hall. But they were nearly always for receptions, where the guests must have numbered in the hundreds. Lila had explained it to me: "It's because of this accursed Corridor. Since our castle is, so to speak, at the heart of the problem, all those invitations are more political than they are personal." And when he heard of these parties, Tad would grumble, "The drowned forest …" It was the title of a Walden poem that told the story of a submerged forest, from which the melodies of its drowned songbirds echoed each night.

I forced myself to contain my anger and show the phlegmatic English stoicism I admired so much in the novels of Kipling and Conan Doyle. Even today, I still wonder what feelings of pettiness and insignificance made up Stas Bronicki's daydreams of grandeur. He stood before me, a glass of whiskey in hand, an eyebrow raised high above the blue and slightly glassy eye of a man "under the influence." Perhaps at the bottom of it all was some mortal anxiety that nothing could transcend.

"As you wish, sir," I replied. I nodded to him and left the room. It was as I descended the great, solemn staircase—one had the impression of stepping down centuries, rather than stairs—that I began to wish ardently for this war, which, according to Tad, would really be "the end of a world," and would shake all those condescending monkeys down from the high branches of their family trees. I didn't breathe a word of this interview to Lila; I wanted to spare her the shame and the tears. I discussed it with Tad, who reacted with one of those thin smiles, which were for him a kind of arm for the disarmed; three years later, we found in the pocket of a fallen SS officer a now famous photograph, of a Resistance fighter, his hands bound and his back against a wall, facing an execution squad—and on the face of this Frenchman who was about to die, my memory immediately recognized Tad's smile. He refrained from any comment, probably because his father's attitude seemed so natural to him, so self-evident in a society that was hanging on to the bulk of its sinking past as one clutches at a life preserver, but he ended up speaking to his sister about it; I found out that Lila had burst into her father's office and called him a pimp. I was touched, but what appeared significant in Tad's retelling of the scene was that Lila had reminded Stas Bronicki that, according to the local gossip, he was a bastard himself, the son of a stable boy. I could not help finding something amusing in the idea that even from the heights of her egalitarian indignation, Lila saw "son of a stable boy" as the worst of insults. In a nutshell, I was learning irony, and I don't know if I owe it to Tad's teachings, or whether, as I matured, I had begun spontaneously arming myself for life.

The result of this interview was that Lila began "dreaming of herself" in an entirely new way, and one that delighted Tad; she would enter my room loaded up with "subversive" literature, which until then Tad had unsuccessfully endeavored to get her to read; my bed was littered with pamphlets printed clandestinely by Tad's "study group"; curled up beneath its canopy, which had sheltered the sleep of princes, her knees tucked under her chin, she would read Bakunin, Kropotkin, and excerpts from the work of a certain Gramsci, whom her brother ardently admired. She questioned me about the Popular Front, of which I knew almost nothing beyond the Léon Blum kite my uncle kept in a corner of his workshop; suddenly, she wanted to know everything about the Spanish Civil War and La Pasionaria, whose name she pronounced with lively interest, for in her new approach to the search, as she would say to me, there might be some possibilities there. She smoked cigarette after cigarette, stubbing them out with fervid resolve in the silver ashtrays I held out for her. I understood this manner of reassuring me, of displaying her tenderness toward me, and perhaps of loving me; I suspected strongly that there was, in her sudden revolutionary blaze, more elegance of sentiment than any actual conviction. We would end up tossing the books and pamphlets onto the floor and taking refuge in far less theoretical passions. I knew also that my simplistic vision of things, which could well have led me to the life of a rural postman, returning home every evening to Lila and our many children, was attributable to the same comical naïveté that had caused our distinguished visitors to laugh so heartily at the "certified postman" and his childish kites. I recognized in this quality the survival of some primal ancestral strain that could not be eradicated—and that couldn't have fit more poorly with Lila's expectations for the man to whom she would tie her fate. Timidly, I asked her one night: "If I graduated from the Polytechnical Institute at the top of my class, would you ..."

"Would I what?"

I held my tongue. It was not a question of what I would do in life, but what a woman was going to do with mine. And I didn't understand that my companion was intuiting the possibility of an entirely different "me" and an entirely different "we," in a world she vaguely sensed was drawing near every time she sought shelter in my arms and murmured, "The earth will shake."

Squadrons of cavalrymen crossed Gródek with their swords and their flags, singing as they went, to take up their positions on the German border.

It was said that a superior officer from the French General Staff had come to inspect the fortifications at Helm and had declared them "worthy, in certain ways, of our own Maginot Line."

Nearly every week, Hans von Schwede continued to make clandestine, forbidden border crossings on his handsome gray steed to spend a few days with his cousins. I knew that in so doing he was risking his career and occasionally even his life to be near Lila. He told us that he had been shot at several times, once on the Polish side, once on the German. His presence was difficult for me to bear; even more difficult was his friendship with Lila. They took long rides through the forest together on horseback. I didn't understand this aristocratic fraternizing above the fray; in it, there seemed to me, was an absence of principle. I would go to the music room, where Bruno practiced the piano the whole day through. He had been invited to participate in the Chopin competition in Edinburgh, and was preparing for his departure for England. England, too, during those perilous days, was attempting to lavish on Poland encouraging signs of its serene power.

"I cannot understand how the Bronickis could welcome a man who is about to become an officer in the enemy army into their home," I declared to Bruno, flopping into an armchair.

"There's always time to be enemies, old man."

"Bruno, someday you'll die of kindness, tolerance, and gentleness."

"Well, given the options, it isn't a bad way to go."

I would never forget that moment. I would never forget his long fingers on the keyboard, that tender face under its thatch of hair. When fate finally laid its cards on the table, nothing would have prepared me for the change it signaled: Bruno's card really must have been drawn from another deck. But then again, fate sometimes does play with its eyes shut.

18

SUMMER WAS PAST ITS PRIME — NOTHING BUT clouds and fog; the sun just barely nibbled at the horizon line; the pines quieted, their branches stilled by the seaside damp. It was already the windless season that awaits the equinoctial gales. There were butterflies we'd never seen, velvety dark brown, bigger and heavier than those of summer. Lila remained nestled in my arms and I'd never yet felt myself so present in her silences.

"We're making memories for ourselves," she would say.

Of all the hours of the day, five o'clock in the afternoon was my worst enemy, for the air became too cool and the sand too damp. We had to get up, to part, to cut ourselves in two. There was still one last good moment when Lila would draw the blanket over us, pressing herself a little closer to me for warmth. At around five thirty, the Baltic would suddenly grow old; its voice would become crankier, more cantankerous. The shadows would swoop down on us with vaporous wing strokes. One last embrace, until Lila's voice died on her lips, unmoving and half-open; her widened eyes would lose their quick; her heart would slowly calm against my chest. In those moments, I was still stupid enough to feel like a master builder, proud of his force. All of these conceits would disappear when I understood that I loved Lila in a way that accepted no limits, including the limit of sexuality, and that there is a dimension to a couple that never ceases to grow, even as everything else dwindles away.

"What's going to become of you when we part, Ludo?"

"I'll die like a dog."

"Don't be silly."

"I'll die for fifty years, eighty years—I don't know. The Fleurys are long-lived, so you don't need to worry: I'll take good care of you, even after you've been gone a long time."

I was sure I'd keep her and I did not yet have any idea of how comical the reason for my certainty really was. Contained in this faith in my virility was all of the naive "triumphalism" of my eighteen years. Each time I heard her rising moans, I told myself that I was what was going on in there and that no one could do any better. These were probably the last moments of my adolescent naïveté.

"I don't know if I should see you again, Ludo. I want to stay whole."

I kept quiet. Let her go on "searching for herself," she would find only me. The twilight thickened around us; the gulls' cries came from very far off and already resembled memories.

"You're wrong, my dear. My future is in the bag. With my uncle's prestige, I'm almost certain to get a nice job with the postal service in Cléry, and then you can finally see what life is really all about."

She laughed. "Well, now there's a class struggle. That's not what it's all about, Ludo."

"What is it all about? Hans?"

"Don't be petty."

"Do you love me, yes or no?"

"I love you, but that's not where everything ends. I don't want to become your other half. Do you know that horrible expression? 'Where's my other half?' 'You haven't seen my other half, have you?' When I see you in five years, or ten, I want to feel my heart ringing out. But if you come home every single evening, year after year, it won't ring out anymore—it would just be the doorbell jingling."

She pushed away the blanket and got up. Sometimes I still wonder what happened to it, that old Zakopane blanket. I left it there because we were going to return, and we never returned.

19

ON JULY 27, TEN DAYS BEFORE MY DEPARTURE, A SPE-
cial train from Warsaw brought Genitchka Bronicka home, in the
company of the commander in chief of the Polish army and marshal
of Poland, Rydz-Śmigły himself, a man with a shaven head and fero-
cious, bushy eyebrows, who spent all his time at an easel, painting del-
icate watercolors. It was the famous "weekend of confidence," whose
calm assurance was celebrated by the entire press. The idea was to display proof to the world of the commander in chief's serenity about the
future, just as Hitler's vociferations from Berlin were reaching a fever
pitch. A photograph of the marshal sitting peacefully in the middle
of the "Corridor," painting his watercolors, was reproduced with ad-
miring comments in the British and French presses. The other guests
Genitchka had brought with her from Warsaw included a famous
psychic, an actor who was introduced to us as the "greatest Hamlet of
all time," and a young writer whose first novel was, any minute now,
going to be translated into every language. The psychic was invited
to read our futures in a crystal ball, which she did, but she refused to
tell us what she saw, for, given our youth, it would have been fatal to
incite us to passivity by showing us the paths in life that had already
been traced out for us. She did not, on the other hand, hesitate to
predict the Polish army's victory over the Hitlerian hydra to Marshal
Rydz-Śmigły; however, she concluded her prophecy with a rather
sibylline remark: "But everything will turn out well in the end." Hans,

who had been at the castle since the day before, remained discreetly in his room for the duration of this "weekend of confidence," as the press described the event. The marshal took a return train that evening, followed by the greatest Hamlet of all time, once the latter had, at the end of dinner, recited to us with incontestable sincerity the famous "to be or not to be" monologue, which, while being quite apropos, was not really in keeping with the atmosphere of optimism that everyone was supposed to be displaying. As for the young novelist, he sat among us with a distant expression, examining his fingernails and smiling somewhat condescendingly from time to time whenever Madame Bronicka attempted to tackle a literary subject; that was sacred ground, which he did not intend to defile with the banality of society chatter. He disappeared the next day, escorted to the station after an incident that had occurred in the steam baths reserved for the domestic staff; the precise nature of the "incident" was kept quiet, but for the writer it had resulted in a black eye, as well as a trying interview between Walenty the gardener and Madame Bronicka, during which Genitchka attempted to explain that "talent must be forgiven certain vagaries, without anger." It was a disastrous weekend in every way: six golden plates, as well as a Longhi painting and a miniature by Bellini, had disappeared from Madame Bronicka's little blue sitting room. Suspicions first came to rest on the psychic, who had departed the day before, since Genitchka could not resign herself to incriminating great literature. My stupefaction may be understood when, on Monday evening, I opened my closet to remove a shirt and discovered a hatbox containing the Longhi painting, the Bellini miniature, and the six golden plates. I stood there uncomprehendingly for a moment, but the stolen objects really were there, in my closet, and the reason they had been put there occurred to me suddenly, in a searing flash of horror: someone was trying to dishonor me. It didn't take me long to find the name of the only enemy capable of hatching such a plot: the German. An odious but clever way of getting rid of the little Norman hayseed who had committed the unpardonable crime of loving Lila.

It was seven o'clock. I tore into the corridor. Hans's room was located in the eastern wing of the castle, overlooking the sea. I remember that when I arrived at his door, I had a curious surge of the "good manners" I'd caught rubbing shoulders with elegant company: should I knock at the door, or not? Given the circumstances, it seemed to me that I should consider myself in enemy territory and shrug off convention. I pressed down on the heavy bronze door handle and entered. The room was empty. Like mine, it was all nobility and grandeur, its walls covered with imperial eagles, its furniture whose every empty seat evoked an image of some lordly fundament, and the lances of the Polish Imperial Guardsmen crossed over the fire burning in the fireplace. I heard the sound of a shower running. I hesitated to enter the bathroom—it wasn't the place to settle an affair of honor. I returned to the door, opened it, and closed it again, noisily. A few more seconds and Hans entered. He was wearing a black bathrobe with some sort of insignia of his military academy on the collar. His blond hair and face were dripping with water.

"You bastard!" I cried. "It was you."

He had his hands in the pockets of his bathrobe. That imperturbability, that total absence of emotion—they belonged to a man not only accustomed to treachery, but for whom it was second nature.

"You stole those things and you put them in my closet to dishonor me!"

For the first time, there was the trace of an expression on his face. The beginnings of ironic surprise, as if he were incredulous at the idea that honor could be a question for me. It was all that disdainful superiority, hereditary as syphilis, of people who had possessed the privilege of disdain since birth. "I could knock you out right here, with my bare fists," I told him. "But that's not enough. I'll be waiting for you in the gun room at eleven o'clock tonight."

I left the room and returned to mine, where I found Marek, the valet, had come to fetch my shoes, which he shined morning and evening. He was a stocky lad, with pomaded hair and a *czub* shaped into a kiss-curl in the middle of his forehead, always cheerful and a great fan of the ladies. He made my bed, attempting as usual to communicate with me by reducing his Polish to the few rudimentary words he deemed likely to figure in my vocabulary. Since my arrival in Gródek, I had felt great friendliness toward the castle's domestic staff, who were, after all, like me, just peasants in disguise. Nothing is harder to vanquish than prejudice, and favorable prejudices are no less tenacious than the others.

Marek beat the pillows back into their nice obese form, turned down the coverlet, and then moved toward the closet. He opened it, and, apparently paying no attention to the hatbox and its contents—you could see the gold tableware sparkling—removed my pair of spare shoes. Then he shut the closet again and went away, my shoes in hand.

It was useless for me now to signal the presence of the stolen art in my room to Madame Bronicka, as I had intended to do. Marek had seen them, so it would have been presumed that, all being lost for me, I was attempting a preemptive strike.

At eight, when the dinner gong rang, I went downstairs. I was always seated to the right of the countess, in honor of France. Hans was seated at the foot of the table. I had always found that there was something feminine in his facial features, although it would have been impossible to use the word "effeminate." He looked at me from time to time with the trace of a smile. I was so nervous that I could neither eat nor speak. There were two enormous candelabra on the oaken table, and our faces darkened or glowed at the will of the breezes, in a play of shadow and light. Tad had just turned nineteen, and was suffering from his position at the crossroads in life where virility has already begun aspiring to accomplishments that adolescence still forbids; he was speaking of the war that the Spanish Republicans had lost against Franco, in passionate tones that must have matched those of Byron's followers, or Garibaldi's. Madame Bronicka listened to him in consternation as she fiddled

with the crumbs on the table. That her son would allow himself such
fervor in memory of Catalonia, where the anarchists had danced in
the streets with exhumed nuns' corpses, only confirmed in her eyes,
as she often repeated to us, the nefarious influence of Picasso on today's youth. There was no doubt in her mind that all of the horrors
that had taken place in Spain were, directly or indirectly, his work. It
had all begun with the surrealists, she told us, with an air Tad called
"definitive."

As soon as dinner ended, I kissed Genitchka's hand and returned
to my room. Several times, Lila had looked at me with surprise, for,
never having learned the polite art of masking my emotions, it was
difficult for me to hide my fury. When I left the dining room she followed me, stopping at the foot of the stairs. "What's wrong, Ludo?"

"Nothing."

"What did I do to you?"

"Leave me alone. You're not the only one who matters."

Never had I spoken to her in that way. Had I been ten years older,
I would have wept with rage and humiliation. But I was still too
young: my idea of virility had marked tears as feminine, refusing
manliness its full portion of brotherhood.

Her lips trembled slightly. I had hurt her. I felt better. Less alone.

"I'm sorry Lila, I have a heavy heart. I don't know if that expression exists in Polish."

"*Ciężkie serce,*" she said.

"I'll explain everything to you tomorrow."

I climbed the stairs. I felt as if I had finally spoken to Lila on equal
terms. I turned around. It seemed to me that there was a trace of
anxiety in her expression. Perhaps she feared losing me—she did
have an overactive imagination.

It wasn't just me: I felt wounded in the deepest part of my family.
Not one single Fleury had been left unsullied by the insult. That I
had been taken as a readymade victim by Hans, with what credibility
my humble origins might lend me the *natural* role of the guilty party,

plunged me into a state of frustration and fury that, in history, has always caused the roles of the victim and executioner to flip back and forth on a metronome of hatred. I had fallen prey to a febrile impatience that turned every passing minute into another enemy. Time, it seemed to me, that shabby old nobleman, was dragging itself along with premeditated slowness and perhaps even hostility toward me, as if it were some kind of venerable accomplice to its own aristocratic past.

I believe I owe my first dawning of social awareness to Hans.

20

AT FIVE MINUTES TO ELEVEN, I WENT DOWNSTAIRS.
The gunroom was low-ceilinged, fifty yards long and ten yards
wide. You could see the brickwork through the plaster. At the apex
of the vaulted ceiling was an incongruous Venetian chandelier, dis-
figured on one side, where it had lost some of its branches. The floor
was covered with a big, worn Carpathian rug. Suits of armor stood
in rows against the walls, which were covered with pikes and sabers.

Hans was waiting for me at the other end of the room. He wore
a white shirt and the trousers of his dinner suit. A cigarette burned
away between his fingertips: everywhere he went he carried one of
those round metal boxes of English cigarettes, with a picture of a
bearded sailor on the top. Players, they were called. He was very
calm. Obviously, I told myself, he knows I've never handled a sword
before, and like a good Prussian, he's been fencing since childhood.

I removed my jacket and let it fall to the ground. I looked at the
walls. I didn't know which weapon to choose: what I really needed
was a good old Norman stick. In the end, I picked up what was in
reach: an old Polish *szabelka*, a curved, Turkish-style saber. Hans
set down the box of Players on the carpet and went to stub out his
cigarette in a corner. I took up a position beneath the chandelier and
waited as he took another sword from the wall.

As is often the case when you find yourself alone, face-to-face with
a man you have spent a long time hating, who your imagination has

punished over and over, my anger had cooled off quite a bit. The reality of an enemy is always disappointing compared to the idea you have put together of him. And suddenly something dawned on me that disturbed and nearly paralyzed me: his vague resemblance to Lila. It was that same blondness, that same coloring, and a certain similarity in their traits. I realized that if I stayed there without reacting for a few seconds longer, I was going to lose an enemy. I had to rekindle the flame quickly.

"Only a Nazi could have come up with something so low," I spat at him. "You can't accept the idea that she loves me. You can't accept the idea that she and I are forever. So, like all Nazis, you needed your Jew. You took those things and you put them in my closet. But your miserable plan is idiotic. Even if I were a scoundrel, Lila would still love me. You don't know what it is, to truly love someone. It pardons nothing, and at the same time it pardons everything."

There was no way for it to occur to me that two years later, I would be able to say the same thing about France.

I raised my weapon. I was vaguely aware that you had to advance with one foot and keep the other behind you, as I had seen in *Scaramouche* at the Gródek cinema. Hans observed me with interest. He looked at my right foot, which I had placed in front of me, my left foot behind me, and at the saber I had raised above my head like a woodsman's axe. He kept his weapon lowered. I bent both knees and bounced up and down in place a few times. I sensed that I must have looked like a frog. Hans bit his lips and I understood that it was to keep from laughing. So I let out a sort of inarticulate cry and rushed at him. I was stupefied when I saw the blood spurting from his left cheek. He had not moved, and he had not yet lifted his sword. I straightened myself slowly, lowering my arm. The blood flowed more and more abundantly on Hans's face, soaking his shirt. The first clear idea that occurred to me was that I had probably gone against all of the rules of dueling. All at once, the feeling of boorishness overtook me again, and my shame was so monstrous that it metamorphosed into rage, and I raised my saber once more and gave a desperate yell: "You can all go to hell!"

Hans raised his sword at the same time as I did, and, in the second that followed, my *szabelka* was torn from my hand and flew through the air. Hans lowered his weapon and looked at me with furrowed eyebrows and tightened jaw, without the least bit of attention to the blood that was running in rivulets down his face.

"Asshole!" he said. "Goddamn asshole!"

He threw his sword against the wall and turned his back on me. There was blood on the carpet.

Hans picked up his box of Players and took out a cigarette. "You were wrong to rush things," he told me. "It'll happen soon enough anyway."

I found myself alone. I stared stupidly at the bloodstains at my feet. I'd managed to empty myself of my vengeance and rancor, but they were replaced with an unease I couldn't shake off. Hans's attitude had a dignity to it that unsettled me.

I didn't really get what was troubling me until the next morning. Marek had been arrested with the purloined objects. He had confessed. He had taken advantage of the presence of guests he saw as disreputable in the castle—namely, the writer and the psychic—to pilfer the contents of Madame Bronicka's office and little sitting room; interrupted by a manservant who had come into the bedroom, he had placed the box in my closet, intending to return for it later on. But my presence had disturbed him in his first attempt and he had only been able to recover the loot during dinner.

It was nine in the morning when Bruno gave me this news in the dining room, where I had joined him for breakfast. I felt a chill overtake me, and I'd forgotten about the teapot in my hand until my cup overflowed onto the tablecloth. I pushed back my chair and left the table with Bruno gazing after me in surprise. Never before had I experienced such hatred, and the man I hated with such intensity was myself. I understood that in imagining I was the victim of such an ignoble plot at the hands of my rival, there was no one to find guilty but me. And yet, there could be no question of my seeking out Hans and apologizing to him. I quite preferred recognizing the mediocrity of my own soul to humiliating myself in front of *them*.

I did not come down for lunch, and at around four o'clock in the afternoon, I began packing my suitcase. I almost regretted not having stolen the objects, not having been exposed publicly as the thief—for there would have been a kind of aggression to it, an almost triumphal manner of breaking with a milieu that was not mine.

I left my room only at the end of the afternoon, to make arrangements for my departure. I didn't want to see or thank anyone; I didn't even want to say goodbye. But I ran into Tad in the corridor; he asked me what I was doing there with my suitcase. He told me that Hans had had an accident during a late-night ride; in the moonless dark, a branch had given him a deep scrape on the cheek—but again, he asked, what on earth was I doing there with my suitcase in hand? I explained to him that I wanted to be driven to the station; there was a nine o'clock train for Warsaw; I was returning to France; if war broke out, I didn't want to run the risk of being cut off from my country. It was at that moment I saw Hans, at the other end of the corridor, walking slowly toward us, holding his everlasting round box of English cigarettes; a bandage covered his left cheek. He stopped near to us, very pale, but strangely peaceful, and glanced at the suitcase I held in my hand.

"I'm leaving tonight," he announced, then turned on his heel and walked away.

21

I REMAINED IN GRÓDEK A FEW MORE DAYS. THE RAIN had come to blur the landscape, and above our heads, the sky croaked with the voices of invisible crows. It was on one such foggy afternoon, as we were walking along the beach, while the wind stuck sea drops to our faces, that the future signaled to us. It was a Jew, dressed in a long caftan known in Polish as a *kapota*; on his head was one of those tall black hats that millions of Jews then wore in their ghettos. He had a very pale face and a gray beard, and he was seated on a mile marker by the side of the road to Gdynia. Perhaps because I was not expecting to find him there at the edge of that empty road, or because his appearance, in the vague, misty shades of the air, had something ghostly about it; or maybe the bundle tied to a stick he was carrying on his shoulder made my memory flood with the legend of millennia of wandering—suddenly, I felt an apprehension and an unease whose premonitory nature I would recognize only much later. At the time what I saw there was one of history's most banal and on the whole normal conjunctions: a Jew, a road, and a marker.

Timidly, Lila called out to him. "*Dzień dobry panu*, hello, sir."

But he did not respond, and turned his head away.

"Tad is convinced we are on the verge of an invasion," Lila murmured.

"I don't know a thing about it, but I just can't believe there could be a war," I told her.

"There always have been."

"That was before …"

I was going to say, "That was before I met you," but it was presumptuous on my part to launch into such an explanation of the origins of war, hatred, and massacre. I still lacked the authority it would have required to bring people to share in my understanding. "Modern weapons have become too powerful and too destructive," I declared. "No one will dare to use them, because there wouldn't be any winners or losers, only ruins …" I had read that in an editorial in the *Times*, to which the Bronickis subscribed.

I wrote a thirty-page letter to Lila, starting over several times; I ended up throwing it into the fire, because it was only a love letter—I didn't manage to do any better than that.

It was Bruno, on the day of my departure, as the fog drove its woolen flocks through the air outside, who spoke to Lila in my name.

I had just entered the sitting room with her. I took a last look at the butterfly collections in their glass cases, which covered an entire wall. They reminded me of my Uncle Ambrose's kites: little scraps of dreams.

Bruno was sitting in an armchair, paging through some sheet music. He lifted his eyes and watched us for a moment, smiling. I never once saw anything but kindness in his smiles. Then he got up and took a seat at the piano. His hands already resting on the keyboard, he turned to us and observed us a long time, attentively, like a painter studying a model before sketching his first line. He began to play.

He was improvising. He was improvising *us*. It was Lila and me, our separation and our certitude, that his melody spoke of. I heard myself love, despair, and believe. I lost Lila and I found her. Misfortune raised its black shadow over us and then all became joy. And it took me a few minutes to understand that Bruno was giving me the brotherly gift of what he himself was feeling.

Lila fled, weeping. Bruno got up and came over to me, in the light of the great, pale windows, and hugged me.

"I'm glad I could talk to you one last time. As for me, really all I have left is music..." He laughed. "Obviously, it's a bit frightening to love and to know that all you can do with your love is play another concert. But at the same time, it's given me a source of inspiration that's not likely to dry up anytime soon. There are at least fifty years in it, if my fingers hold out. I imagine Lila so clearly, sitting in the audience in her old age; I can see her listening to me as I tell her about herself, traveling back to when she was twenty." He shut his eyes and, for an instant, held his hand over his eyelids. "Oh, well. There are loves that end, apparently. I read that somewhere."

I spent my last hours with Lila. The presence of happiness was almost audible, as if hearing had broken with the superficialities of sound and finally penetrated the deepest parts of silence, which before had been hidden by solitude. Our moments of sleep had that kind of warmth where you cannot tell the dream from the body, the nest from the wings. I can still feel the imprint of her profile on my chest—perhaps invisible, but my fingers find it faithfully in the leaden hours of this physical error that is one body alone.

My memory seized every instant, setting it aside. Where I come from we call that a nest egg; there was enough for me there to last a lifetime.

22

LEANING OUT OF THE WINDOW AS WE APPROACHED
Cléry, I knew who'd come to meet me as soon as I saw the Polish
eagle floating high above the station. When I looked carefully, however, I noticed the old pacifist had made it so the bird, too warlike
for his taste, resembled a beautiful two-headed dove. It had been
five weeks since our parting and I found Ambrose Fleury worried
and aged.

"Well, well, look who's a society gent now! What's this?" He
brushed his finger over the insignia of the Gdynia Yachting Club,
which had been solemnly presented to me the day before my departure from Gródek as a symbol of Poland's free access to the sea. Never
more than in that month of August 1939 were doubts and anxieties
so closely accompanied by gesticulations and ostentatious displays
of confidence.

"It'll be any minute now, apparently," I told him.

"That's what you think. The people will never allow themselves
to be led to the slaughterhouse again." Ambrose Fleury reeled his
dove back down to the ground—as usual, as soon as he showed up
somewhere, he was immediately swarmed by children—and tucked
the kite under his arm. We walked a little ways and my uncle opened
the door of a small automobile.

"That's right," he said, seeing my surprise. "Lord Howe gave it to
me, you remember, he came to visit us before."

At sixty-three, my uncle was now a nationally respected figure, and his reputation had garnered him decorations from the Academy—recognition he had always refused.

As soon as we got to La Motte, I ran to the workshop. In my absence, maybe because the threat of war troubled him more than he was willing to let on, Ambrose Fleury had returned to his "humanist period," enriching its ranks with all that France has to offer those who believe in its lights. The "Encyclopedist" series looked especially good as it hung from the beams, if a bit listless, as is always the case when they lack wide-open spaces.

"I've been working a lot, as you can see," my guardian told me, smoothing his mustache and looking pleased with himself. "The days we're living through right now are making us lose our heads a little. We have to remember who we are."

We weren't Rousseau, we weren't Diderot, we weren't Voltaire: we were Mussolini, Hitler, and Stalin. Never had the "Enlightenment" kites of Cléry's former postman seemed so trivial to me. All the same, my love was a blindness, from which I could draw all I needed to continue believing in the wisdom of men; nor did my uncle doubt for one second that peace would hold, as if his heart alone could triumph over history.

One night, when I was off with Lila on the Baltic shore, I felt a tug at my arm pulling me back. There was Ambrose Fleury, dressed in a long shirt that lent amplitude to his body, sitting on my bed with a candle in his hand. In his gaze was more pain than is really strictly necessary to make a man look like a man.

"They've given orders for general mobilization. But of course mobilization isn't war."

"Of course not," I replied. Still not entirely awake, I added, "The Bronickis are coming back to France for Christmas."

My uncle raised the candle so he could see my face better.

"They say love is blind but who knows—with you blindness might just be another way of seeing…"

In the hours leading up to the invasion of Poland, I stuck to my role in the great collective turkey ballet being performed across the country with impeccable stupidity: everyone was straining to see whose leg could reach the highest for our imaginary kick in the Germans' pants, dancing the French cancan on a cabaret stage that stretched all the way from the Pyrenees to the Maginot Line. POLAND WILL STAND, clamored the newspapers and the radio, and I knew with happy certainty that a barricade of the world's most valiant chests was puffed up around Lila; I remembered the battalions of cavalrymen who'd marched singing through Gródek with their swords and their flags. The "historical memory" of the Polish people, I told my uncle, was an inexhaustible fount of courage, honor, and fidelity; turning the dial of our old wireless, I waited impatiently for hostilities to begin, for the first victory bulletins, and grew irritated when the commentators discussed "last-ditch attempts to salvage peace." I saw my older comrades off at the station as they were mobilized; together, we sang, "We'll win glory like our fathers"; I felt my eyes grow misty when I saw strangers shaking hands in the street and shouting, "Long live Poland, sir!" I listened as our priest, old Father Tachin, announced from the pulpit that "heathen Germany will be felled like a rotten tree"; I went and admired my old teacher, Monsieur Leduc, who'd put on his old horizon-blue uniform and decorations to remind young people of what a tough old veteran of the Great War looked like, vouchsafing our new victory. I barely saw my uncle, who remained shut up in his room, and, when I came and knocked at his door, I heard him bark at me, "Leave me alone and go ass around with the others, you little snot."

On September 3, I was sitting by the empty fireplace, black with burnt-away fires. From the workshop I heard strange cracking noises. They didn't sound like what I usually heard when my uncle was at work. I got up, vaguely worried, and crossed the courtyard.

Broken kites trailed their shreds and tatters everywhere. Ambrose Fleury had his beloved Montaigne in his hands; in one swift motion he broke it over his knee. I spied among the mangled pieces some of our best work, notably my uncle's favorites: *Jean-Jacques Rousseau* and *Liberty Lighting the People*. Not even the works from his "naive period" had been spared, all the dragonflies and children's dreams that had so often lent their innocence to the sky. Ambrose Fleury had already smashed a good third of his collection to smithereens. Never before had I seen such an explosion of distress on his face.

"They declared war," he called out to me in a strangled voice. He ripped his *Jean Jaurès* off the wall and crushed it with his heel. I leapt forward, tackled my uncle bodily, and pushed him out the door. I felt nothing, I thought nothing. The only thing I knew was that we had to save the last of the kites.

23

THE FIRST NEWS OF THE POLISH DEBACLE PLUNGED
me into a state of shock from which I have kept just one memory: my
uncle sitting on my bed, his hand resting on my knee. The wireless had
just announced that the entire region of Gródek, on the Baltic shore,
had been flattened by bombs. The battleship *Schleswig-Holstein*,
with no declaration of war, had suddenly opened fired with its cannons. A historical detail was carefully added regarding this moment
of honor for the German navy: a few days prior, the battleship, dis-
guised as a training ship, had requested permission from the Polish
authorities to drop anchor "for a courtesy call."

"Don't cry, Ludo. They'll be counting misery in the millions before too long. Of course it speaks to your heart with just the one
voice; that's normal. But since you're such a math whiz, you ought to
consider the law of large numbers. Right now you can't count higher
than two; I understand that. And then again, who knows ...

"It's still possible that the war will be over in a few days," he went
on, his gaze lost in some depths of hope—he was, after all, a Fleury,
one of those crazies whose vindication of human rights sometimes
means denying rights to excessively odious realities. "Europe's peoples are too old—they've suffered too much to let themselves be
forced to go on with this indignity. They're saying that secret ne-
gotiations are already underway in Geneva. The German masses are

going to sweep Hitler from power. We have to trust in the German people, just like we do all the other peoples."

I lifted myself up on one elbow. "Kites of the world, unite," I said.

Ambrose Fleury did not seem hurt by my hostility. And I knew better than anyone that there are things you can't break in men's hearts because they are unattainable.

I ran to enlist. My pulse was racing at 120 beats per minute and I was declared unfit for service. I attempted to explain that it wasn't a physical problem — it was one of love and tragedy, but at that the military doctor only fixed me with a severer look. I wandered through the countryside, indignant at the serenity of those fields and woods — never had this nature seemed further away from man's. The only news that reached me of Lila was the news that an entire people had been crushed. A kind of shattering femininity emanated from the body of martyred Poland.

People looked at me a little strangely in Cléry. Rumor had it that I had been declared unfit for military service because, like all the Fleurys, I was a little wrong in the head: "It's hereditary in them." I was beginning to understand that what I was feeling was not common currency, as they say, and that for the sound of mind, love is not the meaning of life, but only a little side benefit.

The moment finally came when Ambrose Fleury, although he was the very man who had devoted his life to kites, began to be seriously concerned. During the evening meal, beneath the oil lamp that hung over our heads, he said to me: "Ludo, it can't go on like this. You've been seen walking through the streets talking to a woman who isn't there. They're going to lock you up one of these days."

"Well, so let them lock us up. In or out, she'll stay with me."

"Shit," said my uncle, and it was the first time that he spoke the language of reason to me in this manner.

It was, I believe, to reel me back down to earth that he asked Marcellin Duprat to take me in hand. What the two men said to each other I never did find out, but the chef of the Clos Joli invited me to accompany him on his morning rounds from market to farm, throwing vigorous winks my way from time to time as if to reassure himself that the healthy reality of the Norman soil's sturdy produce—by nature a powerful antidote to the loss of reason—was having the desired curative effect upon my "state."

During those winter months in 1940, when the war was limited to sorties, patrols, and the occasional ambush along the Maginot Line, when "time was on our side," you had to reserve your table at the restaurant several days in advance—"to put in your application" as Curnonsky, the Prince of Gastronomy, liked to say. Every evening, after he closed up, Marcellin Duprat would page with satisfaction through the big red leather volume he kept in his office, stopping on a page that bore the fresh signature of some new minister or as-yet-unvanquished military chief, and say to me: "You'll see, kid. Some day they'll come and study the guest book of the Clos Joli to write the history of the Third Republic!"

He was short-staffed. Most of his kitchen assistants and employees had been drafted, replaced by the old guard who had, in solidarity—you might almost say patriotically—agreed to come out of retirement in these darker hours of our nation and maintain the service from which they'd departed so many years ago. Duprat had even managed to rally Monsieur Jean, the sommelier, who was nearly eighty-six.

"It's been a long time since I employed a sommelier," he explained to me. "Sommeliers always seem so obligatory, if you see what I mean—it's just irritating when they bear down on the customer with that wine list in their hand. But Jean knows what he's doing and he can still hold down the front end of the restaurant."

I would arrive on my motorbike every morning at six. When he caught sight of my defeated face and my lost look, Marcellin would growl, "Come now, come along with me. This'll bring you back down to earth." I would take a seat in the van and we would drive through the countryside and the markets, where Duprat would inspect the vegetables. He would hold peapods to his ear and "listen for the crickets," that is, see if they were crunchy; look to see whether the beans had "that velvet look," choosing "black broad," "Italian," or "Chinese" beans according to their "tint"; or decide whether the cauliflowers were "worthy to appear." Duprat served his vegetables whole — "proud," as he put it. He had a horror of purees, which were coming into fashion at the time, as if France had a premonition of what was in store for it.

"Everything's puree these days," he'd grumble. "Puree of celery root, puree of broccoli, of watercress, of onion, of green peas, of fennel … France is losing respect for the vegetable. Do you know what this is a sign of, this puree craze? Puree, my little Ludo. That's what it's a sign of. We'll all end up in it, you'll see."

It was above all with butchers that Marcellin Duprat revealed himself at his most demandingly imperious, especially when it came to his beloved Norman tripe. I saw him go white with rage because he suspected Monsieur Dullin—who years later, in 1943, was shot by a firing squad—of giving him tripe from two different cows.

"Dullin," he'd roared, "the next time you pull that will be the last time you see my face! Yesterday you stuck me with the tripe of two different oxen. How on earth could they possibly cook the same way? And you'd better take it as gospel that I want the foot off that very same ox!"

He snickered when he saw the butcher presenting a housewife with a rolled veal shoulder, all nicely trussed up, a sight to behold.

"You can bet they've stuffed the middle with fat to add weight — they'd throw in the hoofs and the horns if they could!"

Going "back to the land" under the care of Marcellin Duprat did me good. I continued to see Lila, but more privately. I even learned to laugh and joke with others in order to hide her presence. Dr. Gardieu was pleased, even if my uncle suspected that I had simply gotten better at faking.

"I know very well that you're not over it—it's incurable with our kind," he would tell me. "And a good thing, too. Some cures bring you down lower than the sickness."

I was doing my best. I had to hold firm and it was Lila herself who demanded it of me. If I let myself go, I was certain to end up in despair, and that was the surest way to lose her.

The Clos Joli was located just off the intersection of the road to Noisy and the road to Caen, across from the farthest outskirts of the hamlet of Ouvières, set back in a little garden where spring and summer met you with magnolias, lilacs, and roses. There were doves everywhere to "calm the customer," as Duprat said. "I give people their money's worth in my restaurant, but they feel good when they see a dove. For a while I had pigeons, but seeing a pigeon on the way into a restaurant—that just puts the client on edge." For the same reason the cash desk, where I often worked, was set off to one side, slightly concealed from view.

"You can't start thinking about the bill as soon as you walk in. Some tact is required."

Sometimes, he would come and lean on the desk, in his full whites—"we haven't changed uniforms since Lent"—and confide in me: "I'm holding firm, but things are going downhill, they're going downhill," he complained. "Now the fire's bothering them. They're complaining about the heat. A kitchen with no fire is like a woman with no ass. Fire is our father, the father of all the chefs in France. But some of them are switching to electricity now, and with automatic timers, no less. That's like making love and checking your watch to see when it's time to climax."

I noticed that the embroidered insignia on his jacket had changed. Where once it had said, "*Marcellin Duprat, Clos Joli, France*" in tricolor letters, it now said "*Marcellin Duprat, France.*" Writing "Clos Joli" and "France" must have seemed like tautology to him.

In the kitchen, every pot bore the initials C. J. and a vintage in Roman numerals. His enemies liked to say he believed he was a descendent of the Caesars. He did not tolerate anyone saying "the kitchens."

"There's a plural that stinks of hospitality. I say the place where I work is *the* kitchen. They're out to multiply everything, these days."

At the entrance to the restaurant was a big map of France, with pictures of the products that were the crowning glory of each province. For Normandy, he had chosen tripe.

"After all, that's what makes a Frenchman. And French history."

His prices were steep. Minister Anatole de Monzie said to him one day, "My dear Marcellin, to taste your dishes is erotic; to see your prices is pornographic!"

Duprat was criticized from the very beginning of the "Phony War." People whispered that there was something indecent in the ongoing gastronomic fete being held at the Clos Joli while the enemy bayed at the door. Duprat shrugged with disdain.

"Point is holding firm in Vienne, Dumaine in Saulieu, Pic in Valence, La Mère Brazier in Lyon, and I am here in Cléry," he'd say. "Now more than ever, every man must give his best to the thing he does best."

Ambrose Fleury seemed to share this opinion. He had gone back to his kites with a determination that resembled a kind of declaration of faith. He had redone his "humanist" series: Rabelais, Erasmus, Montaigne, and Rousseau once again floated above the Norman woodlands. I watched my uncle's strong hands making adjustments to the spars, spines, and sails; in the paper and strings of the kite's body you could already begin to recognize some immortal figure of the Enlightenment. Jean-Jacques Rousseau was his favorite, it seemed: in his lifetime, it has been estimated that Ambrose Fleury assembled more than eighty of them.

I sensed that he was right and that Duprat was, too. Now more than ever, everyone had to give the best of himself. I smiled, remembering those hours of our childhood when Lila, in the attic of Le Manoir des Jars, would predict our paths in life based on each of our gifts: "Tad will be a great explorer, he'll discover Scythian warrior tombs and Aztec temples; Bruno will be as famous as Menuhin and

Rubinstein; Hans will seize power in Germany and assassinate Hitler; and you—as for you …" She would look at me solemnly. "You're going to love me," she would tell me, and I still felt on my cheek the kiss that accompanied this revelation of my raison d'être.

I announced to my uncle that I would not be returning to Duprat's.

"I'm going to Paris. It's easier to get news there. Maybe I'll try to make it into Poland."

"There is no more Poland," said Ambrose Fleury.

"Well, anyway, the Polish army is reforming in France. I'm sure I'll manage to find something out. I've got hope."

My uncle lowered his eyes. "What do you want me to tell you? Go ahead. With our kind, hope is always the one to decide. That bastard—it never lets up."

When I returned to say goodbye, we stayed together in silence for a long moment; seated at his bench, with his old leather apron and his tools, he resembled every old master craftsman in the history of France.

"May I take one as a memento?" I asked.

"Pick one."

I looked around me. The workshop was twenty-five yards long by ten yards wide, and the words that sprang to mind at the sight of those hundreds of kites were "an embarrassment of riches." They were all too big for me, much easier to fit into memory than into a suitcase. I took a tiny little one, a dragonfly with iridescent wings.

24

I ARRIVED IN PARIS WITH FIVE HUNDRED FRANCS IN my pocket and wandered for a long time through this city I didn't know, in search of a place to live. I found a room for fifty francs a month, above a dance hall in the rue Cardinal-Lemoine.

"I'll give you a break on the rent because of the noise," the landlord told me.

The Polish officers and soldiers who had made it to France through Romania had been met with some condescension, and they answered my questions wearily: no, there was no Bronicki among them; I should inquire at the staff headquarters of the Polish army, which was regrouping at Coëtquidan. I went there every day, to rue de Solférino, and was politely turned away. I renewed my efforts at the Swedish and Swiss embassies, and the Red Cross. I had to leave my lodgings after I slapped the landlord across the face: he had told me we ought to come to terms with Hitler. "You've got to admit he's a leader. We need a man like that."

His wife called the police, but I managed to get out before they arrived and found myself a hideout, a furnished room in the rue Lepic. My new digs were in a hotel frequented by prostitutes. The woman in charge was tall and thin, with dyed-black hair and a hard, straight gaze that made me feel scrutinized, studied, even searched. I rarely saw her without a pack of Gauloises in close reach, and without a cigarette dangling from one corner of her mouth—so much so that her face, in my memory, remains wreathed in smoke.

Her name was Julie Espinoza.

I spent all my time lying in my room: liberating Poland and holding Lila in my arms on the Baltic Coast.

The day came when I no longer had the money to pay my rent. Instead of throwing me out, the madam invited me to eat with her in the kitchen every day. She chatted about one thing and another, asked no questions, and observed me attentively, stroking Chong, her Pekinese, a little creature with a black muzzle and brown-and-white fur, who always sat in her lap. Her inflexible gaze made me uneasy; her eyes always seemed to be on the lookout for something; her eyelashes made me think of spiders' legs crouching in the depths of time. I learned that Madame Espinoza had a daughter who'd studied abroad.

"In Heidelberg, in Germany," she added, in a tone that sounded almost triumphant. "You see, my little Ludo? I knew what was going to happen. I've known since Munich. My girl has a degree that will come in very handy when the Germans show up."

"But ..." I was going to say, "Your daughter's Jewish like you, Madame Julie ..." but she cut me off.

"Yes, I know, but her papers are as Aryan as they come," she proclaimed, one hand resting on Chong, who was curled up in a ball on her lap. "I had it seen to and she has the right kind of name. You'd better believe we're not handing it over to them on a platter this time around. Not me, at any rate. Our kind has a thousand years of training and experience. Some of us have forgotten, or they think it's all over and done with, that it's civilization nowadays—what they call human rights, in the newspaper—but not me. I know what your human rights are. They're roses. They smell nice, that's all."

Julie Espinoza had spent several years as an assistant madam in the "houses" in Budapest and Berlin, and she spoke Hungarian and

German. I noticed that she always wore the same brooch pinned to her dress, a little golden lizard, which she seemed very fond of. Whenever she was worried, she fiddled with it.

"It's lovely, your lizard," I remarked to her one day.

"Lovely, schmovely—the lizard is an animal that has survived since the beginning of time, and when it comes to slipping off between the rocks it can't be beat."

She had a manly voice, and when she was upset she swore like a cattle drover—they say "like a cattle drover," but I came from cattle country and I'd never heard anyone use language like that—and sometimes her talk became so vulgar that it would end up bothering Madame Julie herself. One night, she stopped short in the midst of a modest "dammit to hell" followed by some other words I prefer not to write, out of respect and gratitude to the woman to whom I owe so much. Interrupting her own diatribe, which had to do with some sort of trouble with the housing authorities, she reflected, "It's funny, when you think about it—it only comes to me in French. Never came to me in Hungarian or German. Maybe I didn't have the vocabulary. Then again, in Buda and Berlin it was a different clientele. The best kind of people. They'd come in tuxedos sometimes, or even frock coats, straight from the opera or the theater, and they'd kiss your hand. Here, they're just garbage."

She looked pensive.

"This won't do at all," she declared firmly. "I can't allow myself to be vulgar."

And she concluded with this mysterious sentence, most likely a slip of the tongue, because she hadn't yet accorded me her full trust: "It's a matter of life and death."

She took her pack of Gauloises from the table and departed, leaving me bewildered. I didn't see how a dirty mouth could seem like such a threat to her.

My bewilderment turned to stupefaction when, at her advanced age, she began taking comportment lessons. An old maid who had once been the director of a boarding school for young ladies appeared twice a week to help her acquire what she called "class," a word that awoke in my memory the worst of my humiliations in Gródek: the episode of the stolen objects, my relationship with Hans, and that asshole Stas Bronicki—to use Madame Julie's terms—and his solemn warning, his unreserved assent to his daughter's taking me as a lover, accompanied by an invitation to me to banish any mad hope I might have of marrying Lila, given my humble origins and the elevated distinction of the Bronicki name. My irritation grew when I heard Madame Julie's tutor explaining to her what she meant by "class": "It is not enough, you see, to adopt behavior that differs from that of the lower levels of society. Quite the contrary, in fact: it should never appear to have been *acquired*. It must seem utterly natural—inborn, as it were."

I was outraged by the affable smile with which Madame Julie accepted these remonstrations—the very same woman I'd so often heard bawling out a customer who had "taken liberties." She was very obedient, displaying not the least bit of impatience. I would come across her reciting La Fontaine fables with a pencil clenched between her teeth, or pursed in her lips, stopping regularly to greet an arriving couple, which happened often, since each of her girls saw easily fifteen or twenty customers a day.

"Apparently I have a street accent. You know—Pigalle. That old grasshopper calls it 'popular speech,' and she's giving me exercises to get rid of it. I know I look like a jackass, but what can I say? You do what you have to do."

"Why are you going to so much trouble, Madame Julie? It's none of my business, but …"

"I have my reasons."

The way she walked troubled her a good deal, as well.

"I look like a guy," she acknowledged.

It was a kind of roll, from one leg to the other, shoulders swinging, forearms forward, elbows out; it was, it's true, a walk with nothing feminine about it, bearing a certain resemblance to the stance used by professional wrestlers in the ring. Mademoiselle de Fulbillac emphatically deplored it.

"You can't go out in the world like that!"

So it was that I began to see the boss moving prudently from one corner of the sitting room to another, with three or four books balanced atop her head.

"Hold yourself nice and straight, Madame," ordered Mademoiselle de Fulbillac, whose father had been a naval officer. "And if you please, avoid the cigarette between your lips. There's nothing so ill-bred."

"Shit," Madame Julie would say when the pyramid of books came tumbling noisily down. And right away she would add, "I've got to get rid of this dirty mouth. Anything could pop out at the wrong moment. I've said 'shit' so many times in my life it's like second nature to me."

Her physique was not "of our kind," as Mademoiselle de Fulbillac had remarked to me on several occasions; to me, there was something gypsylike about her. Many years later, when I had acquired a little learning in the arts, I found that Julie Espinoza's traits resembled the faces of women in Byzantine mosaics, and the wooden effigies painted on the sarcophagi at Sakkara. It was, at any rate, a face from very ancient times.

Once, as I entered the office where customers would come and pay for their rooms before going upstairs, I found Julie Espinoza seated behind the counter, an open history book in her hand. Eyes closed, a finger resting on one of the book's pages, she was reciting, as if from a lesson she was struggling to learn by heart, "… It may therefore be said that Admiral Horthy became regent of Hungary very much in spite of himself … His popularity, already great in …" She glanced down at the textbook. "Already great in 1917, following the battle of Otranto, soared to such heights that, having crushed the Bolshevik Revolution of Béla Kun in 1919, he could only bow to popular opinion …"

She noticed my surprise. "What?"

"Nothing, Madame Julie."

"Mind your own beeswax." She fiddled with her little golden lizard, then softened, adding tranquilly, "I'm practicing for when the Germans get here."

The certainty of the tone with which she announced the unthinkable to me—that France might lose the war, in other words—left me beside myself, and I stormed off, slamming the door behind me.

For a while I thought that Madame Julie was practicing to open a "classy" house, then recalled that she was Jewish and didn't see how such a leap in social status could be accomplished if the Nazis won the war, as she was so convinced they would. Perhaps she was thinking of opening a luxury bordello in Portugal, a country in which she seemed to have an interest.

"Are you going to flee to Portugal?"

The shadow of dark fuzz on her upper lip quivered with scorn. "I'm not the fleeing kind." She crushed her cigarette and looked me straight in the eye. "But they won't have my hide, I'll tell you that."

I was confused by this mix of courage and defeatism. I was also too young to understand such a will to survive. And in the state of anxiety and emotional deprivation into which I was currently plunged, life didn't seem to deserve that kind of attachment.

Julie Espinoza continued to observe me. It was as if she were trying me and preparing to deliver the verdict.

One night, I dreamed that I was standing on the roof and that Madame Julie was standing below, on the sidewalk, her eyes raised to me, waiting for me to jump so she could catch me in her arms. Ultimately, the moment came when, seated across from her in the kitchen, I hid my face in my hands and broke down sobbing. She listened to me until two in the morning amidst the noise of the bidets, which didn't ever really stop in the Hôtel du Passage.

"Who is that stupid?" she murmured, when I informed her of my intent to make it back to Poland at all costs. "I don't understand why they didn't take you in the army, fool that you are."

"I was exempted. My heart beats too fast."

"Listen to me, kid. I'm sixty years old, but sometimes I feel like I've lived—survived, if you rather—for five thousand years, and even like I was there before that, at the beginning of the world. Don't forget my name, either. Espinoza." She laughed. "Almost like Spinoza, the philosopher, maybe you've heard of him. I could even drop the *E* and call myself Spinoza, that's how much I know…"

"Why are you telling me this?"

"Because pretty soon things are going to get so bad, it's going to be such a shitstorm that you and your big booboo are going to disappear in it. We're going to lose the war and we'll have the Germans in France."

I set down my glass. "France can't lose the war. It's impossible."

She half closed one eye, over her cigarette. "Impossible isn't French," she said.

Madame Julie stood, the Pekinese in her arms, and went to pick up her bag from a bottle-green plush armchair. She drew out a roll of banknotes and returned to the table.

"Take this, to start with. There'll be more later."

I looked at the money on the table.

"Well, what are you waiting for?"

"Listen, Madame Julie, there's enough to live on for a year there, and I'm not too keen on living."

She chuckled. "Awww, it wants to die of love," she said. "Well, you'd better get cracking. People are going to start dying like flies, and it won't be from love, I'll tell you that much."

I felt a rush of sympathy for this woman. Perhaps I was starting to sense that when people speak disdainfully of "whores" and "madams," they're locating human dignity in the ass, to make it easier to forget how low the rest of us can sink.

"I still don't understand why you're giving me this money."

She was seated in front of me, with her mauve woolen shawl

drawn across her flat chest, with her dome of black hair, her bohemian eyes, and her long fingers playing with the little golden lizard pinned to her bodice.

"Of course you don't understand. Which is why I'm going to explain it to you. I need a guy like you. I'm putting myself together a little team."

And so it was that in February 1940, while the English were singing "We're Going to Hang Out the Washing on the Siegfried Line," the posters were proclaiming that WE WILL WIN BECAUSE WE ARE STRONGEST, and the Clos Joli was resounding with victory toasts, one old madam was getting ready for the German Occupation. I don't think that anyone else in the country had at that time thought to organize what would later be called "a resistance network." I was charged with making contact with a certain number of people—including a forger who, after a twenty-year sentence, was still nostalgic for his profession—and Madame Julie so thoroughly convinced me to keep it all a secret that even today I barely dare to write their names. There was Monsieur Dampierre, who lived alone with a canary—and here it must be said to the Gestapo's credit that they spared the canary, taking it into their care when Monsieur Dampierre died of a heart attack under questioning in 1942. There was Monsieur Pageot, who would later be known as Valérian, two years before his execution by firing squad with twenty others on a hill that bore the same name; and Police Commissioner Rotard, who became the head of the Alliance network and who spoke of Madame Julie Espinoza in his book *The Underground Years*: "A woman in whom there was a total absence of illusion, born no doubt of the long exercise of her profession. Sometimes I imagined her receiving a visit from dishonor, whom she knew so well, and hearing its confidence: it must have murmured in her ear, 'My hour is coming soon, my good Julie. Get ready.' At any rate, she was very persuasive, and I helped her to organize a group, which met regularly to envision various measures to be taken, from forging paperwork to choosing safe houses where we could meet or hide out during the German Occupation—which she did not doubt for a single instant would occur."

One day, after a visit to a pharmacist in the rue Gobin, who gave me some "medicine" whose nature and intended recipient I would learn only much later, I asked Madame Espinoza, "Do you pay for them?"

"No, my little Ludo. Some things you can't buy." She shot a strange look in my direction, a mixture of sadness and harshness. "They'll be sent to the firing squad—future victims."

Another day I wanted to know why she didn't flee to Switzerland or Portugal, if she was so sure that the war was lost and considered the German invasion a certainty.

"We already talked about that. I told you: I'm not the fleeing kind." She laughed. "Maybe that's what old lady Fulbillac meant when she kept saying I wasn't 'the right sort of person.'"One morning, I noticed some photographs in the corner of her kitchen, one of Salazar, the Portuguese dictator; one of Admiral Horthy, regent of Hungary; and even one of Hitler. "I'm waiting for someone to come autograph them for me," she explained.

Madame Julie never did trust me enough to tell me the new name she intended to adopt, and when the "specialist" arrived to sign the portraits I was asked to leave the room.

She made me get a driver's license.

"It could be useful."

The only thing the boss was unable to predict was the date of the German offensive and the defeat that would follow. She was expecting something "as soon as the weather turns nice," and was worried about what her girls would come to. There were thirty or forty of them, working in shifts around the clock at the Hôtel du Passage. She advised them to take German lessons but there wasn't a whore in France who believed we'd lose the war.

I was surprised at her confidence in me. Why such unhesitating

trust in a boy of twenty? Life might still make anything of me—
which was not necessarily an endorsement.

"I could be making a mistake," she acknowledged. "But you want
me to tell you? You've got that firing-squad look in your eyes."

"Shit," I said.

She laughed.

"Scared you, eh? But that doesn't necessarily mean twelve bullets
to the head. You can live to a ripe old age with it. It's your Polish girl.
She gives you that look. Don't worry. You'll see her again."

"How can you know, Madame Julie?"

She hesitated, as if she didn't want to hurt me. "It would be too
beautiful, if you didn't see her again. It would stay whole. Things
rarely stay whole in this life."

Two or three times a week, I continued to show up at the French
headquarters of the Polish army, and finally, a sergeant, sick of my
questions, called out to me, "We don't know anything for sure but it's
more than likely that the whole Bronicki family died in the bombing." But I was certain that Lila was alive. I even felt her presence
growing by my side, like a premonition.

At the beginning of April, Madame Julie disappeared for a few
days. She returned with a bandage on her face. When the compress
was removed, Julie Espinoza's nose had lost its slightly hunchbacked
look and had become straight—shorter, even. I didn't ask her any
questions, but seeing my astonishment, she told me, "The first thing
those bastards will look at is noses."

I ended up with such complete trust in her judgment that when the
Germans broke through at Sedan, I wasn't surprised. Nor was I surprised when, a few days later, she sent me to get her Citroën from the
garage. Returning and entering her room, I found her sitting among her
suitcases with Chong, a glass of eau-de-vie in her hand, listening to the
news on the radio, which was announcing that "nothing has been lost."

"Some nothing," she observed.

She set down the glass, picked up the dog, and rose to her feet.

"Right, we'll go now."

"Where?"

"We'll go a little ways, together—you're going home to Normandy, and that's in the same general direction."

It was June 2, and there was no trace of defeat on the roads. In the villages we drove through, everything was peaceful. Madame Espinoza let me drive, then took the wheel herself. She was wearing a gray coat with a mauve hat and scarf.

"Where are you going to hide, Madame Julie?"

"I'm not going to hide at all, my friend. The ones who hide are always the ones they find. I've had smallpox twice; the Nazis just make it a third time."

"But what are you going to do?"

She smiled faintly and said nothing. A few miles from Vervaux, she stopped the car.

"Here we are. We'll say goodbye. You'll make it home from here, it's not too far."

She gave me a kiss. "I'll be in touch. Soon we'll be needing little guys like you."

She touched my cheek. "Go on, now."

"You're not going to tell me I've got that firing-squad look, again, are you?"

"Let's just say you've got what it takes. When a guy knows how to love like you do—to love a woman who's not there anymore—then chances are you know how to love other things, too ... other things that won't be there anymore either, when the Nazis start in on them."

I was outside, holding my old suitcase. I felt sad. "At least tell me where you're going!"

She started the car. Standing in the middle of the road, I wondered what would become of her. I was also a little disappointed in her lack of trust, in the end. Apparently, whatever she'd read in my eyes wasn't enough. Oh well. Maybe it was for the best. Maybe I didn't have that firing-squad look after all. I still had a chance.

25

A MILITARY TRUCK PICKED ME UP ON THE ROAD AND I got to Cléry by three o'clock that afternoon. You could hear the radio through the open windows. We would be stopping the enemy at the Loire. I didn't even think that Madame Julie could have stopped the enemy at the Loire.

I found my uncle at work. As soon as I walked in, I was struck by the change of atmosphere in the workshop: Ambrose Fleury was up to his knees in French history at its most warlike. Scattered pell-mell around him were the Charles Martels, the Louis, the Godefroy de Bouillons, the Roland de Roncevaux—all the men who had, in France, ever shown their teeth to the enemy. Everyone was there, from Charlemagne up to the field marshals of the Empire; even Napoleon himself—of whom my guardian had formerly liked to say, "Put a fedora on him and it's Al Capone." Needle and thread in hand, he was repairing a Joan of Arc that must have run into trouble, for the doves that were supposed to bear her to heaven were hanging off to one side, and her sword had been broken following some unfortunate run-in with the ground. For an old pacifist and conscientious objector, it was a conversion that left me dumb with surprise. I sincerely doubted that this change of heart corresponded with some influx of new commissions, for in all of its history, rarely had the country been less inclined to take an interest in kites. Ambrose Fleury himself had changed. Never had I known his face to look harder. He was sitting there, with his mangled Joan of Arc on his lap, offering an excellent example of all the fury that it was possible to muster in an old Norman mug. He did not get up from his bench; he barely even nodded at me.

"Well, what's new?" he demanded, and the question left me speechless, as all defensive effort had just been abandoned and Paris was declared an open city. It seemed to me we ought to be asking each other an entirely different kind of question. But it was only June 1940 and we hadn't yet entered the era when Frenchmen would be tortured and killed for things that no longer existed anywhere but inside their own heads.

"I couldn't get any news. I tried everything. But I'm sure she's alive and that she'll come back."

Ambrose Fleury gave a little nod of approval. "Good, Ludo. Germany won the war. The whole country's about to be overrun by good sense, prudence, and reason. You'd have to be nuts to keep on hoping and believing. To me, this means only one thing." He looked at me. "We'll have to be nuts."

I should perhaps recall that in those hours of capitulation, madness had not yet come into the heads of Frenchmen. There was still only one madman, and he was in London.

It was a few days after my return that I saw my first Germans. We had no funds, and I resigned myself to returning to Marcellin Duprat's, if he would still have me. My uncle had gone to see him at the moment that it became clear that nothing could stop the Wehrmacht's crushing advance any longer; he'd found Marcellin standing with reddened eyes before the map of France that decorated the wall of the entryway, the one with each province featuring a picture of its noblest produce. He had placed his finger on the ham illustrating the Ardennes, and said: "I don't know how far the Germans will get but we've got to keep our lines of communication open with the Périgord at all costs. Without truffles and foie gras, the Clos Joli is fucked. We're lucky Spain's stayed neutral—it's the only place I can get decent saffron."

"I think he's gone crazy, too," my uncle had reported to me admiringly.

There were three tanks on the road in front of the garden and an armored car by the door, beneath the magnolias in bloom. I expected to be questioned, but the German soldiers didn't even glance at me. I crossed the vestibule; the shutters of the rotunda and the galleries were closed; two German officers were seated at a table, studying a map. Marcellin Duprat stood back in the shadows striped with light, in the company of Monsieur Jean, the octogenarian sommelier, who no doubt had made his way to the abandoned Clos Joli to offer what comfort he could to his boss. Duprat had his arms crossed over his chest and his head held high but his eyes looked a little wild, and he spoke in a raised voice, as if wanting to make sure that the two German officers could hear him.

"I'll give you this: it's looking like a good year. Maybe even one of our best. Just as long as there aren't any sudden rains to wash out the vineyards …"

"Well, it's off to a good start anyway," Monsieur Jean said, smiling in the middle of his wrinkles. "France will remember the '40 harvest; I sense it's going to be one of our finest vintages. I've heard good things from all over. The Beaujolais, all of Burgundy, the Bordelais … News has never been this good. This year's wines will have more body than in the entire history of our vineyards. It'll hold."

"In the whole memory of France, we've never seen a June like this one," Duprat acknowledged. "The heavens seem to be with us. Not a cloud in the sky. The vines are starting to flower; in ninety days it will be in the bag. Some people are getting discouraged—they're saying it's too good to last. But me—I trust in the vineyards. That's how it's always been in France. What you lose on one end you gain on the other."

"Alsace wines are toast, obviously," Monsieur Jean remarked.

"And a map with no Alsace is a national disaster," Duprat admitted, raising his voice slightly. "But when you think about it, I have enough in my cellar to hold for four or five years, and after that, with a little luck, we'll be able to supply ourselves again … Point sent someone from Vienne: apparently things couldn't be better up his way, the vineyards are really outdoing themselves. Things are even holding up in the Loire, I hear. France is a funny country, old friend. When everything looks like it's in the toilet, we suddenly realize the fundamentals are still there."

Monsieur Jean raised his hand to wipe away a tear from among the smile wrinkles. "Yes, indeed. I tell you, Monsieur Duprat, in a few years we'll think back to 1940 and say, 'We won't see a year like that again!' I know some folks who are looking at their vineyards and weeping from emotion, that's how good the vines are looking this year!"

The two German officers remained bent over their map. I thought it was a military map of France. I was wrong. It was a map of France, all right, but it was the one from the Clos Joli: *Terrine de fumet aux truffes Marcellin Duprat. Filet de mostelle à l'estragon. Lapereau du bocage normand au vinaigre de framboise. Coquille à la dieppoise.* I knew the map by heart, right down to the bowl of cider. Observing the two German officers, it suddenly occurred to me that the war wasn't actually lost yet. One of the officers stood up and walked over to Duprat.

"The commanding general of the German army in Normandy and His Excellency the ambassador Otto Abetz will be lunching here with fourteen people this Friday," he said. "His Excellency the ambassador Abetz often came to your restaurant before the war and he wishes to remember himself to you. It is important to him that the Clos Joli uphold its reputation, and to this end he will give you all the help that is required. He asked us to send you his best wishes for the future."

Duprat looked them over. "You tell your general and your ambassador that I have no staff, no fresh food, and that I do not know that I will be able to remain open."

"These orders come from very high up, sir," the officer said. "In Berlin they wish to see life continue as normal and we intend to respect everything from which France's greatness and prestige are made; and above all, obviously, its culinary genius. Those are the words of the führer himself."

The two officers saluted the master of the Clos Joli with a click of their heels and departed. Duprat remained silent. Suddenly, I saw a strange expression appear on his face, a mix of fury, despair, and resolve. I hadn't said a word. Monsieur Jean also seemed worried.

"What is it, Marcellin?"

And then I heard from the mouth of Marcellin Duprat words that had probably never crossed his lips before that day: "Motherfucker," he muttered darkly, "what do those bastards think? That I'm going to bend over? For three generations, the Duprat family has had the same motto: *I will stand firm.*"

He announced that the Clos Joli would be reopening the following week. All around us, though, one capitulation followed another; England was expected at any moment, and there were some hours, particularly during the night, when all seemed lost to me. Then I would rise and go to Le Manoir des Jars. I would climb the wall and go to wait for Lila in the lane of chestnut trees. There, the stone bench, which for so long had exchanged nothing but chill and emptiness with the moonlight, extended us a friendly welcome. I would enter through one of the tall terrace windows, whose panes I had shattered; I would climb up to the attic and run my hand over the globe, traveling with my finger over the lines Tad had traced out to mark his future expeditions. Bruno would arrive and sit down at the piano and I would listen to Chopin's *Polonaise,* which I could hear as clearly as if the silence, indifferent old man that he was, had softened just this once. I didn't yet know that other Frenchmen were beginning to live as I did, from memory, and that what wasn't there and seemed to have disappeared forever might remain alive, and present, with so much force.

26

THE WORKSHOP HAD BEGUN RECEIVING ORDERS again. The history of France was in great demand. The authorities looked upon this activity benevolently: the past was in good standing. The Germans had forbidden flying kites more than thirty yards off the ground, fearing they might be a vehicle for coded signals to the Allied air forces or to the first "bandits." We received a visit from Cléry's new mayor, Monsieur Plantier, who came to pass on to my uncle a "recommendation" he'd received. It had been remarked in high places that among the praiseworthy "historical" pieces produced by the workshop of Ambrose Fleury—who had been named *Meilleur Ouvrier de France* in 1937—an image of Marshal Pétain was lacking. For the competition that members of the Order of the Kites of France were planning to hold in Cléry, it had been suggested that for the grand finale, Monsieur Fleury himself might launch a kite in the form of the marshal of France. The event would be highly publicized, with the catchphrase "Throw it up!" to combat low morale and gloom. My uncle accepted, with just the barest hint of a mischievous gleam in his somber eye. I tenderly loved these flashes of gaiety in his gaze, the hint of a wry smile behind his gray mustache: an old gaiety that emerges from the furthest reaches of our past, brushing lightly over a face in passing as it makes its way into the future. And so he assembled a three-yard kite in the image of the marshal of France, and everything would have gone off without a hitch, if the municipal government had not followed my uncle's excellent advice and invited a few German officers and soldiers to the festivities. There were more than a hundred entries—Marshal Pétain, of course, was hors concours—and the first prize was awarded to a two-section kite made by a Dominican priest. It represented a Crucifixion, with a Jesus that detached from the cross and ascended to heaven. I never knew whether Ambrose Fleury premeditated this affair or whether it was simply an unfortunate coincidence, but he seemed to have a bit of trouble launching the kite, whose size was better suited to the historical moment than to the rising air currents, and a German corporal very obligingly rushed over to help him—unless it was my uncle himself who asked for his help. Marshal Pétain finally managed to make it into the air, but when he spread his winged arms thirty yards above our heads, it was a German corporal who ended up in the photograph, gripping the end of the line. No one paid it any mind during the celebration, and it was only when the picture was about to be published that the censors perceived any malicious intent in it. That particular photo never saw the light of day, but another was found, snapped by an unknown photographer, which showed up on underground pamphlets until the end of the Occupation: a magnificent Marshal Pétain floating in the air at the end of a string held firmly by a laughing German corporal.

This affair caused some trouble for us, and my uncle himself reckoned he might indeed have "stuck his neck out too soon." The first elements of the Espoir network were just beginning to be pulled together in Normandy, under the command of Jean Sainteny, who had come in person to visit Ambrose Fleury; the two men, despite their age difference, were made for each other. Within Cléry, the Marshal Pétain incident provoked a variety of different reactions. There were those, at the Petit-Gris or the Vigneron, who greeted "good old Ambrose" with winks and slaps on the back; but others recalled his "Popular Front" period, when he could be seen flying his Léon Blum above the Norman meadows, and remarked that a man whose two brothers had both been killed in the Great War merited a good kick in the ass for mocking the hero of Verdun. Nor were people prepared to forget that he had been a conscientious objector. One fine morning—I still say "one fine morning" because words have their own habits, and the presence of a few German tanks shouldn't make them change—one fine morning, then, we received a visit from Grillot, a childhood friend, who got his throat slit by the Resistance two years later, God forgive him. He and two other youths from the other side spent the morning ransacking our kites, just to make sure that "crazy old Fleury" didn't have any other dirty tricks up his sleeve. My uncle had hidden his entire "Popular Front" series with Father Tachin, Cléry's priest, who'd blustered about it at first but in the end had concealed everything in his cellar, except for Léon Blum, which he'd burned because, "Come on, goddammit, there are limits." My guardian was not bothered, but he saw which way the wind was blowing, and decided, after long reflection, that he had to "go at it from another angle." The meeting at Montoire gave him his opportunity, and his kite representing the historic handshake between Marshal Pétain and Hitler took to the air five days after the event. "Got to strike while the iron is hot," he confided in me. It was reproduced by a team of volunteers, and more than a hundred copies were made, which could be seen flying more or less everywhere in France. No one saw any malicious intent in it, except for Marcellin Duprat, who'd come for a drink at our house. "You old so-and-so," he told his old friend. "When you're taking a piss, everyone had better get out of the way."

27

IN NOVEMBER 1941, AS, WITH EACH PASSING DAY, the silence from Poland yawned into the silence of mass graves, I found myself at the manor for my memory exercises. That very morning, Grüber, the Cléry Gestapo chief, had come to La Motte with his men for a visit: well-meaning tongues had spread the rumor that Ambrose Fleury had made a kite in the shape of the Cross of Lorraine and was preparing to fly it very high, high enough be seen from Cléry to Clos, and from Jonquière to Prost. This was not the case; my uncle was far too sure of himself for such imprudence; the Germans found nothing that did not feature in any of the approved French history textbooks. They hesitated a fair while before a Joan of Arc borne aloft by twenty-four doves, but as Ambrose Fleury laughingly pointed out to them, you couldn't very well stop Joan from ascending to heaven. He offered our visitors a drink of calvados, showed them his *Meilleur Ouvrier de France* certificate, which he had received under the Third Republic, and—since without the Third Republic the Nazis wouldn't have won the war—the *Obersturmbannführer* had said, *Gut, gut*, and departed.

It was five o'clock in the afternoon; I was standing at the center of the attic's dusty wooden floor; the tree branches in their spiny bareness obscured the dormer windows; Bruno's piano remained silent; I closed my eyes in vain; I saw nothing. Good old common sense was working overtime that evening. The Germans were closing in on

Moscow and the radio announced that London was being reduced to dust.

I don't know by what desperate effort I managed to overcome my weakness. Lila was still sulking at me a little—she always had enjoyed putting my faith to the test—and then I saw Tad, spotting the names of our future victories on the globe, and, finally, Lila appeared and threw herself into my arms. A waltz, it was just one waltz, but as soon as my head began spinning, everything became whole again. Lila laughed in my arms, her head thrown back; Bruno played; Tad leaned nonchalantly against one of those globes that describe the earth so poorly, being unaware of its misfortunes; once again, I was certain of our survival and our future, because I knew how to love.

I continued waltzing in this way, eyes closed, arms open, giving free rein to my madness, when I heard the door creak. Up there, the wind had entries everywhere; caught up in my commemoration, I would hardly have paid it any mind had I not committed the error— always a grave one for those who live off faith and imagination—of opening my eyes.

At first I saw only the silhouette of a German officer standing out against a rectangle of darkness.

I recognized Hans. My head was still spinning a little and I thought I'd merely fallen victim to an excess of memory. It took me a few seconds to be entirely sure—it really was Hans. He stood there before me in his victor's uniform. He did not move, as if he under-stood that I was still unsure, and was giving me time to convince myself of his presence. He seemed unsurprised to have found me in the attic, waltzing with the one who was not there. Nor was he moved: misfortune, for victors, is just routine. Maybe he'd been told that I didn't have all of my reason, and surely someone had added, "That poor little Fleury boy, he certainly comes by it honestly." The Resistance was only in its very early stages, and the word "folly" had not yet earned the right to qualify as "sacred."

There was just enough in the way of crepuscular shadows to spare us from too clear a view of each other. Nevertheless, I made out the white scar on my enemy's cheek: the mark of the Polish *szabelka* I had wielded so clumsily. Hans seemed sad, almost respectful: courtesy is suited to uniform. Around his neck, an Iron Cross: no doubt he'd won it during the invasion of Poland. I don't recall what we said to each other, during those minutes in which no words were said. He made a refined gesture, displaying that good upbringing Prussian squires pass down from father to son: he blocked the doorway and then moved aside to let me through. After so many victories, he must have gotten into the habit of observing retreat. I didn't move. He hesitated, then began removing his right glove. For an instant, the expression on his face made me believe he was going to extend his hand to me. But no, there again, he spared me the embarrassment: he went over to the dormer, looked out at the bare branches, while still pulling off his gloves. And then, he turned toward Bruno's piano. He smiled, walked over to it, opened the cover, and ran his fingers over it. A few notes, just barely. He remained motionless for a moment, his hand on the keyboard, his head lowered. Then he turned away from it, walked a few steps, slowly, as if hesitating, as he pulled his gloves back on again. Before departing he stopped, turned partway toward me, as if he were going to say something. Then he left the attic.

I spent the night wandering through the countryside, not even recognizing the paths, although they had been familiar to me since my childhood. I could no longer tell whether I had actually seen Hans or whether I had pushed my remembering exercises so far that I had summoned up one spirit too many. The Jarrot brothers, who found me unconscious in their sheep barn the next morning, brought me back home and advised my uncle to have me admitted to the hospital in Caen.

"Around here we all know the young one is a little disturbed, but this time …"

Their timing was all wrong. *"Aunt Martha will come for a walk at dawn." "The cow will sing with the voice of a nightingale." "The trouser buttons will be sewn on time." "My father is mayor of Mamers and my brother is a masseur."* "Personal messages" from London to the

Resistance, transmitting on long waves of 1500 meters, medium waves of 273 meters, or short waves of 30.85 meters, reached us each day. Ambrose Fleury thanked the Jarrots for their good advice and, having politely shown them the door, came to my bedside and squeezed my wrist: "Be frugal with your folly, Ludo. Don't go squandering it, now. The country is going to be needing it more and more."

I tried to pull myself together, but I was deeply shaken by my encounter with Hans. I returned to prowl the grounds of Le Manoir des Jars; the Germans had not moved in yet; they hadn't even begun getting it ready.

At the start of December, just as I was scaling the wall, I heard the gate open, and, flattening my stomach to the ground, I saw a Mercedes bearing the pennant of the commanding general of the German army in Normandy turn down the main drive. Hans was at the wheel, alone in the car. I didn't know whether he was returning to prepare the place for occupation, or, like me, to think of Lila. That evening, I stole five tanks of petrol from the Clos Joli, which was comfortably supplied by the Germans, and carried them to the manor one by one. I set fire to it the very same night. It wouldn't take; I had to start over several times; I wandered from room to room, removing my memories from harm's way, awaiting the ashes that would preserve them intact. When at last everything went up in flames, all the way to the roof, I found it difficult to depart, so much friendship, it seemed to me, was contained in the blaze.

I was arrested in the morning, brought in to Cléry, and questioned roughly. The French police were all the more excitable because their standing in the eyes of the Germans was on the line. For the authorities, I was the ideal guilty party: it had been the gesture of a madman, without any "terrorist" intentions.

I denied nothing, I only refused to answer; I thought of my comrades Legris and Costes, from the Espoir network, who had refused to speak under torture: if a few slaps and punches could wring a confession out of me, I'd be short on memory for the first time in my life. So I took the thumping, smiled gormlessly, and pretended to sink into a dumb stupor, which discouraged the policemen considerably.

My uncle swore that I had not left my bed for a week; Dr. Gardieu drove eighteen miles in his cart—to the great displeasure of his horse, Clémentin—to confirm this affirmation; but the authorities were set on "the act of a madman" and the questioning resumed the next day, this time in the presence of two Germans in plainclothes.

I was seated on a chair, my back to the door. Suddenly, I saw the two Germans stand to attention, their arms raised, and Hans walked past me, without a glance in my direction. His face was tense, his jaws clenched; one sensed the effort he was making to master both his contempt and his irritation. He did not respond to the heil-Hitler salutes of Grüber's men and addressed the commissioner in French.

"I do not comprehend this arrest. I fail to see how Ludovic Fleury, whom I know well, could have been present at Le Manoir des Jars on the evening of the fire, since I was with him at the time, in the home of his uncle in Clos, and I left them only quite late in the evening, after a long discussion on the subject of kites with the master craftsman Ambrose Fleury. It is therefore totally impossible that he set the fire, since, according to witnesses, the flames were visible from several miles away starting at eleven o'clock that night."

My first impulse was to refuse this help and protection from the stronger man, and I nearly jumped up and yelled out, "It was me, I set fire to the manor." In the tumult of my thoughts, the one that initially prevailed was, yet again, my boorish resentment of his gesture; at first I saw more disdain and aristocratic superiority in it than generosity of spirit. But, just in time, another intuition dispelled this old antagonism: Hans was keeping faith with what united and separated us at the same time—Lila. He truly loved her and, in helping me, was coming to the aid of the very thing that gave meaning to his own life. I could detect the signs of his devotion to remembrance in his haughty air, in the supercilious glance he cast over the faces of my accusers: it wasn't me he had come to defend, it was our shared memory.

He didn't even wait for anyone to ask a question before departing: the testimony of a German officer was indubitable. I was released immediately. My uncle, Dr. Gardieu, and Clémentin brought me back home. No one has ever seen three men more silent in all they had to say to one another. Only after we had been seen home, and Dr. Gardieu and Clémentin had set off over the Cléry road again, did my uncle demand: "Why did you set fire to the place?"

"To keep it intact," I answered him, and he sighed, for he knew that thousands of Frenchmen were already dreaming of setting fire to the place "to keep it intact."

No one in the region doubted my guilt. Some people—the ones who had begun hearing the first calls to "unreason," and not just the ones coming from Radio London, but also the ones transmitted on a different frequency altogether—showed me a kind of timid sympathy. The others avoided me: the ones who, by "playing their cards right," or "putting their heads down till it blows over," were ennobling madness. Few people then believed in an Allied victory: at the very most people spoke of the possibility of a separate peace, piggybacking on the Russians.

I was placed under observation at the Caen psychiatric hospital, where I spent two weeks chatting out loud with the invisibly present, which got me officially certified as mentally unbalanced; nothing could have been more helpful to me in my activities with the Resistance. No one found it surprising to see me gesticulating as I wandered from farm to farm, and Soubabère, my network leader, put me in charge of all the liaisons. My wits would return magically for my accounting work at the Clos Joli, and so I continued, which made people remark to Duprat that "a good kick in the pants or two wouldn't go amiss." He must have suspected my underground activities, for very little escaped him. He was careful not to allude to them in any way—"So as not to be implicated," my uncle said—and limited himself to grumbling, "You people will never change!" And I couldn't tell whether he was speaking only of the Fleurys, or of our whole crazy brotherhood. Our numbers grew across devastated Europe as we began giving in to this aberration, which, in the history of its peoples has so often succeeded in demonstrating the possibility of the impossible.

She is standing at the other end of the room in a shadowy corner; there, on the wall, is a clumsy kite with a pink and pale-yellow body, speckled with silvery white, painted and assembled in the workshop by a seven-year-old child. I cannot tell if it is a bird, a butterfly, or a lizard, for the childish imagination has been careful not to deprive it of any possibilities.

"I haven't always been kind to you, Ludo. So now you're getting back at me. You forgot me for hours yesterday. You know I'm at your mercy and you like to make me feel it. That's so typically masculine. As if you were always expecting me to say, *what would I become without you?* You're making a game of scaring me."

I will admit that I enjoy her fears and worries: here she is, a girl from the oldest of noble families, dependent on a Norman hayseed, on his faithfulness and his memory. But I never abuse my power over her. I allow myself, at the very most, to take the license of infinitely prolonging certain of her motions—like brushing her hand through her hair: I need a few good minutes of that caress each morning. Or I lay hold of her arm to stop her putting on her brassiere.

"Ludo, come on! Will you cut it out?"

I like setting off that spark of anger in her eyes. Nothing comforts me more than the sight of her so unchanged, identical to herself.

"You think you're allowed to do anything, because I depend on you. Yesterday you made me walk twelve miles through the countryside. And I didn't like that stupid green sweater you made me wear either, not one bit."

"It's the only one I have, and it was cold."

And then, slowly, she ebbs, returns to her clandestinity, and I keep my eyelids closed, the better to protect her.

28

I GOT AROUND THE COUNTRY WITH EASE; THE GER-
mans didn't mistrust me, because they knew I had lost touch with
my reason, though that should have been reason enough for them to
shoot me on sight. I stored hundreds of constantly changing names
and "post box" addresses in my head; never did I have even the smallest scrap of paper on my person.

One morning, after a night on the road, I stopped for a breather at
Le Thélème. At a neighboring table, a man sat reading his newspaper.
I couldn't see his face, just the headline through the first page: *Red
Army in Full Collapse*. Monsieur Roubaud, the owner, came over and
set two glasses of white on the table for "poor Ludo"—one for me, the
other to humor me. People around here had grown accustomed to my
peculiarity, and newcomers were invariably reminded that I was even
more "certified" than my uncle, the famous eponymous postman,
with his kites. My neighbor lowered his newspaper and I recognized
Monsieur Pinder, my old French teacher. I hadn't seen him since the
eighth grade. The passage of time had strongly accentuated his features, which still had the admonitory severity with which he'd once
hunted out spelling errors in our notebooks. The same pince-nez and
the same goatee he'd worn back then still adorned his face. Monsieur
Pinder had always seemed slightly imperial, and he still did, though
his illustriousness came largely from the crossword puzzle he'd composed for the *Gazette* for the past forty years.

I got up from my seat.

"Hello, Fleury, hello—please allow me to present my respectful salutations to …"

He rose slightly and bowed to the empty chair. Bricot, the waiter, who was wiping glasses behind the bar, stopped in astonishment, then resumed wiping. He was a nice enough fellow, who never once used his imagination in his entire life; his death at the hands of SS agents fleeing after D-day was therefore totally useless and unjust.

"I salute sacred folly," said Monsieur Pinder. "Yours, your uncle Ambrose's, and that other young Frenchman in this country whose memory has made him lose his head entirely. I am pleased to note that so many of you have retained what rightly deserves to be included in our good old mandatory public education." He chuckled. "One might interpret 'to keep one's reason' in two ways. I assigned you a composition on the subject once, I believe. A *French* composition, if you will."

"I remember it very well, Monsieur Pinder. '*To keep touch with reason: to follow good sense; to act reasonably.*' Or, to the contrary, '*To keep one's reason to live.*'"

My former teacher seemed extremely pleased. Although he'd retired long ago, had grown wrinkly, and his imperial air had sagged a bit, there always has been a wholly different kind of youth, the kind that can get even a seventy-year-old schoolteacher deported.

"Yes, yes," he said, without specifying the object of his approbation.

Lorgnette, the owner's dog, a fox terrier with a black patch around each eye, came and offered Monsieur Pinder her paw. He patted her.

"One needs a great deal of imagination," he observed. "A great deal. Look at the Russians: it would appear that they've lost the war, according to this newspaper here. But they also seem to have enough imagination not to have noticed it."

He stood up. "You're a very good student, Fleury. Keeping your reason to live is sometimes an antonym for keeping touch with your reason. You shall have excellent marks. Come and see me one of these days, and don't wait too long. Waiter!"

He set twenty sous on the table, removed his pince-nez, which was attached to its fob pocket by a velvet ribbon, and put it carefully away. He bowed again to the empty chair, put on his hat, and walked off, his gait somewhat stiff, as his knees were not doing him any favors.

From May 1941 to July 1942, he wrote a good part of the clandestine "literature" distributed in Normandy. He was arrested in 1944, just before D-day, having grown too confident in his crossword puzzles, which were published twice a week on page four of the *Gazette*, and which transmitted coded instructions to members of the Resistance fighting in the west, but whose key had been delivered to the Gestapo by a comrade after the rending of a few fingernails.

All the same, Ambrose Fleury was fingered as a suspect after posters appeared in Cléry one morning on which the words "eternal France" spoke with the fresh and unexpected power of clichés when they suddenly begin molting and emerge transfigured from their old, tattered skins. I was surprised at this unexpected insight from those professionals of heavy-handedness, who, although they knew that what goes up—even a kite—must come down, no matter the force of hope propelling it, somehow identified this old naïf, who could usually be found in a field, surrounded by children, looking up at one of his *gnamas*, which nowadays we were forbidden from flying higher than fifty feet off the ground.

The news that suspicions had landed on my uncle was brought to us by our neighbors' son, the Cailleux boy, who dashed into the workshop one fine morning. Johnny Cailleux was as blond as if he'd been rubbed from head to toe with a sheaf of wheat, and he was all out of breath, more from the emotion than from the running.

"*They're* coming."

Whereupon, having paid this first tribute to friendship, he bolted outside and offered up a second one, this time to Norman prudence, disappearing as swiftly as a terrified rabbit.

"They" turned out to be the mayor of Cléry, Monsieur Plantier, and the town hall secretary, Jabot, whom Monsieur Plantier invited to stay outside; most likely he didn't want his trusty as a witness—trust then was running with the hare and hunting with the hounds. He came in, wiping his forehead with a large red-checked handkerchief—officials were already sweating a lot, with the first sabotages—and sat down on a bench, in his piss-colored corduroy jacket and breeches, without so much as a hello, his humor far from pleasant.

"Fleury, is it you, or isn't it?"

"It's me," my uncle replied, for he was justifiably proud of our name. "It's been Fleury for ten generations at least."

"Don't play dumb. They've got firing squads now, in case you didn't know."

"But what have I done?"

"Pamphlets have been found. Real calls for insanity, there's no other word for it. You'd have to be mad to attack the German forces. Everyone's saying it: only those crazy Fleurys would do such a thing. First the young one sets fire to the mansion where the German staff headquarters is supposed to be set up—fool, don't deny it!—and then the old man spends all his time launching his proclamations in the sky."

"What proclamations, you old noodle?" my uncle inquired, surprised, with tenderness unwonted for an old pacifist whose vocabulary had fought the Battles of the Marne and Verdun.

"Your nutty kites and those pamphlets—it's the same damn thing," shouted the mayor, suffering from the effects of a comprehension that seemed to come more from the heart than from the head. "Clemenceau, the other day—my kids saw that! And that? What's that?"

He pointed an accusing finger at Zola.

"Is it really the time to be flying Zolas out there? Why not Dreyfus, while you're at it? Old man, that kind of kidding around will get you marched before a firing squad!"

"We had nothing to do with the sabotages they're talking about—much less my kites. You want some cider? You're imagining things."

"Me?" roared Plantier. "Me, imagining things?"

My uncle poured him some cider. "No one is safe from imagination, Monsieur Mayor. Pretty soon you'll be seeing de Gaulle floating around up there ... No one is safe from acts of folly, not even you."

"What is that supposed to mean, not even me? You think I don't want to see the Germans out of here?"

"Good Lord, I hope you're not one of those people who listens to Radio London every night!"

Plantier looked at him darkly. "Yes—well, look here, it's none of your business what I do or don't listen to."

He stood up. He was fat. His weight made him sweat even more.

"Remember, it would be very convenient for us all if it could be proven that two nutcases were printing those pamphlets. If they start going after reasonable people we'll never get a moment's peace. I should have let them nab you in the public interest. I don't know what stopped me."

"Maybe it's because you used to come play with my kites when you were little. Remember?"

Plantier sighed. "That must be it." He gazed suspiciously around him. The kites from my uncle's "historical series" of French kings hung from the rafters, and when they dangle like that, with their heads down, they look sad. Plantier pointed at one of them.

"Who's that one?"

"That's Good King Dagobert. He's not subversive."

"Yeah, you go figure what's subversive and what's not these days." Plantier took a step toward the door. "Do some housekeeping, Fleury. They're coming, and if they find one single pamphlet ..."

"They" did not find any pamphlets. It did not occur to them to look inside the kings of France. They didn't find the printing press, either. It was hidden in a hole beneath a pile of manure. They poked around the manure with a pitchfork, and when the manure responded in the usual way, they didn't ask anything else of it.

German soldiers often came to order *gnamas* to send back home to their children as gifts. Certain kites contained not only calls to resist written in Monsieur Pinder's fiery prose, but also notes on the principal locations of German troops and the positions of coastal batteries. You had to be very careful not to mix the "sale stock" with the rest.

Our neighbors, the Cailleux, were perfectly aware of our activities, and Johnny Cailleux often served as a messenger for us. As for the Magnards, I sometimes wondered if they had even noticed France was occupied. They had the same attitude toward the Germans as they did toward everyone else: they ignored them. No one had ever seen them take the slightest interest in what was going on around them.

"They still make the best butter in the region, though," Marcellin Duprat remarked approvingly.

The owner of the Clos Joli recommended us to his new clientele, and once we even received a visit from General Milch, the celebrated German aviator.

Our most frequent visitor at La Motte was Cléry's mayor. Plantier would sit down on a bench in the workshop and remain there, grim and suspicious, watching my uncle give body and wings to the naive pictures children sent to him. Then he would get up and leave. He seemed anxious, but kept his fears to himself. And then one day he took my uncle aside.

"Ambrose, you're going to slip up one of these days. I can feel it coming. Where are you hiding it?"

"Hiding what?"

"Come on, don't play dumb with me. I'm sure you've got it squirreled away somewhere. And then you'll launch it and they'll take you away, I'm telling you."

"I don't know what you're talking about."

"You've made a de Gaulle kite, I know it. I've been expecting it. And the day you decide to fly it, you know what's going to happen to you?"

My uncle didn't say anything at first, but I saw he was moved—there was a softness in his eyes when something touched him. He went and sat down beside the mayor.

"Come now, come now—don't think about it all the time, Albert, or you'll end up on the town hall balcony shouting '*Vive de Gaulle!*' without even knowing what's hit you. And don't make that face …" He laughed into his big mustache. "I'm not going to denounce you."

"Denounce me for what?" shouted Plantier.

"I won't go telling the Germans you're hiding de Gaulle in your home."

Monsieur Plantier remained silent, staring at his feet. Then he left and didn't come back again. He managed to contain himself for a few months, and then, in April 1942, he made it over to England in a fishing boat.

The country was beginning to change. The presence of the invisible grew steadily. People who seemed "reasonable" and "sane" risked their lives to hide English aviators who had been shot down and Free French agents who had parachuted in from London. "Sensible" men—bourgeoisie, working class, farmers, people it was hard to claim were pursuing the blue yonder—printed and distributed papers in which they spoke of "immortality," a word they employed frequently, despite the fact that they were always the first to die.

29

WE'LL BUILD OUR HOUSE AS SOON AS THE WAR IS over, but I don't know where or how I'll come up with the money. I don't want to think about it. You have to keep a sharp lookout for excesses of lucidity and good sense—life has lost some of the prettiest feathers in its cap to them. So I haven't waited; I did all the work myself, and the materials hardly cost me more than a kite. We have a dog but we haven't named him yet. You always have to set a little something aside for the future. I decided not to sit for the entrance exams for the *grandes écoles*; out of loyalty to that good old "mandatory public education," I've chosen the profession of schoolteacher, although when I read the names of executed hostages on the walls I'm not sure it deserves that much sacrifice.

Sometimes, I'm afraid. Then the house becomes my refuge; it's hidden from sight; only I know the way there; I built it in the place where we first met; it's not wild strawberry season but, after all, we don't live off childhood memories. I often come home dead tired from the long days of trekking through the countryside, filled with nervous tension, and then it takes tremendous effort to find it. You can't say enough for the power of closed eyes. One German victory follows another in Russia, which often makes it even harder to overcome my weaknesses, and maybe it's not the time to spend my nights so doggedly building a house for a future that seems to recede further with every passing day. How Lila must hate my moments of solid good sense: she's entirely dependent on what everyone at the Clos Joli calls my aberration. Even my uncle worries about my underground activities. I wonder if he isn't feeling his years all of a sudden—they say wisdom overtakes us with age. But no: he simply advises me to be a bit more careful. It's true that I take too many risks, but there are more and more weapons drops and someone has to collect them, bring them to a safe place, and learn how to use them.

Often, I find the house is empty. It's normal for Lila not to be there waiting for me. We don't know much about the Polish Resistance and the partisan groups hiding out in the forest, but I can only imagine that reality must be even more vigilant there than it is here, more odious, more difficult to vanquish. They're saying it's already chalked up millions of deaths.

It's almost always in my worst moments of discouragement and weariness that Lila comes to my rescue. It's enough for me to see her exhausted face and her pale lips to remember that from one end of Europe to the other, it's the same struggle, the same senseless effort.

"I waited up for you night after night. You didn't come."

"We sustained heavy losses; we had to go deeper into the forest. There were injuries to take care of and almost no medical supplies. I didn't have time to think about you."

"I could feel that, all right."

She's got a heavy military greatcoat, a stretcher with a nurse's red cross; I've kept the long hair and the beret from our happy times.

"How are things going here?"

"The keep-your-head-downs and the play-your-cards-rights. But it'll change."

"Watch out, Ludo. If you ever get arrested …"

"Nothing will happen to you."

"And if you're killed?"

"Well, then, someone else will love you, and that's that."

"Then who? Hans?"

I am silent. She still enjoys teasing me as much as she always did.

"How much more time, Ludo?"

"I don't know. There's always that old saying, 'We're living off hope,' but I'm starting to think hope is the one living off us."

Waking up is our best time: a warm bed is always a little bit of a wife. I draw these moments out as much as I can, but day always comes, bearing its weight of reality, messages to carry, new contacts to establish. I hear the floorboards creak, I watch Lila dress, moving to and fro under my eyelids; she goes down to the kitchen, lights the fire, puts the water on to boil—and I laugh at the thought that this girl, who never did such menial chores in her life, has learned to keep house so quickly.

My uncle grumbles: "There are only two other people living entirely off memory like you—de Gaulle in London and Duprat at the Clos Joli."

And then he laughs. "I wonder which of them will end up winning."

30

THE CLOS JOLI CONTINUED TO PROSPER, BUT MARcellin Duprat's reputation in the area began to suffer; he was accused of serving the occupier too well; as for our comrades, they hated him cordially. I knew him better than that and defended him when my friends called him a bootlicker or a collaborator. Truth be told, as soon as the Occupation began, with the German superior officers and the entire Parisian elite already flocking to his "galleries" and his "rotunda," Duprat made his choice. His restaurant had to remain what it always had been: one of France's proudest landmarks, and every day, he, Marcellin Duprat, intended to show the enemy a thing that could not be defeated. But since the Germans felt so comfortable there, and were unstinting in their protection of him, his attitude was misunderstood and harshly judged. I myself observed an altercation at the Petit-Gris, where Duprat had stopped to buy a tinder lighter and was called out by Monsieur Mazier, the solicitor, who did not mince his words: "You should be ashamed, Duprat. The whole nation's eating rutabaga and you're treating the Germans to truffles and foie gras. You know what we call the menu of your Clos Joli around here? The menu of shame."

Duprat stiffened. There had always been something military in his physique, with a face that would harden all at once, lips clenched beneath his little gray mustache and his steel-blue gaze.

"The hell with you, Mazier. If you're too stupid to understand what I'm trying to do, then France really is in the toilet."

"And what exactly are you doing, you old jackass?" No one had ever heard that kind of legal jargon before.

"I'm holding down the fort," growled Duprat.

"What fort? Fort Scallops Chervil? Fort Lobster Soup? Fort Turbot with Cream of Leek and Mullet Sautéed with Thyme Blossoms? France's young men are rotting away in prison camps, when they're not being shot to death, and you ... *Mousse de sol au beurre de fines herbes! Salade de queues d'écrevisses!* Last Thursday, you served the occupying forces lobster rolls with sweetbreads, shellfish saveloy with truffle and pistachio, and Bresse chicken liver mousse with cranberries ..." He pulled out his handkerchief and wiped his lips. I do believe his mouth was watering.

Duprat waited a good long moment. There was a crowd at the bar: Gente, the civil engineer; Dumas, the owner; and one of the Loubereau brothers, who would be arrested a few weeks later.

"Listen carefully, you asshole," Duprat said finally, in a low voice. "Our politicians have betrayed us, our generals turned out to be fools, but the men responsible for France's great cuisine will defend it to the death. And as for the future ..."

He shot them all a glare.

"Who's going to win the war? Not Germany, not America, not England! Not Churchill, not Roosevelt, not that other guy, what's his name, the one who's always talking to us from London! The war will be won by Duprat and his Clos Joli, by Pic in Valence, by Point in Vienne, by Dumaine in Saulieu! That's all I have to say to you, assholes!"

Never before had I seen such stupor on the faces of four Frenchmen. Duprat flung a few coins onto the tobacconist's counter, put the lighter in his pocket. He looked them all over one last time, and departed.

When I told him about the incident, Ambrose Fleury nodded his head to show he understood. "He's crazy with sorrow, too."

That very night, the Clos Joli's van stopped in front of our house. Duprat had come to seek comfort with his best friend. At first, the two men did not exchange so much as a word, and went to work on a bottle of calvados. It was an entirely different man I saw sitting before me now from the one I'd watched a few hours before at the Petit-Gris. Marcellin's face was ghastly pale and defeated; no trace remained of his determined air.

"You know what one of those gentlemen said to me the other day? He got up from the table and declared to me with a smile, 'Herr Duprat, the German army and French cuisine—we'll build Europe together! With Germany for force and France for flavor! You'll be the one to give this Europe of the future what it needs from France, and we will ensure that all of France becomes a big Clos Joli!' And then he added, 'You know what the German army did when it got to the Maginot Line? It drove right past! And do you know what it did when it got to the Clos Joli? It stopped! Ha, ha, ha!' And he laughed." For the first time, I saw tears in Duprat's eyes.

"Come on, Marcellin," my uncle said gently. "Look, I know these words have often smacked of defeat, but … we'll get them!"

Duprat pulled himself together. His eye recovered its famous steely gleam and you could even see a glint of some cruel irony. "Apparently in America, in England, they're saying France is unrecognizable. Well, tell them to come to the Clos Joli: they'll recognize it, all right!"

"There. That's better," said my uncle, filling his glass.

They were smiling now, the two of them.

"Because," Duprat went on, "I'm not one of those people whimpering, 'Who knows what the future has in store for us!' You ask me. I know: there will always be a France in the Michelin Guide!"

My uncle had to drive him back home. I think it was on that day that I understood Marcellin Duprat's desperation and furor, but also his faith: that very Norman mix of flair and hidden fire, the fire he had once told me was "everyone's common ancestor." In any case, in March 1942, when the idea of fire came up with regard to the Clos Joli—that is to say, of setting fire to it and along with it to all the upper crust of the collaboration rushing for a seat at the occupier's table there, I protested vehemently.

There were six of us at the meeting, including Monsieur Pinder, to whom I had spoken at length. He had promised me he would do what he could to calm the hotheads among us. Guédard was there— he was beginning to scout out clandestine landing spots in the west; Jombey, aggressive and nervous, as if he already sensed his tragic end; Sénéchal, a teacher from Caen; and Vigier, who had come from Paris to study "the Duprat case" with local network heads and make the necessary decisions to proceed. We had met at Guédard's house, on the third floor, which faced the Clos Joli from the other side of the road. The general's Mercedes and the black Citroëns of the Gestapo and their French colleagues were already lined up in front of the restaurant. Jombey stood at the window, the curtain open a crack.

"It can't be tolerated," he repeated. "Look at the image Duprat is broadcasting! For two years, he's been a toady and a whore—it's insufferable. The old cook pulls out all the stops to pleasure the Boche and those traitors …" He came over to the table and opened Duprat's "file." Proof of collaboration with the enemy, as it was called back then. "Listen to this …"

We hardly needed to listen. We knew the "proof" by heart. *Terrine d'anguille sauce émeraude*, served to Otto Abetz, Hitler's ambassador in Paris, and his friends. *Fantaisie gourmande Marcellin Duprat*, served to Fernand de Brinon, Vichy's ambassador in Paris, who was executed by firing squad in 1947. *Feuilleté aux écrevisses et aux pointes d'asperges, mousise de foies blonds aux airelles*, served to Laval himself—the head of the Milice, in the company of his Vichy crew. *Pot-au-feu vieille France*, served to Grüber and his French aides in the Gestapo. And twenty or thirty of the best dishes of the *Meilleur*

Ouvrier de France, in which General von Tiele, the new commander of the German army in Normandy, had already taken his victor's pleasure in the course of a single week the month before. The wine list alone was sufficient evidence of Duprat's eagerness to provide the occupier with the very best of what French soil had to offer.

"Listen to me, I mean *listen!*" Jombey roared. "At the very least he could have hidden his best bottles—kept them for the Allies when they get here! But no, he gave it all up, he handed it all over ... he *sold* it all! From the 1928 Château Margaux to the 1934 Château Latour—even a 1921 Château d'Yquem!"

Sénéchal was seated on the bed, caressing his spaniel. He was a big blond guy. I always try to remember, to bring it back to life—the hair color, if nothing else, of this man of whom, a few months later, nothing would remain. "I ran into Duprat eight days ago," he said, "he was coming back from his rounds of the local farms and the back of his car was chockablock with parcels. He had a black eye. 'Hoodlums,' he said to me. 'Listen, Monsieur Duprat, they're not hoodlums and you know it. Aren't you even a little ashamed?' He gritted his teeth. 'Well, well, you, too, little one? And here I thought you were a good Frenchman.' 'What does that mean right now, a good Frenchman, according to you?' 'We'll, I'll go ahead and tell you, since you don't seem to know. That doesn't surprise me, as a matter of fact. You've even forgotten your history! A good Frenchman, nowadays, is one who stands firm.' I was stunned. There he was, at the wheel of his little van, with petrol supplied by the occupier, bringing the best products in France to the Germans, talking about people who 'stand firm.' 'And standing firm—what does that mean to you?' 'It's someone who doesn't back down, who holds his head high and stays loyal to what makes France France...It's this!' He showed me his hands. 'My grandfather and my father worked for France's great cuisine, and France's great cuisine has never taken a fall. It's never known defeat, and it never will be defeated, so long as there's a Duprat to defend it—against the Germans, against the Americans, against anybody and everybody! I know what they think of me. I've heard it enough times. That I go all out to please the Germans. Shit. Is the priest at Notre Dame Cathedral going to stand in the way if the Germans want to kneel? In two or three decades France will realize who we are—the Pics and the Dumaines and the Duprats, and the few others who salvaged the essentials. One day, all of France will be making pilgrimages here, and the standard of our country's greatness will be borne by its great chefs to the four corners of the earth! One day, my good man, whether it's Germany, America, or Russia who wins the war, this country will be so sunk in the mud that the only hope we'll have of finding our way out will be the Michelin Guide! And even that won't be enough! And then we'll see guides, let me tell you!'" Sénéchal trailed off.

"He's a desperate man," I said. "You've got to remember, his generation fought at Verdun."

He smiled at me. "He's a little like your uncle, with his kites."

"I think he's telling everyone to go *fly* a kite," Vigier put in. "He's just giving everything he has to pursue his passions—for his work, and for rattling people's chains."

Monsieur Pinder looked uncomfortable. "Duprat has a certain idea of France," he murmured.

"What?!" Jombey hollered. "Monsieur Pinder, I can't believe you're saying that!"

"Calm down, my friend. Because all the same, there is, after all, a hypothesis to be evaluated here ..."

We waited.

"What if Duprat is a visionary?" said Monsieur Pinder softly. "What if he's taking the long view? If he's really seeing the future?"

"I don't get it," Jombey muttered.

"Maybe Duprat, out of all of us, is the one who sees the country's future most clearly. And when we've all been killed, and the Germans have been beaten, it will all end in a blaze of glory—culinary glory. We may pose the question as follows: who, here, is prepared to die for France to become Europe's Clos Joli?"

"Duprat," I said.

"Out of love or hate?" demanded Guédard.

"Apparently the two go pretty well together," I pointed out. "Both blind, all's fair in love and war and so on. I think if we got him into a trench with a rifle in his hand like back in '18, he'd be able to show us his true feelings."

"Come see," said Jombey.

We went over to the window. Four faces, three young, one old. The curtains were thin cotton, with pink and yellow flowers on them.

The gentlemen were leaving the restaurant.

There was Grüber, the local head of the Gestapo; Marle and Dennier, two of his French colleagues; and a group of aviators, among whom I recognized Hans.

"A bomb in there," Jombey said. "And burn the Clos Joli right down to the ground."

"The costs of an attack like that would be too high for the local population," I said. I felt uneasy. I really understood Marcellin Duprat and his mix of despair, sincerity, and showmanship, the cunning and authenticity in his loyalty to his vocation, which vastly transcended whatever futility it also contained. I had no doubt that, in all his rage and frustration as a veteran of the Great War, French haute cuisine had become his last line of defense. Actually, his brand of willful blindness was just another way of seeing: the kind that lets a man hold on to something so he doesn't go under. Obviously, I wasn't mistaking cathedrals for custard, but, having been raised among the kites of "that crazy old Fleury," I had a soft spot for anything that allows a man to give the best of himself.

"I know it sounds ridiculous to you but don't forget that three generations of chefs before Marcellin bore the Duprat name. He was completely traumatized by the defeat—it was the collapse of everything he believed in—and so he's given himself completely to what's left, body and soul."

"Yeah, asshat of veal in bugger sauce," Jombey shouted. "What do you take us for, Fleury?"

I had a plan all ready and I had already talked it over with Sénéchal.

"We have to use the Clos Joli, not destroy it. Once the wine starts flowing, the Germans talk a lot around the table, and very freely. We have to plant someone in the restaurant who knows German and who can pass us information. Information, that's what London's asking us for. A whole lot more than flashy attacks."

I underlined the risk of reprisals against the local population, as well, and it was decided that we would hold off on the action. But I knew that sooner or later, if I couldn't prove to our comrades that Duprat could be useful to us, the Clos Joli would go up in flames.

31

I SPENT A FEW DAYS RACKING MY BRAIN. SÉNÉCHAL'S
fiancée, Suzanne Dulac, had a degree in German, but I still couldn't
figure out how to get Duprat to take her on.

For the past few months, I had been in charge of coordinating the
safe houses for the escape route that funneled downed Allied pilots
out through Spain. One evening, one of the Buis brothers alerted me
that a Free French pilot had been found and hidden at their farm.
The Buis family had kept him for a week while things "cooled off,"
and when the Germans became less frequent in their patrols around
the downed plane, they called for me.

I found the pilot sitting at the kitchen table in front of a plate of
tripe. His name was Lucchesi. It seemed like he'd spent a lifetime
tumbling out of the sky, so at ease was he with his red polka-dotted
scarf around his neck and the Cross of Lorraine insignia on his air
force blue battle dress.

"Tell me, sir, is there a good inn around here I could recommend
to my squadron mates? We're losing four or five pilots a month, so if
any end up around here …"

That's when it came to me. I had to stow the pilot for at least eight
days before I could arrange for his passage to Spain.

My uncle accompanied me to the Clos Joli late the next evening.
I found Duprat plunged in somber thought, in the company of his

son, Lucien. Radio Vichy was on full blast, and there was plenty to be upset about. The British merchant fleet was no more, the Afrika Korps was closing in on Cairo, the Italian army had occupied Greece … never before had I seen Marcellin Duprat so preoccupied by bad news. Only when he started talking did I realize my error. The master of the Clos Joli had simply forgotten to turn the radio off. He was meditating on something quite different from such ephemera.

"You know, Tournedos Rossini—I never did want it on my menu. Another Escoffier legacy. What a flimflammer. You know what the Tournedos Rossini is? Trick of the eye, that's what. Escoffier invented it because there were so many questionable steaks. So he just slapped something on top to make them go down easier. Foie gras, truffles *à la brune*—it distracts the tongue. That's pretty much where we're at with politics right now: Tournedos Rossini. Tricks of the tongue. The product is rotten, so they slather it in lies and pretty talk. The more eloquence they pile on, the cleverer they get, the surer you can be that it's rotten on the inside. Personally, I never could stomach Escoffier. You know what he called frogs' legs? 'Nymph wings *à l'aurore*' …"

Two American aircraft carriers downed in the Pacific … three hundred English bombers shot down by German aviators in the past two nights …

Duprat's eyes were slightly glazed. "It can't go on like this," he went on. "Everything's show nowadays. Take presentation. That has got to end. The future is in the dish. But no one ever listens to me. Even Point refuses to admit that presentation is an unnatural act. The dish always loses its spontaneity, its truth, its *moment*, in the presentation. It has to come out fully real, in its dish, straight from the fire. And that Vannier, the nerve of him, telling me that only cheap dives send food out from the kitchen in the dish. And where's taste in all that? What counts is the taste, seared in its moment of truth, the moment when the flesh and the flavor blossom together—you have to seize that moment, you can't let it get away …"

Hundreds of thousands of prisoners on the Russian front... vigorous police reprisals against traitors and saboteurs ... in England, twelve villages razed in a single night ...

It hit me that Duprat was talking to keep himself together; that he was, in his own way, fighting discouragement and despair.

"Hello there, Marcellin," my uncle said.

Duprat stood up and went to shut off the radio. "What do you want from me at this hour?"

"The kid needs to talk to you. It's private."

We left the room.

He listened to us in silence.

"No way. The Resistance has my full support. I've proved that well enough, standing firm in these impossible conditions. But I can't receive an Allied aviator under the Germans' noses. They'll shut me down."

My uncle lowered his voice a little. "It's not just any aviator, Marcellin. It's General de Gaulle's aide-de-camp."

Duprat was struck with a kind of paralysis. If a monument is ever raised to the man who held the rudder of the Clos Joli with a steady hand through the storm, that's how I imagine he'll be immortalized in a square in Cléry, his gaze steely, his jaws clenched. I do believe he felt a certain rivalry with France's greatest Resistance fighter.

He thought about it. I sensed he was both tempted and hesitant. My uncle observed him out of the corner of his eye, which betrayed a hint of mischief.

"That's all very nice," he said at last, "but your de Gaulle is in London, and I'm here. I'm the one who has to face the hardships day-to-day. Not he." He struggled for another moment. I knew it was a question of vanity, but I also knew that the hidden depths of his defiance had more than a bit of grandeur to them. "I'm not putting everything I've salvaged on the line so your man can come here. It's too dangerous. Risking closure just to make a splash—no. But I can do better than that. I'll give you the Clos Joli menu. Your man can give it to de Gaulle."

I stood there, dumbfounded. In the dark, Duprat's tall, white silhouette resembled some kind of avenging spirit. My uncle Ambrose remained speechless for a moment, too, but when Duprat returned to his kitchen he muttered, "We may be loose cannons, you and I, but that one there is the whole damn artillery."

For a while now, the rumble of English bombers had blended with the fire from German antiaircraft guns—the night voice of the Normandy countryside. The searchlights crossed swords above our heads. And then an orange light burst a hole in the sky: an airplane had been hit; it blew up with its bombs.

Duprat returned. In his hand was the Clos Joli menu. A few bombs fell, over towards Bursières. "Here we are. Listen. This is a personal message to de Gaulle from Marcellin Duprat …" To drown out the voice of the German antiaircraft cannons, he raised his own:

> Soupe crémière d'écrevisses de rivière
> Galette feuilletée aux truffes au vin de Graves …
> Loup à la compotée de tomates …

He read us the entire menu du jour, from the foie gras in pepper jelly with warm potato salad in white wine all the way to the white peach with Pomerol granita. The Allied bombers rumbled overhead and Marcellin Duprat's voice trembled a little. From time to time, he stopped and swallowed hard. I think he was a little afraid.

A fracas of bombs near the Etrilly rail line made the ground shake.

Duprat went silent and wiped his forehead. He handed me the menu. "Here. Give this to your pilot. So de Gaulle remembers what it's like. So he knows what he's fighting for." The projectors continued their fencing match in the sky, surrounding the toque of the best chef in France with what looked like flashes of lightning. "I don't kill Germans," he said. "I crush them."

"You talk out of your ass, is mostly what you do," my uncle observed gently.

"You think so, do you? We'll see about that. We'll see who has the last word, de Gaulle or my Clos Joli."

"There's nothing wrong with French cuisine winning the day. As long as it doesn't win out over all the rest," my uncle said. "I just read about a contest a newspaper organized. The subject was, 'What should we do with the Jews?' First prize went to a young woman who answered, 'Roast them.' Now, with all this rationing, she's probably just a good little housewife dreaming of a nice roast. Be that as it may, one shouldn't judge country by what it does with its Jews; for all time, Jews have been judged by what's done to them."

"Oh what the hell," Duprat burst out suddenly. "Bring him to me, your aviator. And for heaven's sake, don't think I'm doing this to make things right with the future. I have nothing to worry about in that regard. Any German with a shred of sense who sets foot in the Clos Joli can see he's dealing with supremacy, with historical invincibility. The other day, Grüber himself dined here. And when he finished, do you know what he said to me? 'Herr Duprat, you should be shot.'"

We left him in silence. As we made our way through the fields my uncle remarked, "When the defeat came, and the country went down, I thought Marcellin was going to lose his mind. Lucien told me that after the fall of Paris, he walked into the kitchen and found his father standing on a stool with the noose around his neck. He was delirious for days, stuttering and muttering a garble of duck with Normandy herbs and his famous *giboulée à la crème*, Foch, Verdun, Guynemer. Then, he wanted to shut down, and then he locked himself in his office with his three hundred menus and the glory they've brought to the Clos Joli for generations. I think he's never really completely recovered, and that was when he decided to set an example for the Germans and the whole country—a French chef who wouldn't capitulate. For sure," he added, "neither of us can accuse him of being unreasonable."

32

LIEUTENANT LUCCHESI'S LUNCH AT THE CLOS JOLI
was memorable. We had procured him a brand new suit and impeccable papers, although since the beginning of the Occupation not one single identity check had ever occurred at Duprat's restaurant. The lieutenant was served at the best table in the "rotunda," among the high officers of Wermacht, including General von Tiele in person. At the end of the meal, Marcellin Duprat walked Lucchesi to the door himself, shook his hand, and said: "Come back to see us."

Lucchesi looked at him.

"Unfortunately, you don't get to choose where you're downed," he replied.

From that day on, Duprat refused us nothing else. I don't think it was in any way because we now "had him," or because he had begun to feel the wind was changing and wanted to prove his loyalties to the Resistance, but because if the words *sacred union* had any meaning for him, it was that such a union ought to coalesce around the Clos Joli. Or, in my uncle's words—which carried more affection than they did sarcasm—"Marcellin may be older than de Gaulle, but he still has every chance of succeeding him."

And so Duprat agreed to take Sénéchal's fiancée, our comrade Suzanne Dulac, a pretty brunette with sparkling eyes and perfect German, into his service as a "hostess"—"no floozies under my watch" was his only qualification. There was no doubt that the table conversation she picked up was of interest in London, where they seemed particularly concerned with what was happening in Normandy: our orders were to disregard nothing. But very soon, we found at our disposal a source of information that turned out to be so important that it profoundly altered the activity of our entire network. As for me, it took me several days to recover from the shock. It was more than surprise: before that day I had never truly understood what lengths a human being—a woman, in this case—could go to in their implacable commitment to struggle and survival.

In my work at Marcellin Duprat's, the name I saw most often on the invoices and in the account books was that of the countess Esterhazy—the *Gräfin*, as the Germans called her—whom my employer held in high esteem: she was an excellent hostess. The buffets at her gatherings were all catered by the Clos Joli, and added appreciable sums to the restaurateur's income.

"She is a great lady," Duprat explained to me, looking over the figures. "A Parisian woman from a very good family, who was married to one of Admiral Horthy's nephews—you know, the dictator of Hungary. Apparently he left her vast properties in Portugal. I was at her house once, she has autographed photos on her piano of Horthy, Salazar, Marshal Pétain—even Hitler himself, believe it or not: 'for the Gräfin Esterhazy, from her friend Adolf Hitler.' I saw it with my own eyes. It's no surprise the Germans take good care of her. When she came back from Portugal after the victory—well, I mean, after the defeat—she moved into rooms at the Stag at first, but when the hotel was requisitioned by the German General Staff, out of courtesy they left her the pavilion in the hotel gardens. The point is, you see almost as much of the upper crust at her place as you do at mine."

Dogs were not permitted to enter the Clos Joli. Duprat was completely intransigent about it. Even the Pomeranian Spitz that followed Grüber everywhere was required to wait in the garden, although it's true that Duprat sent out generous portions of potted meat for the pooch while it waited. One day when I was in the office, Monsieur Jean came in carrying a Pekinese.

"Esterhazy's little doggy. She asked me to bring it in to you, she'll come pick it up afterward."

I glanced at the Pekinese and felt beads of cold sweat form on my brow. It was Chong. Madame Julie Espinoza's dog. I tried to get ahold of myself, to tell myself that it was just a resemblance, but I've never been able to play tricks with my memory. I recognized the black muzzle, every tuft of white-and-brown fur, the little reddish ears. The dog came over to me, placed his front paws on my knees, and began to whimper and wag its tail.

"Chong!" I murmured.

He jumped into my lap and licked my hands and face. I sat there stroking him, attempting to order my thoughts. Only one explanation was possible: Madame Julie had been deported, and the dog, in some bizarre series of mishaps or reincarnations, had ended up with the Lady Esterhazy. I knew how respectfully the Germans treated animals, and recalled an announcement published in the *Gazette* alerting the local population that "the transport of live poultry by tying their feet and hanging them head-down over bicycle handlebars shall be considered torture and strictly forbidden."

So Chong had found a new mistress. But the memories tumbled back impetuously and among them those of the "boss lady," certain of defeat and preparing for the future with meticulous precaution: identity papers "above all suspicion," millions of counterfeit bills, all the way down to the portraits of Horthy, Salazar, and Hitler that had intrigued me so, yet which "hadn't been autographed yet." I continued to sweat with emotion until Monsieur Jean opened the door and Madame Julie Espinoza walked in. To tell the truth, if it hadn't been for Chong, I wouldn't have recognized her. All that remained of the old madam in the rue Lepic was the bottomless depth of her gaze, in which whole millennia and all the hardship of the world lay hiding. Beneath her white hair, her face wore a chilly expression of slight haughtiness; an otterskin coat was slung casually over her shoulders, and a gray silk scarf wrapped around her neck; she'd given herself a majestic bosom, gained a good twenty pounds, and seemed almost as many years younger: later, she confided in me that she had taken advantage of her connections to have herself "dewrinkled" at the military burn hospital in Berck. The little golden lizard I knew so well was pinned to her scarf. She waited until Monsieur Jean had respectfully closed the door behind her, took a cigarette from her handbag, lit it with a gold lighter, and drew in the smoke, watching me. A hint of a smile appeared on her lips when she saw me there, frozen in my chair, my mouth hanging open in astonishment. She tucked Chong under her arm and observed me an instant longer, attentively, and almost with malevolence, as if she hardly approved of the trust she felt forced to place in me, and leaned forward: "Ducros, Salin, and Mazurier are under suspicion," she murmured. "Grüber isn't touching them for the moment, because he wants to know who the others are. Tell them to lie low for a while. And no more little meetings in the back room of the Normand—or at least not always the same faces. You got that?"

I was silent. My vision was foggy and I had a sudden desire to pee.

"Will you remember the names?"

I nodded my head, yes.

"And you will not mention me. Not a word. You never saw me. Understood?"

"Understood, Madame Ju …"

"Shut it, fool. It's Lady Esterhazy."

"Yes, Lady Esther …"

"Not Esther. Esterhazy. Esther is not a name to throw around these days. And hurry, because who knows, Grüber may want to pick them up before the meeting. I've got one of his guys feeding me information, but the stupid git has been laid up with pneumonia for the past three days."

She adjusted her otterskin coat on her shoulders, arranged her scarf, stared at my face for a long moment, crushed out her cigarette in the ashtray on my desk, and left the room.

I spent the whole afternoon running to warn the threatened comrades. Soubabère absolutely wanted to know who my informant was, but I told him that a passerby had slipped me a note in the street and then taken off running.

I was so stunned by the metamorphosis of the madam of the rue Lepic into this imposing revenant—a kind of *statue de commandeur*—that had appeared in my office, and that I tried not to think about it and didn't breath a word of it to anyone, not even my uncle Ambrose. I ended up believing that my "state" had worsened, and that it had been a hallucination. But, two or three times a month, at lunchtime, Monsieur Jean would bring me the Gräfin's little doggy, and whenever his mistress came to collect him, it was always so that she could slip me information, some of it so significant that it was becoming more and more difficult for me to pretend that I was picking it up from notes slipped to me by a stranger in the streets of Cléry.

"Listen, Lady ... I mean, My Lady, how am I supposed to explain where I'm getting this information from?"

"I forbid you to speak of me. I'm not afraid to die, but I'm certain the Nazis are going to lose the war and I want to be around to see it."

"But how do you get ..."

"My daughter is a secretary at the General Staff headquarters, at the Stag."

She lit a cigarette. "And she's Colonel Schtekker's mistress." She chuckled and stroked Chong. "The Stag. Quite the stag party they've got going on there. Tell your guys that you find the information in an envelope on your desk. You don't know where it comes from. Tell them that if they want it to go on, they had better not ask you any questions."

For the first time, I saw a trace of worry on her face, as she observed me.

"I trust you, Ludo. It's always a stupid thing to do, but that's the

risk I took. I've always kept close to the ground, and for once …"
She smiled. "The other day I went to see your uncle's kites. There
was one, a real beauty, that slipped out of his hands and blew away.
Your uncle told me it was gone forever, or if you did find it, it would
be all banged up."

"Pursuing the blue yonder," I said.

"I never thought it would happen to me," said Madame Julie Espinoza, and suddenly I saw tears in her eyes. I think when you've seen
too much darkness, a little blue goes straight to your head.

"You can trust me, Lady Esterhazy," I said softly. "I won't betray
you. You've told me enough times that I've got the firing squad look."

Soubabère didn't believe a word of the envelope story. When I
handed him a map detailing the entire German military presence in
Normandy—the number of planes in every airfield; the location of
every coastal artillery battery and every AA formation; the number
of German divisions that had been pulled out of Russia and were en
route to the West—he all but had me court-martialed.

"You bastard—where are you getting this from?"

"Can't tell you that. I gave my word."

My comrades were starting to look at me strangely. London
demanded imperatively to know the source of the information. I
thought so hard about it that there were times I didn't see Lila for
days and days. I had to find a solution at all costs and convince Her
Ladyship, who I couldn't help calling "the Jewess" in my head, to
give me permission to inform my network commander. In the end,
I resorted to an argument that I wasn't particularly proud of, but
which seemed only fair.

That day, a Sunday, the Lady Esterhazy came to lunch at the Clos
Joli after mass. The Pekinese was duly entrusted to me by Monsieur
Jean. At around three o'clock, the *lieutenant* entered my office and
pulled a note out of her handbag. She glanced prudently at the door,
then placed the paper in front of me. "Learn it off by heart and burn
it immediately."

It was a list of "trusted sources"—that is, informants—the Gestapo was using in the region. I read over the names twice and burned the paper.

"How did you get that?"

Madame Julie stood before me dressed all in gray, stroking Chong. "None of your business."

"Explain it to me, for God's sake. It's not credible, when you think about it. It's straight from the Gestapo."

"Well, I'll tell you. Grüber's deputy, Arnoldt, is a homosexual. He's living with a friend of mine, who's a Jew."

She rubbed her cheek against Chong's muzzle. "I'm the only one who knows he's Jewish. I had Aryan paperwork forged for him. Third-generation Aryan. He can't refuse a thing to me."

"But now that he has the right papers, he can get rid of you. He can denounce you."

"Ah, no, my little Ludo. Because *I* kept his real papers."

There was something implacable and nearly invincible in that dark gaze.

"So long, kid."

"Wait. What do you think will happen to you if I'm arrested and shot?"

"Not a thing. I'll be very sad."

"You're wrong, Lady Esterhazy. If I'm no longer around to corroborate all you've done for the Resistance, they'll be after you as soon as the Liberation comes. And then, there will be no one left to defend you. All that will be left is…" I swallowed and screwed my courage to the sticking point: "All that will be left is Julie Espinoza the madam, who was very cozy with the Germans. The firing squads will be just as busy as they are now, you can be sure of that. I'm the only one who knows what you've done for us, and if I'm not around anymore…"

Her hand froze on Chong's little head, and then continued its caress. I was horrified by my audacity. But the only thing I saw cross the "boss lady's" face was a smile.

"My goodness, Ludo, you've toughened up," she said to me. "A real man's man. But you're right. I have witnesses in Paris, but I probably won't have time to go back there. Fine, fine, go ahead. You can tell your friends. And tell them, too, that tomorrow I want a letter of commendation for the services I've rendered. I'll keep it in a safe place … where no one will go looking, at my age. And you tell your network commander … What's his name again?"

"Soubabère."

"That if there's the slightest slipup, I'll be the first to know, and I'll have the time to get away, but not you. None of you. There won't be a single one of you left—not even you, Ludo. I've been fucked too many times in my life to get fucked over. He'll keep his mouth shut, that boss of yours, or I'll have it shut for him, and for good."

It took me an hour to explain everything to Souba that evening. The only comment he made after hearing me out was, "She's quite a lady, that hooker."

From time to time, I almost came to regret the argument to which I'd resorted to convince the *lieutenant*. I'd hit her where she felt it most: her instinct for self-preservation. What might happen to her in the days following the departure of the Germans really came to haunt her: she all but asked for a receipt every time she passed me information. After her "Resistance Hero" certificate, which was dated and signed by "Hercules"—the code name Soubabère had modestly chosen for himself—she demanded another one for her daughter, and another one, typed out, signed, and dated, but with the beneficiary's name left blank, to fill in later. "Just in case I want to save someone," she explained to me.

Soon, Madame Julie had her own code name in London: *Garance*. After she was awarded her Resistance Medal, her behind-the-scenes role became well known, so I've changed some names and a few details here, so as not to disturb her in the notoriety she gained after the war. She continued as our informant until the Allied landing, and was never bothered or suspected. Right up to the end, her ties to the occupying forces were considered "shameful" in the region: she threw a garden party for the German officers at the Stag just days before D-day. She even grew so bold as to install a transceiver in her maid's quarters, and the maid in question, Odette Lanier, fresh from her training in London, was able to work entirely undisturbed a hundred and fifty yards away from the German staff headquarters.

We had agreed from the start that I would never take the lead in contacting the Gräfin.

"If I have something for you, I'll come and have lunch here, and I'll leave Chong for you to take care of. I'll pick him up on my way out and I'll tell you what I have to say. If I want you to come see me at home, I'll forget the dog and you'll bring it back to me …"

A few months after our first encounter, Monsieur Jean came into the office, where Chong was asleep on a chair. "The Lady Esterhazy forgot the pup. She just rang. She wants you to bring it back to her."

"Goddammit," I said, for form's sake.

The villa, which before the war had been occupied by a Jewish family from Paris, was located in the vast gardens of the Stag. Chong was unenthused by his bicycle ride under my arm, and didn't stop wriggling the whole time. I had to walk part of the way. A chambermaid—a pretty one, at that—opened when I rang.

"Oh, yes, Madame forgot it …" She tried to take the dog, but I refused, sullenly. "Hang on a minute, now, a whole goddamn hour on this bike and …"

"I'll go and see."

Just moments later, she returned. "Her Ladyship begs your pardon. Please come in. She would like to thank you."

The Gräfin Esterhazy, dressed in a discreet shade of gray that went perfectly with her snow-white chignon, appeared at the door of the sitting room accompanied by a young German officer, who was bidding her goodbye. By sight, I knew him well: he was the staff interpreter, who often accompanied Colonel Schtekker to the Clos Joli.

"Goodbye, Captain. And believe me, Admiral Horthy became regent quite against his own wishes. His popularity, which was already considerable in 1917, following the battle of Otranto, soared to such heights that, having crushed the Bolshevik Revolution of Béla Kun in 1919, he had no choice but to bow to popular opinion ..."

It was, word for word, the paragraph from the history textbook I had heard Madame Julie reciting in her bordello in 1940, as she prepared for the German victory.

"But it's said he has dynastic ambitions," the captain said. "He named his son István vice-regent ..."

Chong trotted over to his mistress.

"Ah, there you are."

She smiled at me. "Poor little thing. I forgot him. Come, young man, come ..."

The officer kissed the Gräfin's hand and departed. I followed her into the sitting room. There, on the piano, were the famous "autographed" portraits of Horthy and Salazar I'd noticed at the Hôtel du Passage. Marshal Pétain hung on the wall in a prominent position. The only thing missing was the picture of Hitler I'd also seen "waiting" at the rue Lepic.

"Yeah, I know," said Madame Julie, following my gaze, "but it was making me sick." She glanced at the entryway, then shut the door again. "That handsome captain is *schtupping* my chambermaid," she told me. "Which is quite a good thing—it could come in handy. But I change servants every two or three months. It's safer that way. They always end up knowing too much." She yanked open the door again with a sudden movement and looked outside. No one was there. "Good. We're all clear. Come on."

I followed her to her bedroom. The change that came over her in the space of a few minutes was extraordinary. At the Clos Joli, and just before, with the German officer, she had been a distinguished lady, holding herself very straight, head high, supported by a cane. Now, she advanced heavily, rolling from one leg to the other, like a docker under a crushing load. She seemed to have gained forty pounds and aged half as many years.

She walked over to a dresser, opened a drawer, and pulled out a bottle of Coty perfume. "Here, take this."

"Perfume, Madame Ju ..."

"Do not ever call me that, you idiot. Cure yourself of that habit— it could come over you at the wrong moment. This isn't perfume. It's deadly, but it only takes effect after forty-eight hours. Now, listen closely ..."

And so it was that in June of 1942, we learned that General von Tiele, the new commander of the German army in Normandy, was giving a luncheon at the Clos Joli, whose guests would include the commander in chief of the Luftwaffe, Marshal Goering himself, as well as a pack of ace pilots, including Garland, the English air force's number one enemy, as well as numerous generals of the highest rank.

Our first decision, as soon as we found out the time and date of Goering's dinner, was to make a big hit. Nothing would have been easier than to poison all the dishes. The affair was too important, however, to be undertaken on our own initiative, and we consulted with London. Everything had to be planned for, including Duprat's evacuation to England by submarine. The details of Operation Achilles' Heel have been told several times now, most notably in Donald Simes's memoir, *Nights of Fire*.

The task of talking Duprat into it fell to me, and I approached him with apprehension. The menu General von Tiele had chosen included a seafood saveloy made with truffles and pistachio. I explained our project in what I confess was a feeble voice.

Duprat refused outright.

"Poison my saveloy? Impossible."

"Why?"

He glared at me with the steely blue gaze I knew so well: *"Because it wouldn't taste good."*

He turned on his heel and left the room. When I attempted to follow him into the kitchen, he took me by the shoulders and pushed me out without a word.

Thankfully, London sent us a message to abort the operation. From time to time I wondered whether de Gaulle himself hadn't put a stop to it, for the sake of the Clos Joli's reputation.

33

I SPOKE TO LILA LESS AND SAW HER LESS, AND IN this way concealed her more in the eyes of others: it was the rule of the underground. From time to time, a comrade was nabbed because he was taking too many risks and didn't know how to hide his reason to live. My memory had stored away so many hundreds of constantly changing addresses and collected so much military intelligence that there was less and less room for Lila in there; she'd had to squeeze over a bit and live on less. Her voice barely came through to me now, and when it did, when, instead of thinking of the following day, of meetings, of arrest, of the ever-present possibility of betrayal, my mind was free to listen to her, she spoke with an undertone of reproach.

"If you keep forgetting me it'll all be over, Ludo. Over. The more you forget me, the more I'll be nothing but a memory."

"I'm not forgetting you. I'm just hiding you. I'm not forgetting you, or Tad, or Bruno. You should know that by now. It's not the time to be showing the Germans your reason for living. They'll shoot you for that."

"You've become so sure of yourself, so calm. You laugh a lot, as if nothing could happen to me."

"As long as I stay sure and calm, nothing can happen to you."

"What do you know? And what if I'm dead?" My heart nearly stops, when I hear this insidious murmur. But it's not Lila's voice. It's just the voice of fatigue and doubt. Never before have I needed to go to such lengths to remain unreasonable.

I stop at nothing; I use every trick. At night, I rise, heat water for the bath, and fill the tub. They're dreaming of hot baths over there, in their snowy forest, where it's so cold that every morning you find the bodies of frozen crows curled up beneath the trees.

"You really do think of everything, Ludo."

She is there, beneath my eyelids, soaking in hot water up to her chin.

"It's tough, you know. The hunger, the snow … You know me, how I hate the cold! I wonder how much longer we can hold out. The Russians are being routed, there's no one to help us. We're all alone."

"How is Tad?"

"He's taken command of all the partisans in the region. His name is legend, now."

"And Bruno?"

She smiles.

"Poor thing! If you could've seen him, rifle in hand … He held out a few months …"

"To be near you."

"Now he's in Warsaw, with his music teacher. He's got a piano."

I feel a hand on my shoulder, shaking me roughly. My uncle is there, in the dull rainy gray of daylight.

"Get up, Ludo. They found an English plane near the ponds over at Goigne. It's empty. The crew must be searching for a place to hide. Got to try and find them."

Another month, and another. Around us, reality is becoming harsher and harsher, more and more implacable: the entire team that printed the *Clarté* newspaper was arrested; no one got away. I haven't seen Lila for weeks: I even went to see Dr. Gardieu, to see if something was wrong with my heart. Nope, nothing wrong in that department.

When the discouragement got to be too much for me, when my strength lagged and my imagination laid down its arms, I would go and see my old French teacher in Cléry. He lived in a house with a little garden that looked as if it had been squeezed in around two trees. Madame Pinder would make us tea and serve it in the library. Her husband would invite me to take a seat, and then regard me at length through his pince-nez. He was probably the last man in the world to wear sleeve protectors. He still wrote with the old Sergent fountain pen of my childhood. He would tell me that in his youth he'd dreamed of becoming a novelist, then he'd add that the only work of imagination he had ever successfully produced was his wife. Madame Pinder would laugh, roll her eyes heavenward, and fill our cups. There are some older women who in a single gesture, a laugh, become young girls again. I'd keep quiet. I didn't come to talk, but to find comfort; this couple who'd never left each other reassured me in their permanence; I needed their duration, their old age shared, their promise. The house was unheated, and Monsieur Pinder would sit behind his desk with his jacket draped over his shoulders, a flannel scarf around his neck, wearing a wide-brimmed hat; Madame Pinder wore old-fashioned dresses that went down to her ankles and kept her all-white hair pinned back; I observed the two of them avidly, as if they were auguring the future to me. I dreamed of being elderly, of finding myself with Lila on the threshold of extreme old age. All doubt and worry, everything that was nearing despair in me, would calm at the sight of this old, happy couple. Home was in reach.

"They're still laughing at Ambrose Fleury and his kites," Monsieur Pinder said to me. "It's a good sign. That's one of the great virtues of comedy: it's a safe house where serious things can find refuge and survive. What surprises me is that the Gestapo leaves you alone."

"They've already searched us. They didn't find a thing."

Monsieur Pinder smiled.

"That's a problem the Nazis will never be able to solve. No one has ever succeeded in that kind of search. How is your … friend?"

"We've received several airdrops. A new kind of transceiver, with an instructor. And weapons. At the Gambier farm alone we have a hundred pistols hidden, plus hand grenades and incendiary devices … I'm doing all I can."

Monsieur Pinder nodded his head to show he understood. "The only thing I worry about with you, Ludovic Fleury, is your … re-union. I might not be around by the time it happens, which will no doubt shield me from many disappointments. France, when it returns, will need not only all of our imagination, but a lot of imaginary things, as well. So this young woman you have been imagining for three years with so much fervor, when you find her again … You'll need to keep inventing her, with everything you have. She will surely be very different from the girl you knew … I don't know what wonders our Resistance fighters are expecting of France when she returns, and bleak laughter will often be the measure they show of their disappointment—and even more than that, of themselves …"

"Lack of love," I said.

Monsieur Pinder puffed on his empty cigarette holder. "Nothing is worth the experience if it isn't a work of imagination above all things—or the sea would be nothing but a lot of salt water … Take me, for example, for fifty years I've never once stopped inventing my wife. I haven't even let her age. She must be riddled with faults I've turned into qualities. And in her eyes, I'm an extraordinary man. She's never stopped inventing me, either. In fifty years of living to-gether, you really learn not to see each other, to invent and reinvent each other with every passing day. You do always have to take things as they are, of course. But only because that's how you grab onto them to drag them into the light. That's all civilization is, really—continuously dragging things as they are into the light …"

Monsieur Pinder was arrested a year later and never returned from the camps; nor did his wife, although she wasn't deported. I visit them often, in their little house, and they welcome me just as warmly as they always did, even though they've been gone a long time now, I've been told.

34

IN THE UNDERGROUND STRUGGLE I'D JOINED TO hasten Lila's return, my main responsibilities were as a liaison among my comrades; with André Cailleux and Larinière, I was also in charge of the Normandy section of the network that—when we made it to a landing site before the Germans did—sheltered downed Allied aviators and helped smuggle them through to Spain. In the months of February and March 1942 alone, we recovered five out of the nine pilots who had managed to land their planes or parachute out in time. At the end of March, Cailleux came to alert me that there was a fighter pilot hidden near the Rieux farm; the hideout was secure, but the Rieux were getting impatient, especially the old lady, who was eighty and feared for her family. We set out into the foggy dawn. The damp earth stuck to the soles of our shoes; we had twelve miles to cover, not counting the detours we had to make to stay clear of roads and German checkpoints. We walked in silence; it was only as we neared the farm that Cailleux announced to me: "Hey, I forgot to tell you ..." He winked at me in a friendly way, but not without a hint of mischief: "You might be interested to know. The pilot's Polish."

I knew there were many Polish aviators in the RAF's squadrons, but it was the first time any of them had been picked up by the Resistance. Tad, I thought. It was absurd; there really was no chance of it being him, given the thing we sometimes so tragically call "probability distribution." Hope often plays these kinds of tricks on us, but then again, those are the tricks we live off of. My heart beat wildly; I stopped for a moment and gave André Cailleux an imploring look, as if it were up to him.

"What is it?"

"It's him," I said.

"Who's that?"

I didn't answer. In the forest a half mile beyond the farm was a shed where the Rieux stored wood for the winter; a hundred yards from that, we had dug an underground passage that led to a weapons cache, which also served as a hideout for wanted comrades, or for the aviators we'd managed to pick up. Its outside entrance was hidden beneath a pile of dead wood. We moved away the logs and the branches; lifting the trapdoor, we descended into the passageway, which led for twenty-odd yards to the hideout. It was very dark; I lit my flashlight; the aviator was sleeping on a mattress, under a blanket; I could just make out the "Poland" insignia on the sleeve of his gray battle dress, and his hair. That was all I needed. But the idea seemed so impossible to me, so insane, that I bounded toward the sleeper, and, pulling away the blanket, shone my flashlight in his face.

I hovered over him, holding one end of the blanket, utterly convinced that, yet again, my cursed memory was rekindling the past.

It wasn't an illusion.

Bruno, gentle Bruno, so maladroit, always lost in his musical daydreams, was there, in front of me, in his English aviator's uniform.

I didn't have the strength to move. It was Cailleux who shook him awake.

Bruno rose slowly. He didn't recognize me, in the dark. It was only when I shone the bright beam of the flashlight in my own face that I heard him murmur: "Ludo!"

He embraced me. I couldn't even return the hug. All of my hope was knotted in my throat. If Bruno had managed to make it to England, then Lila must be there, too. Finally, I asked, in a terrified voice, for this time I risked knowing: "Where is Lila?"

He shook his head. "I don't know, Ludo. I don't know."

There was such pity and tenderness in his eyes that I grabbed him by the shoulders and shook him: "Tell me the truth! What happened to her? Don't try to spare me."

"Calm down. I don't know, I have no idea. I left Poland a few days after you, to go to that piano competition in England. In Edinburgh. Maybe you remember …"

"I remember everything."

"I got to England two weeks before the war. Since then I've done everything I could to find news … Like you, I guess … I haven't succeeded."

He had trouble speaking and lowered his head. "But I know she's alive … that she'll come back. You, too—don't you?"

"Yes, she'll come back."

For the first time, he smiled. "Actually, she's never left us …"

"Never."

He'd kept his right hand on my shoulder, and little by little, this fraternal touch calmed me. I saw the ribbons decorating his chest.

"My, my!"

"What can you do," he said. "You change, sometimes, when disaster hits. It can even turn a pacifist daydreamer into a man of action. As soon as the war started I joined the English air force. I became a fighter pilot."

He hesitated, and then said, a little abashedly, as if he were lacking in modesty: "I've racked up seven victories. Yep, old Ludo, the time for music is over and done with."

"It'll come back."

"Not for me."

He withdrew his hand from my shoulder and raised it. There was a prosthesis fixed to it: two fingers were missing. He looked at it with a smile.

"Another one of Lila's dreams bites the dust," he said. "You remember? The next Horowitz, the next Rubinstein …"

"And you can fly a plane with that?"

"Oh, just fine. I brought home four victories with *that* … But what I'll do with my life afterward … that's a whole different question. The war will keep going for a while yet, so maybe it's one I won't need to ask myself."

We stayed together for two days. With excellent German paperwork procured for us by Lady Esterhazy's daughter, we took a few risks, including lunch at the Clos Joli. Marcellin Duprat's face when he saw the "young prodigy," as he had called Bruno, was for me one of the restaurant's tastiest delicacies, an unplanned addition to the chef's menu. His expression was one of astonishment and pleasure—and a healthy dose of fear, as he eyed the German officers and the chief of the Evreux Milice, who were seated at a table in the "rotunda."

"Oh. It's you," was all he managed to say.

"Squadron leader Bronicki has seven victories to his name," I said, not really trying to be quiet.

"Shut up, stupid," Duprat growled, attempting to guard his smile.

"He's returning to England to continue the struggle," I added, raising my voice.

I couldn't really tell whether the good Marcellin was smiling or showing his teeth. "Don't just stand there, for God's sake. Come with me."

He dragged us "portside" as he called it, seating us at the least visible table in the room. "All crazies, those Fleurys," he grumbled.

"If there were no madness, Monsieur Duprat, France would have thrown in the towel a long time ago. You first of all."

We didn't talk about Lila anymore. She was there with us, so present that mentioning her would only have pushed her away. Bruno spoke to me of his admiration for England, and told me about life among these people who were going to win the war because in 1940 they hadn't been willing to admit they'd lost it.

"And they've kept up their kindness and good cheer. Not even a trace of animosity for the foreigners we all are, even the ones who can't help sleeping with their sisters and the wives of the English soldiers fighting overseas. And the French, how are they?"

"They're pulling themselves back together. It was a real punch in the gut for us; it took time."

Marcellin Duprat came circling around twice during the meal, looking both worried and a little guilty.

We ate *poularde en vessie, sauce Fleurette.*

"You see I'm holding firm," he said to Bruno.

"It's very good. As good as before. Bravo."

"Tell them, over there. They can come. I'll take care of them."

"I'll tell them."

"But don't drag it out too much …"

Maybe he meant the meal, maybe he meant the war—we had to give him the benefit of the doubt.

The second time he appeared, he looked prudently in all directions, then asked Bruno, "And your family? Have you heard anything?"

"No."

Duprat sighed and moved off.

After lunch, we made our leisurely way to La Motte. My uncle was standing in front of the farmhouse, smoking his pipe. He showed no surprise when he saw it was Bruno.

"Well, everything happens," he said, "which proves that dreamers sometimes do have the last word. Not all daydreams crash and burn."

I told him that Bruno had become a pilot in England, that he had notched up seven victories with his plane, and that in a couple of weeks he'd be back in the air again, fighting. As they shook hands, my uncle must have felt the two steel fingers of the prosthesis: he shot Bruno a quick, pained look. After which he was overcome by a fit of coughing, bringing tears to his eyes.

"I smoke too much," he grumbled.

Bruno asked to see the *gnamas*, and my uncle brought him to the workshop, where several children were busy with paper and pots of glue.

"You've already seen them all," Ambrose Fleury said. "I'm not making any new ones right now, just sticking to the old. These days, we need memory more than innovation. And we can't fly them any more. The Germans don't give them enough height. First they limited us to a hundred feet, then fifty, and now they're all but demanding that I teach my kites to crawl. They're afraid they might serve as orientation markers for Allied aviators when they're in the sky, or maybe some kind of coded message to the Resistance. They're not entirely wrong, really."

He coughed for quite a while again, uncomfortably, and Bruno rushed to answer his unspoken question: "Unfortunately, I have no news of my family. But I'm not worried about Lila. She'll be back."

"We're all entirely certain of that here," my uncle said, glancing over at me.

We stayed at La Motte for another hour, and my guardian asked Bruno to contact Lord Howe and send a message of friendship and gratitude from Ambrose Fleury to the members of the Order of the Kites of England, to whom the "Cléry chapter" sent a fraternal salute.

"It's extraordinary how they stood firm, all alone, in 1940."

And then he came out with this slightly comical phrase, which surprised me, coming from such a modest man: "I'm happy to have been useful for something," he said.

Bruno set off on the escape route to Spain that very evening, and two weeks later we received a "personal message" from the BBC confirming his arrival in England: "The virtuoso has returned to his piano." Our encounter had shaken me deeply. It was like a first sign of the end of the impossible, the promise of another return. I couldn't help seeing a benevolent signal from God in this breach in probability distribution. Unbeliever that I was, I thought of God frequently—now, more than ever, it was a time when man needed to keep all his most beautiful creations around him. As I've said before, as if in apology, that while being so preoccupied by all the things I was doing to hasten her return, I felt Lila's physical presence by my side less and less often. But even that I took as a good sign, like when she'd stopped writing to me from Gródek, because our reunion was so imminent. I lived in the premonition of this imminence. It seemed to me that at any moment, the door might open and ... It was only an incantation. All it changed was my relationship with doors. Becoming more sure of her survival, I didn't need to invent her anymore, and contented myself with memory. I recalled our walks on the shores of the Baltic, when Lila dreamed of herself with so much frustration and fervor.

"The only way I can make it is to write something amazing. No woman has ever yet written *War and Peace*. Maybe that's what I should do ..."

"Tolstoy already wrote it."

"Stop it, Ludo! Every time I try to do something with my life, you hold me back! Goddammit!"

"Personally, Lila, I have no ambition to become the first woman Tolstoy, but—"

"Oh, sarcasm, now! That's just what we needed!"

I laughed. I was almost happy. From my memory I drew the strength, as Ambrose Fleury put it, "that the French need to pull the sun up over the horizon."

35

WITH SABOTAGES BECOMING MORE FREQUENT, THE Germans began to see "enemy agents" everywhere, an obsession comparable to the hysteria over spying that overcame the French in 1939–40. The occupier tightened its embrace and even Duprat was hassled. This despite the fact that Grüber, the head of the Gestapo in Normandy, was a frequent customer of the Clos Joli. I believe that what interested him more than anything was the relationship between the Wehrmacht's senior officers and the French.

Grüber was a thickset man with pallid skin and dirty blond hair cut close to his ears. From time to time I would observe him tasting the restaurant's delicacies, and be struck by his attitude, which was attentive and contemptuous all at once. The looks on the faces of certain Germans, the highly cultivated ones, such as General von Tiele or Otto Abetz, were expressions of admiration mixed with profound satisfaction, as if, having conquered France, they had come to our table in order to savor its peerless uniqueness. For many Germans, then as now, I think that France was and remains a place for delectation, meant entirely for that. All of this is to say that I was accustomed to the whole spectrum of expressions with which our conquerors savored even a simple *coq au vin* or a *cassolette duchesse*. As for what was actually going through their heads, I had no idea. Perhaps it was a kind of symbolic rite, not all that different from the rites of the great dead civilizations of the Incas or the Aztecs, in which the victor tore out the heart of the vanquished and ate it in order to possess his soul and spirit. But the face Grüber made as he chewed was very different from what I was used to observing: it contained, as I have said, the skeptical and slightly disdainful—or at any rate sardonic—awareness of a man who was not easily intimidated.

It was Lucien Duprat who put his finger on it: "Look at him. He's *investigating*. He wants to know what's in it."

That was exactly it. I think a lot of Germans stationed in France during the Occupation were asking themselves that question.

And yet it was hard to understand how a man as uncultivated as Grüber could be so fascinated by the Clos Joli. Duprat's expression—"he senses the enemy"—did not seem to line up with the man's unsophisticated nature, especially since he never missed an opportunity to say how "decadent" the restaurant was.

Marcellin Duprat didn't trouble himself much over Grüber, despite the fact that he was the one making sure that the Clos Joli was kept supplied, in total disregard of all the regulations at that time. Duprat knew he was protected from high up, and, to be sure, the Germans had been trying to accommodate the French elites and assure their cooperation since the beginning of the Occupation. For Duprat, the explanation for this policy was simple: the talk among leaders of the Third Reich was of "building Europe," and they were trying hard to show that within this Europe, France would occupy the place that was rightfully hers. But even supposing that Grüber did have strict instructions regarding the restaurant, and was respecting them in spite of himself, this did little to explain the spiteful and almost hateful air with which he ate his *boudin d'huîtres*, as if hidden inside it was some kind of challenge to his Nazi faith. According to Duprat, who would observe him occasionally with a quietly mocking air, he behaved like a man who was being defeated on the Russian and Western Fronts all at once.

All that notwithstanding, it came as a surprise to everyone when, on March 2, 1942, with total disregard of all the orders about "collaboration," he arrested Marcellin Duprat. The restaurant was closed for eight days, and the affair took on such proportions that after the war they found indignant telegrams from Otto Abetz to Berlin, including this one, cited by Sterner: "The führer himself has given orders that major landmarks of French history be respected."

Duprat returned from his week in prison furious and somewhat proud—"I stood up to them, and that's that"—but he refused to tell us what had led Grüber to question and detain him. In Cléry, it was rumored to have something to do with the black market, some sort of hike in the price of palm-greasing that Marcellin had balked at. There was also the fact that Duprat was protected by von Tiele—relations between the Nazis and the Wehrmacht "caste" were at that time deteriorating rapidly. Personally, I was convinced that Grüber had wanted to remind everyone who was really in charge at the Clos Joli.

My uncle seemed to have another idea entirely. I never knew whether the good turn he did for his pal Marcellin was deliberate or not—he did like a good laugh. Maybe he'd simply had one glass too many with his friends at the bar of the Petit-Gris when he tossed out to them: "They questioned that old Marcellin for days. He stood firm."

"But what did they want from him?" demanded Monsieur Meunier, the owner.

"The recipe, doggone it!"

There was a long silence. At the bar that night, in addition to the owner, was Gaston Cailleux, our neighbor, along with Antoine Vaille, the one whose son's name is now on the war monument.

"What recipe?" Monsieur Meunier inquired, at length.

"The recipe," my uncle repeated. "The Krauts wanted to know what's in it: *lapereau du fermier au vinaigre de framboise, blanc de volaille cathédrale de Chartres*—the whole damn menu. And that old devil wouldn't talk. Even under torture—they tried their worst, even the bathtub—but he stood firm. He wouldn't even let slip the recipe for his *panade aux trois sauces.* Kids, some folks will fold after the first wallop, but not our Marcellin. They nearly killed him, but he wouldn't say a word."

The three old men laughed. My uncle didn't even have to wink at them.

"Personally," said Cailleux, "I was sure that old national treasure wouldn't talk. The recipe of the Clos Joli is sacred. God almighty, that sure is something, isn't it?"

"We all feel it," said Vaille.

The owner refilled their glasses.

"Got to let people know," murmured my uncle.

"And how!" Vaille roared. "Your grandchildren will tell their grandchildren, they will. And on down the line."

"Right on down the line," Cailleux agreed. "It's the least we can do for him."

"Have to do what it takes," my uncle concluded.

As you may recall, the story of the great French chef who refused to give his recipes to the Germans, even under torture, was published in September 1945 in the *Stars and Stripes*, the American Armed Forces' newspaper. It made a big splash in America. When they asked Marcellin Duprat for his own thoughts on the matter, he shrugged. "They say all kinds of things. What can be said is that I represented something the Nazis couldn't stand: an invincible France that was going to pull through yet again. That's all. So they tried to give me a rough time. But as for the rest ... I'm telling you, it's nonsense."

"You're too modest, Marcellin," my uncle would tell him.

I was there for some episodes in the birth of "the legend," when Duprat would grow angry and deny "all that bullshit." At those times my uncle Ambrose would put his arm around Duprat's shoulders and say gravely: "Come now, Marcellin. Come now. Some things are bigger than all of us. Show a little humility. The Clos Joli lived through some terrible times, and it needs to rebuild."

Marcellin Duprat grumbled about it for a while, but in the end he let it be said.

36

ON MARCH 27, 1942, THE WEATHER WAS COLD AND gray. I had a transport to deliver in Verrières, six miles from Cléry: two new AMK II receivers, and a number of "curiosities," including timed explosive devices in the shape of goat cheeses, and exploding cigarettes, all of it hidden in the wagon box between the boards and under the hay. I had picked the materials up at the Buis' and Dr. Gardieu had lent me his cart; Clémentin the horse was walking along at a steady clip. Just for show, I had placed a few kites on the hay; Ambrose Fleury's workshop still had a good reputation, and was even listed among the Youth Department's "activities to encourage," as the mayor of Cléry himself had let us know.

My route followed the road that ran along the grounds of Le Manoir des Jars; arriving before the gate, I noticed it had been left wide open. I had a rather strange proprietary feeling about the manor—or, more precisely, a feeling that I was the keeper of its memory. I accepted no intrusions, although I was aware there wasn't much I could do about them. I stopped Clémentin, got down from the wagon, and made my way up the main driveway. There were about a hundred yards to cover. I was some twenty paces from the fountain when I noticed a man seated on the stone bench, to my right, beneath the bare chestnut trees. His head was lowered and his nose was hidden in the fur collar of his coat: he had a cane in his hand and was using it to trace signs in the dirt. It was Stas Bronicki. I felt no emotion; my heart did not skip a beat; I'd always known that life was not without meaning, and that it was doing its best, even if fell short from time to time. *They* had returned. I moved closer. Bronicki did not appear to see me. He was looking at his feet. He had traced out several numbers with the tip of his cane, and had pushed a dead chestnut over one of them.

Von Tiele's Mercedes was parked in front of the ruined manor; brambles had grown up through the half-crumbled veranda and stairs; the roof and the attic had disappeared. The upper floors had gone up in flames; all that had remained intact, blackened by fire, was the lower portion of the façade around the entrance, its windows gaping with emptiness. The only rooms that had escaped the flames were those on the ground floor. The door had been ripped off its hinges by someone scavenging wood for the winter.

From inside the building, I heard Lila's laughter.

I stood there motionless, my eyes raised. I saw first Hans, then General von Tiele emerge; another moment, and I saw Lila. I walked forward a step or two and she saw me. She didn't seem surprised. I remained immobile. There was, in this apparition, something so simple and so natural that even today I can't say whether this absence of reaction was the effect of a shock so great that it emptied me of all sensation. I lifted my cap, like a servant.

Lila was wearing a white, fur-lined jacket and a beret; she had several books under her arm. She descended the steps, walked over to me, and held out a gloved hand, smiling.

"Oh, hello Ludo. I'm happy to see you again. I was just thinking about coming to visit you. Are you well?"

I remained silent. This time, I began feeling a bewilderment rise within me that metamorphosed into fear and panic. "I'm fine. And you?"

"Oh, you know, what with all these horrors and everything that's happening, I can say we've been lucky. Except for my father, who's ...

Well, it's medical, and they think it will get better. I'm sorry I haven't been by La Motte yet, I promise I've been thinking about it."

"Really."

All of this was so polite, so well mannered, that it was starting to feel like a nightmare to me.

"I came here to see what remained," she said. I think she was talking about the manor. "Almost everything burned, but I was able to salvage some books. You see: a Proust, a Mallarmé, a Valéry … There's really not much left."

"No," I answered. And then murmured: "But it will come back."

"I'm sorry? What do you mean?"

"It will come back."

She laughed. "You haven't changed, have you? Still a little strange."

"I suffer from an excess of memory, as you know."

This seemed to irk her, she appeared slightly flustered, but she pulled herself together and looked at me with kindness.

"I know. You mustn't. Obviously, with all this … misfortune, the past is even happier, because it's even further away."

"Yes, that's true. And … Tad?"

"He stayed in Poland. He didn't want to leave. He's in the Resistance."

Von Tiele and Hans were just steps away and could hear us.

"I always knew Tad would do great things," Lila said. "Actually, we all thought so. He's one of the men who will take Poland's destiny in hand one day … Well, whatever's left of it."

Von Tiele had turned discreetly away from us.

"Did you think of me a little, Ludo?"

"Yes."

Her gaze disappeared somewhere among the treetops. "It was another world," she said. "It seems centuries since then. Well, I won't keep my friends waiting any longer. How is your uncle?"

"He keeps at it."

"Still with his kites?"

"Always. But he's not allowed to fly them very high anymore, now."

"Give him my love. Well, see you soon, Ludo. I'll be sure to drop by and visit. We have so much to catch up about. You weren't drafted?"

"No. I was declared unfit. Apparently I'm a little crazy. Runs in the family."

She brushed my arm with her fingertips and went to help her father into the car. She sat down between him and General von Tiele. Hans seated himself behind the wheel.

I heard crows laughing.

Lila waved at me. I waved back. The Mercedes disappeared down the drive.

I sat there for a long time, trying to locate myself again. The feeling of not being there anymore, not elsewhere, not anywhere, and then a slow wave of despair rose in me. I struggled. I didn't want to cross over to the enemy. Despair is always a surrender.

Numb, incapable of movement, I stood upright on the gravel, my cap in my hand, and as the minutes ticked away, the feeling of unreality intensified before the ruins, in these ghostly grounds with their frost-whitened trees, where everything swam in immobility and lifelessness.

It wasn't true. It wasn't possible. My imagination had played this trick on me, it had tortured me as revenge for all I had demanded of it for so many years. Just another vision, another waking dream I had let myself enter too easily—and now it was having my head. This apparition couldn't be Lila—so politely sophisticated, so indifferent, and so far removed from the woman who had lived with such intensity in my memory for nearly four years. That detached voice, her very politeness while conversing with me, the total absence of any trace of our past in the chilly blue of her gaze—no, none of that had actually happened, my malady had simply worsened with the weight of solitude; I had overnourished my "folly" and was now paying the price. A phantasm of horror, brought on by nervous exhaustion and passing discouragement.

In the end, I managed to wrench myself out of my collapse, and made for the gate.

I had walked a few steps when I noticed the bench where I had first thought I'd seen Stas Bronicki sitting a little while earlier, tracing imaginary roulette numbers into the dirt with the tip of his cane.

I hardly dared lower my eyes to look, to be sure.

The numbers really were there, with a dead leaf bet on the number seven.

Barely conscious of what I was doing, I managed to drop my delivery off at Verrières, and made it home. My uncle was in the kitchen. He had a drink or two in him and was seated near the fire, stroking Grimaud the cat, who was asleep in his lap. I had trouble speaking.

"She hasn't left me for a single instant since she's been gone, and now that she's back, she's another …"

"Another lady, my man. You invented her too much. Four years of absence leaves way too much up to the imagination. The dream has landed, now; that always does some damage. Even ideas quit looking like themselves when they're embodied. Wait till you see our faces when France returns! Everyone will be saying, 'That's not the real France, it's different!' The Germans have given us a lot of imagination. The reunion will be cruel once they're gone. But something tells me you'll get her back, your little lady. Love has genius, and it has the gift of taking everything you throw at it. As for you, you thought you were living off memory, but you were actually mostly living in your imagination."

He laughed.

"And imagination, Ludo, is no way to treat a lady."

At one o'clock in the morning, I was standing at my window, my face in flames, awaiting I don't know what maternal caress from the night. I heard a car, a long silence, the steps creaking, the door open behind me. I turned around: my uncle stood there alone for an instant, lamp in hand, and then he disappeared and I saw Lila. She was sobbing, and the sounds of her weeping seemed to emerge from the night of some dark forest. A moan that seemed to ask to be forgiven for itself, because no one had the right to so much sorrow, to so much suffering. I rushed toward her, but she gestured me away.

"No, Ludo. Don't touch me. Later, maybe, later. First you have to know ... you have to understand ..."

I took her hand. She sat down on the edge of the bed, wrapped in her fur jacket, her hands folded demurely in her lap. We were silent. Outside, we heard the creak of winter branches. In her eyes was an inquisitive expression, almost supplicating, and a hesitation, as if she still wasn't sure she could trust me. I waited. I knew the cause of her hesitation. Most likely I was still the Ludo she had known, the little Norman country boy who had spent the three years of war near his uncle and his kites, and who couldn't understand her. And in everything she would tell me that night, the words, "Do you understand, Ludo? Do you understand?" returned without cease, her tone anxious and almost desperate, as if she were certain that these admissions, these confessions, were beyond anything that I could conceive of or accept, let alone forgive.

She looked at me imploringly again, then began to speak; it felt to me that her need to talk was less about letting me know as it was about attempting to let herself forget.

I listened. I sat on the other end of the bed and listened. Trembling a little, but I had to face it somehow. She smoked cigarette after cigarette, me lighting them for her as she continued. The petrol lamp conjoined our two shadows on the wall.

On September 1, 1939, at 4:45 a.m., the German battleship *Schleswig-Holstein*, without a declaration of war, had opened fire on the Polish garrison that was located on the Gródek Peninsula. In the hours and days that followed, the rest of the dirty work had been finished off by the German air force.

"We were all caught in the bombing ... Tad was able to join his combat group—you know, the one that was holding political meetings when you were staying with us ..."

"I remember."

"Bruno had left two weeks before that for England ... We were able to take refuge on a farm ... My father was in a state of shock, my mother was completely hysterical ... Luckily, I met a German officer who was a gentleman ..."

"There are some."

She glanced at me fearfully.

"First off I had to survive, save my family ... Do you understand, Ludo? Do you understand?"

I understood.

"It lasted three months ... then he was sent somewhere and ..."

She trailed off. I didn't ask her: And after that one, who? How many others? With the memory I had, I wasn't about to start keeping those kinds of accounts. *First off I had to survive, save my family ...*

"If Hans hadn't found us—we were able to flee to Warsaw—I don't know what would have become of us ... He'd fought in the French campaign and had managed to have himself stationed in Poland, just so he could take care of us ..."

"Of you."

"He wanted to marry me, but the Nazis forbade marriage with Polish women ..."

"And to think I might have killed him!" I exclaimed. "First I could have strangled him, when he jumped me at Vieille-Source when we were kids, and then in our duel at Gródek ... There really is a God!"

I shouldn't have put so much sarcasm in my voice. I was taking the easy way out.

She looked me over.

"You've changed, Ludo."

"Forgive me, darling."

"When Hitler attacked Russia, Hans followed General von Tiele to the Smolensk front ... We managed to flee to Romania ... At first, we had some jewelry left, but then ..."

She had become the mistress of a Romanian diplomat, then of a doctor who had seen to her—an abortion that had almost cost her life ...

"Do you understand, Ludo? Do you understand?"

I understood. You had to survive, to save your family. She had made "friends" in diplomatic circles. Her mother and father had wanted for nothing. All in all, she had made out all right in the survival game.

"In 1941, we were finally granted French visas, thanks to someone at the embassy who I ... who I knew ... But we didn't have a single cent left, and ..."

She trailed off.

I felt a tranquility grow and smile inside of me, as if I knew that, fundamentally, nothing could happen to us. I couldn't really say what I mean by "fundamentally," and since we never know how others love, I don't want to seem like I'm boasting. Fluttering briefly across my mind appeared an image of our lovely kite Fourseas, sailing magnificent in the blue sky, and then vanishing, then turning up again, covered in scrapes and bumps, shattered and torn. Maybe the suffering had called out some ancient Christian fiber in me, but as I've said, I'd acquired an acute sense of insignificance. And besides that, to hell with that dear old saw, "to understand all is to forgive all," which Monsieur Pinder long ago assigned to us as a composition topic in class. "To understand all is to forgive all" loiters in the dark corners where renunciation and resignation are found. Really, I didn't show any "tolerance" with Lila. The line from tolerance to the intolerable is all too easy to trace, and we're usually led there by the nose. I loved a woman with all her sorrows, that's all.

Her eyes, when she lifted them to me, were intense.

"There were so many times I wanted to get in touch with you; I wanted to come here, but I felt so ... I felt ..."

"Like a tramp?"

She said nothing.

"Listen to me, Lila. In this time and place, being a tramp is no kind of sin. In any time and place, really. Where your ass has been is the least of our worries. Tramphood is pretty much sainthood, compared to all the rest."

"You've changed so much, Ludo!"

"Maybe. The Germans helped me a lot. The inhumanity of it is what makes Nazism so horrible—that's what people always say. Sure. But there's no denying the obvious: part of being human is the inhumanity of it. As long as we refuse to admit that inhumanity is completely human, we'll just be telling ourselves pious lies."

Grimaud the cat made his entrance, tail up, rubbing himself against our legs, demanding to be petted.

"In Paris, those first six months, you can't imagine ... We didn't know a soul anymore. I worked as a waitress in a brasserie, as a shop-girl at the Prisunic supermarket ... My mother was suffering from terrible migraines ..."

"Ah. Migraines. They can be awful."

As for Lila's father, he had, so to speak, lost his sight. A kind of mental blindness. He had closed his eyes on the world.

"My mother and I had to care for him like a child. He was a friend of Thomas Mann's, of Stefan Zweig's, a man for whom Europe was an incomparable light ... And when that light went out and every-thing we believed in crumbled, he retreated from reality, so to speak ... A complete atrophy of the senses."

Well, shit, I thought. That's very convenient.

"The doctors tried everything ..."

I almost asked, "Even a kick in the ass?" but you had to respect that old aristocratic porcelain. I was sure that Bronicki had found the thing he needed to let him off-load all responsibility onto his wife and daughter. He could not, after all, allow himself to know what his daughter was doing to "survive, to save my family." He was defending his honor, you might say.

"Then I was able to find work as a mannequin for Coco Chanel …"

"Coco who?"

"Chanel … You know, the famous clothing designer …"

"Oh right, of course … The Clos Joli!"

"Pardon?"

"No, nothing."

"But I wasn't making enough to take care of my parents and all that …"

A pause. Grimaud the cat moved back and forth between us, surprised at our indifference. The pause lasted, slipped inside me, invaded me entirely. I waited for the "Do you understand, Ludo? Do you understand?" But there was only the mute distress of that gaze, and I lowered my eyes.

"Georg saved us."

"Georg?"

"Georg von Tiele. Hans's uncle. Our estates bordered each other on the Baltic …"

"Yes, yes. Your estates. Of course."

"He was posted in France. As soon as he heard we were in Paris, he took care of everything. He moved my parents into an apartment near the Parc Monceau. And then Hans came back from the Eastern Front …" She perked up.

"You know, I even got to go back to my studies. I got my *baccalauréat* from the French Lycée in Warsaw. I'm going to apply to the Sorbonne and maybe the École du Louvre, as well. I'm fascinated by art history."

"By … art history?"

I was having trouble swallowing.

"Yes. I think I've found my calling. Do you remember how I was looking for myself? I think I've found myself now."

"At just the right time."

"Obviously, it'll take a lot of courage and perseverance, but I think I can do it. I would have liked to go Italy, to Florence more than anything, to see the museums … The Renaissance, you know. But it'll have to wait."

"The Renaissance can wait, it's true."

She rose.

"Shall I see you out?"

"No, thank you. Hans is outside, in the car." She stopped at the door.

"Don't forget me, Ludo."

"I don't have much of a gift for forgetting."

I followed her down the stairs.

"Bruno's in England. He's a fighter pilot over there."

Her face lit up.

"Bruno? But he was so clumsy!"

"Not in the sky, apparently."

I didn't tell her about the fingers.

"I owe you everything," she said.

"I really don't know why."

"You kept me whole. I thought I had lost myself, and now I feel like that's not true and that I was here all along—three and a half years!—here, with you, safe and sound. Whole. Keep me like that, Ludo. I need it. Give me a little more time. I need to put myself together again."

"Art history can really help you with that. Especially the Renaissance."

"Don't tease me."

She lingered a moment more, then left me, and there was only one shadow left on the wall.

I was calm. I was, with millions of other men, crossing over on a path along which each of us would gather up his own supply of sorrow.

I went to join my uncle in the kitchen. He poured me a glass, observing me discreetly.

"It sure will be funny," he said.

"What will?"

"When France returns. I hope we'll recognize her."

I clenched my fists.

"Yeah, well, I couldn't care less what she looks like or what she did while she was away. Just so long as she comes back, that's all."

My uncle sighed.

"No talking to this one anymore," he grumbled.

I was not spared the rumor that Lila had become von Tiele's mistress. I remained as indifferent to this idle gossip as I was to the other voices whining about how "France was done for," that it "would never be the same," that it had "lost its soul," and that the Resistance fighters were "dying for nothing." I felt too deeply certain of the need to trot it out for a breather, as we say around here about the kind of people who need to give everything an airing.

37

I NO LONGER HATED THE GERMANS. FOUR YEARS AF-
ter the defeat, it was difficult for me to engage in the routine of reducing Germany to its crimes and France to its heroes, given all the
things I'd seen happen around me. I'd learned a fraternity very different from those glossy platitudes: it seemed to me that we were
indissolubly linked by what made us different from one another,
which could be upturned at any moment to make us cruelly similar.
Sometimes I even believed that in the struggle I'd signed up for, I was
helping our enemies, as well. There are consequences to being raised
by a man who spent his life looking heavenward.

I saw a German killed for the first time in the fields beyond La
Gragne, where we had cleared out a landing strip. There were three of
us that night, awaiting the arrival of a Lysander, which was supposed
to escort an unnamed politician to England. The surroundings had
been carefully inspected several times since sunset; our orders were
to proceed with the utmost caution; just two weeks prior, a team in
Haute-Seine had been taken unawares while receiving an airdrop, and
we'd had to add five more names to our list of firing-squad victims.

The beacons were lit at one in the morning, and precisely twenty
minutes later the Lysander made its approach. We helped the passen-
ger board the plane; the Lysander lifted off; and we set out to collect
the lamps. We were on the way back, three hundred yards from the
strip, when Janin grabbed my arm; I saw a metallic flash in the grass

to our right and heard a furtive movement; the metal gleam moved and disappeared.

There was a bicycle, a girl, and a German soldier. I recognized the girl: she worked at Monsieur Boyer's bakery, in Cléry. The soldier was lying flat on his stomach beside her; he stared up at us with no expression in his face.

I don't know whether it was Janin or Rollin who pulled the trigger. The soldier simply lowered his head and remained that way, his face to the ground.

The girl pulled away abruptly, as if he had become disgusting.

"Get up."

She rose quickly, arranging her skirt.

"Please don't say anything," she murmured.

Janin looked surprised. He was from Paris and didn't know village life. And then he got it, smiled, and lowered his gun.

"What's your name?"

"Mariette."

"Mariette what?"

"Mariette Fontet. Monsieur Ludovic knows me. Please don't say anything to my parents."

"Okay. We won't say anything, take it easy. You can go home."

He glanced at the body.

"Hope he didn't have time," he said.

Mariette broke down and sobbed.

It was a bad night for me. I felt as if I'd gone over to the other side. I tried to think of all our men who'd been killed, but this only made it one more.

A few days later, I walked into the bakery and stood there, as if I had something to apologize for. Mariette blushed and hesitated. Then she came up to me and murmured anxiously, "They won't go telling my parents, at least?"

It wasn't proper for a girl to lay in the hay with some man. I think that was the only thing that bothered her. We had nothing to fear.

Several times, I saw Lila come through Cléry in von Tiele's Mercedes; once in the company of the general himself. One morning, as I was bicycling home from a drill at the Grollet's farm, where we were learning how to handle some new explosives from a comrade who had trained in England, the Mercedes passed and then stopped. I stopped, too. Lila was alone in the car, with the driver. She had dark circles under her eyes; her eyelids were puffy. It was seven in the morning; I knew there had been a party the night before at Lady Esterhazy's, whose order from the Clos Joli included champagne and Norwegian salmon, and that Duprat himself had been at the house to oversee his *sauté d'agneau de lait* and his *coq au vin*, which "the tiniest bit of garlic—too much or too little—could kill." The utmost care was to be taken; all the German top brass would be there. "In this line of work," he'd growled, "your reputation goes back on the line every goddamn time."

Lila needed my help getting out of the car: she had some drink in her. Beneath her white trench coat she wore a very chic red dress and red shoes with high heels. There was a thick red-and-white woolen shawl around her neck and shoulders. The colors of Poland, I thought. She was excessively made up, as if she'd wanted to hide her face. Perched on her hair, as if forgotten there by another life, was her beret. Only her gaze, in its blue distress, was locally grown. She held a book in her hand: Apollinaire. We had all of Hugo at La Motte, but not a single Apollinaire. One always forgets things.

"Hello, my Ludo."

I kissed her. The military driver had his back to us.

"There's a lot of talk about me around here, isn't there?"

"I'm a little hard of hearing, you know."

"They say I'm von Tiele's mistress."

"They do say."

"It's not true. Georg is a friend of my father's. Our families have been joined since forever. You have to believe me, Ludo."

"I believe you, but I don't give a damn."

She began speaking feverishly of her parents. They lacked nothing, thanks to Georg.

"He's an admirable man. He's openly anti-Nazi. He's even saved Jews."

"That's normal. He has two hands."

"What does that mean? What are you talking about?"

"It's not me, it's William Blake. There's a Blake poem about that. *One of his hands was covered in blood. The other carried the torch.* Why don't you come see me?"

"I'll come. I have to find myself again, you know. Do you think of me a little?"

"Every so often I don't think about you. I draw a blank—it can happen to anyone."

"I feel a little lost. I don't even know where I am with my life. I drink too much. I'm trying to forget myself."

I took the book from her hands and leafed through it.

"Apparently Frenchmen are reading more than ever before. You know Monsieur Jolliot, the bookseller …"

"I know him very well," she said, with unexpected vehemence. "He's a friend. I go to his shop nearly every day."

"Well, he says that the French have taken to poetry with the courage that's born of despair. How's your father?"

"He's completely retreated from reality. A total atrophy of the senses. But there's hope. Occasionally he shows signs of consciousness. Maybe he'll come back to himself."

I couldn't help feeling a certain admiration for Stas Bronicki. The way that aristocratic pimp had figured out how to shield himself from base circumstance was pretty breathtaking—protected from all contact with a repugnant historical era by his wife and his daughter. A real elitist.

"Never saw such a clever old rogue," I said.

"Ludo! I forbid you to—"

"Sorry. That's my country ass talking. I must have some kind of hereditary grudge against nobs."

We walked a few steps, to get a little distance between ourselves and the driver.

"You know, things are going to change soon, Ludo. The German generals don't want a war on two fronts. And they can't stand Hitler. One day—"

"Yeah, I know that theory. I already heard it from Hans, right before the invasion of Poland."

"Just give it a little more time. Things aren't going badly enough for the Germans yet …"

"Well, no, they're not."

"But I'll pull it off."

"Pull what off?"

She was silent, gazing directly in front of her.

"I need more time," she said again. "Of course, it's very difficult, and sometimes I get shaky and lose my nerve … So I drink too much. I shouldn't. But I'm sure, with a little luck …"

"What? What, with a little luck?"

Shivering, she pulled her Polish colors closer around her.

"I always wanted to make something of my life. Something grand and … terribly important …"

The dream was still crawling.

"Yes," I said. "You always did want to save the world."

She smiled, "No, that was Tad. But who knows …"

I knew that slightly mysterious, impenetrable air so well, the one Tad used to call "her Garbo face."

"Maybe it'll be me," she said placidly.

It was pitiful. She could barely keep herself upright; I had to help her back into the car. I arranged the blanket around her knees. She remained silent another moment, the little volume of Apollinaire in her hands, a smile on her lips, her gaze lost in the distance. And then suddenly she turned to me in a burst of warmth, with a voice so grave, almost solemn, that it took me by surprise.

"Trust me, Ludo. You all have to trust me, just a little longer. I'll pull it off. I'll leave my mark on history. And I'll make you proud."

I kissed her on her forehead.

"There, there," I told her. "Don't be scared, now. They lived happily ever after and had lots of children."

I have no excuses. I paid absolutely no heed to the words of the woman everyone at the Clos Joli called "that poor little Polish girl, with her Germans." Just as fantastical, just as wildly fanciful as she ever was. I stood by the side of the road with my bicycle, watching sadly as the Mercedes drove off. "I'll leave my mark on history. And I'll make you proud …" It was so terribly pathetic. It seemed to me that, in her free fall, Lila's need to dream of herself was even greater than before, at Le Manoir des Jars, on the shores of the Baltic—fallen, crushed on the ground, the broken dream continued to feebly flutter its wings. I had not the slightest suspicion, no inkling, no trace of a premonition. Perhaps it was the years of struggle and their implacable demands—maybe with all that pressure to "live reasonably," I was beginning to run short on folly. I had no idea that of all the far-flung kites, lost in search of the blue yonder, the Polish one would fly the highest—and come the closest to changing the course of the war.

38

I DIDN'T SEE LILA AGAIN FOR SEVERAL MONTHS.

The summer of 1942 was a turning point for the underground. In a single night, in the Fougerolles-du-Plessis region, "the devil passed six times," according to the coded message: that meant six airdrops, mostly antitank mines, bazookas, and mortars. The supplies had to be hidden away within a few hours. In Sauvagne, my classmate André Fernin was arrested for possession of fifty incendiary devices; he barely had time to swallow his cyanide. Nowadays these stories are so well known they've been forgotten. They carried out search after search in our area, and didn't spare La Motte—either someone denounced us, or maybe the Gestapo sensed a natural enemy in Ambrose Fleury. None of their searches produced anything—the Buis cache, for example, where Bruno had been hidden, functioned all the way to V-E day. In the workshop, Grüber had gotten his hands on our old Zola, forgotten in a corner, with the words *J'accuse* radiating in a halo around his head, but he hadn't recognized the likeness, and merely asked, "Who's he accusing, *der Kerl*?"

"It's the title of a very famous song from the turn of the century. The woman walks out with her lover, and the man accuses her of being unfaithful."

"He doesn't look like a singer."

"All the same, he had a very good voice."

The Cléry police commissioner himself had issued a friendly warning to Ambrose Fleury, with a bit of a smile—it seemed comical to him, the idea that this gentle pacifist might be mixed up in some kind of subversive activity.

"My good Ambrose, any minute now, they probably imagine you'll be flying the Cross of Lorraine!"

"You know me—that sort of thing…" my uncle observed.

"I know, I know."

But dreamers have a kind of ill repute; there's an everlasting and organic link between dreaming and rebellion. We were kept under surveillance, and for a while our weapons cache was unusable. It was located under the manure pit and beneath the outhouse, which we had been careful not to empty for some months.

And yet it was during this particularly dangerous period for us that my uncle let himself go with a gesture of madness. News of the Vel' d'Hiv roundup made it to Cléry toward the end of July 1942. We were at the Clos Joli that evening, meeting around an old bottle, as the master of the place frequently invited his friend Ambrose Fleury to do. Duprat, who had a way with words, would on some of these occasions read us a poem he had written in alexandrines. But that evening, he seemed to be in a particularly dark mood.

"Did you hear the news, Ambrose? About the Vel' d'Hiv roundup?"

"What roundup?"

"They rounded up all the Jews and deported them to Germany."

My uncle was silent. In that moment, there were no more kites for him to hang on to. Duprat slammed his fist on the table.

"The children, too," he growled. "They handed over the children, too. We'll never see them back alive."

Ambrose Fleury was holding a glass of wine. It was the only time in my life I saw his hand tremble.

"Well, there you go. I'll tell you what, Ambrose. It's a real blow to the Clos Joli. You might ask what the one thing has to do with the other—but it has *everything* to do with it. *Everything.* Goddammit. For a man such as myself, working my way into an early grave to preserve a certain image of France, it's impossible to accept such a thing. Can you imagine? Children. They're sending children off to die. Do you know what I'm going to do? I'm going to close this place for a week. In protest. Obviously, I'll open up again after that—nothing would please the Nazis more than to see me shut my doors for good. They've been trying to break me for a long time. All they want is for France to give up on itself. But my mind is made up. I'm closing down for eight days. They don't go together, the Clos Joli and handing kids over to the Boche."

No one had ever yet heard Duprat utter the word "Boche."

My uncle set his glass down on the table and stood up. His face had gone gray and the number of his wrinkles appeared to have doubled. We rode our creaky bicycles through the night. The moon shone brightly. When we reached the house, he left me without a word and shut himself in his workshop. I couldn't sleep. I suddenly understood how much we'd been using the Germans, and even the Nazis, for cover. For quite a while now, an idea had been working its way into my mind, one that I had a lot of trouble getting rid of afterward; maybe I never really managed to shake it off. The Nazis were *human beings.* And the thing that was human in them was their inhumanity.

I left La Motte at four in the morning: I had to go to Ronce, to see Soubabère. We were supposed to map out some new landing strips together. Also, I wanted to let our comrades know they should steer clear of La Motte for a while. As I set out from the house, I noticed the lights were still on in the workshop. With no little irritation, I remarked to myself that you had to be a real bullheaded Frenchman to be assembling kites in such a despicable time. Children had always been their best friends. If Ambrose Fleury took it into his head to launch his Montaigne or his Pascal into the sky right now, it seemed to me that the sky would spit it right back in his face.

I returned to the house the next day, at around eleven in the morning. I walked the last few miles, pushing my bicycle. I had already patched up both tires a dozen times, and I had to make thrift of what was left. I'd arrived at the place known as Le Petit Passage, where there's now a monument to Jean Vigot, sixteen, who was arrested by the Milice just after the Allied landing with his weapons at the ready, and was shot dead on the spot. I stopped to light a cigarette, but it fell from my lips.

There in the sky above La Motte, were seven kites. Seven yellow kites. Seven kites in the form of Jewish stars. I dropped my bike and began to run. My uncle Ambrose stood in the meadow in front of the house, surrounded by a few kids from Clos. His eyes were raised to the sky, at those seven stars of shame floating there. Jaws tightened, brow furrowed, his hardened face clenched between his gray crew cut and his mustache, the old man looked like a figurehead that had lost its ship. The children, five boys and a little girl—I knew them all, the Fourniers, the Blancs, and the Bossis—all looked grave.

I murmured, "They're going to come …"

But it was the others who came first. Oh, not many of them: the Cailleux, the Monniers, and old man Simon. He was the first to take off his cap.

My uncle was arrested that evening, and held for fifteen days. It was Marcellin Duprat who got him out. All of us were certified, in the Fleury family, from father to son—it was a known fact, he explained to them. A hereditary madness. It was what they used to call "the French sickness," it came from way back. You couldn't take us seriously, or if you did, you were risking serious trouble. Duprat pulled every string, and he had a lot of them to pull, from Otto Abetz to Fernand de Brinon. The day after the arrest, Grüber's Citroën stopped in front of the house, followed by a truck full of soldiers. They threw all the kites into the meadow and set them on fire. Grüber, his hands clasped behind his back, watched as the flames consumed what old French hands had so lovingly assembled.

La Motte was searched like never before. Grüber had recognized the enemy. He went at it himself, nosing around everywhere, as if there were something palpable, something physical he could destroy. My uncle was released on a Sunday. Marcellin Duprat brought him back to La Motte. Upon seeing the empty workshop, all his creations turned to smoke, his first words were, "Well, let's get back to work."

The first kite he assembled represented a village against a backdrop of mountains, surrounded by a map of France so that you could tell exactly where it was. The name of the village was Le Chambon-sur-Lignon, and it was in the Cévennes. My uncle didn't explain why he had chosen this village in particular. All he would say to me was: "Le Chambon. Remember that name."

I didn't get it. Why take an interest in this village, where he'd probably never set foot? Why look up at a Le Chambon-sur-Lignon kite with such pride as it flew in the sky? I kept on asking, but all I got out of him was: "I heard about it in prison."

My surprise had only just begun. A few weeks later, having reassembled a few of his historical pieces, my uncle announced he was leaving Clos.

"Where are you going?"

"To Chambon. Like I told you, it's in the Cévennes."

"Christ on a crutch, what's going on here? Why Le Chambon? Why the Cévennes?"

He smiled. There were now as many wrinkles on his face as there were hairs in his mustache.

"Because they need me over there."

That evening, after supper, he kissed me.

"I'll be leaving very early in the morning. Don't give up, Ludo."

"Don't worry."

"She'll be back. There will be a lot to forgive her."

When I woke up, he was gone. He had taken his toolbox with him. On the table in the workshop, he had left me a note: "*Don't give up on her.*" I couldn't tell whether he was talking about Lila or France.

Only a few months before the Allied landing did I get any answer to the questions I was constantly asking myself: *Why Le Chambon? Why did Ambrose Fleury take his toolbox and leave us for that place, for that village in the Cévennes?*

Le Chambon-sur-Lignon was a village where, under the leadership of Pastor André Trocmé and his wife Magda, and with the help of the entire population, several hundred Jewish children were saved from deportation. For four years, all of life in Chambon revolved around that task. I'll write once more those names of great faith: Le Chambon-sur-Lignon and its inhabitants. And today, if any forgetting about this subject has taken place, let it be known that we, the Fleurys, have always been prodigious rememberers. They say exercise is good for the heart, so I recite their names often, without forgetting a single one.

But back then, on the day I received a photograph of my uncle in Le Chambon, a kite in hand, surrounded by children, I knew none of that. Written across the back were the words, "All is well *here*." "*Here*" was underlined.

39

I HADN'T HEARD FROM LILA, BUT GERMANY WAS RE-
treating from the Russian front and its army had been defeated in
Africa. Resistance had ceased to be "folly"; reason was beginning to
catch up to the heart. Marcellin Duprat himself now took part in our
secret meetings, even as his standing with the authorities reached its
zenith: in May 1943 the idea of naming him mayor of Cléry had even
been mentioned. He refused.

"There is history and there is permanence, and then there are
things that come and go, like politics. It's important to know which
is which," he explained to us.

The celebrity of the master of the Clos Joli had at least as much
to do with the occupier's fascination with him as it did with the
quality of his cuisine. He had an erudition and a way with words, as
well as a personal dignity that came not only from his actual physical
bearing but also from the task he'd set for himself in the midst of terrible hardship and the calm confidence with which he'd shouldered
it—these things impressed even the people who, in the beginning,
had called him a collaborator. The man who held him in the highest esteem was General von Tiele. The two of them had a curious
relationship, one you could almost call a friendship. The general, it
was rumored, looked down his nose at the Nazis. One day, he had
remarked to Suzanne, "Mademoiselle, you are aware that the führer
claims that the fruits of his labor will last a thousand years. If you ask

me, I would rather bet on those of Marcellin Duprat. And they will certainly have a better taste."

Once, as the Luftwaffe's chief was arriving, a lieutenant permitted himself to announce him by saying: "Herr Duprat, one of your greatest connoisseurs can thus personally confirm that France has lost nothing of what defines its genius."

Von Tiele, who was present at the time, took the officer aside and poured several ounces of invective over him. The man, standing at attention as he listened, went very pale. After this, the general came and presented his personal apologies to Marcellin. When I saw the general arm in arm with Marcellin, strolling around the little garden of the Clos Joli as they chatted, I sensed that the two men had managed to surmount what Duprat disdainfully called either "the circumstances" or "the contingencies," and had found some common ground, where a Prussian aristocrat and a great French chef could speak on equal footing. But I didn't fully understand how far these two elite natures had gone—not only in their mutual appreciation, but in a kind of real bond above the fray—until the day I learned from Lucien Duprat that his father was secretly giving cooking lessons to the general *Graf* von Tiele. At first, I didn't want to believe it.

"You're kidding me. Von Tiele must have other things on his mind right now."

"Well, maybe that's why. Come and see."

I shrugged. If someone had told me that the general played violin to take his mind off things, I would have found that unremarkable: a taste for music has always been one of the best-known and most widely recognized clichés of the German soul. And nothing has been more convenient, during and since the Occupation, than reducing Germany to its crimes and France to its heroes. But that one of the most prestigious commanders of the Wehrmacht might, deep down, be so convinced that defeat was nigh that he would seek oblivion in cooking lessons from a French master chef—this seemed to contradict everything that the term "German general" signified to us.

Hatred feeds on generalizations, and nothing sets us more at ease than a "typical Prussian face" or a "perfect specimen of the race of overlords" when the time comes to broaden our field of ignorance.

My questioning of Lucien Duprat bordered on the brutal.

"Your father said so, huh? That's just the kind of thing he'd come up with to make himself seem more important—that's him in a nutshell. 'Yessir, ladies and gentlemen, that's right: you know General von Tiele, the victor at Sedan and Smolensk? I taught him everything he knows.'"

"I'm telling you, the general comes for cooking lessons with my father two or three times a week. Obviously he doesn't want word to get out, since things have been going seriously downhill for them—it might seem a little desperate. Even defeatist. They started with fried eggs and omelets. I don't see what's so surprising to you about that."

"Nothing surprises me. The rest of us are up to our ears in shit and blood and these two panjandrums are communing with each other above the barbarous fray. German power needs French finesse and fine living. Goddamn, I'd like to see that."

"I'll let you know."

That very day, I was leaving the restaurant's business offices when Lucien whispered to me, "Tonight, around eleven. I'll leave the hallway door open a crack. But keep quiet. They're very good friends and my father would never forgive me for this."

I went over on foot. I feared the patrols that had begun roving through the meadows and woods each night in search of airdrop lamps.

I slipped into the hallway that led to the kitchen. The door was ajar. I crept forward, shoes in hand, and peeked inside.

Von Tiele was in shirtsleeves, an apron wrapped around him. He appeared to be well soused. Beside him, Marcellin Duprat, haughty and stiff beneath his chef's toque, was in a state of excessive dignity also attributable to the two empty bottles of Pomerol sitting on the table alongside a significantly tapped bottle of cognac.

"There's no point in coming here if you don't listen to what I tell you, Georg," Duprat grumbled. "You've got no particular gift for this, and if you don't follow my instructions to the letter you'll never come to anything."

"But I learned it off by heart. A glass and half of white wine …"

"*Which* white wine?"

The general went silent, looking slightly befuddled.

"Dry!" Duprat scolded. "A glass and a half of dry white wine! Good God, man, it's not all that complicated!"

"Marcellin, you're not telling me it will be completely fouled up if the white wine isn't dry?"

"If you want to make a real Norman-style stuffed rabbit, the white wine has to be dry. Otherwise it's just bilge. And what in the name of all that's holy did you put in the stuffing this time? I can't believe you. I do not understand, Georg, how a man of your learning …"

"It's not the same learning, Marcellin. That's why we need each other … I put in three rabbit livers, a hundred grams of cooked ham, fifty grams of fresh breadcrumbs … a cup of chives …"

You could hear the groan of the Allied bombers flying up the coast.

"Is that it? My dear general, your mind is clearly elsewhere. In Stalingrad, most likely. I told you to put in a teaspoon of allspice … We'll start over again tomorrow."

"This is the third time I've failed."

"Well, you can't win the battle on every front."

The two men were completely drunk. For the first time, I was struck by their resemblance. Von Tiele was smaller, but they had almost the same fine-featured face, the same little gray mustache. Disgustedly, Duprat pushed away the dish with the offending rabbit in it.

"Pure shit."

"Yes, well, I'd like to see you command a tank corps, Marcellin."

They were quiet for a moment, each one as somber as the other, and then they passed the cognac bottle again.

"How much longer will this go on, Georg?"

"I don't know, old man. Someone will win the war, that's certain. Probably your Norman-style rabbit."

Cautiously, I departed. The very next day, a message was sent off, alerting London that the commanding general of the Panzer corps in Normandy was beginning to show signs of weakened morale.

Chong the Pekinese should have been awarded an official title as liaison for the French Resistance. Each time his mistress came to pick him up in my office—except when Monsieur Jean or Marcellin Duprat himself paid their respects by seeing her out—she passed me information on what was cooking with the Gestapo or gave me details of the German "welcome preparations" along the Atlantic Wall. Several of our comrades owed their lives to these warnings. The Gräfin also apprised me that Lila was living in Paris with her parents, but that she regularly spent time in a villa near Huet.

Lila soon reappeared at the Clos Joli, always in the company of Hans and von Tiele. We called them "the trio." "Reserve a table for the trio at one," Lucien Duprat would call out. I always learned of her presence from Monsieur Jean, who would assume an apologetic air as he let me know. The "little lady" was there with her Germans, it must be breaking poor Ludo's heart. It wasn't. They say that love is blind, but that wasn't the case for me; quite the contrary, in fact. There was something about the trio's interactions that I couldn't quite put my finger on. I was certain that Lila was not von Tiele's mistress and I wasn't even convinced that she was Hans's. In my head, the comical phrase "our estates neighbored each other on the Baltic," which she'd snapped at me to explain her relationship with her German "cousins" was beginning to resemble those "personal messages" we received from London: "*The birds will sing again this evening*" or "*The sunken cathedral will ring its bells at midnight.*" These two Prussian squires and this no less aristocratic Polish girl had a kind of complicity whose true nature I could glimpse, but not quite grasp. Once, I happened to run into Lila as she left the place with her two Junkers. I hadn't seen her for several months and was struck by the change that had come over her. The proud and almost triumphant expression on her face when she saw me seemed to say, "You'll see Ludo, you'll see. You were wrong about me."

My impression was confirmed the following week—and in the most puzzling of ways. Lila breezed into my office, and, before I even had time to stand up, she was kissing me.

"Well, my Ludo, what have you been doing with yourself?"

It had been years since I'd seen her so cheerful and happy.

"I don't know what I'm doing with myself, actually. Not much. I keep the books at the Clos Joli and I see to the kites, when I have the time. My uncle's gone, and I'm doing the best I can."

"Where did he go?"

"Le Chambon-sur-Lignon. It's in the Cévennes. Don't ask me what he's off doing at the other end of the country—I have no idea. All he told me is that they need him over there. So he took his tool-box and he left."

I could tell she wanted to talk to me, that she was holding back; I could even detect a hint of irony in her eyes, as if she pitied my ignorance as to what was making her so happy.

"Hans has been posted to the staff headquarters in East Prussia," she told me.

"Ah!"

She laughed. "You couldn't care less, naturally."

"That's the very least you could say."

"Well, you're wrong. It's very important. I have a lot of influence over Hans, you know."

"I don't doubt it."

"Great things are afoot, Ludo. You'll know soon."

I sensed that she wanted to tell me more. I also sensed that it would be better if she didn't.

"You always thought I had a foolish heart—ever since you met me. And I know what people say about me around here. You're wrong to listen to them."

"I listen to no one."

"You're wrong about me, my little Ludo."

"But …"

"You'll apologize to me soon enough. I think I'm finally going to pull off something extraordinary in my life. I always said I would, as a matter of fact."

She gave me a quick kiss and departed, stopping at the door, of course, to glance triumphantly back at me.

A few days later, I saw her at the Cléry train station, getting out of a car, accompanied by von Tiele. She waved at me and I waved back.

40

ON MAY 8, 1943, AT AROUND TEN O'CLOCK AT NIGHT, as I sat reading, I heard a car pull up. Walking to the window, I saw the blue gleam of headlights. The motor stopped; there was a knock at the door; I lit a candle and opened it. General von Tiele was standing on the doorstep; his eyes, which were what people would conventionally call "steel gray," looked out with a pale fixedness from his precise face, with its clean lines. He wore his Iron Cross, studded with diamonds, around his neck.

"Good evening, Monsieur Fleury. Please excuse my visiting you unannounced like this. I wish to speak with you."

"Come in."

He walked by me, stopped, glanced up at the kites hanging from the rafters.

"There is someone you know in my car."

He ceased speaking and sat down on the bench, his hands clasped. I waited. It was the hour when Allied bombers crossed over the coastline on their way to raze German cities. Von Tiele lifted his head a little and listened to the firing of the coastal artillery.

"Twelve hundred bombers over Hamburg yesterday," he said. "You must be pleased."

I did not understand what this great war chief wanted from me.

"You know the man I am bringing to you," he said. "But I do not know if you consider him a friend or an enemy. Nonetheless, I have come to ask you to help him."

Von Tiele rose. He looked at his feet.

"I want you to help him escape to Spain," he said with the trace of a smile, "as you are so good at doing with the Allied aviators."

I was so floored that I didn't even protest.

"Of course you have no reason to save the life of a German officer, Monsieur Fleury. I understand that all too well. It was Lila who advised me to come see you. This may also seem strange to you. But Hans is—like you—very much in love with her. A rival, in sum. Perhaps you would be happy to see him gone. In which case, all you need to do is phone the local Gestapo chief, Herr Grüber …" He didn't dignify Grüber with his military rank. "But perhaps in the expression 'to love the same woman' there is … how shall I say it? What you might call … a kind of fraternity."

He observed me attentively, with an unexpected warmth in his haggard, almost ghostly pale face.

I was silent.

Von Tiele raised his hand.

"Listen to the sky. How many children will be killed tonight? We'll say no more of that. I'm only telling you that I am trying to save a young man who is my nephew, and whom I love like a son. I must leave now. We have about … twenty-four hours. I have arrangements to make. You still haven't given me your answer, Monsieur Fleury."

"Does Lila know?"

"Yes."

Hans was in uniform. Childhood and adolescence really do leave their mark on you: we did not shake hands. But I had to slip my arm under his shoulder to hold him up. He walked a few steps and collapsed. Von Tiele helped me carry him to my room.

"You must not keep him here, Monsieur Fleury. You are risking your life. Try to hide him somewhere else tonight. However, as I told you, I do think we have twenty-four hours …" He smiled at me.

"I hope you don't feel like a traitor, hiding a German officer?"

"I feel like you owe me one hell of an explanation."

"You'll get it. Hans will explain. And in any case, I'll explain it to you myself. I'll be lunching at the Clos Joli, as I do every Friday."

Hans was sleeping when I returned to my room. Even in sleep his face remained fraught; from time to time, his chin and lips would tremble convulsively. For a long time, I contemplated his face, whose beauty had once raised such animosity in me. He wore a locket around his neck. I opened it: Lila.

It was one in the morning; sunrise was at five. The ticktock of the clock was beginning to give me goose flesh. I put some coffee on and woke Hans. He looked at me uncomprehendingly for an instant, then sprang up.

"Don't keep me here. They'll shoot you."

"What did you do?"

"Later, later."

The coffee was ready. "We don't have much time," I informed him. "It's a three-hour walk."

"To where?"

"Vieille-Source. Do you remember?"

"Do I ever! You almost strangled me. What were we … twelve? Thirteen?"

"Something like that. Hans, what did you do?"

"We tried to kill Hitler."

"Jesus!" That was all I could say.

"We put a bomb in his plane."

"Who is we?"

"The bomb was defective. It didn't go off, and they found it. Two of our comrades had time to kill themselves. They'll get the others to talk. I managed to get out with my plane to warn …" he trailed off.

"I see."

"Yes. I was able to land on the Ouchy field. I wanted to take the general to England …"

I shook myself, snorted like a startled horse, took a deep breath. And then I began to laugh hysterically. Hans wanted to bring General von Tiele to England to establish Free France there. Free Germany, that is. With the Cross of Lorraine as its emblem, maybe. "Shit," I said. "It's May. You're a month early for June 18. You sure do know how to dream, you Germans. It must be heads or tails with your dreams: sometimes you end up with Goethe and Hölderlin, sometimes with millions dead. If I'm getting this right, your elite officers still believe you can come to some sort of gentleman's agreement over this? An aristocratic peace? June 18, 1940, but German-style, in London, in 1943, on the back of the Russians, no doubt?"

He lowered his head.

"All our traditional officers have opposed Hitler and the war since 1936," he said.

"And then of course it was too late, because you were already in Paris, and already halfway to Moscow. Well, come on, let's go. You'll be all right at Vieille-Source for a few days, and then we'll see. Can you make it? It's four miles."

"I'll be all right."

I took my precious flashlight—I had only one extra battery left— and we went outside. A lovely night, just right for the stars' ironic gleam. A French Resistance fighter helping a Gaullist German officer. The moonlight was still strong and I didn't light my torch until we reached the bottom of the ravine. At the end of our childhood path, overgrown with brush and brambles, the source, too, had aged, and no longer had the strength to gush from its wellhead.

In single file, we slid along the mossy walls to where the ravine ended in a cul-de-sac. The wigwam was still right where my uncle Ambrose had helped us build it eleven years ago—listing a little, but still upright. And it was only when we were standing before this structure of our childhood that Lila's phrase rose up in my memory, the one she had murmured to me in my office, so cheerfully and so certainly: *"I think I'm finally going to pull off something really extraordinary in my life. I have a lot of influence with Hans, you know."* I looked at Hans. *It's her*, I thought. *He did it for her.* I crouched down and tried to find a little water at the bottom of the spring well. My throat was so dry, I could barely speak.

"I'll come once or twice a week with supplies. After that we'll try and get you over the Pyrenees. I have to talk to my friends about it."

The air smelled of earth and damp. Above our heads, an owl dreamed. The sky was growing lighter. Hans took off the jacket of his uniform and tossed it on the ground. In his white shirt, he was not very different from the young man who had stood before me in the weapons room at Gródek during our duel.

"I owe you my life and I will repay you with my life," he said.

"Life will be the one to decide that, old man."

It was the only time we ever spoke to each other of Lila by name.

At eleven o'clock, I was at my desk, at work on the ledgers, unable to think of anything but the events of the previous night. And everything Lila had said, every sentence, every phrase, every intonation, continued to echo through my head. *"I'll pull it off ... I'm sure that with a little luck ... I have a lot of influence with Hans, you know ... I always wanted to do something grand and terribly important ..."*

Monsieur Jean opened the door. "General von Tiele put a call in for his monthly bill ..."

"Sure ..."

"Trust me, Ludo ... I'll leave my mark on history ..."

She had talked Hans into it, patiently, and probably without too much difficulty, since even before the hostilities had begun, he was always talking about "saving the honor of the German army." And von Tiele knew that the war would be lost if Germany had to keep fighting on both fronts. With Hitler gone, a separate peace with the United States and England, and then ...

"Check for table five," came Monsieur Jean's voice.

"Yes … Right away …"

"What's wrong, Ludo? Are you ill?"

"No, nothing, I'm fine …"

"One day, you'll be proud of me … I'll leave my mark on history …" The plot had failed and Lila's life was in danger. *"I have a lot of influence with Hans, you know …"* I had to get them into Spain, both of them. I wondered how I would go about it. The two aviators hidden at the Buis' were supposed to be smuggled through Bagnères in a few days, but I didn't even know where Lila was; if Hans were to be part of the convoy, Soubabère would have to sign off on it, and there were no "good" Germans in Souba's eyes. Also, the details of this first plot by officers of the Wehrmacht to overthrow Hitler had to be communicated to London as soon as possible.

Through my distressed confusion, I heard a whimper — Chong was sitting at my feet, wagging his tail and looking at me reproachfully. I'd completely forgotten him. When the Lady Esterhazy came to lunch at the Clos Joli, it was my job to give him his doggie dinner. I left my office and called out to Lucien Duprat.

"Is the Lady Esterhazy still here?"

"Why?"

"She forgot the pooch."

"I'll go see."

He returned to tell me that the Gräfin was having her coffee. I went to the kitchen, grabbed a dish of meat, and returned to feed the dog. As I crossed the entry hall I saw von Tiele's car pull up in front. The driver opened the door and the general emerged. Von Tiele's face was drawn, but he seemed to be in a good mood, and he climbed the steps quickly, waving back to someone I could not see. That morning, Duprat had received a note, which he pasted into the guest register after the Liberation: *"My friend, Marcellin, I am about to be transferred elsewhere and will come say my goodbyes to the Clos Joli this Friday afternoon at two."*

All that his presence signified to me was that the Gestapo didn't know yet. Twenty-four hours at the most, he had told me. I had just a few hours left to locate Lila. But Hans or von Tiele had certainly taken care of her.

Seconds later, the Gräfin made her entrance in my office. She picked up the dog. "Poor little creature. I nearly forgot him."

She placed a ball of wrinkled paper in front of me. I unfolded it. Lila's handwriting. *"I almost succeeded. I love you. Farewell."*

Madame Julie opened her lighter and set fire to the paper. A little pile of ashes.

"Where is she?"

"I don't know. Von Tiele packed her off to Paris yesterday evening. He had her driven to the midnight train in his own car, the fool."

"But that paper …"

She was tense, and tugged at her gloves.

"What about the paper?"

"How did you get it?"

"Well, there was a very nice reception yesterday evening at the Stag, thrown by the subordinate officers for the civilian personnel and the secretaries. All the top brass were there. Even General von Tiele dropped by for a few minutes. Your little lady drank a lot and danced a lot. And then she gave my daughter a letter for you, laughing. It was a love letter, apparently. You know me, love letter, schmove letter, I open everything, nowadays. So there you have it. You're a lucky guy. If she'd passed that note to anyone else …"

"They … they already know?"

"The Gestapo has known since nine o'clock this morning. My little 100 percent Aryan friend—real name Isidore Lefkowitz—let me know at noon. They haven't locked up von Tiele yet because they don't want word to get out. The hero of Smolensk, you know—that would make waves. They have orders to send him to Berlin, with all the honors …"

"But the general is here …"

"Not for long."

Lovingly, she pressed Chong's muzzle to her cheek. "Come along, my pet. Mommy must still have a heart hidden somewhere in there, because she's starting to act like a dope."

She gave me a hard look.

"You can't do a thing for her, so sit very tight and tell everyone else to do the same. There's a shitstorm brewing."

The Gräfin Esterhazy turned on her heel and departed.

I was on the verge of leaving my office to hightail it over to Soubabère's when Monsieur Jean came to tell me that General von Tiele wished to speak with me.

"He is in the Ed …" The old man caught himself. The "Édouard Herriot Room," where the radical socialist leader had once been a regular, had been dechristened. But Duprat, with great courage, had not given it another name. He had simply taken down the Édouard Herriot plaque and set it aside in a drawer.

"You never know," he'd explained to me. "It could come back."

There were lots of Parisian and local officials in the restaurant, both in the "rotunda" and in the "galleries." It was chic to go lean on Fridays: with the country undergoing such hardships, piety and religion had come back into fashion, and to keep business booming on meatless days Marcellin Duprat had gone in for fish specialties with all the subtlety and all the resources of his art. I had to cross through the rotunda and its hoi polloi to get to the dechristened room, which was upstairs—something I never did on ordinary occasions, since my sloppy attire prompted dressings down from the boss whenever I ventured out into the front of the house.

I found von Tiele at his table. Duprat, very pale, a napkin under his arm, was uncorking what he considered to be his finest bottle: a 1923 Château Laville. Never before had I seen the great chef so emotional. To have given in to that kind of sacrifice he must have been touched in the furthest depths of his soul. Clearly, von Tiele had brought him up to speed as to the exact nature of his "transfer." From time to time,

Duprat would glance toward the window at the two Gestapo cars parked in the drive, one of them Grüber's black Citroën.

"Have no fear, my good Marcellin," the general said to him. "I've had them as my escort since nine thirty this morning. I've been transferred to Berlin, the plane is waiting for me. The führer wishes to avoid any undue public attention. Being named to General von Keitel's staff is indeed a promotion. But most likely my plane will crash before we get to Tempelhof, as my feeling is they're not too concerned for the lives of the crew. My three direct subordinates are supposed to accompany me on the flight; not Colonel Schtekker, though. He is a good Nazi, and he will continue to frequent your establishment, I hope. But not everything will go as they've planned. For one thing, I don't see why I would let a perfectly innocent flight crew perish when the Luftwaffe is already short on pilots. But more than that, I refuse to play along—to collaborate, if you prefer. I want it to be known. Corporal Hitler believes himself to be a brilliant strategist, and he is leading the German army to defeat. So my comrades must learn of my 'treachery.' And, if I may allow myself some small immodesty, given my military reputation, all of my fellow commanding officers will understand my reasons, which most of them agree with, moreover. This is a warning, and I want it heard. But—let us speak of more agreeable things."

He tasted the 1923 Château-Laville.

"Wonderful," he cried. "Ah, the spirit of France!"

"I prepared a *ragoût de coquillages Saint-Jacques* and a *turbotin grillé à la moutarde*," said Marcellin Duprat, his voice trembling. "It's a bit routine, obviously. If I'd known …"

"Well yes. Obviously you couldn't know, my good Marcellin. Neither could I, when it comes to that. You see, our failure was caused by … how shall I put it? Not enough trust in the common man. We stayed a cut above them, kept to ourselves, among elite officers. We didn't dare entrust a simple sergeant or a corporal artificer, and that was a tremendous mistake. If we had gone for help among the …

let's not say *inferior*, let's say *subordinate* ranks, the bomb would have been set correctly and it would have done its job. But we wanted to restrict things to our level: that old caste spirit. Our bomb wasn't … democratic enough. We didn't have a squaddie."

This little speech by the general Count von Tiele would return to my mind a few months later. On July 20, 1944, when Colonel Count von Stauffenberg, another "elite officer," left a bomb in a napkin at Hitler's headquarters in Rastenburg, and the explosion barely turned a hair on Hitler's head, I told myself that once again, all those lordly officers were missing was a simple munitions officer, someone who would have been able to give the bomb the necessary strength. It was a bomb that lacked popular will.

Von Tiele finished his *turbotin grillé à la moutarde*. He turned to me.

"Well, my young Fleury … Did it go off all right?"

"So far, so good … He's well hidden—" I hesitated, and for the first time in my life I said to a German: "*my* general."

He gave me a look of friendship. He understood.

"Mademoiselle de Bronicka is in Paris," he said. "In a safe place. Well, as long as she doesn't try and risk a visit to her parents. You know her!"

"General, sir, could you …"

He nodded, drew a notebook from his pocket and scribbled an address and a telephone number. He tore out the page and held it out to me.

"Try to get them to Spain, both of them …"

"Yes, sir, General."

I put the paper in my pocket.

Von Tiele took one more bite of the *coquilles Saint-Jacques* and finished with the famous sour apple soufflé, a coffee, and a glass of cognac.

"Ah, France!" he murmured again, a shade ironically, it seemed to me.

Duprat was weeping. With a trembling hand, he offered the general a box of real Havana cigars. Von Tiele declined them with a wave of his hand. Then he looked at the time and rose.

"And now, gentlemen," he said tersely, "I must ask you to leave me."

Duprat left the room before me and ran to the toilets to wash his face. If the Gestapo found him in tears before von Tiele was dead, there would be some difficult explaining to do.

The shot rang out just as I was climbing onto my bicycle with Chong tucked under one arm. I just glimpsed Grüber's men leaping from their cars and dashing toward the restaurant.

Marcellin Duprat remained in bed for the rest of the day, his face turned to the wall. That evening, before the dinner service began, he said something extraordinary, and I never knew whether it was a slip of the tongue or simply his highest praise: "That was one great Frenchman."

41

I PEDALED SO HARD — HOLDING THE PEKINESE WITH one hand and the handlebars with the other — that when I finally arrived at Her Ladyship's residence, my knees suddenly gave out as I was climbing off my bike, and I fell flat on my face, my head swimming. Most likely fear and emotion had their part to play in it, because despite the "safe place" von Tiele had mentioned to me, and even with the address in my pocket, I had a hard time seeing how Lila could escape the Gestapo and the French police working at the beck and call of the occupying forces. I spent several minutes sobbing while Chong licked my hands and face. I finally managed to pull myself together, picked up the dog, and climbed the three steps to the entrance. I rang, expecting to see Odette Lanier, the "chambermaid" who had arrived from London with the new transceiver nine months prior, but the cook opened the door for me.

"Oh, there you are, dearie. Come along now …" She held out her hand for Chong.

"I would like to speak to Lady Esterhazy myself," I murmured, still trying to catch my breath. "The dog is sick. It keeps throwing up. I went by the veterinarian's and …"

"Come in, come in."

I found Madame Julie in the sitting room, with her daughter. In Cléry once or twice I had seen von Tiele's general staff "secretary," who was widely known to be Schtekker's mistress. She was a pretty brunette, with eyes whose unfathomable depths seemed to descend from her mother's gaze.

"Hermann always suspected the general," she was saying now. "He thought von Tiele was decadent, with Francophile tendencies that were becoming intolerable—and his language, when he was speaking of the führer … unacceptable. Hermann sent report after report about him to Berlin. If what people are saying is true, he'll be promoted."

"Betraying his country! How completely horrifying," Madame Julie exclaimed.

The two women were alone in the sitting room. The conversation was clearly intended for me. I concluded that Madame Julie, who believed mistrust was the key to survival, was inviting me to pay very close attention to what I said. You never knew who might be standing by, with an ear pressed to the door. Both mother and daughter, moreover, seemed fairly tense. I even thought I saw Madame Julie's hands tremble ever so slightly.

"Oh good heavens," she said, raising her voice. "I see I forgot the poor darling at the Clos Joli again. Here, my dear."

She took her handbag from the piano. On the piano were all the autographed portraits I knew: in one corner, the picture of Admiral Horthy was wreathed in black crêpe. The crêpe had been there since the death of his son, István Horthy, in 1942, on the Russian front.

She held out a ten-franc note.

"There you are, young man, and thank you."

"Madame, the dog is very ill, I saw the veterinarian, he prescribed a treatment, I have to tell you about it, it's quite urgent …"

"Well, it's time I got back to the office," the daughter remarked nervously.

Madame Julie walked her to the door. She glanced outside, most likely to make sure I hadn't come "accompanied," shut the door again, turned the key in the lock, and returned.

She motioned for me to follow her.

We went to her bedroom. She kept the door wide open, alert to the tiniest noise, and yet again I told myself that if France had been as concerned for its survival as this old madam, things never would have come to this.

"Come on, quickly now, what is it?"

"Von Tiele killed himself, and …"

"Is that all? Obviously he killed himself. When you go at things like a ham-fisted jackass …"

"He gave me Lila's address and phone number. Apparently it's a completely secure location."

"Hand it over." She snatched the paper from my hands and glanced at the address. "You call that a safe house—it's his little love nest." I must have blanched because she softened.

"Not your girl. Von Tiele loved the ladies. He kept bachelor's quarters in Paris. The last one was a whore from Fabienne's, that hooking shop in the rue Miromesnil, but she had nice manners—raised by the nuns at Our Lady of the Birds—so he didn't notice. The Gestapo knows the place, you can be sure of that. They keep files on the private lives of their generals and they've always spied on von Tiele—trust me, I know. If the kid is really there …"

"She's lost," I murmured.

Madame Julie said nothing.

"Can't we warn her? There's a telephone number …"

"Are you kidding? You don't actually think I'm going to let you make a call from here, do you? The switchboard notes every number you ask for, the time, and the number calling."

"Help me, Madame Julie!"

She leaned over, picked up Chong, and hugged him, glaring at me with hostility. "Unbelievable. I must have a soft spot for you. At my age!"

She thought.

"The only safe line is the Gestapo's," she mused. "Wait. There's another place. Arnoldt's house—Grüber's deputy."

"But…"

"He lives there with his little friend—the one I told you about. It's 14, rue des Champs, in Cléry, third floor on the right. They have their own line, and the calls aren't logged. Go ahead. It's good timing—I forgot to send his medication over… Well, when I say forgot … My little Francis hasn't had much time for me lately…"

"Francis?"

"Francis Dupré. It's as far as you can get from Isidore Lefkowitz. Wait right here …"

She went and rummaged through a dresser drawer, returning with two vials.

"It's been eight days. He must be climbing the walls, poor thing. But that'll teach him."

I took the vials.

"He's diabetic. It's insulin."

"It's morphine, you mean."

"What can you do, he's been scared to death for nearly four years, now. He's always been a little uneasy in his own skin, actually. Tell him I won't forget him again, unless he starts forgetting me again, too. And to let you use the phone."

She sat down in an armchair, legs parted, with Chong in her lap.

"And give me the thing you've got in your pocket, Ludo."

"What thing in my pocket?"

"The cyanide capsule. If they search you and they find that on you, it's as good as a confession. And what are you going to do, pop a cyanide capsule just because they're about to search you? There's always the chance you might get away."

I placed my cyanide capsule on the night table.

Madame Julie looked dreamy all of a sudden.

"It won't be long now," she said. "I can barely sleep at night I'm so impatient. It'd be a damn shame to get nabbed at the last minute."

Distractedly, she fiddled with her golden lizard.

"If things heat up too much around here, I'm out of here. I'll stick a yellow star where I need to, head down to Nice or Cannes, and turn myself in to the Germans. They'll deport me right away, of course, but I'm sure I can hold out for a few months, and then the Americans will land. You know, like those movies with the redskins, where the cavalry always shows up at the end."

She laughed.

"Yankee-doodle-doodle-dandy …" she hummed. "Well, something like that. Even the Germans think so. Apparently it'll be in the Pas-de-Calais. I'd like to be there to see it. So if they bust you …"

"Don't worry, Madame Julie. I'd let them torture me to death before I'd …"

"Everyone always thinks that. Well, we'll see. Now you scram."

In three-quarters of an hour I was at number fourteen, rue des Champs. I left my bicycle a few hundred yards away and mounted the stairs to the third floor. I was so agitated that for the first time in my life my memory actually blanked: I couldn't remember whether it was the door on the right or the left. I had to think back through my entire conversation with Madame Julie to locate the words *third floor on the right*. I rang.

A gaunt man came to the door, good-looking enough if you liked the tango dancer type, but ghostly pale and with dark circles smudged under his nervous eyes. He was wearing pajamas and had a little cross on a chain around his neck.

"Monsieur Francis Dupré?"

"That's me. What do you want?"

"The countess Esterhazy sent me. I brought your medication."

He perked up.

"Finally … It's been at least a week … She forgot me, that bitch. Give me that …"

"Madame … I mean, the countess Esterhazy asked that I telephone Paris from your house."

"Go right ahead, come on in … the telephone is over there, in the bedroom … Give me that."

"I don't know German, sir. You'll need to ask for the number yourself..."

He dashed to the telephone, asked for the number, and passed me the receiver. I gave him the two vials of morphine and he ran and locked himself in the bathroom.

A minute later, I heard Lila's voice at the other end of the line.

"Hello?"

"It's me..."

"Ludo! But how..."

"Don't stay where you are. Get out right now."

"Why? What's wrong? Georg told me..."

I could barely speak.

"Get out immediately... They know the place... They'll be there any minute now..."

"But where am I supposed to go? To my parents?"

"Dear God no, absolutely not... Hang on..."

Dozens of names and addresses of comrades flashed through my head. But I knew that none of them would ever shelter a stranger without a previously arranged password. And maybe Lila was already being tailed. I picked the least dangerous solution.

"Do you have any money?"

"Yes, Georg gave me some."

"Get out immediately, leave all your things there. Don't wait a single second. Go and book a room at the Hôtel de l'Europe, 14 rue Rollin. It's right next to the Place de la Contrescarpe. I'll send someone to you tonight, he'll ask for Albertine and you'll say his name, Roderick. Say it back to me."

"Albertine. Roderick. But I can't just leave here, I have all my art books—"

I barked: "You drop everything and you get out! Say it back to me!"

"Roderick. Albertine. Ludo..."

"Go!"

"I almost pulled it off…"

"Go!"

"I love you."

I hung up.

Physically and emotionally drained, I fell back onto the unmade bed. No sooner had I lain down than Francis Dupré emerged from the bathroom. I would never have believed that a man could change so much in a few minutes. He exuded happiness and serenity. All trace of terror had disappeared from his eyes, with their languorous lashes. He sat down on the bed at my feet, smiling and friendly.

"So young man, everything all right?"

"All right, yes."

"That Lady Esterhazy, she's quite a woman."

"That's true. Quite a woman."

"She's always been a real mother to me. You know, I'm diabetic, and without insulin …"

"I understand."

"And of course there's insulin and insulin. The insulin she gets me is always the best quality. Will you have a glass of champagne?"

I stood up.

"I beg your pardon, I'm in a rush."

"Too bad," he said. "You seem so charming to me. I hope I'll have the pleasure of your company again. See you very soon."

"See you very soon."

"And please, whatever you do, tell her not to forget about me. I need it regularly, every three days."

"I'll tell her. But I was given to understand you had forgotten her a bit, too."

He chuckled a bit.

"True, true. I won't do it again. I'll let her hear from me more often."

Again, I found myself in the stairwell.

It took me several hours to establish contact with "Roderick" in

Paris, to beg him to go to the Hôtel de l'Europe at 14 rue Rollin and ask for Albertine.

We heard back the next evening. There was no Albertine at the Hôtel de l'Europe. All day Saturday and all day Sunday our comrade Lalande called the number von Tiele had given me. He never got an answer.

Lila had disappeared.

42

I COULDN'T GET TO VIEILLE-SOURCE FOR SEVERAL days. The entire region was being turned upside down: thousands of soldiers were combing the countryside for the traitorous officer. My feverish and vain scramble to trace Lila cost me a great deal of time, as well; a few of my comrades even risked a trip to the rue de Chazelle to question the neighbors. All they got were doors shut in their faces. Only a neighborhood café owner recalled seeing a police van across the street, at number 67, but he thought they had departed empty-handed. In Duprat's papers I managed to turn up the Bronickis' Paris address, which Lila must have given him: they, too, had disappeared.

I succeeded in convincing myself that the whole family had managed to flee for the countryside, to the home of trusted friends. After all, the Bronickis had any number of connections with the French nobility, and now there was a groundswell of eleventh hour support for the Resistance, even among those who had until then kept prudently out of things, and despite the many assurances from Radio Vichy that "if they dare to make a landing, the Anglo-Saxons will immediately be tossed back into the sea."

So I managed to calm down a little. If something had happened to Lila, the Cléry Gestapo would be the first to know, and "Francis Dupré" would certainly have alerted the woman who was "like a mother" to him, as he had put it to me. And I had seen the Lady

Esterhazy sweep into the Clos Joli, haughty, dressed in gray: she had walked right by me without so much as a look and didn't even have the Pekinese with her. She had nothing to tell me; there was nothing new to report.

Every day, therefore, I grew more certain that Lila was safe. Whether or not this conviction was entirely sincere I have no idea; what mattered was that it saved me from despair. For now, I had to see to Hans. First I had to find him a safer hiding spot, then arrange for him to be smuggled into Spain with the next convoy. I went to see Soubabère. I found "Hercules" in a particularly sour mood.

"The Boche has never hunted so hard for anything. Our hands are completely tied until they find this guy. If things go on like this, we risk total disaster. They've already stumbled on two weapons caches in Verrières and they arrested one of the Solié brothers and their sister. There's just one thing to do: we have to collar their Kraut for them and turn him in." It knocked me right down to the ground.

"You can't do that, Souba."

"And why not?"

"Because he's a resister, too. They tried to kill Hitler …"

His eyebrows shot up: "Yeah, after Stalingrad. And you can be sure they're going to give it another go. The generals have figured out the ship is sinking, and they're trying to jump while they still can. But let me tell you, Fleury: it's a good thing they screwed up. Because if they'd pulled it off, or if they pull it off the next time, the Americans will negotiate with them to co-opt the German army against the Russians, believe me …"

"You're not actually going to do the Gestapo's job for them?"

"Listen, kid. I have four weapons caches to protect. A printing press. Five radios. And as long as the Boche keeps beating the bushes day and night, we can't bring in a single airdrop. This guy has thrown off our entire organization. So it's him or us. I've given orders. He has to be found. You should get on that, too. No one knows this country better than you."

I went away without answering. Later, I tried to work a little. I started to assemble a kite, but I couldn't even imagine a shape for it. I sat there with the blue paper in my hand. Souba was right. As long as the Gestapo hadn't found Hans, the entire Resistance was stalled out. And it was just as clear that I could not betray him. At eleven o'clock in the morning, there was a knock at the door and Souba entered with Machaud and Rodier.

"They're searching everywhere. Our hands are tied. Your childhood friend—where have you stashed him? Apparently you were buddies—he spent his holidays here, this Hans von Schwede. So you're going to talk now."

"The bathtub's down the hall, Souba. I don't know whether I'll talk—I always did wonder how I'd hold up under torture."

"For God's sake, you're not going to toss it all in the shitter for a German officer, are you?"

"No. Give me twelve hours."

"Not one more."

I didn't wait for nightfall. I preferred to go to Vieille-Source in broad daylight, to be sure none of my comrades were tailing me. I had prepared civilian clothes for Hans, but there was no point now. I found him sitting on a stone, reading. I didn't know where he could have gotten the book, and then I remembered, he always had one in his pocket, and it was always the same: Heine.

I sat down beside him. I must have looked pretty terrible, because he smiled, turned a page, and read:

> Ich weiss nicht, was soll es bedeuten
> Dass ich so traurig bin;
> Ein Märchen aus alten Zeiten
> Das kommt mir nicht aus dem Sinn ...

And then he added, laughing, "The translation doesn't matter—Verlaine said more or less the same thing:

Je me souviens
Des jours anciens
Et je pleure ... *

He set the book down beside him.

"So, tell me."

He listened attentively, nodding occasionally.

"They're right. Tell them I understand perfectly."

He rose. I knew I was seeing him for the last time. And that I would never forget the light playing around the face of my "enemy." Cursed memory. It was one of spring's most beautiful days, with a serenity and warmth that transformed nature into a foreign power.

"Please tell your friends to come for me here—before nightfall, if possible. It's a question of ... hygiene. There are a lot of insects."

He grew silent and waited; for the first time, I read a trace of anxiety in his face. He didn't even dare ask the question.

I don't know if I was lying to him or to myself when I answered: "She must be in Spain by now—you can set your mind at ease."

His face lit up. "Phew. That's one less thing to worry about."

I left him. Right up to the end, we remained faithful to our childhood: we did not shake hands.

The next day, Souba brought me the Heine book and the locket with Lila's photo. They turned the rest in to the police. The Maheu kid had stumbled over the body in a ravine, in a place called Vieille-Source, while gathering lilies of the valley; that was the story they gave.

---

* No indeed, the translation doesn't matter; Gerard Manley Hopkins said more or less the same thing: "Margaret, are you grieving / Over Goldengrove unleaving? / ... / It is the blight man was born for, / It is Margaret you mourn for." —Tr.

43

SOON AFTER, SOUBA ALSO WAS THE ONE TO GIVE ME
news of my uncle. He came to see me one Sunday, in a getup he
himself qualified as unsafe: he dreamed of dressing in uniform, a
real French uniform, "out in the open"—he was a reserve officer, as
he constantly reminded us. He never specified his rank; most likely
he had set aside some stripes for later, just in case. In a beret, boots,
cavalry breeches, and a khaki battle jacket, his fat face looking as
sullen as ever—his fury at the moment of capitulation seemed to
have marked his facial features with a permanent angry expression—
Souba sat down heavily on a stool and, without preamble, declared
gruffly to me: "He's at Buchenwald."

Back then I knew very little about the death camps. My mind did
not yet feel the word "deportation" with all its horrible weight. But
I'd believed my uncle to be safe and sound in the Cévennes, and the
shock hit me so hard that Souba took one look at me and got up,
returning with a bottle of calvados and placing a glass in my hands.

"Come on, pull yourself together."

"But what did he do?"

"Something with Jews," Souba grumbled darkly. "Jewish kids,
from what I understand. Apparently there's a whole village devoted
to it, in the Cévennes. Can't remember what it's called. A Huguenot
village. Those people were really persecuted in their day, so they all
got involved, and from what I hear they've kept up with it, even now.

And of course Jewish or no, if there are kids, Ambrose Fleury will wade right in, with the kites and all that."

"All that."

"Yep, all that." He tapped the side of his head. "Well, we're all certified these days. You have to be crazy to risk your life for others, because we might not be around to see France when it's free. With me though, it isn't my head—" he touched his belly, "—it's in my guts.

"So I can't help it. If it were in my head, I'd make arrangements—like Duprat. Well, anyway, the point is they deported him. They pinched him between Lyon and the Swiss border."

"With children?"

"Not a goddamn clue. I've got someone who's just come from there who can give you details. I'll introduce you. Get up. I'll take you."

I rode behind him on my bike, crying from my nose. It's no use, wanting to hold back tears—they always find their way out.

Monsieur Terrier was waiting for us at Le Normand, in Clos, and Souba presented him to me. During a bombing, he'd taken a uniform from a fallen German soldier and escaped with the help of what he called "a perfect knowledge of the language of Goethe, which I taught at the Lycée Henri IV." First he described what he, bizarrely enough, termed "camp life," and then told me that even under the worst duress, my uncle never gave in to despair.

"True, he lucked out in the beginning..."

"What luck is that, sir?" I yelled out.

Monsieur Terrier explained about my uncle's luck. It so happened that one of the camp guards had spent a year stationed with the Occupation forces in the Cléry area and remembered Ambrose Fleury's kites, which the Germans would come to admire, and often purchased to send back home to their families. The camp commander, with the idea of using inmate labor, had supplied him with the necessary materials. My uncle was ordered to go to work. At first, the SS officers brought the kites home as presents for their children or their friends' children, and then he came up with the idea of turning it into a business. My uncle ended up with an entire team of assistants. And thus, floating above the shameful camp, it was possible to see bouquets of kites whose gay colors seemed to proclaim the inextinguishable hope and faith of Ambrose Fleury. Monsieur Terrier told me that my uncle worked from memory, and that he had managed to make some pieces look like Rabelais and Montaigne, which he'd assembled so many times. But the highest demand was for kites in the naive shapes of children's book characters, and the Nazis even furnished my uncle with a whole collection of juvenile literature and fairy tales, to help out his imagination.

"We liked him a lot, good old Ambrose," Monsieur Terrier said. "Of course he was a bit original, not to say a little touched—at his age, and undernourished as we all were, there's no other way he could have come up with such carefree, jolly shapes and colors and expressions for those creatures. He was a man who didn't know how to despair, and the ones among us who expected that nothing but death would deliver us felt humiliated and almost defied by his strength of soul. I believe the image has been burned into my eyes: that untamable man, in our concentration camp stripes, surrounded by a few shreds of human being who were hanging on to their lives with something that has no body. I can still see him steering a ship with twenty white sails at the end of the lead, fluttering above the crematoria and over the heads of our torturers. Sometimes a kite would get away—it would fly toward the horizon and our eyes would follow it with hope. Over the months, your uncle must have assembled three hundred kites. Like I said, most of his ideas came from children's stories the camp commander gave him. Those were the most popular.

"And then it went bad. You haven't heard the business about the lampshades made out of human skin. Not yet. You will. But to make a long story short, Ilse Koch, a beast who was a guard in the women's camp, had them making her lampshades from the skins of dead prisoners. No, don't make that face: it doesn't prove *anything*. And it never will prove anything, however much proof there is. All we'll ever need is one Jean Moulin, or a single d'Estienne d'Orves and the defense will have the stand again. So as I was saying, it was Ilse Koch who came up with the idea: she asked Ambrose Fleury to make her a kite out of human skin. Oh, yes. She had found one with some nice tattoos. Now, obviously, Ambrose Fleury said no. Ilse Koch stared at him for a second, and then she said: "*Denke doch.* Think about it." She walked away, with her famous whip, and your uncle watched her go. I think that our foe had figured out the meaning of the kites and had decided to break the spirit of this Frenchman who didn't know how to despair. All that night, we tried to talk Ambrose into it: what was one more or one less skin? No one was keeping score in this skin game; we'd lost count. And at any rate, this particular guy wasn't in it anymore. But he wouldn't hear of it. "I couldn't do that to them," he kept saying. He didn't actually say who "he couldn't do that" to, but we understood what he meant. I don't know what his kites meant to him. Maybe some kind of invincible hope."

Monsieur Terrier trailed off, a little uncomfortably. Brusquely, Souba stood up and went over to the bar to discuss something with the owner. I understood.

"They killed him."

"Oh no, no, I can reassure you on that count," Monsieur Terrier hurried to console me. "They just transferred him to another camp."

"Where?"

"In Oświęcim, in Poland."

I didn't know it then, but as is only fitting, the world would eventually know Oświęcim far better by a German name—Auschwitz.

44

TWO MONTHS HAVE PASSED SINCE LILA WENT BACK to sharing my life underground. By sleeping little—this state of nervous exhaustion favors her presence—I manage to bring her to me nearly every night.

"You warned me just in time, Ludo. Thank goodness, Georg had arranged for our paperwork and I could flee with my parents, first to Spain, then Portugal…"

A few times a week I go to the Cléry public library to be closer to her. Leaning over the atlas, one finger on the map, I keep her company, in Estoril and the Algarve, celebrated for its forests of cork trees.

"You should come here, Ludo. It's such a beautiful country."

"Write to me. You talk with me, you comfort me, but when you leave me, you leave me with no sign of life. You've not done anything silly, at least?"

"Anything silly? I've done so many silly things."

"You know … *First off I had to survive, save my own …*"

Here, her voice becomes severe. "See—you think about it all the time. You've never really forgiven me, deep down."

"That's not true. If I don't want it to happen to you again, it's that—"

Her voice takes on a mocking tone, "—it's that you're afraid it'll become a habit for me."

"Not a habit ... A hopelessness."

"You'd be ashamed of me."

"Oh, no! Sometimes I'm ashamed to be a man, to have the same hands, the same face as them ..."

"Who's them? The Germans?"

"Them. Us. You need a lot of faith in my uncle Ambrose's kites to look any man in the eye and say: he is innocent. He's not the one who tortured Jombey to death, he's not the one who commanded the firing squad last week, when they shot six 'communist' hostages to death ..."

The voice sounds far off, now.

"What do you want? First off you have to survive, to save your own. Do you understand, Ludo? Do you understand?"

I get up, I take the lamp, I cross the courtyard to the workshop. They're all there, always the same, and yet you always have to start again. I must have reassembled them twenty-odd times each: Jean-Jacques Rousseau, Montaigne. There's even Don Quixote, that great, misunderstood realist, who was so right to perceive hideous dragons and monsters in the familiar, tranquil-seeming world—ones that had perfected their camouflage, successfully learned to hide behind the faces of nice guys "who wouldn't hurt a fly." Since the dawn of humanity, the number of "flies" who got their wings ripped off thanks to that reassuring cliché must be up in the hundreds of millions. Long ago all trace of hatred for the Germans deserted me. What if Nazism isn't an inhuman monstrosity? What if it's *human*? What if it's a confession, a hidden truth, suppressed, camouflaged, denied, crouching deep within us, but always ready to reappear in the end? The Germans, yes of course, the Germans ... It's their turn in history, that's all. We'll see, after the war, once Germany has been defeated and Nazism has bolted or been buried, whether other peoples, in Europe, in Asia, in Africa, in America, don't pick up the torch. A comrade over from London brought us a chapbook of poems by a

French diplomat, Louis Roché. He wrote this verse about after the war, and it will remain forever in my memory:

> *The dawn it will be pearly,*
> *But heed your mother as she croons:*
> *There will be colossal killing*
> *Before the bells toll noon.*

I light my lamp. The kites are still there, but flying them is still forbidden. At head height, no higher—that's the rule. The authorities fear signs in the sky, they fear a code, messages exchanged, location markers, signals to the Resistance. Children barely have the right to drag them along by a string. No rising up. It's painful to see our Jean-Jacques or our Montaigne dragging over the ground, it's hard to see them crawling. Someday, they'll be free to take off again, in pursuit of the blue yonder. Then they'll begin to reassure us about ourselves again—to shake off these earthly pursuits and pursuers. Maybe kites don't have any real reason to exist other than this one: to put on airs and look heavenly.

I never let myself get too far out of hand. It was simply an instinct for self-preservation: whether it really was a sacred folly or the Fleurys were just plain crazy didn't matter much. What counted was the act of faith. There is no other key to survival. "*Do you understand, Ludo? Do you understand?*" I would wipe my eyes and go on.

Sometimes a few children still came and helped me when their parents' backs were turned: La Motte was three miles from Cléry and everyone was frugal about shoes. We would assemble kites, setting them aside for the future.

And then one morning I got a message from the Lady Esterhazy. She continued to come to the Clos Joli regularly, despite the cruel loss she was grieving: Chong had died. She told me the news herself, her eyes still reddened. "I'm going to buy myself a dachshund," she concluded, sniffing into her handkerchief. "You've got to keep up appearances."

It was May 12, 1944. During the lunch hour, my office door opened and Francis Dupré's face appeared at the door. With his padded shoulders, his slicked-back hair, his unnaturally long eyelashes, and his big tender eyes, he seemed like a character straight out of a Tino Rossi film. No doubt he had a decent dose of his "medication" in his veins, for he was in grand form. Madame Julie must've been "not forgetting" him rather carefully; times were more and more dangerous and the Gestapo was visibly nervous. The Gräfin needed her "100 percent Aryan" friend more than ever, and he could not let himself forget her, either. It's hard to imagine a reciprocal dependence more absolute—or more tragic.

"How are things, young man?" He came and sat down on my desk. "You should watch out, my friend. I saw a little list the other day, with names on it. Some of them were marked with an 'X.' Yours just had a question mark. So be careful."

I was silent. He swung one of his legs.

"I'm pretty worried myself. My friend, Commander Arnoldt, is expecting a transfer to Germany at any minute. I don't know what I'll do without him."

"Well, you could follow him to Germany."

"I don't see how."

"Surely he'll find a way."

I shouldn't have allowed myself to be so bitchy, because Isidore Lefkowitz became very pale.

"I'm sorry, Monsieur Dupré."

"It's nothing. I didn't know she'd told you."

"I've been told nothing. As for that question mark by my name... I've done nothing wrong."

"It all depends on the point of view from which one regards the idea one has of things..."

I finished the sentence: "... for the most perspicacious and circumspect of men is no less subject to a quantity of necessities whose importance is not in any way diminished by their lack of consequence."

We both began laughing. It was a silly game of rhetoric that every high school student knew.

"Janson de Sailly, year ten," he murmured. "My God, it all feels like it was so long ago, now!" He lowered his voice. "She wants to see you. At three o'clock this afternoon, in front of Le Manoir des Jars."

"Why at the manor? Why not at her house?"

"She has errands to run and it's on the way. And ..." He glanced down at his manicured fingernails, "I have no idea what's come over him, but dear old Grüber has gone completely over the top. Can you imagine, the day before yesterday, he had the audacity to search the countess's villa."

"No," I said, my heart in my throat.

I thought of Odette Lanier the "chambermaid" and our transceiver.

"Unbelievable, isn't it? Just a formality, of course. I'd let her know about it, in fact. There's a storm brewing, clearly. There's even word of an imminent landing ... My friend Franz—Commander Arnoldt—has a lot on his mind. The English and the Americans, if they dare such a thing, will obviously be tossed back into the sea. Well, one has to hope."

"We're living off hope."

We exchanged a long look and he departed.

It was one thirty in the afternoon. I couldn't sit still; I was at the manor an hour early. The ruins of what had been the Bronickis' Norman Turquerie were overgrown with weeds, and had taken on a curiously premeditated look, as if they'd been placed there with a studied abandon by some thoughtful artistic plan.

I was aware that the petrol shortage had sent us back to the age of the horse and carriage, but all the same, I was astonished to see Julie Espinoza pull up in a yellow phaeton, seated behind a coachman dressed in a blue livery and feathered Gibus hat. She descended majestically from the contraption, holding her head up beneath a two-story red wig, her bust thrown out like a ship's prow and her bottom like the stern. She had on a corseted dress of the kind no longer found anywhere but on postcards from the Belle Époque. Her virile-featured face looked even more determined than usual. With her pack of Gauloises in hand and a half-smoked cigarette dangling out of the corner of her mouth, she looked like a mind-boggling cross between Toulouse-Lautrec's La Goulue, a distinguished lady, and a firefighter. I could only stare at her stupidly as she explained. She sounded angry, which with her was a sure sign she was nervous.

"I'm throwing a 1900s garden party. I think that little shit Grüber is starting to suspect me, and when that happens you really have to pull out all the stops. I don't know what they're cooking up—the orders say it's a *Kriegspiel*—but all the Wehrmacht bigwigs from miles around have turned up here. They arrived at the Stag yesterday. I went big—I invited them all. Von Kluge is here, Rommel, too. Von Kluge was a military attaché in Budapest; he and my husband were quite close …"

"So what …"

"So what? Either we weren't married yet, or it was a different Esterhazy, it was his first cousin—that's what. It just depends on how the conversation goes. You think he'll have read up on it? He sent me flowers. The garden party is in his honor. Ah, Budapest in the twenties, the good old days, Admiral Horthy … I was assistant madam in one of the best whorehouses in Buda in '29. I know all the names."

She dropped her cigarette and crushed it out with her heel. "It was a close call with Grüber, but Francis warned me in time. Your Odette and her transceiver, if they'd found her … *Ssstt*!" She slid her thumb across her throat like a knife.

"Where did you hide them?"

"I kept Odette, she's my chambermaid. She has all the right paperwork, but the transceiver …"

"You didn't dump it, did you?"

"It's at Lavigne's—you know, the deputy mayor."

"Lavigne? Are you out of your ever-loving mind? He's a known collaborator!"

"Exactly. And now he can prove he was an authentic member of the Resistance."

She smiled ever so slightly at me, with pity. "You don't know the world yet, Ludo. You'll never know it, actually. Which is a good thing. We need people like you. If there weren't any men like your Uncle Ambrose and his kites, or you …"

"You know, for someone with the firing squad look in his eyes, like you were always saying to me … It's 1944. I've done all right so far."

My voice broke a little. I was thinking about the man who didn't know how to despair.

"He's in Buchenwald, I heard," Madame Julie said softly.

I was silent.

"Don't worry. He'll come back."

"What, you think your friend von Kluge will get him out of there?"

"He'll be back. I can feel it. I *want* him to come back."

"Look, I know you're a little witchy around the edges, Madame Julie, but a fairy godmother …"

"He'll be back. I have a sense for these things. You'll see."

"I'm not sure you and I will still be around to see it."

"We'll be here. Like I was telling you, Grüber didn't find anything. He even apologized. It's just for all of the big fish at the Stag, apparently. Exceptional caution is required. And it's true … one good bomb in there and … See what I'm saying?"

"I see. Well, we'll let London know, but there's nothing we can do for the moment. The Stag is too well guarded. It's impossible. Is that why you called me out here? We're not set up for that."

"You're right to lie low for a little while. I'll admit even I have been thinking about making a break for it. I arranged for a fallback position in the Loiret. But I've decided to stay. I'll hang in there. For now, the only thing shitting me …" She must have been really anxious, for her original vocabulary to resurface like that.

"The one and only thing shitting me right now is that guy."

She jerked her head toward the liveried coachman perched on the seat of the carriage, reins and whip in hand, blinking his eyes and looking completely bewildered.

"He doesn't speak a word of French, the bastard."

"An Englishman?"

"Not even. A Canadian, but the son of a bitch isn't a Francophile …"

"A Francophone."

"Your little friends dumped him with me yesterday, in a German uniform. I told them one night and no more. They've been passing him around for three weeks, now … I got him out easily enough with the phaeton and the livery for the garden party, but I don't know where to stash him. She gazed meditatively at the Canadian. "A shame—it's a little early. No one can say whether it's due to arrive this summer or in September. If we did know, I'd auction him off. Soon enough there'll be plenty of people—and you know who— who'd line up and pay good money for an Allied aviator to hide."

"What the hell do you want me to do with him in that getup?"

"You figure it out."

"Listen, Madame Julie …"

"Goddammit, I've told you a hundred times, there is no Madame Julie," she roared like a trooper. "It's Your Ladyship!"

She was so upset that her faint mustache was quivering. It really is a curious thing, I thought, the way hormones can lose their heads and go to ours. And right at that moment, for no apparent reason— maybe because Madame Julie only lost her temper when she was upset or worried—I understood. There was another reason for this meeting, and that reason must be Lila.

"Why did you send for me, Madame Julie? What do you have to tell me?"

She lit a Gauloise, the flame in the hollow of her hands, careful not to look at me.

"I have good news for you, kid. Your Polish girl is … well, she's safe and sound."

I stiffened, waiting for the blow. I knew her. She didn't want it to hurt too much.

"They arrested her after von Tiele's suicide. They really put her through the mill. I think it even affected her mind a little. They wanted to know whether she knew about the conspiracy. People thought she was von Tiele's mistress. People say stupid things."

"It's all right, Madame Julie. It's all right."

"They let her go, in the end."

"And then?"

"Well, after that I don't know what she did. Not the foggiest clue. There was her mother, her asshole father—that one, I tell you!—and they had nothing to live on. Well, anyway, to make a long story short…"

She seemed truly uneasy; she was still avoiding my gaze. She really did like me, Madame Julie.

"Our girl ended up with a friend of mine, Fabienne."

"Rue de Miromesnil," I said.

"Yeah, well, so what, rue de Miromesnil? Fabienne found her wandering the streets."

"Walking the streets."

Do you understand, Ludo? Do you understand? Above all I had to survive, save my own …

"Not at all, what are you trying to say? It's just that, rather than leaving her in the street, Fabienne took her in."

"Well, obviously a luxury bordello is better than the street."

"Listen, my little Ludo, the Nazis are making soap with Jews' bones, so worrying about cleanliness right now … You know Martini, the cabaret singer? In front of a house full of Nazis, he walked out on stage and raised his arm, as if he were doing the Nazi salute.

The Germans applauded. And then he raised his arm even higher, and said, 'All the way up to *here*, in shit!' What I'm saying is, there's no point in using inches to measure where the level is right now. And if Fabienne called me, it's because the girl doesn't fit in there. It takes skill to be a hooker—I'd even say it's a calling. It's not something you make up as you go along. Fabienne wanted to know what to do with her. So you go get her and bring her back to your house. Here, I brought you some cash. Go get her, bring her back home, be nice to her. It will fade. There's been enough black and white. Gray is the only thing that's human. Well, I'm off to my garden party. I brought in all the best whores. I'm going to try and save my skin. And get rid of this jerk for me. The Canadians had better learn French for the next war, otherwise I won't lift a finger for them."

She motioned the guy off his seat, lifted her skirts, and climbed up in his place. Then she grabbed the reins and the whip, and the phaeton moved off at a trot, carrying the old, undefeatable Madame Julie Espinoza to the countess Esterhazy's garden party. I left the pilot in the rubble of what had once been the manor's small sitting room, got word to Soubabère to have him seen to, and began gathering the necessary paperwork to get to Paris as quickly as possible.

45

I WAS SPARED THE TRIP TO MADAME FABIENNE'S *FÉE-ria* in the rue de Miromesnil. I regretted it a little, as the idea of testing my "insignificance" in this way made me feel rather proud. On May 14, I was in the workshop with the few children who still came to work with me, making provisions for the future, for the day when, the Nazis defeated, we would once again be permitted to take to the skies with our kites. The door opened, and I saw Lila. I got up and went to greet her, my arms open.

"Well, this is a surprise!"

Lightless, lifeless, her hair faded—only her beret, which she seemed to have carefully kept with her through all the vicissitudes, was like a smile from a bygone era. Her eyes, with their widened stare, the high cheekbones pushing up from under the muddy cast of her hollowed cheeks—all of it cried out for help, but it wasn't that distress that shook me. It was Lila's anxious, questioning gaze. She was scared. She must have been wondering whether I would throw her out. She tried to speak, her lips quivered, and that was all. When I held her to me, she remained tense, not daring to move, as if she didn't believe it. I sent the children away and made a fire; she remained seated on a bench, her hands clasped, staring at her feet. I didn't speak to her, either. I let the heat take its effect. All that we could say to each other said itself; the silence bustled about, doing its best, a true and faithful friend. At one point, the door opened, and Johnny Cailleux came in, most likely with some kind of urgent message or mission for me. Looking startled, he left without a word.

The first words Lila said were: "My books. We have to go get them."

"What books? Where?"

"In my suitcase. It was too heavy. I left it at the station, just sitting there. There's no checkroom."

"I'll go tomorrow, don't worry."

"Please, Ludo. I want them right now. It's very important to me."

I ran outside and caught up with Johnny. "Stay with her. Don't move."

I leapt onto my bike. It took me an hour to pedal all the way to the Cléry station, where I found the big suitcase in a corner. When I lifted it, the lock broke, and I stood there looking at the glory days of German painting, the Munich Art Gallery, the legacy of Greece, the Renaissance, Venetian artwork, the impressionists, and all the oils of Goya, Giotto, and El Greco, all tumbled out over the floor. I put everything back as best I could. I had to walk the whole way back, balancing the suitcase on my bicycle.

I found Lila sitting on the bench just as I had left her, with her fur-lined coat and her beret; Johnny was holding her hand. He squeezed my arm affectionately and left us. I set the suitcase down in front of the bench and opened it up.

"There you go," I said. "You see? Nothing's missing. Everything is there. Look for yourself, but I don't think anything is lost."

"I need it for my exam. I'm going to start at the Sorbonne in September. I'm studying art history, you know."

"I know."

She leaned over, picked up Velázquez. "It's very difficult, but I'll make it."

"I'm sure you will."

She set Velázquez down on El Greco and smiled with pleasure.

"They're all there," she said. "Except for the expressionists. The Nazis burned them."

"Yes, they've committed some atrocities."

She remained silent for a moment, then asked, in a tiny voice: "Ludo, how did all of this happen to me?"

"Well, first of all, they should have built the Maginot Line all the way to the sea, instead of leaving our left flank exposed. Then, we should have taken action as soon as they occupied the Rhineland. And then, our generals were all knuckleheads, de Gaulle was discovered too late…"

A ghost of a smile appeared on her lips and I felt like a good Fleury.

"I'm not talking about that … To me … How could I …"

"But that's exactly what it is. When things explode, there's always fallout. They even say that's how the universe was made: an explosion, and then fallout. Galaxies, the solar system, the earth, you, me, the chicken soup with vegetables that must be ready right about now. Come on. Let's eat."

She kept her fur-lined coat on at the table. She needed a shell.

"I have a magnificent rhubarb tart. Straight from the Clos Joli."

Her face brightened a little. "The Clos Joli …" she murmured. "How is Marcellin?"

"Admirable," I told her. "The other day, he said something magnificent. Legendre, the pastry chef, was complaining that all was lost — whinging about how the country will never fully recover, even if the Americans do win. Marcellin blew his top. He yelled, 'There will be no despairing over France in my kitchen!'"

Her gaze remained haunted. She held herself very straight, her hands clasped on her lap. In the fireplace, the fire kept to itself.

"We need a cat here," I said. "Grimaud died of old age. We'll get another one."

"I can really stay?"

"You were never gone, lady. You stayed here the whole time. You never left my side."

"Don't be angry with me. I didn't know what I was doing anymore."

"We won't talk about it. Actually, it's just the same for France.

After the war, they'll say, she was with those guys, she was with these guys. She did this, no, she did that. It's all talk. You weren't with *them*, Lila. You were with me."

"I'm beginning to believe you."

"I haven't asked you about your family."

"My father is doing a bit better."

"Ah, he deigned to regain consciousness?"

"When Georg died and we ended up penniless, he found work in a bookshop."

"Always was a bibliophile."

"Obviously, it wasn't enough to live on." She lowered her head. "I don't know how I ended up doing that, Ludo."

"I already explained it to you, my darling. General von Rundstedt's tank corps. The Blitzkrieg. You have nothing to do with it. It wasn't you, it was Gamelin and the Third Republic. If they'd asked *you*, you would have declared war on Hitler as soon as he occupied the Rhineland—I know that. Right at the moment Albert Sarraut was proclaiming to the National Assembly, 'We will never abandon the Cathedral at Strasbourg to the threat of German cannons.'"

"You make fun of everything, Ludo. But I've never seen a more serious heart."

"You hold up better, pretending to laugh."

She waited, then murmured, "And … Hans?"

I tugged my shirt collar open a little way and she saw the locket. Outside, we could hear birds singing, with their strong idyllic tendencies. Sometimes a little irony goes a long way.

"And now I'm going to make you some real coffee, Lila. You only live once, so they say."

She suffered from insomnia, and spent her nights curled up in a corner with her art books, studiously taking notes. During the day, she did her best to "make herself useful," as she called it. She helped me with the housework, looked after the children, who came not only every Thursday but also after school on most days; the kites piled up everywhere, waiting for the day they could rise again. Comically enough, the Cléry school director qualified these courses as "applied learning," and we even began receiving funds from the town council—provisions for the future. Word on the street was that it was due to arrive in August or September.

She slept in my arms, but following a few timid attempts I no longer dared to touch her—she accepted my caresses, but holding still, with no reaction of any kind. It wasn't just her sensuality that seemed to have been snuffed out. It was something deeper, something in her very senses. I understood how deeply her guilt tortured her on the day I noticed there were burns covering her hands.

"What on earth is that?"

"I scalded myself."

It wasn't believable: the burns were each distinct from one another, separated and regularly spaced. The following night, I woke up, sensing that her side of the bed was empty. Lila wasn't in the room. I went to the door and leaned over the stairs.

There was Lila, standing with a candle in her right hand, deliberately burning the left one with the flame.

"No!"

She dropped the candle and lifted her eyes.

"I hate myself, Ludo. I hate myself!"

Never before, I think, had I experienced such a shock. I remained frozen in the stairwell, unable to think, to act. This horrible and childish attempt at punishing herself, an atonement—it seemed so unjust to me, so revolting, when so many of our comrades were fighting and dying to restore her honor. My legs gave out from under me and I fainted. When I opened my eyes, Lila was leaning over me, her face in tears.

"Forgive me, Ludo, I won't do it again ... I wanted to punish myself ..."

"Why, Lila? For what? Punish yourself for what? You're not guilty. You're not responsible. None of that will remain. I'm not even asking you to forget. Not at all. I'm just asking you to think about it sometimes and shrug. My God ... My God, how could a person lack so much ... insignificance? How could you be so inhuman—so intolerant toward yourself?"

She slept, that night. And the next day I saw a great deal of lightness and gaiety in her face. She had taken a turn for the better, I thought, and I was soon proven right.

Every morning, Lila took her bicycle to run errands in Cléry. Every morning, I would walk her to the door and watch her go: nothing made me smile more than that skirt, those knees, that flying hair. One day she came home and put her bike away; I was in front of the house.

"Huh," she said.

"What is it?"

"I was coming back from the grocer's with my basket, and this lady was standing there waiting for me. I said hello to her, I didn't remember her name—I know so many people around here. So I set my basket on my bike and I was getting ready to go when she came up right beside me and called me a *Bochesse*."

I examined her carefully. She was *truly* smiling. It wasn't one of those smiles you wear in defiance, or put on so you don't cry. She wrinkled her nose, and ran her hand through her hair.

"Huh," she repeated. "Huh. Bochesse. And there you have it."

"Everyone can feel victory coming, Lila—so everybody's getting ready for it in their own way. Don't give it another thought."

"Oh no, I have to think about it."

"Why on earth is that?"

"Because feeling like the victim of an injustice is so much better than feeling guilty."

46

IT WAS JUNE 2. FOUR DAYS LATER, WE WERE FLAT ON
our stomachs one mile to the east of La Motte as the bombs fell around
us. Even today, I remain convinced that the first successful hit made
by the thousands of Allied boats and airplanes engaged in Operation
Overlord was my bicycle: I found it in twisted ruins in front of the
house. "They're coming," "They're on the way," "They're here," were
the only sentences I believe I heard all day. As we ran past the Cailleux
farm, old Gaston Cailleux was outside, and, having informed us that
"they're coming," he added a sentence he couldn't have heard on Radio London, as de Gaulle only uttered it a few hours after that: "My
little Ludo, this is the battle of France, and it's France's battle!"

But I guess historic statements are like everything else in life: once
in a while, the impossible draws a winning hand.

We left him there, with his crutch, jumping for joy on his one and
only leg.

There wasn't a German soldier in sight. All around us the fields
and woods were being barraged with fire, most likely to prevent enemy reinforcements from reaching the beaches.

I hadn't yet learned to distinguish between the whistle of a bomb
falling from an airplane and the whistle of shellfire, so it took a while
for me to figure out; just as you might expect, hell comes from the
sky. There were more than ten thousand sorties made that day by the
Allied air force over Normandy.

We had only covered a few hundred yards when I saw a body lying across the path, unmoving, arms spread-eagled. It was a body I was used to seeing; I recognized it from far off: Johnny Cailleux. Eyes closed, head bloodied; he was dead. I was certain of it. I loved him too much for anything else to be possible.

I turned to Lila. "Come on, what are you waiting for? Examine him, for God's sake!"

She looked surprised, but crouched down beside Johnny and pressed her ear against his chest. I actually think I laughed. In all those years of her absence, I'd spent so much time imagining her caring for the wounded in the Polish Resistance that I expected her to perform her duties as a nurse. And that's exactly how she looked just then, bent over the body of my comrade, searching for a sign of life. She turned to me. "I think …"

Right at that moment Johnny moved. He sat up on his rear end, snorted, shook his head three or four times, his eyes still a little hazy, and shouted, "They're coming!"

"Goddamn son of a bitch!" I yelled out in relief.

"They're here! They're coming!"

I grabbed Lila by the hand and we started to run.

I wanted to find shelter for Lila and then join my comrades. The "Green Plan" had long ago given us our mission: we were to attack convoys and sabotage rail lines and high-tension lines. We were to meet in the Orne—but nothing went off as planned. When, the next day, I finally managed to locate Souba, I found our dear commander in a blind rage. Dressed in a magnificent uniform—he'd promoted himself to colonel—he stood there shaking his fist at the sky, in which Allied planes were circling.

"Those bastards screwed it all up," he shouted. "They screwed up all our communications. All our guys are wandering the countryside! If that isn't a horrible goddamn waste I don't know what is!"

He wasn't far off cursing the Allied landing. Even many years later he would still grumble whenever it was mentioned in his presence. I think he would have liked to resist for another twenty years.

Each time a bomb showered us with earth, Lila would stroke my face: "Are you afraid of dying, Ludo?"

"I'm not afraid, but I'm in no hurry for it, either."

We left La Motte at six in the morning, and by six that evening we were still only two miles past the milepost at Clos. It was there, lying flat on our stomachs behind an embankment, sniffing the air to try and guess where the next wave of the assault would be coming from, that we were treated to a spectacle. To this day, I don't know whether it was pathetic, heroic, or both at the same time. Four Percheron horses filed past us, the first one harnessed to a wagon and the others to carts, all plodding along with an indifference to the world around them that they must have caught from their owners. The Magnard family was moving house. There they were, piled together in the wagon, the two daughters seated on crates of provisions, the father and son standing at the front. The carts behind them were piled with the furniture, beds, chairs, mattresses, chests, wardrobes, bundles of linens, and barrels. Three cows followed up from behind. They jostled along the road, their expressions just as closed as ever, without so much as a glance toward the sky or the earth. I will never know whether the Magnards were bovine or superhuman. Who knows, maybe it was just their own brand of kite.

This procession of invulnerable humans left me embarrassed and a little ashamed, since I was sweating bullets, but Lila laughed.

"You're all the same, you Polish folk," I grumbled. "The worse things get the better you are."

"Give me a cigarette."

"I'm all out."

The incident that occurred just then returned all hope to me. A few isolated shots rang out from behind us, followed by machine gun fire. Quickly, I spun around. An American soldier backed slowly out of the woods, his machine gun in hand. He waited a moment; then, looking reassured, he touched his side and examined his hand. He appeared to have just been slightly wounded. It didn't seem to concern him; he sat down on the ground beneath a bush, took a packet of cigarettes from his pocket—and then exploded.

He literally exploded, all at once, for no apparent reason, disappearing in a rain of earth that fell to the ground as quickly as it had flown upward—but without him. I think that same bullet that had caused his minor wounds must have touched the pin of one of the grenades hanging from his belt. When he sat down, it must have dislodged the pin the rest of the way. He had disappeared.

"Too bad," Lila said. "They must be all gone."

"All what?"

"He had a whole pack in his hand. I haven't smoked an American cigarette in years."

At first I was horribly upset. I was on the verge of saying, "Darling, that's not keeping your cool, that's downright cold," when suddenly, happiness washed through me. It was the Lila of our childhood, the Lila of wild strawberries and little provocations: she had returned.

We lay flat there, behind the embankment, for nearly an hour. There was no trace of the Germans anywhere, and I couldn't understand why the bombs and shells would be coming down so hard in the woods and fields.

"You'd think it was us they were after!"

Calmly, she pulled clumps of dirt out of her hair. "You know Ludo, I've already been killed several times in my life."

A few days later, Souba explained the reasons for this nearly continuous bombardment of a dozen square miles of the Norman countryside, so far from the landing beaches. An American airborne division had been dropped and scattered too far inland by mistake, and so a German unit had been pulled from the coastal regions to fight off what they thought was a premeditated maneuver. We had been caught in its fire, as well as that of the English regiment guarding the two bridges over the Orne River as the Allied air force bombed all of the region's roads and railways.

We took advantage of a moment of calm to advance a little in the direction of the Orne, when about a hundred yards ahead of us, we saw a line of German tanks appear. It was the armored division that had, at four o'clock that afternoon, received orders from Hitler to cut back the Allied bridgehead.

My only thought was, "They'll shoot at anything that moves," which cropped up from an account of some massacre or another. I took Lila's hand. We froze in the middle of the field. Not one of my fallen comrades had been lucky enough to have his hand held in this way. In a manner of speaking, this was my last thought. And the brightness, the burst of sunlight among heavy, gray clouds, that little scrap of blue sky that always knows to shine the very best of itself at just the right moment. And Lila's profile, her blonde hair falling over her neck and shoulders—her face, in which fear had chosen a smile.

There was a German officer standing in the gun turret of the tank at the head of the formation. As they drove by, he raised his hand in a minute gesture of friendship. I will never know who he was or why he saved our lives. I don't know whether it was out of scorn, or humanity, or if it was merely a matter of style. Perhaps the sight of a couple of lovebirds holding hands had caused him, too, for just a moment, to yield to higher faith. And then again, maybe he just had a sense of humor—I don't know. Once he had passed us, he turned, laughing, and gave us another little wave.

"Phew," said Lila.

We were exhausted and starving; more than that, in the chaos, there was no particular reason to pick one place over another. We weren't far from the Clos Joli, which was about two miles to the south, but the bombing seemed most intense in that area, most likely because of the Orcq Bridge and the highway; nevertheless, if anything remained of the restaurant, we were sure to find something to eat, even among the ruins. Emerging onto the Ligny Road, we stopped up short: there before us was an armored car, upended and burnt, still smoking. Two German soldiers lay dead beside the vehicle; a third one was sitting with his back against a tree, holding his belly, his eyes rolled back, emitting the groaning hiss of an empty hose. His faced seemed familiar to me and at first I thought I knew him, and then right away I understood that what was familiar to me was the expression of suffering. I had already seen it on our comrade Duverrier's face after he escaped from the Cléry Gestapo and dragged himself to the Buis' farm to die there. German or French, in those moments, it's actually interchangeable. I thought of that later on, every time I heard the term "blood bank." He had a beseeching look. I tried to hate him, so I wouldn't have to finish him off. It was no good. You have to have it in you. I had no talent for it. I took his Mauser, cocked it in front of him, and waited, to be absolutely sure. Something approaching a smile appeared on his face. "*Ja, gut...*"

I lodged two bullets in his heart, one for him, and one for everything else.

It was my first gesture of Franco-German brotherhood.

Lila had blocked her ears, closed her eyes, and turned her head, in a movement that was feminine, or childlike, or both.

I felt, rather stupidly, that I had made friends with this dead German.

Six American planes flew over us and dropped their bombs in the place where the armored division must have been. Lila watched them. "I hope they didn't kill him," she said.

I think she meant the tank commander who had spared us. My nerves were so frayed that I was overcome by my weakness for mental math, which emerged as a defense mechanism for my sanity when it felt threatened. I told Lila that we had covered about twelve miles, when we'd actually only advanced about three or four, and I estimated our chances of survival at around one in ten. I placed the number of shells and bombs we had dodged at a thousand, and the number of planes we'd seen overhead at thirty thousand. I'm not sure if I was trying to prove my godlike equanimity to Lila or if I was actually beginning to lose my head. We were sitting by the side of the road, exhausted, drenched in sweat, bleeding here and there where we'd been grazed, reduced to the merely physical presence of our bodies. We were pulled out of our torpor by a bombing so violent that the entire forest two hundred yards ahead of us was pulverized before our eyes in the space of a few seconds. We took off running through the fields toward Ligny and ended up in front of the Clos Joli a half hour later. I was struck by the immutability of the place. It had not been marred in any way. The chimney smoked quietly. The flowers in the garden, the orchard, the old chestnut trees—they had a serenity which to me bore witness to some sort of deep certainty. I was hardly in a meditative mood in that moment, but for the first time since the day had begun, I remember feeling the both bizarre and soothing impression that everything was saved.

The intact, red-curtained rotunda was completely empty. The tables were set, ready for service to begin. The crystal sang with each explosion. The portrait of Brillat-Savarin was in its place—a little off kilter, it's true.

We found Marcellin Duprat at work in the kitchen. He was very pale and his hands were trembling. He was just pulling a *panade aux trois viandes*—which requires several hours of cooking—from the oven. He must have started at the beginning of the shake-up. I don't know whether it was an attempt to soothe fear with familiar gestures, or a loud report for duty. His eyes shone from his haggard, worn-looking face with a gleam I recognized as the madness so dear to me. I thought of my uncle Ambrose. I went over to Duprat, and, with tears in my eyes, embraced him. He appeared unsurprised, perhaps even unconscious of my gesture.

"They all left me in the lurch," he croaked, his voice hoarse. "I'm all alone. No one to run the front of the house. I'll be in fine fettle if the Americans show up now."

"I don't think the Americans will be here for a few more days," I told him.

"They should have let me know."

"About the landing, Monsieur Duprat?" I stuttered.

He thought about it. "Do you not find it interesting that they chose Normandy?"

I looked at him in astonishment. But no, he wasn't pulling my leg. He was crazy, splendidly crazy.

"They must have studied the Michelin Guide and picked the best spot," Lila observed

I glanced at her furiously. I almost thought I heard Tad's sarcastic voice. It seemed to me that sacred flame of such grandeur deserved a bit more respect, if not downright piety.

Duprat gestured to the big back room. "Sit down."

He served his *panade* to us himself.

"Taste it, taste it. I had to make it from leftovers. How is it? Not too bad, given the circumstances. There were no deliveries today. Well, what can you do?" He went to get the tart from the oven. As he was returning, I heard a whistle I had learned to recognize. I just barely had the time to grab Lila, push her to the ground, and lie down on top of her. The explosions continued for several minutes, but they were happening somewhere near the Orcq, and just one window was broken.

We got back up. Duprat had remained standing, holding the tart in its dish. "It's safe here," he stated in a voice I didn't recognize as his. It was muted, mechanical: it came from the very depths of his refusal, and he underlined it with his fixed glare. *"They wouldn't dare,"* he added.

I helped Lila to her feet and we returned to our seats at the table. Never, I imagine, has Duprat's Norman tart been less appreciated. The Clos Joli trembled from top to bottom. The glassware sang. After a day of hesitating, Hitler had, at that late hour, given the order to launch two strategic reserve divisions to support his Eighth Army.

Duprat hadn't budged. He was smiling—and with what scorn, with what superiority!

"See," he observed. "It missed us. And it will always miss us."

I attempted to explain to him that I was planning to reach Neuvet before nightfall and then continue along the Orne River to join my combat unit.

"Mademoiselle Bronicka can stay here," he told me. "She'll be safe."

"Come on, Monsieur Duprat, haven't you thought about it? You're going to take a hit at some point."

"Oh, please. You think the Americans are going to destroy the Clos Joli? They can't afford to. The Germans didn't touch it."

I was speechless. Such crazy confidence in his three stars inspired an almost religious respect in me. Clearly, in his mind, the Allied troops had received orders, possibly from General Eisenhower himself, to ensure that this hallowed place in France remain intact.

I tried to convince him: the Clos Joli was going to be caught up in deadly crossfire. He should leave the place. All I got out of him was, "No way. You've hassled me for long enough with your Maquis and your Resistance. Now it's my turn to show you who is, and always has been, the true leader of the French Resistance!"

I couldn't resign myself to leaving him like that, in cloud-cuckoo land; I was sure he had lost his mind and was going to die among the ruins of the Clos Joli. In my head was a map of the area's roads, bridges, and railways, and I knew that if the Allies weren't pushed back to the sea, then the most intense fighting would have to take place right where we were. But Lila had reached her limit; a glance at her face affirmed that she was in no state to follow me. I knew that if there really was a God, as they say, then she had as much chance of getting out alive here as anywhere else: it was one of those moments where you think of God, who's a past master at the art of biding His time. It also occurred to me that it wasn't the level of risk that was making me unsure about leaving Lila with Duprat—it was because

I didn't want to leave her. And yet I was desperate to join my comrades. How could I hesitate? We had waited for this moment with too much hope and for too long. It was Duprat who decided it for me. He appeared to emerge from his daze, put his arm around my shoulders, and said, "My good Ludo, you can rest assured, Mademoiselle Bronicka will be safe and sound here. I have the best cellars in France. I'll put her in the safest spot, right with the best wines, where nothing can happen to her. I don't know who said, 'happy as God in France,' but I'm sure that God will know to watch over what's His."

This time, I could discern a tiny gleam of amusement in the old fox's eyes. Perhaps someday I should sit down and have another good think about Duprat, to try and figure out how much of his "folly" was good old Norman cunning. I embraced Lila. I knew myself: I knew that nothing could happen to her. I wanted to cry, but it was only from exhaustion.

I made my way to my unit without too much trouble. At one in the morning, as I was crossing the marshes, I ran into a group of black American parachutists who had gotten their landing wrong and didn't know where they were. I brought them to Neuvet, which was our rallying point, where I found Souba and twenty-odd comrades. As I've said, our orders were to carry out sabotage missions, but for many of us, the temptation to engage in armed combat was too great. Most were killed. From June 8 to June 16, we had one submachine gun for ten men, with a hundred cartridges, and two light machine guns with a hundred and fifty cartridges. Added to that, for the survivors, were the weapons they managed to capture from the enemy. As for me, I stuck to blowing up railways, bridges, and telephone lines. I didn't want to kill any men, and unfortunately, by the time you manage to figure out whether it's a man or an SS officer, it's always too late—he's already dead. I also think I was a little paralyzed by the memory of that tank commander who spared Lila and me. But I did good work, in the rear guard, as the Wehrmacht retreated.

47

I HAD NO NEWS OF LILA FOR THREE WEEKS. LATER, she told me that Duprat had been extremely kind to her, although once he had done something that surprised her enormously: he'd pinched her bottom. He'd seemed terribly abashed about it—but one had to lose some battles to win the war, even at his age. She stayed at the Clos Joli for two weeks, helping Duprat to greet the Americans and trying to translate the map of France into English—which, according to Duprat, was entirely unthinkable. Then she returned to La Motte, where I found her on July 10. The next day, we made our way into Cléry together. The fighting continued, but its rumbles in Normandy now resembled little more than a far off thunderstorm. I pasted a notice to the door of the town hall: the workshop in La Motte would be starting up again the next day and any local children interested in what Ambrose Fleury called "the kindly art of the kite" were welcome. Lila had kept her bicycle and its basket, and she went to the Americans to try and get chocolate for the children. She wanted to celebrate the reopening of "classes" at La Motte with a real gala afternoon tea.

As for me, I hitched a ride on a military truck bound for the Stag, where the Americans had set up their headquarters. It dropped me off at the entrance to the grounds. I wanted to say goodbye to Madame Julie, who was returning to Paris.

I found her in tears, collapsed in her armchair beside the piano, where the photographs of the Gräfin Esterhazy's old "friends" had been replaced with portraits of de Gaulle and Eisenhower.

"What's wrong, Madame Julie?"

She could barely speak.

"They ... shot ... him!"

"Who?"

"Francis ... I mean, little Isidore Lefkowitz. And I had taken every precaution ... You remember the 'Great Resistance Fighter' certificate, the one Soubabère left blank so I could fill in the name myself?"

"Of course I do."

"It was for him. I'd given it to him. He had it in his pocket when they shot him. They stuck him in a truck with two other Gestapo collabos—real ones—and they murdered him. They found the certificate afterward. Izzy never showed it to them! He was probably scared out of his mind and so doped up he forgot!"

"That might not be it, Madame Julie. Maybe he was just sick of it all."

She stared at me, stupefied.

"Sick of what all? Of life? Have you lost your mind?"

"Maybe he was sick of himself, the dope—everything."

She was inconsolable. "Those bastards. After everything he did for you ..."

"We didn't shoot him, Madame Julie. It's the new guys. The ones who joined the Resistance after the Germans left."

I tried to hug her but she pushed me away. "Get out of here. I never want to see you again."

"Madame Julie ..."

There was nothing for it. For the first time since I'd known her, this indomitable woman gave in to despair. I left her there, an old woman in tears who, like poor Isidore, must've been suffering from a momentary lapse in memory: she couldn't recall where she'd left her "toughness."

A Jeep brought me back to Cléry and dropped me off in the rue Vieille-de-l'Église. I was supposed to meet Lila in the Place du Jour, which had recently been renamed La Place de la Victoire. As I entered the square, I found myself at the edge of a crowd pushing toward the fountain. There were shouts and laughter, children running about, and two or three people walking away, most of them older. One of them was Monsieur Lemaine, a friend of my uncle's and a veteran of the Great War, who'd had a stiff knee since Verdun. He limped past me, stopped, nodded his head, and walked away, grumbling. I couldn't see what was happening by the fountain. I would hardly have paid it any mind had I not noticed the strange looks I was getting. Leleu, the new owner of the Petit-Gris; Charviaut, the grocer in the rue Baudouin; Colin, the stationer, and others—they all stared at me with a mixture of discomfort and pity.

"What's going on?"

They each turned away without a word.

I dashed forward.

Lila was sitting in a chair by the fountain, her head shaved. Chinot, the barber, his clippers in hand, a smile on his lips, had stepped back a little to admire his handiwork. Lila was sitting quietly on the chair, wearing a summer dress, her hands clasped in her lap. For a few seconds, I couldn't move. Then something tore at my throat, a cry. I threw myself at Chinot, punched him in the face, grabbed Lila's arm, and dragged her through the throng. The people stepped aside: it was over and done with, the "little lady" had been made to pay for sleeping with the enemy. Later, when I was able to think about it, what remained, beyond the horror, was the memory of all those familiar faces, faces I'd known since childhood. They weren't monsters—that was what was so monstrous.

The memories are there, ineffaceable. I ran through the streets, tugging Lila by the arm. It felt as if I would never stop running. I wasn't running toward the end of the earth: we were already there.

I didn't know where I was going, and indeed there was nowhere to go. I screamed.

I heard steps behind me. I swung around, fist cocked. I recognized the face of Monsieur Boyer, the baker, panting, with his big belly.

"Come to my place, Fleury, it's right here."

He pulled us into the bakery. His wife looked at Lila, horrified, and began crying into her apron. Boyer took us upstairs and left us alone. Closing the door, he said to me: "Now the Nazis have really won the war."

I helped Lila onto the bed. She didn't move. I sat down beside her. I don't know how long we stayed like that. From time to time, I stroked her head. It would grow back, of course. It always grows back.

Her eyes had a fixedness that seemed to reflect the indelible image inside her. The jeering faces. The clippers in the hands of a brave village barber.

"It's nothing, darling. It's just the Nazis. They've been here for four years and they left their mark."

That evening Monsieur Boyer served us a meal, but it was impossible to get Lila to eat. She remained prostrate, her eyes wide open, and I thought of her father, who had retreated from reality, "heart and parcel," as Lila had put it to me. These aristocrats—really, when you think of it, what is one young woman's shaved head? It's almost friendly considered alongside everything the others did—the extermination camps, the torture. The others, you know—but what others, actually?

Sometimes shared humanity is pretty damn ugly.

In the middle of the night, I got up and set fire to the Clos Joli. I soaked the old walls in gasoline, and when they began to crumble, I finally fell into peaceful sleep. Luckily, it was just a bad dream.

Monsieur Boyer went and got Dr. Gardieu, who told us that Lila was in a state of shock. He gave her an injection so that she would sleep. When the door opened, I could hear the radio announcing news of our victories.

That afternoon, she woke up, smiled at me, and raised her hand to run her fingers through her hair.

"My God, what ..."

"The Nazis," I said.

She hid her face in her hands. Tears bring comfort, it's often said.

We stayed with the Boyers for a week. And, every day, I went out with Lila and we walked though the streets of Cléry, holding hands. We'd walk slowly, for hours and hours, so that they could all see us, straight ahead, a young woman with a shaved head and me, Ludovic Fleury, twenty-three years old and known throughout the country for my memory. I told myself that we'd really miss the Nazis, that it would be difficult without them, because we wouldn't have any excuses anymore. On the fifth day of our demonstration, Monsieur Boyer arrived in our room with the newspaper *France-Soir*, looking very moved: there was a picture of us, strolling hand in hand through Cléry. I hadn't known that my face was capable of such hardness. The next day, our demonstration was interrupted by three men wearing FFI armbands. I knew them. They had joined the official "Resistance" eight days after the Allied landing.

"Are you done with your little show yet?"

"Well, they did do it for show, didn't they?"

"You're going to end up with a bullet in the ass, Fleury. Enough is enough. What are you trying to prove?"

"Nothing. The proof's been there for a long time." They let it go at that, and walked off calling me a nutter. We continued our "walk" for a few more days. It was Monsieur Boyer who made me decide to quit.

"They're used to seeing you. It doesn't affect them anymore."

We went back home to La Motte, and stayed put until October, when we left to get married.

Johnny Cailleux brought us supplies every morning, and gave us a puppy from a litter they'd had at the farm; Lila named it Darling, which caused a fair amount of confusion at home; every time she called out, we'd both come running. Those days were not without unhappiness, though—it's needed in life; you can't live without it. We learned that Bruno had been reported missing in combat in November 1943. He had notched up seventeen victories by then and was one of the most decorated aviators in the Royal Air Force. We sent letter after letter off to Poland to try and obtain news of Tad, but in vain.

Lila decided to put off going to the Sorbonne for another year, so that she would be better prepared. She studied a lot. *Trends in Contemporary Art, Treasures of German Painting, The Complete Works of Vermeer, Masterpieces across the Centuries, The Western World through Its Museums*—the books piled up around the little table she had set up near the workshop window.

Her parents didn't come to our wedding. The difficult circumstances they'd endured hadn't caused them to forget their rank, and they disapproved of Lila marrying beneath her station. Social stock had risen rapidly to its prewar value and Stas Bronicki had bounced right back again. Instead, our witnesses were Duprat himself and the "countess" Esterhazy, who, with democracy's return, had become Julie Espinoza again. She arrived at the town hall in an American army car driven by a GI, in the company of two ravishing young ladies.

"I'm rebuilding my network," she explained to us.

She looked magnificent in her towering Christian Dior hat and with her little golden lizard, which had never left her and was now tucked into the hollow of her shoulder.

Madame Julie was disappointed that we weren't having a church wedding.

Duprat wore a morning coat, with an orchid in his buttonhole. *Life* magazine had just featured him in an article that is still on display—above the portrait of Brillat-Savarin—with Robert Capa's famous cover shot of the Clos Joli with its lord and master. He's standing by the door in his chef's uniform, beneath the headline, "A Certain Idea of France." The article provoked great ire in the Parisian press. It's true that in 1945, the country didn't hold haute cuisine in quite the same esteem as it does today. I don't know what idea the Americans had back then of the role they'd leave for France in the new world order, but they admired the Clos Joli and its illustrious proprietor at least as much as the Germans had.

The morning before the ceremony, Lila stared at herself in the mirror for a long time. Then she made a face: "I need to go to the hairdresser …"

Her hair had barely grown an inch. At first I didn't understand. There was only one hairdresser in Cléry, and it was Chinot, the barber. I looked over at her and she grinned back at me. I understood.

Duprat had lent us one of his vans for the day, and at eleven thirty we pulled up in front of the barbershop. Chinot was alone inside. He backed away a little when he saw us.

"I'd like you to cut my hair in the latest style again," Lila announced. "Look. It's grown back. It doesn't show anymore."

She walked over to a chair and sat down, smiling. "Like last time, please," she said.

Chinot still hadn't moved. He had gone pale.

"Come on, Monsieur Chinot," I told him. "Our wedding is later today and we're in a hurry. My fiancée would like you to shave her head, just like you did six weeks ago. Don't tell me you've lost your inspiration so quickly."

He glanced at the door but I shook my head. "Come on, come on," I said. "I know those heady first days are over and your heart's not in it anymore, but you've got to keep carrying the torch."

I picked up the clippers and held them out to him. He stepped back.

"I told you, we're in a hurry, Chinot. My fiancée had an unforgettable experience and that's exactly why she wants to be seen looking her best."

"Leave me alone!"

"I have no desire to let you have it, Chinot, but if you insist …"

"It wasn't my idea, I swear to you! They came to get me and …"

"We're not here to talk about whether it was 'them,' 'me,' 'I,' 'their guys,' or 'our guys,' old pal. It's always *us*. Come on. Go ahead."

He walked over to the chair. Lila was laughing. *Intact*, I thought. *It always stays intact.*

Chinot got to work. In a few minutes, Lila's head was shaved as closely as it had been in those first days. She leaned forward and admired herself in the mirror.

"It really suits me."

She stood. I turned to Chinot.

"How much do I owe you?"

He was silent, his mouth hanging open.

"How much? I don't like being in anyone's debt."

"Three francs fifty."

"Here's four, for tip."

He threw down the clippers and fled to the back of the shop.

When we arrived at the town hall, everyone was waiting for us. There was a great silence when they saw Lila's shaven head. Duprat's mustache quivered nervously a few times. Seeing the faces of my comrades from the Espoir network, you would have thought that the Nazis had returned and we had to start all over again. Only Julie Espinoza rose to the occasion. She walked up to Lila and gave her a kiss.

"Darling, what an excellent idea! It looks fabulous on you!"

Lila was very cheerful, and the slight unease that had overtaken the guests lifted immediately. After the ceremony, we went to the Clos Joli, and at the end of the luncheon Marcellin Duprat spoke with feeling about those who had "remained at their posts," without a single reference to himself. He simply recalled the trials "we all had to face, each at his own battle station," and then said something I couldn't quite hear; I couldn't tell whether he was speaking of his joy at being able to return the Clos Joli to France or France to the Clos

Joli. At the end, he turned to the American officers we had invited and glared at them in silence for a moment, darkly.

"As for the future, we can't help feeling a certain degree of worry. Already, my good sirs, from your great and beautiful country, I hear rumors that make me fear the worst. Our France, which has known such suffering, will now be put to a new test. I'm already hearing talk of chickens fattened with hormones, and even, may God forgive me, frozen and ready-made dishes. Never, my American friends, will Marcellin Duprat bow down to ready-to-eat cuisine. Anyone who wants to turn our France into a feeding trough will have me to deal with first. *I will stand firm.*"

There was cheering. The Americans were the first to applaud. Duprat raised his hand.

"There's no use denying it. After the years we've just been through, the road will be a rocky. We haven't been able to train our youth. Nevertheless, I remain convinced that what I have given everything to defend will grow stronger each day, and that in the end it will take root and triumph in a way we have yet to imagine. As for you, Ludovic Fleury, who fought so hard for this future, and you, Madame, who I've known since you were a little girl, you are young enough to be certain of seeing the France that I, old man that I am, can only dream of. And when you do, have a little friendly thought for me and say, 'Marcellin Duprat got it right.'"

This time, the applause lasted a good minute. Madame Espinoza wiped her eyes.

"One more thing. Someone is missing from this table. A friend, a great soul, a man who did not know how to despair. You guessed it: I'm talking about Ambrose Fleury. We miss him. Ludo, I know how your heart must be grieved. But let's not lose courage. We may get him back. Perhaps we'll see him appear again among us, the man who was able to express, with such constancy, through the kindly art of the kite, everything that remains eternally pure and inalterable on this earth. I raise my glass to you, Ambrose Fleury. Wherever you are, know that your spiritual son is continuing your work, and, thanks to that, the French skies will never be empty!"

It was true that I had returned to our workshop. Never, since my uncle's departure, had it been so active. The country needed to rebuild its spirits, and orders were coming in from all over. Our stock had suffered a lot and we more or less had to start from scratch. Most of the pieces had been burned, but the ones my uncle had managed to hide with neighbors, a good fifty of them, served as our models. They had been poorly cared for, however, and they, too, had wasted away and lost their shapes and colors. I knew the craft and worked quickly. The only question was whether, after all that I had seen and experienced, I might be lacking in inspiration. A kite requires a great deal of innocence. There was also the problem of supplies, and we were penniless. Duprat helped us a bit—it was vital, he said, to maintain this local attraction—but it was Madame Julie Espinoza who really got us afloat again. In liberated Paris, Madame Julie turned over the brightest new leaf of her career, the one that would, in the thirty years that followed, make her the celebrity she is today. I had hesitated a little—I wondered what my uncle would have thought if he'd known that our kites were being financed, after a fashion, by Paris's number one madam. But patronage has always existed, and it seemed to me that if I refused this help because of where it came from, I would end up in league with those people who sanctify what we do between the sheets, making them into the twin sources of good and evil. So we went to see Madame Julie in Paris. She had set herself up in the beautiful apartment she'd managed to have requisitioned for herself, decorated in the style of Louis XV. She served us tea and we chatted about her problems with the competition, particularly from Le Chabanais and 122 rue de Provence—she was indignant that the same houses that had entertained the Germans had stayed open for business and were now entertaining the Americans.

"They've got a lot of damn nerve, some of these ladies," she growled.

I saw that she was all the more ready to help because, the day before, she had witnessed an admirable scene between Duprat and Madame Fabienne, the madam at the rue de Miromesnil. She had come to lunch at the Clos Joli in the company of the American military attaché, and she'd had the nerve to inform Duprat that he had not been the only one, as he liked to put it, "to remain at his post."

Duprat had flown into a black rage.

"Madame," he had shouted, "if you don't see the difference between a paragon of civilization and a bordello, I must ask you to leave at once!"

Madame Fabienne didn't budge. She was a small, myopic woman with a thin smile.

"And may I point out to you," Duprat had roared, "that right here, under the very noses of the Germans, I took in Resistance fighters and Allied pilots!"

"Well, Monsieur Duprat, I can claim some merit in that department, as well. Indeed, it's what allowed me to hold my head high when I went before the Purge Commission. Do you know how many Jewish girls I saved, during the Occupation? A good twenty of them. From 1941 to 1945, I had twenty Jewish girls staying in my establishment. When they sent me to the Purge Commission, those young ladies came and spoke in my favor. In fact, I took in four Jewish girls when they were doing that horrible Vel' d'Hiv roundup. My establishment might be a bordello, but how many Jews did you employ under the Germans, Monsieur Duprat? What would the Nazis have done to me, pray tell, if their officers had learned that they were sleeping with Jewish girls? I'm not saying I have a noble craft. I don't put on any airs. But where, other than my place, would these young ladies have been taken in and helped?"

Duprat—there's an exception to every rule—was speechless. After a moment of silence, all he could do was mutter, "Goddammit," and beat his retreat. I recounted the incident to Madame Julie, who seemed fairly disconcerted.

"I didn't know Fabienne had saved Jewish girls," she said.

She announced to me that nothing would make her happier than helping me continue the work of Ambrose Fleury.

"At least the money will be going to something clean," she said.

Madame Julie also showed a lot of understanding and benevolence toward Lila's parents. "There's nothing more unpleasant than the fate of exiled aristocrats," she explained to us. "I can't stand the thought of people who are used to a certain lifestyle falling victim to hard times. I've always had a horror of the fallen."

So she entrusted Genitchka Bronicka with the management of a *hôtel particulier* in the rue des Marronniers, which, over the years, achieved a global reputation. This allowed Stas to return to his old stomping grounds at the gaming tables and horse tracks. He succumbed to a heart attack in 1957, at the Deauville roulette table, as the croupier pushed the three million chips he had just won over to him. It may therefore be said that he died happy.

The embassy of the new Polish People's Republic could give us no information concerning Tad. We never got any. To us, he is still alive, and still fighting in the Resistance.

We took the train back to Cléry, and finally made it back in the early afternoon, following numerous stops on the still damaged railway. We walked home to La Motte through the fields. The rain had helped the sky with its morning ablutions, and it was a beautiful day.

The Norman earth was still gashed and bruised, but the peaceful autumn was already at work healing it over. The sky, arching over the toppled tanks and gutted houses, had regained its look of beautiful detachment.

"Ludo!"

I had seen him. He was floating in the air, his arms raised in a V for victory. It was the General de Gaulle kite, flying above La Motte. There was a little wind, to help him gain height, and he was pulling hard at his moorings—he must not have appreciated being tied down. He floated majestically, a little heavily, slanting, bathed in crepuscular light.

Lila had already begun running toward the house. I stayed where I was. I was afraid. I didn't dare. I had just knocked on every door in Paris: the Ministry of Prisoners and Concentration Camp Inmates, the Red Cross, and the Polish Embassy, where it was confirmed to me that the list of prisoners held at Auschwitz had indeed included the name Ambrose Fleury.

Hope is a shock. My entire body was ice-cold, and already I was crying with disappointment and despair. It wasn't him, it was someone else, or the children had wanted to surprise us. Finally, unable to face it, I sat down on the ground and hid my face in my hands.

"It's him, Ludo! He's back!"

Lila pulled me by the arm. The rest was a kind of happy haze. My uncle Ambrose couldn't hug me, because he couldn't let go of his de Gaulle, but he gave me a look in which tenderness and good cheer had finally found their home again.

"Well, Ludo, what do you say? Pretty great, isn't he? I haven't lost my touch. We'll need hundreds—the whole country will be asking for them."

He hadn't changed. He hadn't aged. His mustache was as long and thick as ever, and his eye just as solemn in its gaiety. There isn't a thing they can do about that. I don't know what I mean by "they." The Nazis, maybe. Or simply anyone.

"I've been worried about you," he said. "And you, too, Lila. Kept me up some nights. Can you imagine, twenty months without a word..."

Christ, I thought. *He spent twenty months in Buchenwald and Auschwitz, and he was worried about us.*

"I came back through Russia," he said. "I worked there for a few months. With all they've been through, the kids over there really need kites. I see you've been busy, but there's a lot to be done."

We spent the evening making an inventory to see what we still had.

"We can patch up a few of them," my uncle said. "But the whole historical series needs to be reassembled. Will you look at that!"

Pascal and Montaigne, Jean-Jacques Rousseau and Diderot, whom we had recovered from the neighbors, were hanging from the ceiling, moth-eaten and covered in spots, ailing and eaten away by the poor climate.

"Well, we'll put it all back, that's all …"

He thought for a moment.

"And then again, I wonder if it's really worth redoing the past. Well, yes, of course, for memory's sake. But we need some new blood. We'll do de Gaulle for the time being—that'll be it for a while. But then we'll have to find something else, look to the horizon, reach for the future …"

I wanted to tell him about the Clos Joli and Marcellin Duprat, for something in me suspected that the future was located in that direction, but no man is a prophet in his own land, and we still had a long way to go.

The return of Ambrose Fleury was celebrated like a national holiday, and for everyone, it was as if France had finally found its true face again. The children helped us secretly assemble an Ambrose Fleury kite, and it floated for an entire Sunday above the square that now bears his name, near the Cléry Kite Museum, which, I regret to observe, is better known abroad than it is in France—and whose reputation far from equals that of the Clos Joli. You won't find the Ambrose Fleury kite in the museum's collection, though. My uncle vehemently refused to become a museum piece, despite the fact that, in Marcellin Duprat's slightly catty words, "he had it coming to him." Relations between the two men aren't what they once were. They may be a bit jealous of each other, and at times they appear to be tussling over the future. "We'll see who has the last word" is a sentence I've heard both men grumble from time to time.

And I end this story by writing—just once more—the names of Pastor André Trocmé and Le Chambon-sur-Lignon. Because there isn't anything better to say than that.